Proper Goodbye

Connie Chappell

BLACK ROSE
writing™

The final approval for this literary material is granted by the author.

First printing

This is a work of fiction. Names, characters, businesses, places, events and incidents are either the products of the author's imagination or used in a fictitious manner. Any resemblance to actual persons, living or dead, or actual events is purely coincidental.

ISBN: 978-1-61296-780-6
PUBLISHED BY BLACK ROSE WRITING
www.blackrosewriting.com

Printed in the United States of America
Suggested retail price $19.95

Proper Goodbye is printed in Adobe Garamond

Your Wildest Dreams

Once upon a time
Once when you were mine
I remember skies
Reflecting in your eyes
I wonder where you are
I wonder if you think about me
Once upon a time
In your wildest dreams

*Lyrics by Justin David Hayward, lead singer and guitarist
in the rock band, The Moody Blues*

The theme of reflecting on one's dreams and memories, especially for lovers, is one that runs through *Proper Goodbye*.

The fondest memories I have of my father are the moments I found him captivated by two black-and-white photographs of my mother. So young, she was pregnant with their first child, not me, but my brother David.

While he studied these pictures with white, scalloped edges, music played in the background. The love songs seemed to transport him to another place in time where he'd been the photographer, a young husband and sailor in bell-bottom pants. In the image, an unseen wind blows Mother's hair and accentuates her pregnancy. It was easy to see how his memories entranced him again.

His unwavering devotion and a scene very similar to the one shared here made their way into *Proper Goodbye*.

Proper Goodbye

Forget-Me-Nots

Sunrise quietly made its way into Abigail Walker's life. Its hazy, golden rays eased into her bedroom and prodded her to open an eye. In the breath of a second before Abigail complied, she sensed what she would see. If the dawn could do more than prod, the worrying dawn would have said that its peek around the forget-me-nots printed on cotton curtains in the room next door found the child's bed cold and empty.

A foe in the darkness had not snatched the child away. There was no reason for alarm, no reason to rouse her husband Cliff, lying beside her, from sleep.

Abigail opened her eyes to smile at a scene that was repetitive in her life: Her nine-year old daughter Beebe was curled into the cushion of the oversized chair spaced little more than the width of a nightstand away.

Folding back the covers, Abigail slipped her feet to the rug. She wore a pretty pair of mint-green pajamas. When she stood, the hems of the silky pant legs dropped down, skimming her ankles. Two short steps brought her within reach of her daughter. She lay a hand on her shoulder. The child stirred. Her gray eyes had just focused on her mother's when Abigail said, "Morning, sweetie. Make room."

With their coordinated efforts, Abigail managed to slip onto the chair with Beebe half-sitting, half-laying on her, her knees drawn up, and safely held in place by Abigail's arms. This maneuver was easier achieved when Beebe was smaller.

"Daddy asleep?"

Their conversation was held in low whispers, more because the gentle moment called for it rather than to preserve the peace for the sleeping man.

"You know him. I'm not sure he would wake if the bed fell through the ceiling into the living room," Abigail said. "Hopefully, they would land sunnyside up." Both of them giggled.

Abigail had long since stopped asking her daughter about the circumstances that brought her into her parents' room. Beebe simply didn't sleep well. Cause unknown. She admitted to no bad dreams. Neither did the dark or anything in it frighten her.

Beebe's wakeful nights occurred with no predictability. They weren't as noticeable on mornings when Abigail found the cheerful one-year old in her crib, sitting up before she entered. The crib had at least contained the child where, when the time came, the standard bed did not.

Their chair was angled with its back to the window. Dawn extinguished the night, but cradled between the wingbacks, mother and daughter still sat in shadow. "I remember the first time I got up and found you asleep in the hall with your dolly." It was a ragamuffin thing Beebe adored. "You'd climbed out of bed and played on the floor next to the night light. Do you remember sitting on that stool in the bathroom to watch Daddy shave?"

The head against Abigail's shoulder nodded. "Why'd I stop?"

"Kindergarten. Catching the bus. One day, I realized you were more than merely smart, you were an exceptionally bright little girl."

"What'd I do?" Abigail could tell her daughter smiled as she spoke.

"You were three when you carried the stool to this chair and used it for the climb up."

"You didn't make me go back to bed?"

"The chair was better than the chilly, hard floor. At least I had an eye on you and was pleased you used the flannel shirt Daddy left in the chair as a blanket." As the midnight journeys continued, the mother's trained ear, alert to sounds in the house and her child's restless movements, became desensitized to the occasions when Beebe settled down in the chair.

"Don't need the stool now," Beebe said, her arm tightening around her mother, which Abigail sensed to mean nothing in this world could separate them.

"That's because my bright little girl grew longer legs." She kissed the top of Beebe's head.

Neither of them mentioned how Abigail always kept a throw and small pillow in the crook of the chair arm for her daughter's nocturnal visits. Neither of them mentioned how someday, Beebe would truly outgrow the chair. She was almost there now. Soon, she would be ten. Double digits. A division in time.

With the mother's nudge, the two began to move, unfolding themselves, like twin butterflies emerging from the same cocoon, their faces images of the other.

Barefoot, neither of them bothered to step over that one creaky floorboard on their way to the door. Cliff Walker would rise only at the alarm clock's ringing persistence. He'd push his feet into battered slippers and begin his day without ceremony. No stretching, no moaning, no yawning.

Then one day, he'd scuff across the bedroom in the trailing shadow of his child's abandoned habit. Without a glimmer of conscious thought, Beebe would forsake overnight stays in the chair.

Farewell

After forty-six years on God's earth and nineteen years with the church, Pastor Beebe Walker was sacked on the first Monday in March.

She couldn't say the turn of events was totally unexpected that afternoon. From her office window inside Trydestone Lutheran Church, she watched two men out in the parking lot. They shook hands at the bumper of a silver Toyota. The Toyota bore Tennessee plates and belonged to Phillip Dixon, the man who would move to Cassel, Maryland, and replace her in the pulpit. The other man, Norm Rogers, was Trydestone's head deacon. Another few strands of dialogue passed between the men. Through the glass, she clearly recognized the future camaraderie they would know. Deacon Rogers genially slapped Phillip Dixon on the arm, then turned and hurried to the church's side entrance.

Trydestone's pulpit had not been given without reservation when she moved to Maryland from Kansas nine months before. Her arrangement with Trydestone consisted of filling an existing void as interim pastor while the search for a permanent one ensued. She had a better-than-even shot at snaring the job. The problem was, a rather ominous void existed simultaneously inside of her.

Today, Beebe's focus remained fixed on the Toyota as it exited the lot with its thin line of exhaust trailing behind. When it was gone from view, she pulled in a deep breath that straightened her backbone. By now, she thought Norm must be reseated in the deacons' board room, where two other deacons waited, all worthy representatives of Trydestone. A glance at her watch told her it was time for her appointment with the search committee.

There was a strategy to the order of the appointments that day. The committee met with Dixon first, made the offer, received acceptance, then brought Beebe in to relay the bad news.

Slipping away from the window, she followed a dimly lit hallway to the board room. Once inside, she was surprised to find Norm Rogers alone, standing at another expanse of windows, looking out. The demeanor in the room felt casual, not what she anticipated. Twisting his wide torso slightly toward her when she entered, he said, "Come in. The wind's picking up."

A large meadow adjoined this side of the church. It was open and flat. A rush of brittle, dry leaves whisked through the air, then dropped to tumble against tufts of field grass, listing to the right, surrendering to the wind.

Beebe took a place beside Norm. His fists were bunched in the pockets of dress slacks. The top button of his shirt was undone; the knot in his necktie loosened. A sports coat lay folded over a nearby chair back.

Matching Norm's relaxed stance, Beebe slipped her hands into the side pockets of the dress she wore. The curious discomfort she felt in the last weeks and months was oddly at bay. When Norm offered no more than the weather report, she said, "You released Raymond and Stan early." The Morrow brothers were the other two deacons who made up the committee.

"Yeah. Didn't need them really. They were just dragging me down." He turned his teasing eyes her way. "In all honesty, it seemed like triple teaming, given the circumstances, because, Beebe, my friend, as of now," he said, draping an arm around her shoulders, "you're fired. I hope that doesn't come as too much of a shock."

"I'm glad I heard it from you, not from someone at Lutheran Central." Her hand patted his before he withdrew his meaty forearm. "That's how it went in Kansas."

"Kansas. Yeah. That was a tough sell."

Trydestone's board of deacons knew about Kansas. When church elders removed her from Kansas and sent her to Maryland to be Trydestone's interim pastor, they forwarded a work history composed of their words. Norm and Beebe sat on many occasions while she reprised the story, adding a dalliance of emotion here and there, and not just sideswiping the heartache.

The more she rehashed the Kansas story, either verbally or in the privacy of her thoughts, the more cynical the telling became. The Blessed Lutheran Church In All Its Wisdom sent Beebe to Bixler, Kansas, with an assignment. She was to infiltrate the four Lutheran churches there. (On those occasions when cynicism ran rampant, she used infiltrate rather than counsel as a descriptor.) Her mission was to set the four churches on a path to merge into a single, more viable one. She was not only the emissary for the Blessed Lutheran Church In All Its Wisdom, but a replacement pastor at one of the four.

She spoon-fed the Bixler Lutherans. She broke down barriers. It took eighteen hard-fought months, but eventually, the membership at all four churches accepted the idea. The actual vote was sixty-six percent in favor. Majority rules.

Her intervention perpetuated the future survival of the Lutheran church in Bixler, creating a more potent vessel to complete God's work. She made Bixler's community of Lutherans understand that the day of a landscape dotted with a multitude of church steeples had disappeared. Their losses were numbered alongside the quaint corner drugstores and corner groceries.

Corner bars seemed a bit more prolific in Bixler. She nearly frequented one last July when she drove east with her suitcases packed and riding in the trunk.

Her disappointment at being relocated rose to the point of anger and tears. Church elders blindsided her with the news of her relocation after the merger's success initially brought nothing but accolades. They couched their decision in the guise of a reward. She balked nonetheless. Yes, Trydestone was a healthy, growing church, but she wanted the Bixler church.

Her heart and soul were wedged inside that living, breathing triumph. As an elder on high explained, excising her from the Bixler church was strategic. (*Elder on high* and *excising*: yep, more cynicism.) The church's post-merger stratagem provided just compensation for the thirty-four percent who disagreed with the plan, but had it stuffed down their throats. Not seeing Beebe in the pulpit made the merger more palatable for those in the minority. Less palatable for Beebe was the chunk of choking deception caught in her throat. It never entered her mind that she would not be the one to take the reins once the merger was nothing but a bad taste. That measure of masked deceit she laid at the elders' feet.

Norm fished out Beebe's feelings over the last few months, concurrently with Tyrdestone's search efforts. The elders expected her to be a shoo-in. However, a congregation expected its pastor not to be shoehorned in. That's where the Morrow brothers stood, she suspected. Norm, though, wanted Beebe's wounds to heal. He counseled her to accept Trydestone. Every heart is asked at some point to leave something or someone behind while it yearns and aches for a different outcome. Despite her attitude, Norm encouraged her to remain in the pulpit as part of his recovery plan for her. She agreed, but knew she only gave Trydestone her best imitation of a good pastor.

"I can't get it back, Norm," she said one evening after a board meeting broke up and the others went home. By "it," she meant the internal fire necessary to ignite her faith.

"Politics was played back in Kansas. I won't deny that. The situation was difficult. How could it not be? People's lives. Their faith. *Their* support of *their*

12

church. Changing times counts for a lot of it, but you fought through it all and left Bixler better than you found it. *You* did that."

She shot him a sideways glance. "The church betrayed me, Norm, after I did its bidding. I wanted God to step in. I wanted a miracle."

After a thoughtful pause, he said, "It is my profound opinion that God goes silent on us all at some time or other."

She allowed the words the insightful layperson spoke to the ordained minister to sink in and make their mark. She remembered them again today while they watched eerily brilliant sunbeams shine through a hole punched into thick clouds, the color of an ugly bruise. Then as God had gone silent, the opening to the heavens slammed shut and the afternoon mimicked the darkness that shadowed Beebe's heart.

"We're not in Kansas anymore, Toto," she mumbled to herself.

As if adopting the little dog's persona, her funny friend scratched the skin behind his ear. "No, we're not." The tone Norm used wasn't humorous. It said, that's the point. "You know, your first few months here were fine. I thought that."

"I tried, but I couldn't let go despite the fact that Trydestone offered everything I wanted in Kansas. Everything. It was billed as the prize. But the prize was a misfit for the battle. They didn't mesh," she said. "This work I've chosen shouldn't be about me, I know. But my feelings have come front and center. And yet, in that framework, I've lost myself entirely." The sentiment she described gave her a jittery feeling as if electricity prickled her spine.

"I'm here, Beebe, if you ever want to talk. I'll continue to pray for you."

Norm's words sounded like a conclusion to the issue. Beebe's conclusion ran another course entirely. It was apparent to her that an undercurrent of cynicism doesn't work from the pulpit. It'll get you fired every time. Once was enough for her. "You know what this means."

"Still waiting for that miracle?" He grinned.

"It means I'm done, Norm."

Her simply stated pronouncement vanquished his grin. "You don't mean done with the church? Don't say that. There are other options."

"I don't want you to feel guilty about my decision in the least."

"How can I not?"

"Don't, Norm."

"Take a furlough," he said, anxious, "but don't turn in your shield. You may be disillusioned by the church, but give God another chance."

"I don't think I'll find God inside the church. If I find Him again, I think I'd rather find Him outside the church. We might be able to reconnect on neutral ground. It'll take some getting used to. It'll be hard on Olney."

"Olney will work through it. I'll have a talk with him."

"No. Let me do it." Truth was, she already prepared him.

"I'm sure, by now, he's waiting outside."

"Well, this is it." Beebe put out a hand. It rested in Norm's for a moment. While the dark afternoon loomed beyond the glass, she wound back around the board table toward the door.

When her hand rattled the knob, Norm rushed to say, "You may not think you touched us at Trydestone. Know that you have. Olney is just one example. There are others. Don't forget about your Sunday morning walks with little Jonah. He's your true-blue."

Mentioning Jonah Young made her smile. The six-year old liked to meet her at her office door on Sunday mornings and walk her in to services. "Thanks, Norm. This is my first firing. It wasn't so bad."

"Aw, shucks, ma'am, credit's gotta go to the quality of the person I had to work with." He winked.

She adjourned their mutual admiration society on that note and stepped out into the hall, but not quickly enough for her peripheral vision to miss his crestfallen expression and his chin drop to his chest.

Closing the door softly, she found a worried Olney Jones waiting with his trusty dust mop and his trashcan on wheels. Olney was friend, custodian, member of Trydestone's flock, and expectant to the point of pain. By the slump of his shoulders, he finally believed the outcome Beebe predicted: She was not the deacons' pick.

Throughout the last few weeks when prospective pastors walked Trydestone's halls, Beebe tried to ease Olney down the path that would ultimately lead to her resignation from the Blessed Lutheran Church In All Its Wisdom. (She tried to be less cynical in Olney's presence, but was not always successful.)

Olney was the first church member she met who was not a deacon. Her first memory of him was kneeling before the monument sign out at the corner of the church yard, where the sidewalk met the street. He added her name, letter by letter, beneath the church's name. She could imagine his misery when he replaced her name with Phillip Dixon's. Given his duties at the church, she saw Olney on a daily basis. They knew a kinship. He correctly interpreted her sighs, struggles, and lackadaisical efforts when her dissolving faith worked against her. His never faltered.

Olney's dull eyes followed Beebe's approach. He fell into step alongside her. The dust mop hitched a ride on his cart, its one wheel squawking in opposition.

He was an older gentleman, his timidness oversized for his small frame. Olney appeared stooped as if Beebe's battle with God hovered weightily over him. Cynicism aside, God did nothing, she wanted Olney to understand. What she felt was supreme indifference. It was a one-sided venture. That fact sparked an inkling of guilt. She was the reason Olney no longer stood tall.

Olney was a casualty of the mistake she made many years ago. The ramifications of which, she strangely felt, were just beginning to surface. She was never cut out to be a minister. She got that wrong. Her rebellious attitude proved that.

She pegged the church as a refuge for a young woman's loneliness. As a minister, she would always have a church family within reach and be the guiding hands in its spiritual well-being. For a long while, she flourished. The blossom began dying on the vine during her last days in Kansas.

Beebe and Olney strode away from the board room without a word between them until they stared in at her office through the doorway.

"I'm going to need some boxes. Can you round up three, four? Not too big," Beebe said.

Olney grumbled something, then disappeared.

Beebe walked over to the office window to again peer out at the lot, empty except for her red Ford Taurus. It sat forlorn in the small parking alcove set aside for the pastor's car.

Olney returned, apologizing. He scrounged up only two decent boxes. Beebe gathered personal items and transferred them to the desk. Olney packed them. When Beebe's activities slowed, Olney picked up the nameplate from the desk's front edge.

"No, Olney, I don't want that." Along with her name on the engraved plate was the title she cast aside: Pastor. She took the nameplate from him and lay it face down on the oaken desktop.

His face fell. "Why can't this be fixed?"

She laced compassion into her voice for his sake. "I know my giving up the church hurts you, my good, good friend, and I'm sorry."

"But why?" Olney truly couldn't understand. He was a simple man with simple fixes. Something for stains, something for shine, a squirt of something to replace elbow grease.

"Olney, please. We talked about this. We knew what was coming. I want you to make peace with it."

"I won't, Pastor Bee—"

She waved a hand, cutting him off. "Not pastor. Not anymore. Not ever again." Then she tempered her tone. "Don't you understand? I can't find myself. I can't find the pastor I used to be."

Olney hung his head. She turned away from his grief, but from the corner of her eye, she saw Olney slip her engraved nameplate out of its wooden holder and tuck the plate in his left breast pocket, over his heart. He lay a hand on both.

For a moment, she squeezed her eyes tight, then opened them to scan the room. They slid from the extended desk drawers, to the closet with its door standing open, to the twin bookcases. There was nothing else she wanted. Everything with any thread of religious connotation was left in place for the incoming Phillip Dixon.

The packing was done. It took—she looked at her watch—less than ten minutes. Olney spent more time than that hunting down boxes.

She gave the carton on her desk a resolute thump. Another closed carton sat in a guest chair.

"Looks like I have everything. One box for each of us. You don't mind helping me get these to the car?"

"I don't want to, but I will."

Olney Jones got one box up in his arms. Beebe Walker hoisted the other. The chubby woman and the slight man strolled side by side down the tiled corridor that would intersect the front hall and push her out into a blustery afternoon with her bosom drained of spirit.

* * *

Gauzy moonlight drizzled across the country road. Yates sat with Terri in what passed for transportation, his banged-up Jeep Cherokee. They were parked across from a cemetery and what Terri termed the caretaker's house.

For the three-hour road trip, Yates bundled Terri into the back seat, cushioning her on all sides with blankets and pillows. She sat up now. Yates could almost feel Terri's will to live slip from her body with each labored breath. An eerily cold sensation slithered over Yates's shoulder, before being pulled through the driver's window, lowered a few inches, and out. It made sense to Yates that nearness to all the natural haunts of a graveyard would lure her will away.

That spring, he drove Terri Miller to Larkspur, Michigan, to die. He knew why the woman of sixty-six would die. She had AIDS. And not much time left. He didn't know why the caretaker's house. Why the cemetery. And he didn't know why Larkspur, for that matter. Why would she come back to this place he learned just today was her hometown? It was possible an extremely old and quite faded wanted poster for her hung on the post office wall. The charge was levied thirty years ago, and she avoided the town since then.

This was the extent of his knowledge about her distant past. He asked her for more often enough over the last ten years. She could be one stubborn woman. Stubborn enough to disappear from his young life when school started each year, though he begged her not to. Tough enough to live on the streets.

Yates Strand shivered. "How long are we going to sit here?" By his calculations, they were close to their eventual destination.

"We'll sit here until I'm ready." Her squawk brought up a cough.

He tried to keep a small pot of anger brewing over her contrariness because if he didn't, he'd cry like a baby.

After another few minutes, the upstairs light was doused. It was early, but the house slept. Yates watched Terri through the rearview mirror.

"Okay, let's go into town." Her words eked out through a held breath and the uncompromising pain brought by the movement of leaning back against the pillows.

He bit his lip. Her condition was so fragile.

The Jeep sputtered and shook, then started. Its headlights cut through the darkness. He followed the road that veered closer to Lake Huron and the heart of Larkspur's compact downtown.

Yates still wore his nursing duds. He went straight to Gaven House that March afternoon, as he did every afternoon after school, to check on Terri.

Gaven House was a large residence in an old and deteriorating neighborhood. The house doubled as a hospice for people suffering the last stages of AIDS and who would receive no care elsewhere without the benefit of insurance. Gaven House was a privately run charity ward. More than charity, Eddie Gaven provided love and comfort. Eddie Gaven afforded respect to the people he and other volunteers nursed. He was afflicted with the disease himself. Well, the earlier version. Eddie carried the HIV virus.

Gaven House was a blessing. Gaven House gave Terri a home and a level of care. Yates volunteered several hours each week. He owed the establishment whatever he could give.

Today, and for as long as her energy lasted, Terri promised to help him cram. Yates, twenty-three and on track to graduate from college, was scheduled to take the nursing boards tomorrow and the next day. Instead, when he arrived at Gaven House, he found Eddie out front.

Eddie pushed himself off the porch steps and met Yates halfway down the front walk. He carried his smile with him. But smile or not, Yates's heart beat at a rib-breaking crescendo. Eddie was heading Yates off. That could only mean one thing: Something was wrong with Terri.

"What happened?" Yates's voice shook.

"It's nothing like that." Eddie waved Yates's fearful thoughts away. "Terri and I had a long confab today. A long, long confab. Hell, she wore me out."

"What about?"

"Terri wants to be moved."

"Moved? Where? Why?"

"She'll tell you. Her mind is made up. I can't hold her here. I can't force her to stay. This is what she wants."

When Yates entered Terri's small room, he found her sitting in an old recliner wedged in the corner beside her bed. She presented him with a piece of paper, the results of an internet search.

Had she rallied enough that day to sit at the computer? he wondered. Gaven House kept one in the common area. Then he noticed the print date encoded along the paper's bottom edge. A month ago. She'd been significantly stronger in early February.

He scanned the sheet that provided driving directions to another hospice, along with other general information. "What's this?"

"We're going there. Get me ready."

"Why? Why are you doing this?"

"Come on. We don't have a lot of time." Her attempt to collapse the recliner's footrest lacked the strength to complete the task.

"Talk to me, Terri. Tell me what prompted this." Yates looked around. The extra pillows and blankets Eddie promised for the move lay on the foot of Terri's bed. These items represented Eddie's firm conviction that nothing would alter Terri's decision. Stubbornness would never drain out of her.

"I'll tell you along the way." For a woman whose clothing hung on her slight frame, she could be wearisome.

"But does it have to be right now?"

"Yes, today. We've got a long trip, and I'm high maintenance." She paused to catch her breath. "You can see the place closes at nine."

"This place is in Larkspur?"

"I know. Get me ready."

The full brunt of realization dawned. He thought he prepared himself for her eventual death, but this option never entered the realm of possibility. This was unfair. "Terri, you can't do this. No."

"Yes, I can, and you'll help me. Now get moving. Stat."

He stared, he knew, with sad spaniel eyes. She commented on those the first day they met. He'd been thirteen and scared.

"This is the nursing life, Yates. Get used to it. We can cram for those boards along the way."

So, this had been her plan all along, Yates thought.

Now they crept forward, looking at the numbers painted, nailed, and otherwise affixed to Larkspur's downtown businesses. He steered the Jeep to the curb, several parking spots back from the hospice named Crossroads. It also doubled as a homeless shelter, senior center—and based on the advertisement written on the sandwich board out front—a bingo hall on Tuesday nights. This was Tuesday. The place looked full.

In an earlier day, the old bricked storefront looked like it operated as a department store. It was located on Battlefield Road, which ran parallel to the main drag, and intersected with Standhope. The street names signified the weighty counter-pull of life. In Terri's case, though, she could neither stand, nor hope; Battlefield spoke for itself.

They sat and watched lights again, and the clock. Twenty-two minutes before nine.

"Should I get you inside?" he asked.

"No. Let's wait."

"What for?"

"For the people to clear out."

He gave a slight nod. He'd honor her pride and privacy issues.

With these few moments, he reminisced one last time about the past, about the tail end of his childhood, about summers at his house, about her never-wavering impact on his life since the car accident, when she saved his father with her own nursing skills.

"Every day. Every day of your life, Yates," his father, Arthur, told him, "pray for Terri Miller. Thank God she helped me."

Yates stood by his father's hospital bed when Arthur accomplished so much with a few simple words for the wandering Terri. "Come back and see us," he said.

An invisible tether tugged at Yates. He sensed its tug at his father and Terri, too. A handful of hospital visits took them through that last week of summer. When school let out each year thereafter, Terri Miller returned, and she stayed until classes took up again.

Yates prayed for her still. It was natural that she came to him when the merciless disease put up a better fight than a warrior-of-one could combat. They were close, like family, but not.

Yates turned some in the front seat. "Remember the summer I learned guitar, me and Bobby from up the street? We were pretty good, huh?"

He saw Terri's grin. "You two stank that first summer. But I admit, your fingering improved. I said so the next June. You and Bobby stuck to it."

"When school was ready to start that first summer, I said, 'All we need is a drummer.' Remember, you were there." The conversation took place in the garage.

"I was right there on the stool by the workbench," she said.

For a male in his first year of teenage life, sensitive Yates accepted Terri without reservation. She was the cushion of adult supervision that summer, since his mother began working again at the county library's research desk. Terri checked in, hung for a while, like that day in the garage, then left Bobby and him alone to admire her because they knew she lived life on the lam. For Yates, it was more. He loved her outright. She saw through him at the hospital, clear through to his soul and his sadness at even the thought of losing his father.

"I still can't believe what you did. The next June, you arrived in a pickup with a drum set in the back. Where'd you find that lady?"

"I told all this before. She owed me a favor, so I asked her to drive me with the drums."

"Yeah, but you took lessons. You were awesome, Terri."

"A natural," she said. "Who knew?"

"Now, that was one radical summer." Yates and Bobby called themselves Metal Mouths, for the braces. "The next summer, there wasn't much time for music. Bobby and I were business magnates. Still using Metal Mouths. Metal Mouths Lawn Service."

"I cut more grass that summer than I ever imagined."

"But it was fun."

"It was fun, but not as much fun as the next summer."

"I couldn't believe when Dad came home with that ice cream truck. Mom had a fit, but we drove it every day." Yates's mother's fit was quickly curbed by his father. Such a curbing was not standard practice in the Strand household. "It was you, me, and Bobby that summer, all summer long."

When Yates was ready to move chronologically to the following summer, Terri spun out on a tangent.

"Where is Bobby?"

"West Coast, still. He asks about you."

"He's a good kid. You both are."

Yates wanted to tell her he loved her, that she was a good soul, but he knew she refused compliments of any kind. Something else to honor.

"Before the crowd leaves, Yates, get me out. Sit me on that bench up there, then back the Jeep up, so you can't be so easily seen."

His eyes passed from the sidewalk bench to Terri, dragging shock with them. Summer memories crashed to the concrete. "No, Terri, please."

"Do it. I'll be all right."

She would not be all right. That was the point of this entire exercise. He blinked and suddenly all he could see and feel was his own misery, not hers. During his childhood summers, she looked after him in her own way. But she'd done *this* to herself, damn it. Got AIDS. Who knew how. She was leaving him and asking him to fast-forward the ending. Only respect made him open the Jeep's door. Respect, and the summer she avoided speaking of.

He climbed out. Words did not come. Something was balled in his throat. Anger, he told himself. Anger for the needless loss: his, with their imminent and final separation. Anger for the lost need: hers, the drugs now behind her, and yet those addictive days ruled her through the disease. Another breath, another heartbeat. By his own hand, he facilitated her abandonment of him. That was tantamount to emotional abuse, and testament to the strength of character she knew he possessed. She never asked him to perform more than his capabilities. That was how Terri honored him.

Yates lifted Terri out, giving extreme care to the process. He carried her to a sidewalk bench thirty feet or so from the senior center. He placed a blanket over her and kissed her cheek. She nodded. Their eyes met. Love rebounded. The child and the drug addict.

"Go back," she whispered.

"Please," he begged.

"Go. Back."

"But Terri—"

She pushed him. "Hurry now. Be a good boy."

The boy who first loved Terri did hurry. He jumped in the Jeep and started it. For a moment, the boy thought about peeling out. For that rash move, the man would hate himself forever. Self-loathing funneled through Terri, too, he knew, for what she did to someone in her past. And how she tried to make up for that grating mistake with him. He slammed the transmission into reverse and parked in front of the drycleaner, three doors down.

He waited and kept his eye on Terri. She looked like a pitiful waif, sitting in the shadows, the light from the closest streetlamp was blocked by a curbside tree. He could see that Terri's head was turned toward the bricked storefront and away from him. Just as with the start of school each fall, Terri passed out of his life. She returned to the homeless world and, he fully suspected, took up her addiction again. He always wondered, always worried that she would not return the next summer, and was always delighted when she did.

The summer after the ice cream job eased into his memory. Terri's pattern of *summers only* in town changed without ceremony when Yates was seventeen. Yates's mother was slowly dying. Between Yates, his father, and Terri, they nursed his mother and kept the small neighborhood hardware store his father owned going. From Yates's seventeenth birthday to his next, Terri remained a constant in his life, housed, dressed, and fed in his parents' home. She saved his father's life, and now she would make the loss of his mother's life easier for the Strand family. When the end came, that closely held cluster included Terri, too.

He was absolutely sure she remained substance-free throughout the ordeal. Yates's mother, Naomi, was never a fan of Terri Miller's presence, despite her heroic rescue of Naomi's husband. Terri strapped a tourniquet around his leg to save it. She groped through the car's wreckage for his cell phone and placed the emergency call. Then she conned the paramedics into letting her ride up front in the ambulance taking Arthur to the emergency room. Yates and his mother arrived after a call came from hospital admissions to find Terri hovering outside the treatment cubicle.

Terri's stint at sobriety lasted over a year, all while Naomi's pain medication sat within easy reach. Yates thought when Terri got through that ungodly period, she'd remain free of the addiction. But old haunts, like the cemetery, preyed on her, coaxed, and cajoled. Terri was gone, just gone, three days after the funeral. None of his mother's unused medication was missing. Terri wouldn't let Yates experience that. Never did she use during those childhood summers, nor any summer between his years at college.

Summer memories faded abruptly when the bingo crowd disbursed. Laughing and talking, they headed away from Terri and toward the parking lot across the street. Then, a man came out and stood on the stoop under the porch light. Yates tilted the folded website page he used for directions toward the moon's glow. The man's face was there. Vincent Bostick. He operated the center.

On the stage before Yates, the tragedy played out. Terri pushed up from the shadowy bench. She stood in silhouette and found enough strength to pitch her voice through the still night air. Even from this distance, Yates swore he heard her. "Please. Help me."

Vincent Bostick ran. He caught her just before her knees gave out. Quickly, he got her up in his arms, took a few seconds to look around, then carried her to the door, kicked it open, and disappeared inside.

Like her departure from his life on school's first day, Terri entered a world that didn't welcome him. She timed her exit to coincide with his nursing boards, miles away in Lansing. She would never forgive him for missing the test. If any person could die on command, that person was Terri Miller.

The flame went out under his small pot of anger, and he wept.

Yates fled the town, back past the cemetery, where, no question, she would be buried. His headlights grazed the nameplate on the mailbox in front of the caretaker's house. Walker, it read.

Propositions

It was a dewy April morning in Cassel, Maryland. Beebe sat at her dining room table with her second cup of coffee. Six weeks passed since she said goodbye to Olney Jones in Trydestone's parking lot. Out in front of her house, the rising sun winked off the windshield of a car pulling to the curb. It caught her eye. A man got out. Just the way he pushed his glasses up into his thick and curly crop of chestnut-colored hair told her who he was.

Vincent Bostick, her ex-fiancé, looked up at her wood-shingled bungalow with its covered front porch. For several moments, Beebe sat transfixed while Vincent's elongated shadow preceded him across squares of concrete that led to her front door. He rang the bell. Beebe set her coffee cup down hurriedly with a thud. She crossed the living room and swung the door wide.

The man who was Beebe's first love in high school and through college peered in. Her heart channeled through a range of emotions in record time: from inquiring, to astonishment, which bowed to disbelief, and finally, the smile she never denied him broke onto her face.

"Vincent! Wow! What a surprise. Come in." She stepped back.

The tall forty-six-year old man, neither stocky nor thin, reached for the screen door's handle. Once he was inside, she gave him a tight hug that still felt familiar, but the warm hello emanated only friendship at this point in their lives.

When the embrace ended, Beebe stared up at his tentative smile. "Sorry to just drop by unannounced," he said.

Still stunned by his turning up on her doorstep, she wrestled with a moment of speechlessness before she managed, "No. I'm glad you did." Although in truth, Beebe knew she looked a little rough. This was a day off, so she hadn't tried too hard. She wore a T-shirt that hung over baggy pants, the hems of which met a pair of pink clogs.

"Here, let's sit down." She cleared the cushions of her afghan-covered couch. The living room was Beebe's center of operations, and it showed. Some of her clutter extended to the dining area beyond. Two cardboard boxes were stacked behind an easy chair, angled into the room, the same two Olney and she loaded into her car.

After they settled themselves on the couch, he read the expression printed on her white shirt. "Where are you taking me? And why am I in this hand basket?" it said.

"I hope you don't believe I'm here to take you to hell in a hand basket?" he teased, unscrambling the quote.

"No. Of course not. Well, I hope not." Her hand jumped out and squeezed his arm. "I can't believe it's you."

"It's me. Believe it." He flicked a glance out the picture window across from the couch. "I was, um, down at the church. I met a man named Dixon." Vincent took pains to keep up with her over the years, the places she lived and the churches she pastored. He still resided in Larkspur, the town in Michigan where they were raised.

"Trydestone. Yes. Dixon's the new pastor. I took an interim post. The board of deacons thought Dixon suited better," Beebe said, purposely short on details.

"So what are you doing now?" Vincent's conversational chatter followed a logically curious path.

"I made a change. I'm a grief counselor," she said, upbeat.

"A grief counselor? Not a minister. No church." He frowned.

"No church. I'm at Swanson's. It's the local funeral home. Swanson's offers counseling services to the community. You know me: I thrive at a slower pace. There's nothing slower than recovering from grief." She added a smile to the playacting that was intended to steer him toward her new life. This temporary misdirection would eventually bend to Vincent's prying. He would want the story that severed her relationship with the church. Oh, how she didn't want to go into that today.

Her comment about grief's slow recovery was true, not only for people who lost loved ones, but for those who lost a house to fire or flood, a friend to a long-distance move, a loss of livelihood, or, in her case, the loss of the only way of life she knew. As the boxes still sat behind the chair, largely ignored, she made no attempt, once the dust settled, to reexamine her decision to give the church the mighty heave-ho. And the dust had certainly settled on that, now a month and a half later.

The curious discomfort she felt at Trydestone was a precursor to the stages of recovery that left her feeling ill at ease in her own life. Just because she counseled people about the grieving process didn't mean she mastered her own grief with no effort and no repercussions.

The classes Beebe led taught that grief was comprised of three distinct stages. Each stage contained three characteristics. She liked the symmetry of her formula: three by three. She stressed to those who attended her classes that the characteristics often overlapped, ebbed, and then rose again. The characteristics of the stages were shock, denial, and numbness, followed by fear, anger, and depression, then understanding, acceptance, and moving on. On different days, she regressed. On others, she could be all over the chess board.

"So, you're busy?" Vincent said.

Initially, the question struck her as banal, then its double-edged element made her sit up. She knew him. He was hunting, but not about her resignation from the church. "I'm mostly busy. This is a two-week hiatus between sessions."

"Nice."

"And you, Vincent, how are things with you?" She could hunt, too.

"Well, that's why I'm here." His tap dance stopped sooner than she thought it would.

She closed one eye. This was a tell he would remember about her. It meant she attempted to read his thoughts.

"I don't quite know how to say this." He emitted a nervous laugh. "I practiced my speech all the way in the car, but now, none of the phrasing seems right. It's not Cliff," he jumped to say. "He's fine." Beebe's father, Cliff Walker, still lived in Larkspur, too. "But the problem sort of includes Cliff. He needs to hear something. After that, he may not be fine. I've come to enlist your aid."

Even without the tap dance, he was being too circumspect, forcing Beebe to react. "With what? Stop driving the wagons in a circle, Vincent."

"You're not going to believe this, but I swear it's true."

"Tell me."

He drew in a breath. "One night a few weeks ago, bingo let out for the seniors. I stepped out front. Down from Crossroads, a very ill woman sat on a bench. She got up, calling out for help. I rushed over and caught her just before she collapsed. I got her inside and into a bed. She told me she had AIDS and was living her last days. I was struck by her phrasing: Not dying, but living her last days. That's how she put it. I sat with her day and night. After the second night, well, early the next morning, she died."

"Why are you telling me this? What does this have to do with Daddy?" In the time it took for a sour chord to sound, Beebe put it together. She felt the blood drain from her face. "Mother. The woman was Mother. Oh, my God." Her hands flew to her face. He touched her back. In the next second, she was up. She went to the desk across the room and stared down at a jumble of papers, the telephone, a potted cactus, all while her heart pounded in her chest.

"Beebe. Beebs. I didn't know who she was until just before she died. Well, just before she slipped into a coma. It was like she knew she was heading that way. At first, she gave her name as Terri Miller. I didn't know your mother. You and I dated after she, well, left."

Beebe spun around. "Abandoned us! We were a family!" Vincent knew the full course of events. That knowledge came after the fact. Beebe was nearly sixteen when her mother disappeared. The next year, Vincent came into her life.

She felt herself losing control. Why was she so upset? But God bless it, she felt caught in an endless loop. Every time she completed a cycle, she passed her mother, then her father, then the church. She wound back to the starting block with her mother again, the nurse who fled town with her addiction in tow, not her daughter, and not a word of explanation.

Maybe her break with the church would break the cycle. Or would it leave her to grind around with her grief indefinitely? Which now reached out, thanks to Vincent's visit, to incorporate past grief: her missing, and now dead, mother. And her father, who raised lack of understanding to an art.

Her eyes closed and her stomach sank. If the grief passed, she'd be stuck with her father. Which squarely matched Vincent's proposition.

"Beebe, I know it all hurt back then. She knew it, too, of course. She told me stories about her life. I thought she really was Terri Miller—"

"Terri Miller," Beebe scoffed. "An assumed name. A fake name. Why? AIDS?" She threw up a hand that slapped her thigh when it fell.

"Come sit down." He patted the couch cushion, which lured her over. He turned his knees toward hers. When he spoke, his voice was soft as a prayer. "She couldn't seem to play out the scene she'd written, so she came out with the real story. Beebe, she begged me not to tell you or Cliff. I argued. But she begged me."

"Not to tell?" He nodded. "You agreed?" He nodded. "When was this?"

"A month ago."

"In March! And you're just telling me now."

He cringed at her response. "It takes a while to build enough courage to break a promise to a dying woman."

She pinned him with a glare. She didn't want to hear about courage or promises related to her mother.

"You have to understand," he said, "for a woman as sick as she was, she grabbed my hand with the power to break bones. She was dying. This was her last wish."

"I appreciate the fact that you came to tell me about Mother face to face. I do. But a wish?" she spat. "She gets to have wishes. It was a lie."

"She begged me, Beebs. What could I do? I promised to keep her secret. But I couldn't. In the end, I couldn't. I'd see Cliff, and..." His eyes dropped to the triangle of cushion between them. "Pretty soon, I avoided him. I crossed the street. I saw him going into church one morning... And I went home."

When he renewed eye contact, she said, "Ashamed, were you?"

She saw his lips tighten. That was the effort necessary to push past her hardness. "You've got to come with me. You're off for two weeks. It's perfect. We can tell Cliff together. You've got to be there. He'll need you. And you haven't been home for a while."

"No. I can't."

"You can't? How can you say that?"

"I'm suffering a bit myself, Vincent. It's not that I have no church, it's that I left the church. That's not easy."

"What?" Vincent jerked back with the revelation.

"I'm not going to bawl my eyes out for my father. I'm not going to leap to my feet and run pack a bag. This is your complicity, not mine. *You* feel loyalty; *you* want closure."

"Look, I know things with Cliff became strained over the years. You grew apart. This could bring you back together. I'd love to see that. I'd love to see you spend time in Larkspur. A lot of time."

"No. No. No. I'm running on the dregs of emotion these days. That's not pretty." She indicated her clothing and untidy home. "I give what I have to the people in my grief sessions. There's nothing left for my father."

"How can you be that cruel?"

"You should have thought about cruelty before you joined forces with my mother."

"What do you mean, joined forces? She was sick. She needed help. I would never walk away."

"I mean, get in league with her, when you knew the story."

"Beebe, you've got to forgive."

That stopped her, but she offered not a shred of compliance.

"What about your father?"

"What about him? He's blissfully ignorant. Why ruin that?"

"You don't get it, or you don't want to: He's caring for her grave. He doesn't know his wife is buried under the headstone engraved Terri Miller. How long can you let that go on?"

Ever since Beebe was quite little, her father acted as caretaker for Larkspur Cemetery.

"Me. You're putting this on me. You did this. You let it get this far. You tell him. He wasn't there for me after Mother left."

"Aw, come on," he said, getting up and crossing the room, "that was thirty years ago. Give it up. He tried. He misses you. You two should have had the counseling you're giving people now. You just need some time to think about this. It's a lot to digest. You'll reconsider."

"I doubt that day will come."

The eyes he turned on her were so full of disbelief bordering on horror that she found it hard to keep from dropping her gaze. "What's happened to you? Why aren't you with the church any longer?" He gave those questions a good long wait, but Beebe couldn't find the desire, because it required strength, to answer. When he moved toward the door, she thought he accepted the impasse. She was wrong. "I refuse to give up so easily. Please, Beebe, think about coming home. I'll call you tomorrow."

Beebe pushed herself off the couch. "Give it longer than that."

Shaking his head, Vincent Bostick let himself out.

Before he was off the porch, Beebe felt her knees unhinge. She put a hand down to the couch arm to ease her collapse onto the cushion.

Way too much baggage churned inside her. Her mother. Her father. All the reasons she chose the church. All the reasons she left it...rocked her life again.

* * *

About once every six weeks, Cliff Walker drove with Rosemary Olmsted and Vincent Bostick to Newton, Michigan, after Sunday services for the barbeque ribs at Omar's. They always felt a little overdressed for Omar's when they wedged themselves into the restaurant's dingy lobby, but not after they crowded around one of the small round tables in the main room. By then, they'd donned the bibs provided and sported the same uniform as all the other diners.

The threesome decided to make the trip to Omar's on the first Sunday in July. Their routine varied in two respects: First, Vincent drove his own car, so he could continue on to the auction house down the pike in Harrelsburg. The second change-up was Rosemary's request to stop at Larkspur Lake on the way back to walk the trail winding through the quiet, recreational area. Rosemary didn't ask to stop until they passed the main entrance and were coming up on a lesser-used road with little parking.

Cliff's stomach fluttered when he heard her idea, but he acquiesced. He would have rather just taken Rosemary on home. He pulled off the county road and onto the back lake road. His was the only vehicle parked on the dirt shoulder, and they were the only walkers. A fickle breeze, warm, then cool, escorted them along the trail.

"Don't you think Vincent seemed a little quiet at lunch? I really had to push him to get him to come with us," Rosemary said, squinting up to Cliff and blocking the afternoon sun with her hand.

He stood a shade over six foot. At fifty-eight, she remained easy on the eyes, although she carried a few extra pounds. The cause was probably Omar's ribs; the cure was probably a little extra exercise on Sunday afternoons.

"I suppose he just wanted to get to the auction house," Cliff said.

"I thought he was just there."

"Evidently, the auctioneer has more items Crossroads could use." Cliff knew that as Crossroad's director, Vincent tried to outfit the organization's hospice and senior center with gently-used furniture. He was bound by a meager budget.

"Yeah, well, he's a good man." Rosemary elbowed Cliff. "You're a good man, too." Then Cliff felt her fingertips glide across his palm and slip between his digits.

Uh-oh, Cliff thought. He should have listened to his stomach, which fluttered wildly again, instead of allowing Rosemary to lure him to the unpopulated side of the lake. "What's this?" he asked, in stride, holding up his hand loosely laced to hers.

"Can I hold your hand?"

Now she asked permission, he thought. "You already are." He didn't furnish consent.

"Don't like the forward girls?" Her face creased where her smile made inroads.

"I don't quite think of you as a girl."

"What am I then? Just a buddy. Like Vincent. We could have something here if you'd let it happen. It doesn't need to always be the three of us."

He turned away from the impossible scenario she described. He looked out across the rippling water, fully aware her eyes hung on him. He felt her warm palm against his, the pressure of her fingertips. He debated his answer. She tugged him to a stop.

"They call it taking the next step. Let's try. Don't say no. Say you'll think about it."

"Everything will change."

"We won't let it."

"I like our friendship the way it is." He pulled his hand from hers.

She stared at her empty hand. "Now, I've ruined it, I suppose."

"No, not at all."

"You don't embrace change, Cliff Walker. I know that. I also know what's best. I see right through you. We could be good together. And it's high time we got together."

Rosemary, normally on target with her ideas and insights, missed the mark on this occasion. Despite his wife's long absence, he was not tempted to enter a relationship. Without trying, his spark for Abigail Walker never went out. It felt like betrayal to even hold hands with another woman. Everything about Rosemary's hand felt foreign. If blindfolded, he swore he would know if Abigail's fingers slipped through his.

"Take some time," Rosemary said. "Think about it."

"I don't need time. We can't date."

"What would be different, except that Vincent may or may not be there, depending. And you'd kiss me at the end of the evening. Of course, Vincent wouldn't be there for that." She feigned shyness by digging her toe in the dirt. "We're private people. I get that."

"Rosemary, ah..."

She grabbed his hand again. "Think about it."

"Geez, you're pushy for a Sunday-after-church buddy," he said teasingly.

She looked up at him with those soft gray eyes that signaled she was a good person. She lay her other hand gently on his cheek. "Think about it," she repeated. "Now, take me home. These shoes were a bad choice for this much walking." She chortled.

With that, she released her hold on him and turned. Her skirt twirled. She headed back up the path, ahead of him. She gave him no choice but to follow.

It was true. Cliff Walker and Rosemary Olmstead were private people. Rosemary moved to Larkspur from Kerr, forty miles north and a jog east, ten years ago. Someone wanted the family restaurant she owned in Kerr for a development deal. The money was good, so she took it, looked around, and purchased the empty downtown diner in Larkspur.

In contrast to Cliff's one-and-only hometown life, Larkspur represented a bold new start for Rosemary. She was a woman of determination. That quality notwithstanding, his decision was already made. The buddy system would prevail.

Wandering Delirium

It was Tuesday. Vincent Bostick steered his freshly serviced Chevy down Town Street. He spent the last hour at the Lube and Oil, south of Larkspur's city limits. Since his stomach was sending out hints that he should not turn up Standhope, but hurry on to Rosemary's before the lunchtime rush, he followed that course.

A month and a half passed since his visit to Beebe Walker. The only thing shorter than his engagement to Beebe was the conversation in her living room.

He stayed in town for two days and attempted to pursue a resolution to his request, but his calls went unanswered. On the third day, he drove to her street and parked several houses down. He called again. Her car sat in the driveway, but she didn't pick up. Two weeks later, he reached out from Larkspur, and three weeks after that. Every attempt went to voice mail. He always left a message.

All the while, he tried to conduct himself as normally as possible with Cliff. Since he hadn't mentioned his visit to Cliff's daughter, Vincent merely loaded more secrets into the gaping barrier between them. Granted, only Vincent perceived the barrier's existence, and only Vincent heard Beebe's silence.

The downtown restaurant lay within his sights, just a half block away, when a man with a full crop of white hair stumbled out between a van and a tall truck parked at the curb. The truck was delivering to McKinley's Hardware. Right behind the older man came a lanky gent, wearing a McKinley uniform shirt, his two arms outstretched toward the first man's shoulders. Vincent's heart leapt. Fear endorphins produced instantaneous reactions: His foot slammed the brake pedal to the floor. His arms stiffened, and his grip tightened on the wheel. With his backbone pressed into the seat cushion, he got the Chevy's bumper stopped just inches from striking both men.

He recognized the older one as Reverend Mosie Razzell, the former pastor of First Lutheran Church. Cliff Walker, Beebe's father, wore the McKinley uniform. He worked his duties as the cemetery's caretaker around his full-time job at the hardware store.

Vincent threw the car door open and got out with only a few seconds delay. He needed to get his breathing jump-started again and yank the transmission into park. Cliff tugged on Rev. Razzell, trying to get him back to the curb, but the seventy-seven-year old man resisted. He looked frightened of Cliff and slapped at his arms.

Vincent rounded the car's fender. "I nearly ran you both down," he chided before the scene playing out in the middle of the street registered.

This was the first time he observed Razzell's odd behavior. Others had to some degree. The majority of them were seniors who were in and out of Crossroads as Razzell was. None reported anything as serious as the situation Vincent just witnessed.

Razzell was a golden fixture in Larkspur and of an age that made him unwilling to accept the idea of dementia. Vincent hated the thought, but what other explanation could there be. Neither was he particularly enamored by the fight—fistfight, most likely—that would ensue trying to get the obstinate senior before a geriatrician.

Razzell whipped his head around at the sound of Vincent's voice, then he gave Cliff a double-take. Razzell knitted his brows. It appeared to Vincent that Razzell struggled to bring Cliff into focus, slow on recognizing him. "Well," Razzell stammered, then picked up some steam, "it's Cliff's fault."

The reverend's tentative blame-passing bounced off patient Cliff with his one-track mind. "Come on, Mosie. Come back up on the sidewalk, so Vincent can get through. We're blocking traffic." Two vertical worry lines cut into the space between Cliff's dark brows.

Vincent saw that a second car waited. He and Cliff each took one of Razzell's arms and led him to safety. Razzell seemed to stare hard at the curb before he lifted his foot.

"Let me get out of the road. Stay here, Rev. Razzell, until I get back. Wait for me. Okay?" Vincent said.

Razzell gave him a jumpy nod, his eyes unfocused behind rimless glasses.

Vincent found a parking place for his car four spaces up. He hurried back along the sidewalk. Razzell still fussed with Cliff.

"I saw him out here," Cliff said to Vincent when he reached them. "He nearly tripped over the ramp."

An angled metal ramp jutted down from the back of the delivery truck to the asphalt. Crossing here meant Razzell attempted to jaywalk. Where was he headed? A women's dress shop faced the hardware store across the street. That didn't make sense.

"It shouldn't be there, in the road," Razzell argued.

"You're right," Vincent said. He looked inside the truck's doorway. An orange traffic cone sat there. Grabbing it, he marked the obstruction. Razzell still seemed flustered to Vincent, now by how quickly Vincent solved Razzell's immense problem. "It's lunchtime, Reverend. I thought I'd stop at Rosemary's. Cliff, can you get away?" Good manners required Vincent to include him. "We'll all go. My treat. It's Tuesday. Rosemary serves Swiss steak on Tuesday."

"I don't want to eat. I'm not hungry." At that moment, a transformation occurred. Razzell's long distinguished face took sturdy form. He puffed out his chest, as round as a robin's and clothed in a button-down shirt. "Will you unhand me?" He glared at Cliff, who dropped his arm. "What, were you going to carry me off against my will?" His next salvo fired at Vincent. "And I've got plenty of food in my Frigidaire. I'll feed myself, if you don't mind. I can't imagine what got into you two." He employed his contagious grin. "But I forgive you. Bingo tonight, Vincent?"

"Yeah, sure." A confused Vincent flashed a tentative smile. Behind Razzell, Vincent watched Cliff scratch his head, which Vincent interpreted as Cliff also wondering about the minister's sudden clarity of mind.

Razzell's expression was a pleasant one when he turned to Cliff with a question. "Why don't you come?"

Vincent clenched his teeth. He hoped Cliff wouldn't accept the invitation. He still avoided Beebe's father when he wasn't literally running into him.

"Thanks for asking, but I can't manage tonight," Cliff said.

"The cemetery?"

"Keeps me busy."

"You're one of God's good servants." Razzell patted Cliff's arm. To Vincent, he said, "See you at Crossroads."

Off Razzell strode, toward home, agile, like a twenty-year old.

"That was bizarre," Cliff said, staring after Rev. Mosie Razzell, now out of hearing distance.

"I'll keep my eye on Mosie. Something's definitely wrong there. Crossroads needs to be involved."

Vincent's mind was conjuring up something like a Facebook page for each senior in Larkspur. Access to the individualized page would be limited to Crossroads. There, he could cross-reference, make comments, and add tickler notes. The idea felt like a top-notch organizational tool. While it still rummaged around for size and color, the newborn idea already gained weight. Crossroads' board of directors would no doubt bless his official proposal at the next meeting, then he could put the full force of Crossroads behind getting Razzell in front of medical attention.

"Well, how about lunch?" Vincent felt he had to follow through on his invitation despite his ongoing efforts to steer his guilt about the Terri Miller/Abigail Walker situation around Cliff. To add to his guilt, Vincent felt relief when Cliff turned him down.

"The delivery needs tending to." Contrary to his answer, Cliff gave a long look down to Rosemary's.

* * *

Vincent walked back up the sidewalk, passing his car. He crossed Town at the intersection, then waited for the walk light at Cramer, crossed again, and pushed through the door into the diner. An array of delicious smells teased his palate, pushing all guilty thoughts about Cliff Walker off to the side.

For over three months, he kept Abigail Walker's death a secret from her husband. Was he really obliged to keep a deathbed promise? He wrestled with that on a continuous basis. If Beebe would simply relent, find some compassion for her father, and come home, they could team up to break the news. Whether she wrestled too, or buried the obligation, he didn't know. All was mum on the Beebe front. In the meantime, though, Cliff Walker remained innocently unaware.

Although Rosemary handled all the waitressing chores, she would have been easily recognizable to Vincent when he entered if the restaurant employed a host of female wait staff. A woman in a spiffy white uniform dress and starched apron with its neatly tied bow, faced away from the door. The long, thick honey-brown braid that plunged down her back would always set Rosemary apart in a crowd. The cord of hair nearly met the knotted bow. She poured coffee from one glass pot into another. She set the empty pot on the coffee machine's burner, then flipped the switch. Immediately, the machine began filling the pot with brewed coffee.

Turning, she spied him. "Hey, Vincent. A booth?"

Four of the eight booths along the windows were taken, but several empty seats remained at the counter. It would be easier to talk with Rosemary from there. He took the seat most segregated from the other diners.

"Just you today?" she asked.

"Afraid so."

"Why is that? Why just one?"

"I tried to increase my number, but no takers."

"Who refused you? What woman would turn you down?"

"Boy, did you get that wrong!" Vincent's tone was upbeat, but mentally, he wondered how Rosemary could slip like this.

Vincent's wife, Carolyn, died seven years ago, three years after Rosemary's arrival in Larkspur. Carolyn had been thirty-six. Vincent remembered those days after he lost his wife. He wore wrinkled clothes and kept a messy house. Most days, his face carried stubble, and his hair was generally in need of a barber.

Carolyn had also been a Larkspur transplant. She relocated to care for her uncle in his waning years. In her free time, the young woman wrote and published poetry. They met when he redelivered a poetry periodical mistakenly left in his mailbox, a block from its intended destination. After Uncle Karl's passing and a short courtship, they married. Carolyn's headaches preceded the vision problems. All the medical tests led to the same diagnosis: a fast-growing and inoperable brain tumor. The only course of action the oncologist offered was a chance to slow the tumor down. After four chemotherapy sessions, weight-loss, and hair-loss, the tumor's rampage remained unstilted.

Vincent remembered how from the minute the two women met, Carolyn and Rosemary hummed with rapport. Rosemary knew how much Vincent suffered after Carolyn's death. And yet this wasn't the first time Rosemary talked as if the most natural thing in the world was for Vincent to date and with vigor and regularity. How could she, of all people, not know he wouldn't ever be ready?

"No," he said, sloughing off her mental slip, "I was just chatting with Rev. Razzell. Then I asked Cliff, but he had a delivery coming in. He's usually game for lunch."

"No. That figures. I can tell you. He's not happy with me. We had a disagreement after we left Omar's."

"Well, I'm sorry to hear that. Things seemed okay at lunch. I hope you patch it up," Vincent said seriously. He never knew Cliff and Rosemary to utter a cross word to the other. Naturally, he wondered about the subject of their disagreement. Rosemary clarified that.

"Pig-headedness. Sometimes it doesn't pay to be blessed with insight when others are blessed with pig-headedness."

Vincent moved Rosemary toward the positive portion of her declaration. "Say, I'd like to test out your insight." He described the near miss on Town Street and Rev. Mosie Razzell's confusion. "What's your take?"

"Clearly, Vincent," she said, "you've been Razzelled."

"What?" Then he laughed at her manufactured term. It felt good. "You're more than insightful, you're clever."

"You've got to admit, Mosie has always been a character. The crazy ties. The Sunday night he wore clown shoes to preaching and the boutonniere that squirted water."

Vincent enjoyed Rosemary's glittering eyes. His recent memory of the buttoned-down man was replaced with the minister preaching on the Sunday evening Rosemary spoke of. It was six years ago. Razzell was near the tail-end of his career. His sermon was titled, Case in point: Taking ourselves more seriously than God.

"For me, this isn't something that came with his old age—which I suspect you'd agree is the general category of his problem," Rosemary said, "but a wandering delirium, too."

"That's apt, based on today's antics. Sometimes he's in there, sometimes he's not. Trick is, how to get him in front of a doctor?"

Vincent's mind snapped out another idea for Crossroads' members. In addition to the accountant Vincent lined up to assist seniors at tax time, and the local caterer who invited groups to her kitchen for Cooking For One lessons, he thought he'd organize a Health Fair day for seniors. Vincent could certainly issue Rev. Razzell a personalized invitation to attend, but that might trigger Razzell's suspicious nature. Vincent definitely wanted to waylay that. Instead, he'd give the good reverend some part to play, like on bingo night, when he called the numbers.

"A doctor. That's the trick, all right. Um, Vincent," Rosemary stammered. Vincent raised his eyebrows. "I'm just wondering how you're doing. Is everything okay?"

"Me? Why?

"Well, Sunday, it took a little prodding to get you to join Cliff and me at Omar's. You worried about something?"

"Nah. That was just me trying to manage my time. You know, what with needing to get to the auction house." It took every ounce of fortitude he could muster to keep his gaze trained on this caring and intuitive soul, given the fact he told her a boldfaced lie. In the future, he must try harder to mask his feelings regarding his position at the center point of the Walker family triangle.

A few seconds later, she was back with his Swiss steak luncheon special. He ate with a little less fervor than he expected he would when he sat down.

Rosemary walked him out the door after he paid the bill. Like Cliff, she cast a gloomy look down to the hardware store. He hated that something came between the two friends, since he knew exactly how that weighed on one's spirit. Carolyn always said Rosemary and Cliff felt like family. On the Father's Day before she died, Carolyn gave a card to Cliff, saying just that. Cliff grieved her loss as solemnly as Vincent.

Rosemary showed her love for Carolyn early into the chemo treatments. She placed some phone calls and learned how her cut hair could be fashioned into a wig for Carolyn. Carolyn admired Rosemary's beautiful hair so. What could be a greater gift?

Vincent was there when Carolyn heard Rosemary's plans. She cried and pulled Rosemary into a tight embrace on the living room sofa, but she wouldn't permit the sacrifice. She flat-out said no.

A few months later, when the dismal test results came back, she raised a hand to her chest. She spoke more to herself than to Vincent. "I'm so glad I didn't let Rosemary cut her hair." Carolyn and Vincent held each other in the dining room of their home. Their days were running out. Their moments together were precious ones.

The next week, Vincent let Rosemary into the house and led her down the hall to Carolyn's bedside. His wife reached out. Her vision was as smoky as the restaurant owner's eyes by then. Her hand found Rosemary's thick hemp of hair, braided to one side, so it draped easily over her left breast.

"It soothes my heart to know that Vincent can lean on your strength," Carolyn said.

Twenty-four hours later, she lapsed into unconsciousness. Four days after that, she was gone.

All those memories flashed through Vincent's mind the instant he bid Rosemary goodbye, his palm lay on her back, his fingertips touching the braid.

Proper Goodbye

* * *

Beebe Walker sank low into one of the easy chairs in the meeting room that occupied the largest portion of the carriage house behind Swanson Funeral Home. The converted carriage house accommodated the grief counseling classes Swanson provided.

In reality, she suffered grief right along with the fourteen people who attended the Tuesday afternoon session she led. She knew this, but she sought out no one to tell her troubles to. Like the foolish lawyer who was also the client or the doctor diagnosing his own symptoms, she was a counselor confiding only in herself. She didn't grieve the loss of faith, but rather the full days she remembered her faith filling.

Beebe would never be immune to another's sorrow. But a grief counselor for years? She couldn't picture that. While she held the job, and the hearts of those in need of healing rested in her hands, she would work tirelessly. She gave attention to all phases, every detail, right down to the fifteen easy chairs positioned in a circle for her classes.

These chairs were an enhancement over the folding chairs provided by the funeral home. Soon after Beebe took the reins, she put out a call for the gently-used upholstered chairs family and friends of group members might be replacing. She thought it would take time to assemble a comfortable array, but word spread. Chairs arrived from all points. In a few short weeks, an eclectic selection pushed the cold metal chairs into a storage closet in the corner.

With every chair for her afternoon session filled, Beebe looked to the man on her left. She asked him to get the conversation started. The exchange that played out was as easy and sweet as the summer day outside.

"I never thought I'd be sitting here talking about the rest of my life without Pat," a widower said.

"People are just snatched to heaven," a woman observed.

"I want to back up and live those years again," a wife said of her married life.

"What would you change?" another asked.

"Would anything need to be changed?"

"If everyone thinks about it, there's always something they would change."

"No love, no relationship is perfect."

"Everyone has regrets."

Connie Chappell

"Two roads, or three?" The question was sent across the circle.

"If we could back up a little earlier."

"That's a nice thought."

"Yes, if we could just go back and rewrite our mistakes."

"Maybe just tiny changes."

"Maybe just a few."

"Before people are snatched to heaven."

Beebe said not a word. For someone who sought no one to tell her troubles to, this perceptive group found and counseled her with a better-than-average gift on this sweet summer day.

The phrase that got her humming was, "go back and rewrite our mistakes."

Hadn't she fearlessly admitted her mistake? Beebe Walker, a minister preaching in the Lutheran church, veered disastrously off-target. She ended up at odds with the church and with God. The parting was not amicable. She felt remorse and grief. Today, this afternoon class tamed much of that. They touched her heart and with such poignancy. With her next breath, she knew she would rewrite her mistake.

That mistake was set in motion in her hometown, after her mother left, before high school graduation, when railways were laid to the future because it arrived fast, on hot steel, and was obscured by swirling smoke.

Fortuitously, she was handed an opportunity, and before it was gone—snatched, if you will—she would right the wrong.

* * *

"I sort of pictured you calling before now." Vincent Bostick's voice came through the cell phone pressed to Beebe's ear.

She placed the call two seconds after the door closed on the last group member to exit the carriage house. She headed toward her office, guilt going with her. "I answered all your earlier calls in my head. I said a few things. I heard your replies."

"I'm that easy to read?"

"I think so. Sometimes," she said, taking a seat behind her desk.

"So why the extra effort now? There must be a reason. Something that benefits you."

"Ouch! That hurts." She paused, waiting for Vincent to come back with a softening touch. He didn't. Maybe she didn't know this older version of Vincent

41

Bostick as well as she imagined. "I guess that hurts because it's true. Today, I sat through a particularly insightful counseling session. I offered nothing of value, but I received a jewel. One that got me thinking."

She looked up to the bulletin board on the wall by the door. This was one of Beebe's enhancements to Swanson's grief counseling program. The board was slowly filling with pictures. She encouraged her counselees to bring two photographs. A collage formed with the faces of loved ones that could no longer be touched, and the faces of those who missed that touch dearly.

"My mistake was in choosing the church. Back when we were just starting to date, I had a conversation with Rev. Razzell."

"Geez," she heard Vincent say.

"What?"

"I just saw him."

"He must be getting up there in years."

"He retired, what, six years ago. Now he calls the numbers on bingo night at Crossroads."

That was nice, Beebe thought, but she needed Vincent back on track. "I've made a decision," she said firmly. "I've got to go back to where my mistake occurred and begin again. That's home, Vincent. I'm coming home."

A beat passed. "It sounds like you mean for good."

"Yes, I think I do."

"Then sometime soon, we're going to have a conversation with your father about your mother."

Beebe's relief, in hearing Vincent still factored himself into that equation, produced an intake of air to such a degree that it raised her shoulders in the process.

From the moment Vincent said hello, her focus remained fixed on the bulletin board. Now, it blurred as she stepped back in time.

"They say a human being's sense of smell can rekindle a host of memories and emotions," she told Vincent. "When I came home from speaking with Rev. Razzell about studying theology, Daddy was just getting off the cemetery's lawn tractor. I can still remember the smell of cut grass, the heat of sun on my back when I told him I wanted to become a minister."

Beebe didn't share her next thought. It was funny that during that conversation, she and her father never mentioned her mother, but she was there.

She was a barbed wire through every phase of their relationship. Now, Beebe wanted to see that change.

"And to answer your earlier question," Beebe said, "we'll talk with Daddy as soon as I get home. Early August."

As soon as Beebe hung up from Vincent, with her courage stoked, she placed another call. It was answered on the fourth ring.

"Daddy?"

"Beebe?"

She wondered about his tone. Had it sounded somewhat gruff? The pattern of analyzing every nuance formed when her mother left her and her father behind. For today, she kicked old habits aside and pushed on. "It's good to hear your voice."

"It's been awhile."

"I know. My fault. Way too long. Mostly, that's why I'm calling."

Silence hung on the line.

"Daddy, can we talk for a minute? Have you got time?"

"Sure."

Beebe fought against the current that always ran between her and her father, and forced a sliver of cheer into her voice. "Good. I've had some changes in my life. I've talked with some people. Well, listened more than talked." She thought of the snatched-to-heaven circle of thoughts. "And, Daddy, I want to come home. Would you mind terribly if I stayed at the house?"

Her father's response to her inviting herself back into his house and his life was a momentary pause that Cliff concluded by clearing his throat. "Well, there's no problem there. It's not like I've rented your room or anything." He picked up his less-than-exuberant tone by adding a half-hearted chuckle. To be polite, Beebe added one of her own.

Then, when she thought she would blow by with the news that she left the church, his reaction was instantaneous.

"Left the church? Beebe, why? When?"

She was not prepared for the lengthy conversation this discussion would require, not now, not over phone lines, so she truncated the story. "I turned in my shield back in March." She infused a manufactured lilt across the words, while silently thanking Trydestone's deacon, Norm Rogers, for the use of his terminology. "I promise to tell you the rest of the story face to face, okay?"

He did not respond in kind. Into the silence, she forced new topics. She concentrated on the dissatisfaction she foresaw in the long run with the counseling job, and she tried to make light of the fact that her offer to live at home came with no means of income attached. Cliff Walker listened. Said little. His lackluster participation, she felt sure, was tied to her decision to bypass the story of her resignation from the church for another couple of weeks.

Hanging up, Beebe breathed an enormous sigh. The framed bulletin board on the wall before her morphed into gloomy shades of gray.

Elephant in the Room

Cliff Walker flipped the right-turn blinker up. He guided the white truck to a stop in the driveway alongside the caretaker's house that had been his home for more than forty years. He stepped out of the pickup, wearing the blue uniform that marked him an employee at McKinley Hardware back in Larkspur. His day job.

There were times when the day job and the cemetery caretaker's job overlapped. About three that afternoon, Pastor Ned McMitchell stopped by the hardware store. Wayne Downing, a man Cliff could vaguely picture, but didn't know, passed earlier that morning. The pastor and the part-time caretaker discussed the family's plans for burial.

Cliff was pleased to see Hal Garrett's truck parked beside the block building that sat a good fifty yards beyond the rear of the house. For fifteen years now, Hal acted as the cemetery's gravedigger and marker specialist, so there was a need to communicate the specifics of the upcoming interment. Hal came and went as needed. He was trusted and kept keys to the block building that served as workshop and office, with its curtained windows all around. As Cliff passed the low shrubbery that ringed the building, he made a mental note to trim back the offshoots.

Hal looked up when Cliff stepped inside. A desk and filing cabinets occupied one side of the space; a workbench and tools, the other.

The two men greeted each other. Hal wore a short-sleeved denim shirt tucked into Levi's. These were work clothes for the married man and father. The bulk of his week was spent as owner and operator of a heavy equipment company. That more than qualified him for the cemetery duties he undertook back when the heavy equipment company was just toddling about and money was scarce.

"Looks like you got the word." A plot card lay on the desk. Cliff closed the door. The room was small enough and Cliff's eyesight good enough that he saw Downing printed in large letters on the card.

"Yeah, I knew Wayne. Got a call from his brother, Pete."

They confirmed that Hal received the same date and time for services from Pete that Cliff got from Pastor McMitchell. "I can get the day off from the store, unless you want to standby." Most burials were weekdays. Cliff and Hal always coordinated schedules.

"I think I do. I'd like to be here for Pete. The Downings are good people."

"Fine," Cliff said. He took a few hesitant steps, then turned. Since Beebe's call the night before, he accomplished every task he undertook in the shadow of his daughter standing beside him. His sense of her was stronger in Hal's presence because she and Hal were schoolmates.

"Something else?"

"I got a call from Beebe last night."

"Really?"

Cliff thought Hal's response came in the form of a question because most people thought he and Beebe were an enigma where the definition of a family was concerned. "Yeah. She's talking about coming home. I don't think her plans are firm yet about when. She said early August."

"Wow. That'll be nice. I'm glad. I'm glad for you and for her."

Hal's genuineness registered. Of course, the small block building was overcrowded now. It wasn't Hal's sincerity that did it. It was the big white elephant neither man acknowledged. The trunked beast represented Beebe's mother, her departure during Beebe's high school years, and the memories Beebe must deal with upon her return. In the second and a half Hal and Cliff used to make room for the elephant, Cliff thought Hal reached the same conclusion: Surely, Beebe's thought this through.

"Yeah. Thanks," Cliff said to Hal's good wishes.

He made his way to the door, turned the knob, then held the door open somewhat longer than necessary for the elephant to squeeze through. The feeling that he drew everyone's eyes would walk with him into the foreseeable future.

Cliff followed the path made of square concrete stones back to the asphalt road. The stones did not abut each other.

As grassy strips broke up the pathway, snippets of Beebe's words over the phone, last night, cut into Cliff's thoughts. "Test the waters. Don't want to intrude. Your privacy. Stepping on each other's toes."

Beebe spoke as if the size of the house were the problem. It was not. Dancing around the problem was the issue. In reality, he didn't think he could dance with his daughter, nor she with him. They would attempt it, no doubt. But how soon, he wondered, would sore feet inflame their unavoidable past?

The jinx seemed to be in for Cliff. First Rosemary, then Beebe.

Putting off a relationship with Rosemary was purposefully done to keep his life exactly the way he lived it for twenty-five years, since Beebe went off to pastor her first church and rarely returned.

* * *

The next day after the lunch crowd vanished from the diner, Cliff stood on the sidewalk out front of the hardware store. He looked down the street with longing. The diner seemed to beckon. Hands in his pockets, he rattled loose change. His mind told his feet to walk the familiar path to the corner, but his feet resisted the order. Between mind and feet, his heart and stomach held their own conversation. His heart went out to Rosemary; his stomach wanted to yank it back, but the damage was done.

He didn't like being at odds with Rosemary. Their parting Sunday was amicable, but he allowed time to pass. More than he should have. Now a sheen of awkwardness glistened.

Finally, with a few jerky steps, he set off, then his gait smoothed out.

He pushed through the diner door. Rosemary stacked coffee cups. Her sole employee, Larry, nodded a silent greeting. With a wet cloth, he wiped crumbs from a table into his hand. Rosemary turned and saw Cliff. He watched her expression go bland. The internal banter started up again: mind and feet, heart and stomach. Then there was the damage. But it was the plea he felt his eyes convey that overrode them all and brought Rosemary over to the booth he slid into. She arrived with two cups of coffee and sat down across from him.

"Well," she said, "you couldn't avoid me forever. That's good to know."

"I wasn't avoiding you."

"Yes, you were."

"All right, I was, but…"

"But nothing. We've been solid friends for ten years."

"Let's not rehash ancient history. The recent past is where the problem lies."

"Fine. Have you thought about what I said at all?"

"Of course, I have."

"But the answer's still the same, right? We can't have a personal relationship outside this diner, outside church, outside the occasional movie, all of which are accomplished in separate cars. The ride to Omar's being the exception, but more likely than not, Vincent will make a threesome."

"You want to date, Rosemary, and I'm married."

"Oh, Cliff. You're not married. You haven't been for umpteen years."

"I never divorced her."

"It's a bold new world, Cliff. Do people even remember?"

"Sure they do. They'll talk."

Quietly, she said, "I don't care if they talk. We're good for each other. We could make this work. Our lives would be better. No one gets hurt. In fact, a smidgeon of the hurt might go away." She reached for his hand.

"But there's a new wrinkle."

"What?" Her hand pulled back.

"Beebe. She called Tuesday. She's had some changes in her life. I didn't get all the details, but what I heard sounded significant, and it's caused her to want to return home. She wants to live at the house. Timeline on that is up in the air." Before he pushed through the restaurant's door, he decided he would not project any disharmony between father and daughter, although he felt it. His daughter was no longer a minister. Not knowing the story made him think it was an embarrassing one. How would he explain it when people asked? His question was followed by Rosemary's.

"And you said?"

His mouth opened to respond, but Rosemary's hands rose to erase her question.

"Of course, you said yes to her living at home. You had to."

"I wanted to. Well," he paused, "honestly, not at first. But in the last two days, I found I got used to the idea."

"So there's no room for me. No," she blurted quickly. "That's self-centered. What's wrong with me? Good, Cliff, I'm happy for you, especially if you're looking forward to it. I want it to work out. Better lives and all that. That's my wish for you and your daughter."

"Nice speech. But you have every right to think about yourself and your feelings. I've been thinking about them, too. I can't say that I wouldn't like the idea of a woman, you, close. Like now, closer. And you're going to think this is just another excuse," he said, shifting noisily on the vinyl seat, "but I wonder what Beebe will think of me dating. And if she learns we got together just two days after she called, asking if her old room was available, she might take it as an obvious attempt to tamper with the success of our reunion. Was I trying to make her feel like a cog in the wheel?" He knew he was babbling, but he couldn't stop himself. "Quite frankly, I've heard that adult children can be worse with handling their parents' divorce than younger kids. Not that the divorce card is in play, but Beebe is an adult child. That's the connection." His mouth was open to say more when Rosemary cut him off.

"Oh, for the love of God, Cliff, will you listen to yourself? Beebe is an adult. I doubt she'll work collusion into the fact that our first date took place the weekend after she called. How would she even find out? It's a date, Cliff. Dinner. A movie. Nothing X-rated. I promise."

Cliff tried to interrupt several times, but Rosemary rode roughshod over him. Finally, she took a breath. She clamped her lips together, as if to stem the heated flow, and sent her gaze out the window. This Rosemary was a stranger to Cliff. He suspected it was better that he sat quietly. So he did.

She let a few seconds pass. When she brought her eyes back, her voice held more patience. "I get that you're worried. Nervous. About Beebe's return. About me. About us. I'll give you time, and in that time," she said, the stranger wagging a stern finger at him, "believe me, Cliff Walker, I'll be evaluating Beebe's proclivity to accept that her father might want to have a fully above-board relationship with a woman. All I'm asking for is step one: Date night. I'll give you time. A small amount of time. Don't waste it. Because if you do, I'll approach Beebe myself."

The small amount of time equaled about an inch and a half of space between Rosemary's thumb and finger. Cliff thought it best not to ask for an equivalency factor.

* * *

Vincent Bostick's eyes snapped open. It was dark in the one-room living quarters he occupied at Crossroads. He lay in a twin bed. Somewhere in the nether reaches of his mind while he slept, a fantastic idea burst into being. He threw back the sheet, flung his legs over the bed, and crammed his feet into slippers, all in one motion. The illuminated clock on the nightstand read 3:16.

Somehow lost in slumber, an obvious connection was made. More than a connection, he thought. He stood over at the door now, flipping on the overhead light. He married Beebe's return with the needs of seniors in Larkspur—not just those who were members of Crossroads and attended the center's activities, but all the seniors across Stryker County.

Beebe needed a job, and she matched perfectly with the coordinator position Vincent had open for the new programming. Would she accept, given their backgrounds? The time span involved stretched from their brief engagement after college to the unresolved "Abigail Walker, alias Terri Miller" situation with her father.

Wanting to believe she would accept, Vincent grabbed his working papers and laptop from the small round table in the corner. He scuffed down a long hallway and into the agency's main room. The path through the tables and chairs was lit well enough by the outside streetlight eking through the solid-paned storefront window. He found the electrical switch on the kitchen wall and suffered the glare of fluorescent lighting because he desperately needed coffee.

Backed by a firmly defined purpose, he picked up where he left off last evening. His fingers typed program specifications as his mind pictured Beebe performing the associated duties.

Months ago, the organization applied for, qualified, and received grant funding from the Michigan state government for enhanced senior programming. Crossroads overcame its first hurdle when local matching funds, necessary to obtain the state dollars, were identified through a foundation set up by a wealthy Larkspurian. The only drawback there was the duplicate reporting feature.

Vincent thought the grant sustained itself. It provided the funding needed to purchase upgraded computer software to meet state reporting requirements and the salary for the coordinator overseeing the programming. That's where Beebe fit in.

At six o'clock, he slipped off the stool at the bar that separated the kitchen from the main room. He went to start another pot of coffee. The fresh pot waited for him after his shower and shave. Vincent decided to live, work, and sleep at Crossroads after Carolyn's death. The house where his love for his wife overflowed became the old Victorian prison he wandered, hopelessly lost, during the weeks after the brain tumor took her.

Vincent worked off and on throughout the day, rereading and fine-tuning the program specifics. His deadline struck mid-afternoon when Ron Smith and Mona Gabriel, two of Crossroads' board members, arrived for a prearranged committee meeting.

They sat around the table in Vincent's office, one door down from his living quarters. The table was large enough for four. A scratched-up credenza he purchased at an auction sat against the wall inside the door. Earlier, Vincent carried in a tray with a pitcher of water, a carafe of coffee, the associated additives, glasses, and cups.

Ron and Mona listened throughout his summarization of the programming enhancements. While the programming was designed to benefit seniors in all reaches of the county, it was Rev. Mosie Razzell's brush with Vincent's front fender that ran through his mind, making Razzell's presence the honorary fourth in attendance at the table. Vincent left his outline for the senior watch program for last. This provided a natural transition to his proposal to offer Beebe a position with Crossroads.

Ron, clad in a suit and tie, practiced law in Larkspur and acted as Crossroads' legal counsel. "You say she's the ideal person to coordinate these programs," he said, playing with the onyx ring on his little finger.

"Beebe and I went to high school and college together. She's moving back to town. I haven't approached her yet. Before I do, I want to write the job description." Vincent sent his proposal to Mona.

She was dressed for an evening out with her husband and announced such when she swept into the meeting room twenty minutes earlier. When wheels turned behind Mona's large mocha-colored eyes, Vincent thought she would comment on hiring Beebe for the new post, but Mona bypassed that discussion to place herself in the spotlight instead. "I'll take on the task of contacting each board member individually about the new programs."

Vincent worked with Mona Gabriel long enough that he wasn't surprised in the least by how adeptly she formulated a plan to claim this step-up in programming as her triumph. Board members would associate her with their first introduction to Crossroads' new role.

Still in spotlight mode, she went on. "I'll check everyone's pulse—"

"Hold up, Mona." Ron cut her off at the medical term. Dark strands of hair fell and caught on Ron's long eyelashes. His hand whisked the strands away and Mona's plan with them.

She sat away from the table, one knee crossed over the other. Vincent thought she tried to maintain composure, but her jiggling foot told of her annoyance over Ron's interruption. Mona was married to Dr. Hershel Gabriel and, therefore, felt herself qualified to pepper her speech with medical jargon. Dr. Gabriel was a geriatrician, and a man Vincent respected and approached confidentially, several months ago, about being on call for Crossroads. His gratis services were never fully defined. The doctor was still "tossing the proposal around." Vincent hesitated to push.

"I want to review Vincent's documentation thoroughly first, since we're setting off on a new course—"

"Not new, just expanded."

Tit for tat. Vincent groaned to himself. Mona treated Ron to a break in his dialogue. Vincent maintained a neutral expression, but knew this as Mona's game of one-upmanship.

A tolerant smile curled at the corners of Ron's mouth, then he picked up his thought. "Either way, we'll be better off without any false starts."

"But why wait? I've got time this weekend. I can prepare everyone for the programming when the summaries are ready."

"Mona, please." His tolerance stretched now. "Leave me the weekend to get the wording finalized. Then Vincent can ship the files to everyone's inbox Monday."

"There are going to be some naysayers. I know exactly who. Why not make our pitch first, then follow up with the paperwork?"

"I'd rather make a coordinated effort after a full review, then present. You can have the telephone marketing job if you think it's necessary."

"I do."

"Fine. Just wait a few days."

Vincent failed in his effort not to sigh. This was like watching Mommy and Daddy fight.

After a few more jabs between them, Mona Gabriel—Gabby, the behind-her-back nickname used by those who knew her well—finally relented. She would delay in contacting the remaining nine board members. Vincent doubted she'd hear anything negative about the programming ideas identified. If there was any dissention or whining, she would bully said dissenter or whiner into submission in order to effectually pave her way to success. A successful day in Vincent's mind was the day she no longer sat on this board.

Ron, able to keep a handful of organizational points simultaneously alive in his head, pulled the conversation back to Beebe. "Reduce your recommendation of Beebe to writing, Vincent. Not all of the members know her. Even those who do will need her curriculum vitae."

Ron and Mona headed up the group not acquainted with Beebe. They both came to town after Beebe's work with the church began.

In answer to Ron's question, Vincent said he planned an August 1 start date for Beebe, then realized he jumped ahead. He had her actually accepting his employment offer before he made the pitch. He would make that contact yet today.

Above all, concern for Cliff and Beebe Walker rode high on Vincent's list. Their wellbeing was primary. Still, he agonized over breaking his word to Abigail Walker, who begged to remain anonymous under the name, Terri Miller.

"I think we've covered all the bases," Ron said.

That adjourned the meeting. Vincent stood, his antsy feeling sinking into his legs. He filed out of his small office behind the other two.

Old Ways in Good Repair

Vincent returned to his office. He checked his watch. It read 4:20. He called Beebe, praying she'd be free.

She picked up on the second ring. With very little preamble, he gave her the executive summary on the assistant's position and the grant that drove the programming. He left his worries out of it. The excitement that infused his voice didn't seem to catch in Beebe's.

"I'm coming, no matter what, Vincent. You didn't need to do that."

"But you'll need a job, and I've got one."

"I suppose so."

There was a thread of enthusiasm in her tenor that overturned his rising disappointment. "Does that mean I can tell my members you came on board with very little fuss?"

"Yes, Vincent, that's what that means."

He pictured her smile through the phone. "Good, because our senior population is skyrocketing. They are a wonderful volunteer base if they can be focused and funneled into a defined strategy. They need and want to take care of their own. Typically, that's seniors whose health begins to fail, and seniors whose homes become a challenge. I'm asking the board to approve medical checkup days and a canvass to register seniors so no one gets overlooked. The old cooking-for-one class is always well attended. Bingo is great. And the bus trips. But the proposed new programming is the meat and potatoes of what a good core group of seniors can do for each other. Oh, and because men aren't known for their nurturing ability, they'll take on small home repair and maintenance duties for elderly seniors. Nothing too elaborate. Whatever we can fund."

"And preparing and practicing for an emergency. I'm thinking about the homeless. Me, being close to one. One example, and it happened here," Beebe said. "A senior's home needed fumigating. For three days, the man had nowhere to stay. Those situations just come up without warning. Your seniors could be mobilized to respond. I'm thinking the displaced person would stay at the center. Could that happen?"

"You're great, Beebe." Vincent, on his feet, carried the conversation down the hall and into the main room. "I'm going to use that example with the board of how you're already thinking. With your background in grief therapy, seniors can take mini courses to assist older members of the community, see the signs, at least know to involve you."

"Senior Life 101," Beebe assigned a course description.

The positive discussion drew him toward the sunshine. He stood on the stoop. "An excellent name. We're a good team." He made an internal note to change Beebe's job title from community center spiritual assistant to senior life assistant. He asked her to email her curriculum vitae. She said she'd take Sunday and complete it. She had all day. Still not attending church, he thought.

"I'll need to get someone on the hook here to replace me," Beebe said. "Listen to me, talking in fishing terms. Just the hint of going home does it."

Beebe's enthusiasm was throttling up, but Vincent lost some momentum. "I hadn't thought about a replacement. What are the chances?"

"The ministers in town will help out. Some of the larger churches have assistant pastors who are quite capable. It's Swanson's choice."

"The funeral home director?"

"Fourth generation. Robert Swanson. I feel bad about being a short-timer, but maybe Robert had several choices when he asked me to take the job. I'll get with him tomorrow."

"You're sure?" He had to keep asking. He hadn't wanted something to work out this much in a long, long time. He missed Carolyn. He missed someone close in his life. Not that he wanted a romantic relationship with Beebe. He wanted a friend, a friend with depth, someone to talk with about the center's management on his level, not the board members, not the volunteers. Beebe would cross all phases of his life.

"I'm sure," Beebe said. "A session break comes up the first two weeks in August, so my replacement needs to be in place by the third week. That seems doable, somewhat quick, but doable."

"You're helping us out at this end."

"I really appreciate this, Vincent. I will do my best for you."

Vincent heard the sincerity in her words. "I know that."

"But Daddy." Beebe's excited tone drained with those two words. "Remember, the real reason I'm coming home is Daddy. He'll be suffering almost the minute I get there."

Vincent wandered down the sidewalk in front of Crossroads. "You know I'll sit beside you when you tell him. If you want that."

"Yes, I do. He'll want a first-hand account. How's he doing? I'm going to call him later."

"I'm not aware of any problems." Vincent used general terms. He suspected something was amiss between Cliff and Rosemary. There was Terri Miller's grave with his wife's remains buried there. Plus, the fact that Cliff would realize her March death was kept from him for months. Vincent could see Cliff operating under the premise that Vincent's involvement to hire Beebe was equal to scheming behind his back. Which it was. Cliff would not see that the delay to sit and speak with him about his wife's death was in his best interest. No way was he going to see that at the outset. Aloud, Vincent said, "This is his busy time. Summers always are. The hardware store promotes outdoor projects which bring customers in, and the cemetery grows grass with wild abandon."

"Good. If I know Daddy, he'll handle this thing with Mother and stick to his schedule. That is the best medicine. By fall, we should be over the hump."

"Should be." Vincent was a little less optimistic.

"The unknown factor in this is how Daddy and I will get along."

Beebe closed up her conversation with Vincent before he responded. His thoughts drifted to a similar unknown factor: How would he and Cliff get along after Cliff learned the part he played?

Vincent knew how people suffered after the death of a loved one. Unlike Abigail Walker, Carolyn received medical care at Lakeside General. Vincent stayed close at her bedside. Carolyn's invading tumor did not allow her to convert her thoughts to speech. He had so wanted to hear her voice once more before she left him to stumble through life without her.

When he looked around, Vincent found himself sitting on the bench where he first saw Abigail Walker, thinking about the last time he saw Carolyn.

* * *

Beebe hung up. She heard the hope in Vincent's voice. She hadn't heard hope associated with her in a long time. Well, she thought, maybe that was too narrowly defined. She had no hope for herself on the church side of things. Others—those who grieved—found hope through her. That, she admitted, had value.

Hope and value, when the pairing was her and her father, were noticeably absent. Their relationship donned a continually scratchy feel, like a wool suit, and an ill-fitting one. She dialed her father's home number while she ambled across the funeral home's parking lot to her car.

"I just this minute walked in the house to call you for an update," Cliff said.

Beebe slowed her step. She heard a crunch of interest in his voice so she ignored the wooly chafing and provided a rundown of Vincent's involvement.

"Things are coming together for you," he said. "I'll have to remember to thank Vincent. I sort of had my antennae out for something you might like, but this sounds like a great collaboration."

"You sound pleased." Her words carried the scalloped edge of suspicion she'd tried to trim.

"I am. Of course, I am."

His tone seemed positive, but still, she wished she could see his face to determine if believability lived there. Maybe it did, she thought, and felt herself soften by degrees. Cautiously pliant, she asked him about his day, and he told her.

She sat in her car's front seat, the door open, key still in her hand. It surprised her that he focused on the cemetery, not the hardware store. In her malleable state and hearing about the tasks in and around the cemetery jogged a wealth of memories of her early childhood. Every summer night before bedtime, she and her father walked the winding path to the cemetery's back gate. He always held her hand all the way there and all the way back. She looked up at the tall man. He told her stories of symbolism about the ancient markings on the grave stones. She couldn't draw her eyes away. The heavens sparkled with dancing stars just beyond his face, seeming so close, that if he raised her up, she could touch them.

Some of his daylight duties included her company in their completion. There was a block building within view of the caretaker's house. Inside that building, Beebe would often catch her father tending to the oiling of incredibly old and incredibly long leather strips. The oil preserved them.

"When the cemetery was new," Cliff said to his young daughter, "one-hundred-seventy-five years ago, before you, or me, or Mommy, loved ones used these straps to lower caskets into the graves. Back then, that's how it was done."

Beebe's job was to hold her end of the leather strip taut, so her father's large hand and the cloth it grasped could massage the oil in. While he talked, Beebe looked over to the narrow table positioned against the wall. A chisel and hammer lay there. Seven-year old Beebe was squatted beside her father when he opened a dust-covered box he rescued from the attic. Even Beebe knew the tools he lifted out were old.

"Lots of hands have touched these," he said. As they walked through the cemetery over the next few days, he pointed out the headstones with enough age that the chisel and hammer they found were used to engrave the lettering.

On another day after Beebe got home from school, she stood across the floor in the maintenance shack. She held protective goggles to her eyes because its elastic strap was too stretched to do the job itself. She watched sparks shoot off the grinder as her father sharpened the heavy forged-steel chisel.

When he was satisfied with the result and told her she could lay the goggles aside, he said words she remembered still. "It's our job to keep the old ways in good repair."

Beebe learned her sense of duty from her father.

* * *

Right on time, Vincent Bostick crossed the street to Ned and Willa McMitchell's one-story Tudor, shaded by a fabulous cedar. He'd walked the four blocks from Crossroads. The McMitchells were going on seven years in Larkspur. They came to town six months before the date Rev. Mosie Razzell chose for his retirement. None of the members of First Lutheran Church—and Vincent was one—noticed any sparks between the two men of the cloth. They worked together for the congregation, community, and a smooth transition.

Vincent knocked on the front door. The McMitchells expected him. He made the arrangements earlier, after Sunday services. Today, he combined God's work with the center's work. He needed Ned's assistance with a certain retired pastor.

Willa, seven months pregnant with their first child, opened the door, gave Vincent a brilliant smile, and pulled him inside. Ned came up behind them, leaving the door to his study wide. The threesome decided to adjourn to the back patio for the talk Vincent wanted to have about Rev. Mosie Razzell.

"Nice Sunday afternoon," Willa said. She set a tray with a pitcher of iced tea and glasses on the patio table.

Vincent and Ned sat in adjacent chairs with the sun at their backs. The umbrella spearing the tabletop was tipped to assist with blocking the sun's rays.

"Have you started nesting yet?" Vincent grinned up at Willa, accepting the filled tea glass she handed him.

Ned took the question instead. "Oh my word, you should see her. She puts on thick socks and a flannel gown and knits. I sat on the needles last night."

Willa's round features, face and belly contrasted with Ned's straight-arrow physique. Even her hair, its wavy, long locks, barretted in a bundle at the back of her head, posed in opposition to her husband's short cut, with its front section pushed off his forehead into a cowlick.

"Crochet, dear," she said with love in her eyes. Wisps of her golden hair caught the breeze. "I do what I can."

Vincent enjoyed the McMitchells' company often enough to know this was a favored expression of Willa's.

"You see what I'm up against," Ned said. The six-foot-six man was folded at pointed angles into the cushioned patio chair. Willa sat down next to her husband. When they touched hands, Vincent's thoughts snagged on his love for Carolyn and the everyday pleasures living with her brought.

"So you want to talk about Mosie? You don't mind if Willa stays?" Ned asked.

"Fine with me," Vincent said, then immediately included Willa in the conversation. "Have either of you noticed a change in Mosie?"

"We both noticed," Ned said, tugging at his left earlobe.

"He can't seem to hold his focus." Willa added. "He's seventy-seven, but he's always been sharp."

"What have you noticed?" Ned asked Vincent. "More of the same?"

"A little more dangerous," Vincent said. "Have I ever told you the story about the old minister crossing the road? He didn't make it to the other side."

Willa gasped.

Vincent related the story that played out in front of the hardware store. In conclusion, he said, "He was out there initially, then he just snapped back in."

"What do you propose?"

"Well, he's a prime candidate for the new programming I'm designing for Crossroads. Cliff Walker's daughter, Beebe, has agreed to take a position at the center."

"Beebe?" Willa said.

"She grew up here, of course. When she said she was thinking about returning, I approached her. She's perfect."

"So, if I may anticipate, you're recruiting me to help line Mosie up for Ms. Walker's assistance. Are they acquainted?" Ned wanted to know.

"Yes, they are, and so far, all comments are favorable for the board's approval of the programming." Vincent felt a restless eagerness stir. The worthwhile programs established a new and welcoming purpose within him. "But approval or not, Mosie needs someone looking in on him."

"Nearly struck by a car is serious," Willa said. "Will you go to him, Ned? Shouldn't you go right away? It's Sunday. That should play in your favor."

"I doubt it being Sunday will make him any more receptive."

Vincent's mind automatically expounded on Ned's statement. These days, Mosie was often grumpy. One never knew which Mosie would greet them, or on his grouchy days, would, more correctly, bark at them.

Willa gaped at her husband. "Are you saying, why try?"

Ned answered. "Oh, no. We have to try."

In the end, they waited until Monday afternoon.

Road to Larkspur

Dark clouds hung back at the horizon. With spitting rain already coming down, Vincent Bostick and Pastor Ned McMitchell decided to drive to Rev. Razzell's house rather than walk the few blocks. Vincent switched the ignition off. When both men stood on the sidewalk, they looked up at Razzell's cottage-style house with its pitched roof over the door set off to the right, making ample room for a picture window and brick chimney on the other side.

Ned sighed. He moved toward a winding front walkway. "This is going to be an uphill battle. But one worth the effort."

Vincent fell into step behind.

"When I got to town," Ned said with a laugh, "I never heard such praise for a man before. I don't have to tell you. You grew up in Larkspur."

Vincent silently watched the pace of his own beat-up loafers and navy chinos in step on the concrete behind Ned's black and gray Nikes and black nylon sports pants.

"I expected a magnitude of limp handshakes and pasted-on smiles before people accepted me as here to replace Mosie," Ned went on. "That wasn't the case. Just seeing me with him was enough. Folks didn't consider me a competitor or interloper. Their affection was almost instantaneous. I owe that to him."

Ned stopped at the foot of the porch steps. Vincent knew the impact of the difficult situation caught up to him.

Pulling alongside, Vincent patted Ned's back. "This can't wait. I've tried to prepare the words I'll use, but…" Vincent's inability to complete the sentence only proved his struggle to align kindness and tact with the shattering concept he and Ned would deliver to Mosie Razzell. "Damn it! It shouldn't take programming and the state's money to reach out to a beloved community member in need."

Ned's expressive eyebrows tilted up comically at the foul language.

"Pardon my French. I bet I got that accent wrong." Both men laughed. The tension broke.

"Let's do this," Ned said. "My guess is, you won't be the only one swearing before this is done."

Vincent knocked on an aluminum screen door, taking in signs of disrepair. The caulking around the door was dried and cracked; the white paint, peeling. These were the small repairs a maintenance team with a qualified handyman could address.

Mosie Razzell pulled the wooden front door open. Vincent looked up to Ned, then back to Razzell. Despite their smiles, Razzell frowned deeply. Apparently, he interpreted their arrival on his porch for just what it was, a harbinger for bad news.

"What do you want?" Razzell said sharply.

Evidently, Razzell was working on a crotchety day. It saddened Vincent to see such a drastic deviation from the first impression Ned related just a minute ago. "Afternoon, Mosie. Ned and I want to talk about one of the pilot programs Crossroads will undertake when some state funding comes through."

"Can we step inside?" Ned asked.

On guard, Razzell pulled the screen door he'd pushed open back several inches.

"Do you want to come out, then? The drizzle has almost stopped," Vincent said. Razzell's porch held two lawn chairs with seating for a third on the wooden rail.

"No. And I don't want to listen to nonsense either."

"Come on, Mosie. Give us a chance. You shouldn't call it nonsense until we've gotten through our spiel," Ned said.

Razzell sent his cross expression to Vincent. "Can we move this along?"

"I was hoping to appeal to your leadership abilities," Vincent said, "but I can see you want this without any sweetening, so here goes: After I nearly ran you down on Town Street, I got worried."

"You seem confused a lot lately, and Vincent said you were confused that day," Ned tagged on.

Razzell huffed a wordless response.

"In a couple weeks, Crossroads will launch several assistance programs for seniors. We came to ask you to step up in advance."

"Would you sit with a doctor?"

"Are you nuts?" Razzell squawked.

Vincent almost laughed. Razzell got the jump and labeled his visitors mentally incapacitated before he and Ned could lead the angry senior down a path to that reality about himself.

"Don't think it's just Vincent and I who notice changes in you. Willa and Rosemary, too."

"It's a conspiracy," the old minister exclaimed. He started to pull the screen door closed, but Vincent grabbed it. Razzell could have terminated the conversation by shutting the wooden door, but that hadn't occurred to him.

"Okay, Mosie. I'm willing to negotiate. You think about what we've said. I'll give you a week." To Vincent's challenge, Razzell growled. "Because tomorrow, I expect Crossroads will hire someone to implement all these new programs." Vincent grinned. "It's Beebe Walker. Remember? Cliff's daughter. She's moving back."

Vincent wasn't sure, but Beebe's name seemed to rattle Razzell.

His mouth opened and closed, then opened again. "How many times are you going to call me old? No help. I'm fine. I don't want anyone, even Beebe Walker, invading my privacy. Why would I? Nothing's wrong."

In the splutter of his indignation, Vincent thought Razzell was trying to convince himself.

"It's not an invasion, Mosie," Ned said. "It's a visit. I've not met Beebe, but she must be prettier than me. Would you rather I stop by every day?"

"Don't bother."

"What will you do? Not let me in?" Ned's hands went up to indicate his current surroundings, stranded on the stoop.

"A couple of buckets of cold water—no, probably just one—and you'll get the message."

"You're not serious?" Vincent said, almost amused by their cockeyed banter: the former minister, cranky to a fault; the current minister, smiling and unflappable.

"Oh, yeah. He's serious," Ned said. "He'd spill half of it on the way to the door, but he's serious. We're wasting our time, Vincent. Come on."

Vincent climbed down the steps. The banister was still in his hand when he heard Ned speak, his voice held a pleading quality, yet rested firmly against his resolve.

"Don't make me do it, Mosie. Don't make me call apps." Ned laid emphasis on the last word.

Vincent wondered what Ned meant by apps. He couldn't believe it had anything to do with cell phone downloads.

Along with his confusion, Vincent witnessed a bit of Razzell's fire die.

"You remember apps," Ned said.

The repetition was unnecessary. The day's cloudy disposition hovered directly over the Rev. Mosie Razzell. Vincent assumed the men shared a dark memory. It didn't budge Razzell from barring the entrance to his home, but his emotional presence waned for a long moment, during which Vincent thought he heard him say, "Right before taps."

Strange, Vincent thought, putting the two rhyming lines together: You remember apps. Right before taps. But nothing there offered a coherent clue.

Softly, Ned said, "Then let Vincent and Crossroads step in. Don't repeat history."

Vincent waited, hopeful, while another few seconds ticked by, but Razzell remained reticent. When Ned pulled on his earlobe, Vincent knew the conversation between the two ministers reached a bulwark. "Well, Mosie," Vincent said, "we'll pray for you."

Vincent watched something pass between the two men. When Razzell spoke, his genial response surprised Vincent. "Prayers I'll accept." Then he stepped back and closed the door.

Ned's chin dropped to his chest. He breathed a long sigh before descending the steps.

"What was that about?" Vincent said. One behind the other, the two men used Razzell's narrow walkway to return to the car.

"Yes, I suppose I better explain that." Ned's stride slowed. For a moment, he was lost in thought. "Man, I wanted that to work, but it gave him a heads up."

Vincent let Ned's wishful thinking pass and prodded again. "Wanted what to work?"

Ned rubbed his face thoroughly with one hand before he began. "About three months into transitioning me for Mosie, we visited the grandfather of a church family. He was 87 and living by himself. That was the problem. The place was a wreck. He was no longer capable of caring for himself, nor the house. I'm not sure what the family wanted because it was clear they didn't want to take him in. But after seeing the deplorable conditions, Mosie and I couldn't ignore them. Things were unsanitary." He shook his head, as if trying to obliterate an unpleasant memory. "It was all very sad."

Vincent stepped over the curb and rounded the car's bumper to the driver's door while Ned reached for the handle on the passenger side.

"Mosie and I tried to convince the grandfather to consider assisted living. Check into possibilities. We thought he might relent."

"No go?" Vincent said, sliding onto the front seat opposite Ned.

"His obstinate nature prevailed. Sometimes, he'd sit and talk with us like old friends. Sometimes, he got hostile." Ned buckled his seat belt. "Sometimes, he was lucid; sometimes, he wasn't really in there."

"So what's apps?"

"Adult Protective Services."

"Oh," Vincent said, the light finally clicked on. Ned had been pronouncing the acronym, APS, as a word.

"Mosie made the call. He had to. The man's name was Charles Riley. Things moved fairly quickly after Mosie pushed the issue. One day we visited, and Charles sat in the kitchen, wearing nothing but a soiled Depends. It was February. He had the gas jets on the stove turned up all the way. The flames reached a foot high. He used the stove to heat the kitchen. He said the furnace wasn't working, but that wasn't the case. I went to the thermostat, turned it up, and the furnace clicked on right away."

"The stove being used that way was a disaster waiting to happen."

"That caused Mosie to rush APS into action. Funny, I use the term as a word, but Mosie and I didn't assign it. Charles did. The acronym was laid out in bold letters across the top of his social worker's business card. The day the social worker came with the nursing home's rep to, in effect, whisk him away without warning, Charles picked up the card from the table. He said, 'APS, right before taps.'" Ned looked over at Vincent. "He was career military. He died three months later. It was a blow because both Mosie and I thought he would bounce back, become active with proper care and nutritious food."

Vincent started the engine.

"We can't make the call yet, Vincent. We've got to stay close to Mosie. Keep him in that house."

Vincent knew what Ned was thinking. He didn't want to be responsible for placing Mosie in a facility, where he would retreat to an early death. A light rain returned. But for the windshield wipers' regularly timed swish, the ride back to Crossroads and Ned's car was a quiet one.

After Vincent saw Ned on his way home, he checked his inbox for the email he expected from Beebe. It waited with the subject line, "Curriculum Vitae

Attached." He read the document, found it impressive, and thought his board members would have no difficulty approving her employment, even given the short time frame for consideration. He forwarded the message to the members. Their meeting would convene early the next evening.

* * *

Beebe Walker woke, dragged her legs over the side of the bed. She stretched and yawned, then began her morning ablutions.

Her walk to the kitchen for a much-needed cup of coffee was interrupted when she crossed the living room. The answering machine's blinking light caught her eye. She went to the desk and manipulated the controls. She thought the call came in during her shower, but the date and time recorded said she apparently missed the red light when she stumbled through the house after ten o'clock last night, wanting sleep more than anything. The caller's voice belonged to Vincent Bostick.

"Beebe, where are you? The decision's been made. The counseling job is officially yours. The employment contract will come out of Ron Smith's office. He's an attorney and one of my board members. Monday is the start date as planned." Beebe winced and sat down hard in the desk chair.

Yes, they planned on the Monday in question being her first day, but that was before. Just yesterday, Beebe was asked to lead a weeklong grief retreat. The regular counselor was called away on a family emergency. There was nothing Beebe could do but agree to substitute. She was available. The retreat fell during the last week of her two-week hiatus at Swanson's.

Vincent kept talking. "Call me between twelve and one tomorrow. Other than that, my schedule's full. Anyway, congratulations. I'm just as happy as you are. Can't wait to talk."

At the appointed time, Beebe dialed Vincent's number. He answered promptly.

"Vincent, hi," Beebe said.

"Beebs," Vincent said in a comfortable way that made her relish old times. "Perfect timing. I just hung up from Ron. He expects to have the employment agreement ready to mail Monday, but he'd rather email it."

Vincent was scooting ahead, and scooting quickly. Beebe slowed him down. "Maybe we should back up a minute."

"Back up? You mean you're not taking the job." Vincent sounded nervous.

In her mind, she pictured his rather large Adam's apple bobbing.

Beebe spent most of the morning practicing the short speech she would give Vincent, the one that would elicit his complete and utter understanding of the situation involving the grief retreat that would go unsupervised for a dozen paid-up attendees if she didn't fill in.

"Of course I'm taking the job. I just need to delay my arrival by ten days or so. Remember, this past Monday started my two weeks off between counseling classes?"

"But, you're not going to be there for the start of the next class."

"Right, but I need to step in for another counselor at a retreat location out of town. An emergency came up for her. Well, the details aren't important. The long and the short of it is, I'm going to be delayed. Because of the retreat." Funny, Beebe thought, how putting him off another ten days quieted her jitters over the change planned for her life. The calming sensation made her feel like she was breeding a lie to some degree.

There was a bead or two of silence over the line before Vincent said, "Well, okay. I'll explain it to the board. There should be no repercussions. A week or ten days is hardly a problem. I guess I'm just thinking about Cliff. And me."

At first, Beebe was pleased to hear that Vincent sounded on board with her adjusted timeframe, then he added the words that tugged at her heart. "I haven't forgotten about you guys. Don't think I have. I just need a little neater wrap-up here. The counselor I'm filling in for is a friend."

"Got it. I understand."

With Vincent's words, Beebe wasn't too startled to realize that her closeness to him felt warmer than any emotion she felt for her father.

It was after eight that evening when she dialed Cliff Walker's home number. It occurred to her that since he didn't feel the weight of the untold secret she and Vincent hid about Abigail, he wouldn't be so affected by setting the day of return back some. Besides, summer months were always busy ones for Cliff at the hardware store, as Vincent pointed out. His thoughts would be concentrated there.

After an exchange of pleasantries, Beebe said, "It turns out my old employment will delay my arrival by at least one week."

"At least one week, huh?"

Beebe couldn't read her father's questioning tone to determine if more lived in those words. "No more than ten days at the outside," she said.

"Well, I should probably start letting people know you're coming."

There was an implication in that statement, but Beebe couldn't assess its meaning. "No reason to go to any trouble," she said, trying to sound upbeat. "Larkspur probably hasn't changed. Someone's radar will go off the minute I cross the town limits with all my worldly goods in the car. Ding, ding, ding, someone will just know and spread the word. You and I won't need to lift a hand."

Beebe laughed at the conjured scene. When Cliff did not, the jitters made their returning presence known in her stomach. When the time came, she felt sure they would accompany her every mile of the way to Larkspur.

* * *

A week after Beebe made her two calls home, Yates Strand drove back into Larkspur. It was early August. He had a strategy, scanty possessions, and a big yellow dog named Barleycorn.

His landlady hated to see him pack and move from the apartment above her own living quarters that she rented cheap. She kept the dog when he drove Terri Miller to Larkspur in March. She liked Yates, and she liked the idea of a pet to pet who wasn't her pet. Barleycorn, not destructive in any manner, was a quiet mutt. He seemed quieter of late because he mourned the loss of Terri in his life, just like Yates.

Since his heartbreaking first visit, Yates graduated with a nursing degree and passed the state boards in the top ten percent. Then he closed out his life in northern Michigan and his meager bank account. The life of a student with tuition and rent to pay hadn't left much in the way of savings. He was hopeful his plan to move into the Crossroads hospice would give him a place to stay without depleting his pocket money the first week.

When he told his father, Arthur Strand, of his plans, he was more than hopeful in his delivery. He might have led his father to believe room and board at the hospice had been nailed down. Naturally, Arthur Strand worried about his son. Terri Miller possessed some connection with Larkspur, and Yates told his father he aimed to find out what that was. Before he made the trip, he applied online to the local hospital in Larkspur and was patiently awaiting a late August interview. He couldn't know how long it would take so he might as well be gainfully employed. Thoughts of the job interview and the gainful employment appeased his father's concerns to some degree.

It was around two when he looked up at the street signs: Battlefield and

Standhope. He tugged at Barleycorn's leash. A few seconds later, he paused, his hand rested on the knob to Crossroads' door. He turned his head and let his gaze ease down to linger on the sidewalk bench. His memory placed Terri there, a huddled mass of disease and pain. The din of Battlefield seemed to crawl silently by behind him. Swallowing the lump in his throat, he twisted the doorknob.

Man and dog stepped immediately inside a large, open room filled with chairs aligned in rows. He found a slideshow in progress, attended by a rowdy bunch of seniors. He recognized Vincent Bostick, seated in the back row. Vincent noticed them and came over. Introductions followed. Vincent escorted him into an adjacent hallway, away from the noise factor in the main room. Yates and Vincent sat in two chairs that lined the wall.

Yes, in all honesty, Yates was homeless of his own making, since he gave up his small apartment and moved south without making arrangements for another. But he didn't say that to Vincent. Most of his story was truthful, although he started with a nonspecific reference.

"People told me this was a homeless shelter, among other things." Yates tipped his head toward the example of other things winding down in the main room. "I'm a graduate nurse. I've applied to Lakeview General. I have an interview in two weeks, but nowhere to stay, and no money for lodging. I was hoping I could stay here, help out, use my skills in the hospice if needed, or really, anything else, for a roof over my head."

"Well," Vincent said, eyeballing him. Yates presented a good appearance. He wore clean clothes, jeans and a collared shirt. He was clean shaven. He did need a haircut.

Yates reached into the front pouch of his backpack. "Here are two letters of reference. Please. Read them. Call the numbers. Check me out. It would only be for a little while."

Vincent's gaze dropped to the dog, on the high side of eighty pounds.

"Only I can speak for Barleycorn." This was the untruthful part. His landlady would praise the dog, but he didn't want Terri's name mentioned, which was a risk if Vincent called back to the woman. "He's a good dog. He won't cause any problems, I promise. I've got enough money to feed us for a few weeks, but that's it."

Vincent lowered the glasses that rode on top of his head. He read the letters. "I'll make the calls." A bit of sternness clung to his tone. Then, flipping the glasses up, he smiled. "And we won't let you starve."

Yates took the words as a good sign, preliminarily. Often one to over-think situations, Yates wondered if Vincent meant he would see that he and Barleycorn got food, but no bed. For the next twenty minutes, Yates pondered the situation he placed himself in while Barleycorn wandered between him and the doorway where the seniors talked and laughed.

Yates stood when Vincent walked back down the hall and extended a hand. "In exchange for chores, you're welcome to stay. The caveat to that is, the dog must remain well-behaved. There's a park a block over. That's your destination for walks."

Barleycorn's brown eyes looked up at Vincent. The dog tipped his head, trying to understand the man's words.

The pull of the dog's sweet disposition was too much for Vincent. Squatting, he gave Barleycorn rough scratches.

Won over, Yates thought.

* * *

Yates learned that Vincent resided in the center. There were no other guests, either homeless or ill.

Vincent made them pancakes for an early supper. They cleaned up the mess, then began arranging tables and chairs for Tuesday night bingo. It began at seven. They hauled a wire cage filled with white ping-pong balls, all pre-numbered and -lettered, to a head table. The cage sat inside a stand so it swung freely when the crank was used.

At two minutes after the appointed hour, Vincent motioned Yates to the front and addressed the room. "Folks, listen up. Before Rev. Razzell gets started with tonight's festivities, I want to introduce Yates. Yates is staying with me for a couple of weeks. You'll see him here and around town. He's looking for work in our fair community. Les and Doris, you'll see him over at the park with his dog when that monster of yours drags you through." Vincent craned his head to make eye contact with a couple sitting at the last table.

The man wore thick black-framed glasses; the woman's gold-rimmed pair was perched on the tip of her nose. Their simultaneous waves to Yates completed the introduction.

From behind them, a white-haired man made his way to the wire cage. "Everybody ready," he said, giving the crank a spin. Yates correctly assumed that the man was Rev. Razzell.

Yates listened closely as he served beverages, but did not hear any of the players refer to anyone else using the surname Miller. They were all close friends, so first names were primarily spoken.

Whenever someone yelled bingo, the room quieted while the professed winner called out his or her winning spaces. If a bingo was achieved without the use of the free space, then the player won a dollar. That happened only once in the first set of five games, then Razzell called for a break.

The ruckus in the room rose several notches. Yates rushed beverages around and large bowls of potato chips and cheese twists.

Doris stopped him when he passed. "What's his name?" She pointed to the hairy yellow dog laying on a folded-over blanket in the corner. His alert brown eyes never left Yates.

"Barleycorn," Yates said.

"That's an unusual one."

A nearby noise competed with Doris's response, causing Yates to look around. Razzell apparently kicked the leg of an empty folding chair on his passage back to the front of the room. He smiled at the man whose expression remained oddly bland.

Doris went on. "We own a Great Dane."

"Male?"

"Uh-huh. Vincent wasn't teasing. We call him Monster. That didn't start out being his name, but well, he sort of grew into it."

"Vincent said you're just here for a couple of weeks," Les chimed in.

"Hopefully, here at the shelter for a few. I've got an interview at the hospital. I hope to get my own place if I get the job."

"What do you do?" Les asked.

"I passed my nursing boards last spring."

A small gasp distracted Yates. Razzell remained in the vicinity. Their eyes met, telling Yates that the reverend emitted the sound. Covering the gasp with a forced cough, Razzell jerked his eyes forward.

Yates followed his shuffle off toward the cage of bingo balls. Razzell wound the crank. He watched Yates with a funny expression on his face.

The game ended at nine. The seniors cleared out shortly thereafter. Yates tidied the main room without being told. He emptied the wastebaskets into trashcans sitting in the alley out back. After Vincent locked up, he walked Yates to his room for the second time, then moved down the hall to his own.

Earlier, Vincent gave Yates a five-second tour of the barebones hospice facility. It consisted of two patient rooms with one twin bed each, a common bathroom between them, mismatched chairs, nightstands, and lamps. Yates took another five seconds to check out his room. He found it stuffy, cranked a window open, and stored his backpack under the bed.

It was now after ten. The room was no less stuffy. He yanked the bedspread back, knowing it would be unwanted weight. He froze as still as a statue, his arm flung out toward the foot of the bed. A rushing rose in his ears. The blanket beneath the spread was the one he covered Terri with on the bench five months ago.

He faced another summer of memories infused with Terri Miller's presence. What would they bring?

Dead Ends

The next morning, Yates cleaned the center's bathrooms, swabbed the kitchen sink and counters, and washed the front windows inside and out. Vincent and Yates sat down to grilled cheese sandwiches and tomato soup at noon. After the dishes were scrubbed, Yates was released with free time.

He put Barleycorn on his leash. Yates sized up Larkspur's downtown as he led his dog to the park. It was definitely a "walkable" community, and he liked that.

The park was the size of two square blocks dotted with ancient evergreen and deciduous trees. It was a fantastic amenity, really. And roomy. Yates looked around as Barleycorn pulled him toward a tall length of hedge. The crimson leaves reminded Yates that his mother always called such a hedge, "a burning bush."

Yates looked across the way. In one of the houses that faced the park lived the Great Dane named Monster.

The park had its share of benches for those who chose to sit and ponder. Yates tugged on Barleycorn. They crossed the park at an ambling speed, determined by Barleycorn's sniffing nose. Eventually, not following a direct course, Yates approached the one man present and occupying the center of three wooden benches. A patch of wiry hair appeared to grow out of the "V" formed by his plaid cotton shirt, open one button down from the collar.

"Excuse me. I'm new in town. Does Larkspur have a library?" He hoped to find old local phonebooks and crisscross directories shelved there so he could look up the name Miller and see what he could find.

He learned about such things when he visited his librarian mother after school and during summer breaks. Years before Terri's death, he lost the fight with his curiosity and tried an internet search. The search proved quick because the number of results overpowered him. The commonality of the name and the fact that he couldn't narrow down the search parameters were the reasons. Terri never divulged the name of her hometown, not until the afternoon she produced the map and asked to be driven back to Larkspur and Crossroads.

The same rationale negated any positive results from all the Michigan phonebooks stocked in his mother's library and those on microfiche from around the country. He didn't even try. No point in repeating the same process and expecting different results. Wasn't that a test for sanity?

What he needed was a database storing the names of those persons with a longtime homeless disposition. Sanity told him such a compilation didn't exist.

The man squinted up at Yates suspiciously, then down at Barleycorn. "The library's over on Cramer. Two blocks down, one block over." With his head, he gestured first north, then west.

"Thanks."

Yates started to turn when the man said, "Dogs aren't allowed."

He looked back. "What?"

"The library. It doesn't allow dogs."

Yates fixed him with a serious stare. "Too bad because he reads at a third-grade level."

The man puffed out his cheeks to Yates's facetiousness.

Yates stored the library directions away, then retraced his steps to Crossroads. Of course, he would not take Barleycorn into a public facility.

At the community center's front door, Yates and Barleycorn followed another man, dressed in a business suit, inside. His dark hair was shaggy. Yates noticed the onyx ring on his little finger when he waved to three men playing pool. The pool table was positioned to receive a great deal of natural light through the front window.

"Morning, fellas. How's it going?"

Two of the three men responded; the third one just waved. From the return greetings, Yates pieced the man's name together. He was Ron Smith. Ron seemed to know his way around the center. Yates nodded at the pool players, then reduced his pace to slow, and walked in Ron's footsteps down the hall. Yates was headed toward Vincent's office, so was Ron.

Yates hung back when Ron stopped in the office doorway and said, "Just checking on the contract. Did you get it faxed to Beebe okay?"

"Yeah. It went through fine. No answer yet." Ron closed the door on Vincent's voice.

Snapping off the dog's leash, Yates said, "Looks like we'll be waiting our turn. You'd rather stay with Vincent while I go to the library than be closed up in my room, wouldn't you, boy? Give him those irresistibly sad eyes when I ask him, okay?"

Man and dog padded back to Yates's room. Barleycorn went straight to his water bowl and lapped up most of its contents. Yates threw himself on the bed.

Last night while he lay awake in his new surroundings, he decided he would not mention Terri's name to Vincent. He would line up other sources, like the phonebooks and directories, see how far he could get, before breaking down, if need be, and trying to worm information out of his host. Questioning Vincent might raise the suspicion quotient, and Yates was pleased with the bunk space. An overly suspicious Vincent may decide to terminate his goodwill and evict Yates and Barleycorn.

Ten minutes passed before Yates heard Vincent's office door open. He sat up and called Barleycorn over. Eyes forward, Ron sailed past without even a glance their way.

"Come on," Yates said, patting his leg. "Let's go see if we can wrangle an invitation." Barleycorn fell into step alongside his master. Yates stopped short of the office's threshold, but stuck his head around the door frame. Vincent looked up from his laptop and smiled. On the table with the computer were several file folders and loose papers.

"Question," Yates said.

"What is it?" Vincent's voice lured Barleycorn to his side. Tail wagging happily, snout turned up, Barleycorn did his stuff.

"I want to head over to the library. Can Barleycorn stay with you, or should I leave him in my room with the door closed?" By the time Yates finished, Vincent was already stroking the dog's mane.

"Sure, leave him here. I'm writing up some program descriptions."

"Program descriptions?"

"We're about to go into high gear around here with senior programming. Crossroads received a grant and a local entrepreneur made a generous donation. Things are moving fast. That's why you're showing up is definitely a godsend. You taking on the chores around here gives me more free time for defining the scope of the programs. I need my board's approval fairly quickly. I've got a coordinator coming in two weeks."

"Are you sure Barleycorn won't be in the way?"

A whoop went up in the main room.

"No, those guys might be distracting, but Barleycorn is pure company. And the quiet kind."

"Thanks. Be a good dog, Barleycorn."

Barleycorn played the part to the end. His eyes never left Vincent. Yates rushed down the hall and around the corner before Vincent thought to offer the hospice's bookshelves for some easily acquired reading material.

* * *

The library was flanked by a drugstore and quaint bed and breakfast. All sat back from the street with grassy yards that welcomed with the feel of a residential area. Chiseled into the library's cornerstone was the year 1890. Yates thought the library must be one of Larkspur's earliest amenities. A short stone wall bordered the ancient building, its rising tower, and front lawn. Both the building and tower were made of the same style of dark stones used for the wall. A wide walkway led to a covered veranda.

He took his hand off the strap securing his backpack over his shoulder and opened the library's glass and stained-wood door. A high ceiling lifted and opened the closeness of the central room. In addition to regimented aisles of shelves, waist-high shelving created counter space for newspapers and periodicals and cut the room nicely into comfortable reading nooks.

Yates went straight to the circulation desk. A woman with blue-streaked hair and a bundle of wrist bracelets greeted him. "Can I help you?"

"Old phonebooks and crisscross directories?"

"Third aisle." She pointed, her bracelets rattling. "Halfway down. Left side. They can't be checked out."

"Thanks."

Yates knew universal library policies about research material. Almost like osmosis, they soaked in from close contact with his mother. He found the crisscross directories first. The publisher was Polk. These directories, composed annually, were divided into three parts. If the researcher had a Larkspur phone number, street address, or name, he could find or verify information in the other two categories.

Yates's finger dragged across the directory spines, lined-up chronologically, until he came to the edition that preceded the year he met Terri Miller. That would have made him twelve. Had Terri lived in Larkspur that year? He didn't know, but it was possible. He started there and worked back. All he had was the name Miller. *Polk Directory* entries included husband's and wife's names. It didn't take long to check through twenty years' worth. Just to be safe, because Terri was in her sixties when she died, he went back another ten years. He hefted three and four directories at a time and carried them to the nearest table. The amount of time spent in each volume was so miniscule, he didn't bother to sit in any of the chairs provided. His backpack waited in one though.

None of the handful of Miller entries he found listed the name Terri, or Teresa, or any derivative, among them. Not even the initial T.

It became evident the current phonebook would most likely be his best source. Sadly, perhaps his sole source. A Miller presently living in Larkspur might provide a glimmer of information relevant to Terri's past, but so many years had marched by. Surely, Yates thought, a family member would not forget her.

On the shelf below the directories, he found Larkspur phonebooks. The most recent one was there. He slipped it out. Back at the table, he made use of the chair next to his backpack, unzipped the pack's main compartment, and lifted out an electronic tablet. There, he inputted the names, addresses, and phone numbers of the five Millers listed.

With a map of Larkspur, he could put together some logical progression for how to proceed.

He went to speak with the librarian. "Where can I find a street map of Larkspur?"

"One hangs in the lobby."

He looked around at the lobby doors. Yates missed seeing that on the way in. He thanked the woman.

As he returned the phonebook to the shelf and gathered his things, he wondered if he could get around town with the GPS app on his phone. Still, it would help to see an overall layout. He studied the map, retrieved his tablet, and made notes. One location was just two blocks over. He debated going, or returning to the center, picking up Barleycorn, and walking around with him. The dog would make him look less like a stranger. He adopted that plan, but decided not to implement it until early evening, when people were home from work.

His afternoon was spent working with a woman, Bertha Zeller, who authored the Crossroads newsletter. He read it through. Bertha did a nice job and accomplished the goal. The newsletter was newsy. She fitted it to the standard typing page, two columns per sheet. The headline story lobbied for less fat and calories in one's diet. Easy for Bertha to preach. She was yard-stick thin. They walked to the office supply store. A teenage clerk operated the Xerox machine and charged Bertha for fifty copies. The money for duplicating the newsletter and purchasing stamps came from the dues Crossroads members paid annually, Bertha told Yates.

Back at the center, Bertha and he stuffed envelopes, then labeled and stamped the stack. Yates gathered the stack into his backpack. After he and Barleycorn took a jaunt through the park, they delivered the mailing to the post office.

Around six, Yates fed Barleycorn, got a strawberry milkshake at the Dairy Corner for himself, and made his way to the first of the five Millers on his list.

He knocked at 502 Cherry Lane.

"Oh," Yates said, when a black man opened the door. "Are you Thomas Miller?" He was. Yates explained the mistake. Thomas was obviously not Terri's relative. Thomas crossed Peter, Thomas's brother, off the list. That saved Yates a trip.

The first Caucasian Miller Yates located lived on Prospect Street. William J. He listened intently enough, but claimed no real knowledge of outlying family members. He suggested Yates check in with a cousin on Remmer Road, four blocks over.

Yates and Barleycorn walked the distance through a well-established neighborhood of small homes, all single story. The front door to 223 stood open. Yates knocked. Cousin Grace shook her head at the end of his short recital. She could not recall a Terri Miller, and she thought she would have because Grace and Terri were close in age. Grace pointed Yates south toward Michael B. Miller when Yates insisted he wanted to complete his task.

Grace shook her head. "He won't be any help."

That was a true statement. Michael stared at Yates with a glazed look, then referred him back to William, the first Caucasian Miller he visited on Prospect.

The next morning, after breakfast dishes were washed, Vincent asked Yates to mop and wax the kitchen's tiled floor. From a large closet off the kitchen, Vincent got out an old-fashioned rope mop, bucket, wax that squirted from a bottle, and a rectangular sponge applicator affixed to the bottom of a long, blue handle.

Yates looked at the pile of supplies. Leaning on the mop handle, he wanted to ask Vincent, can you say Swiffer?

Instead, he got to the job. After he mopped and while he waited for the floor to dry, he arranged folding chairs from the main room as a barricade across the six-foot entranceway. The chairs kept Barleycorn out. Thirty minutes later, Yates realized he hadn't thought things through when he waxed himself into the corner opposite the moveable chair barricade. Finding no other way out and thankful he was alone, he hopped up onto the counter that cordoned off the kitchen from the main room. He waxed the area his feet just occupied as best he could with his stomach pressed to the Formica, his butt wiggling with the effort, and his legs hanging off the other side. Then he and the wax applicator slid down to the main room's dry floor.

Barleycorn sauntered over. Yates scratched the dog's head. "Lesson learned," he said to the canine.

* * *

The Stryker County Health Department occupied the second floor of the Holmes Building in downtown Larkspur. The building was a product of the eighteen-hundreds when fancy woodwork was a common feature. The doors with skeleton key locks and glass knobs sat under transoms and twelve-foot ceilings. Yates entered the door numbered 201 and went straight to the work counter.

A woman in her mid-forties stood behind the counter, reading some papers. The nametag pinned to her white blouse read Heidi Cranston. Heidi looked up. "Good morning. How can I help you?"

"I'd like to look through some old birth records."

"How old?"

"Sixty-five to seventy years ago."

"Microfilm," she said declaratively. "You sit over there. I'll get the reels. Everything's alphabetical by year. What's the name?"

"Terri Miller."

"Okay. I'll be back."

A five-foot table sat against the wall perpendicular to the counter. A chair was pushed up to the table, and a microfilm reader occupied the center of the table's surface.

Yates leaned his backpack against a table leg, then pulled out and sat in the chair. He always considered Miller Terri's married name, so a birth record match might prove a false lead. The concept of "married name" sparked an idea. What about marriage certificates as a source? That would mean a trip to another government building, he expected.

Heidi returned quickly. "These three reels cover the time frame for the entire county."

He leaned back, and she threaded the first reel. "Let me know if you have any problems."

Yates nodded, although distracted by her comment, "the entire county." He hadn't thought in broader terms. Larkspur was just a subset. The phonebook covered Stryker County. But did the *Polk Directory*, which he remembered now was also referred to as the city directory, cover the county? He might have a hole in his research.

Twenty minutes later, he rubbed his eyes, tired from staring at the screen, but threaded the third reel anyway.

When Yates finished and stood up to carry the boxes to the counter, Heidi noticed and meet him there.

"Any luck?" she asked.

"None, but I'm wondering about marriage certificates."

"For those, you'll need to go to Probate Court." Yates was just forming the word, "Where," when Heidi pointed in a northeasterly direction over his shoulder. "It's the building diagonally across the street at the corner."

The next day, during his break from chores, Yates waited in line at the Stryker County Probate Court clerk's office behind a man he decided was a local minister turning in paperwork for recent nuptials he performed. The minister and female clerk chatted. She apparently attended the wedding.

Everyone in this small town knows everyone, Yates concluded. Terri left Larkspur a long time ago. If she'd been notorious, no one seemed to tremble with fear over her name. For example, the day before, the clerk at the Health Department wasn't struck by fright.

He stepped up when his turn came, made his request for archived marriage licenses, gave the name Terri Miller, and watched. Nope. This clerk didn't gasp, draw back, or quake. Instead, she followed the same drill. She pointed to the microfilm viewer on the table where Yates already stowed his pack. A few minutes later, she carried four boxes of film to the counter. He acknowledged experience with threading the machine and gathered up the boxes. The chair in front of the viewer had one short leg. It rocked when he shifted his weight. Again, he kept his eye out for Teresa, as well as Terri.

Ninety minutes later, he stood outside on the sidewalk. It appeared his escapades raised no red flags around Larkspur, but he gathered no information either. He hit one dead end after another.

Making a quiet nuisance of himself all over town validated his reason to put off a trip to the cemetery. How could he stare down at Terri's grave and think of her there? From a conservation standpoint, he told himself he needed to preserve the Jeep's gas until he had gainful employment. Even he categorized that excuse as lame.

Angel's Prayer

It was midmorning when Vincent poured the last of the coffee from the pot into his mug, overfilling it. He turned too quickly. Brown liquid sloshed out.

Yates stood at the sink, adding water to Barleycorn's bowl. He turned the faucet off with force and a forceful, "Aah."

Vincent looked over. Yates frowned down at the small puddle. "Look what you did to my floor. That's going to take off the wax."

The domestic complaint sounded so incompatible with the young man that Vincent's mind was wiped of the ability to formulate speech. He stared, openmouthed.

When their eyes met a second later, it was quite apparent Yates exaggerated his dismay. A laugh burst out of him. "That sounded just like my mother."

"Mine too." Vincent chuckled.

"Go on. Get out of my kitchen, and let me clean up this mess. I am so unappreciated."

Vincent grinned at the young man's enjoyable nature. He found he liked Yates very much. While complying with his request to vacate, he heard his phone ring. He took a quick and scalding sip from the mug so he didn't repeat the incident before hurrying down the hall to his office. He answered the phone with the center's name, then his.

A woman identified herself. "My name is Callie MacCallum. You don't know me, but I'm Beebe's friend."

A folded-over paper towel complete with old coffee rings lay on the tabletop. He set the mug on the makeshift coaster, then sat himself in the chair. The hairs on his arms rose with the ominous introduction.

"Is something wrong with Beebe? Has something happened? Are you at the retreat?" he wanted to know. Just a few hours earlier, Beebe faxed the signed employment agreement. Now this woman called.

"No, no, no. It's nothing like that. No reason for alarm," she tempered her response. "She's fine. And, yes, I'm with her."

"Good," gushed out on the breath that emitted his relief. "How can I help you? How do you know about me?"

"From the fax."

"Oh, you know about that."

"Yes, I'll miss her greatly after she moves. Beebe and I have grown close."

Vincent knew Beebe traveled for a week of grief counseling, so he ventured with, "You met her through her work?"

"Yes. Beebe started me sewing quilts as therapy for my grief. Now, I sew them for those in her counseling groups. They're memory quilts, made of clothing from the lost loved one."

Vincent thought this was dually impressive, both on Callie's part and on Beebe's. He suffered grief with his wife's death. His heart returned to those days when he slept with Carolyn's down-filled jacket. It was something to hang onto at night when he missed her most. He hoped it would coax her into his dreams. He wanted to remember his wife, healthy and active.

"Beebe always picks the recipient, collects the clothing, and brings it all to me."

"I see."

"Good, because I just learned that Beebe's mother died. She said you knew."

Vincent hesitated. He half-wondered if the statement disguised a guess on Callie's part. In the end, he accepted her words at face value and said, "Yes, I do."

"I know her mother's clothing is still around. That got me thinking. Beebe should have a quilt of her own. I think she desperately needs one although she'd never admit it. Doesn't that sound like her to you?"

"I guess I'd agree. That does sound like her. But what are you asking, Callie?" At the caretaker's house, Vincent knew Abigail's clothing hung in her closet still. Cliff mentioned it to him once. Vincent could see the progression of events: He repeated the comment to Beebe. She must have told Callie.

"Part of the success we need for this week can't be achieved without this gift for Beebe. Can you talk to her father? Explain about the quilts. She's preached the benefits. I want to sew a quilt in memory of her mother. I need to know in the next day or two that her father is willing to part with some clothing. I want to tell Beebe that a shipment is on its way to my house, that there's no turning back. The only way to be sure she gets a quilt is to really not let her in on the decision." Callie paused. "Well, that's the only way to handle the Beebe I know."

With the outset of Callie's plea for success, Vincent carried the remote phone, pressed to his ear, into his bedroom. He opened the closet door. With his free hand, he squeezed the down jacket that hung inside the closet. A draining sadness overwhelmed him, like the sudden whim that caused him to save the jacket and bring it with him when he moved to the center. Carolyn loved the yellow jacket so.

With an absent quality in his voice, Vincent replied to Callie's assessment. "That's Beebe. Always doing good things for others. She would never ask for herself."

"Will you talk with her father then?"

A direct question, Vincent thought, requiring a direct answer. However, timing was the problem: He would ask Cliff for Abigail's clothes before he told the husband his wife lay in a grave outside the kitchen door with another woman's name marking it? Callie did not know that situation, he was sure. Beebe had not told her the full story. His mind ran with a second train of thought. A quilt of Carolyn's clothes. How he would have treasured that. He lifted the jacket sleeve to his nose. It still smelled of her perfume. He knew it would. When the scent faded, he sprayed more on from the bottle he brought to Crossroads from her vanity. Very selectively, he carried a few items to the center from his other life before he auctioned the house that was the home he shared with Carolyn.

"Well," he started. He wanted to fill the growing void in conversation, but Callie had the same idea.

"I know Beebe's mother abandoned her and her father. I know it will be painful for her father and difficult for you, but as you said, Beebe would never ask for herself. Beebe cannot leave for Michigan without knowing there's a quilt in her future. I want her to have that comfort. So will you ask about the clothes?"

With Carolyn's lavender scent swirling inside his nose, he said, "Yes. I'll talk with Cliff."

"And get the clothes shipped soon?"

"I'll make it a priority. I can't promise tomorrow, but soon." Vincent was positively on board, but Cliff was a man who didn't give anything up easily. Still, he heard relief in Callie's voice when she spoke.

"I knew you'd help. She speaks highly of you. Here's the address."

He went back to his office to write the shipping information on a scrap of paper, along with Callie's cell phone number, just in case. After he hung up, he looked at the mug of, no doubt, cold coffee.

That evening, when Crossroads was quiet—Yates and the dog played in the park—Vincent rebuilt his strength concerning the quilt. He squeezed the down-filled jacket once more before he wrote a note for Yates, telling him he expected to be back in a couple of hours and leaving his mobile number if he needed to be reached, should a hospice situation arise.

Vincent fished his car keys out of his jeans. Three good shipping boxes lined the back seat of his car. He repeated his strategy over and over all the way out to the caretaker's house: Swoop in, convince, act, and retreat.

He arrived a little after seven and parked in the drive alongside Cliff's truck. He climbed the steps to the small stoop and knocked at the open front door. Cliff came into view quickly. He appeared to be eating on the run. He carried a hot dog stuffed in a bun. Was he on his way out? Vincent wondered. Possibly to cut grass with the remaining two hours of evening light. Or was there a repair, something that needed fixing?

But Cliff's manner was not rushed. He welcomed Vincent and brought him inside. "I boiled some hot dogs and warmed up some baked beans. Have you eaten? I've got extra."

"No, thanks. I had a bite earlier."

Cliff waved Vincent back to the kitchen. They traipsed through the living room and made a left around the dining room table. Cliff continued his after-dinner cleanup chores.

"Have a seat," he told Vincent. "Are you here to talk about Beebe? I've been meaning to get over to Crossroads to thank you. Beebe told me about the job."

"Yeah, I received her signed employment agreement today. She's ready to start when she gets here."

"Seems she got hung up on a counseling job."

"She's filling in for another counselor," Vincent said, having swooped in, but lingering outside any true effort to convince. He needed to move Cliff toward a serious discussion, one twisted with larceny and subterfuge. He would beg for Abigail's clothes while harboring a lie. Of sober concern was Beebe, who Callie MacCallum claimed was in need of specialized attention. Vincent's plea for the clothing might prove too great for a man who, for thirty years, kept such articles belonging to his runaway wife.

"She called it a retreat. I guess that's the way they do things now. A bit odd. I didn't say that to her. You can keep a secret, can't you?" Cliff laughed as he wrung water out of a dishrag. He ran the rag over the countertop, then threw it over the faucet arm before turning around.

"Actually, I have a request to make that you may find a bit odd in itself," Vincent said, intentionally repeating Cliff's words.

Cliff's facial expression switched to quizzical.

"Sit down, Cliff."

Cliff's eyes remained fixed on Vincent's while he crossed the linoleum and pulled out a chair from the kitchen table. Beyond Cliff, out the kitchen door, Vincent saw the cemetery. His gaze rushed to the approximate location where the body was buried. He attended the funeral for Terri Miller. Cliff Walker and heavy-equipment operator Hal Garrett stood back, attendees only on behalf of the cemetery association. They had duties to perform. Ned McMitchell officiated. Willa came because the numbers were few. The other four thought Vincent was there just because the woman being buried died in Crossroads' hospice. That much was a fraction of the truth.

"There's a therapy Beebe uses in her counseling classes with some of her clients. She collects clothes belonging to the deceased and has them made into quilts. The quilts are remembrances, of course. Beebe shared her situation concerning her mother with a close friend. Callie. She called me today. She's quite fond of Beebe, and she makes all the quilts."

"From the clothes of people who died?"

Vincent could see Cliff catching on. For everyone but Vincent and Beebe, Abigail Walker was a runaway. No one necessarily knew if she died at some point over the years, but Vincent knew Cliff assumed that happened long ago. And Vincent thought Cliff reentered that frame of mind now. "Callie wants Beebe to have a quilt."

Cliff's gaze dropped to the oaken tabletop.

"Others on this special counseling trip have quilts. Beebe arranged them." Vincent waited. Cliff seemed frozen in place. "Abigail's clothes have provided comfort to you all this time. Can you part with enough to make a quilt?"

Cliff raised his chin off his chest. "Is Beebe somehow suffering?"

The word suffering caused Vincent to flash on an old memory. Just as quickly, he swept the memory aside. He kept to his strategy. "I think so. Callie does. Beebe's coming home. I expect that's been a trigger of some kind. I hope you think the move is a good one. She can't help but remember her mother when she thinks of you and this house. This town even. Callie thinks it will help. The quilt won't be sewed in just a few days, but it's a thought, a hope, a tie Beebe can hang onto until the quilt arrives." The table sat next to a window. A bird stopped to eat from the feeder hung on the window frame. "Callie wants the clothes sent right away before the counseling trip ends. I think she wants to use the anticipation of the quilt as a bit of therapy for Beebe."

Vincent watched the look in Cliff's staring eyes intensify.

With Vincent's few seconds of silence, his concentration became distracted. The earlier memory flash disturbed him again. He pushed it down. "Have I explained things well enough? Seems like I went all around the barn." Vincent had no clear sense that he covered the subject adequately, and Cliff studied him still.

"How are *you* doing?" Cliff asked.

This change of subject matter baffled Vincent. In the next moment, though, intuition abounded in the space around the table. Vincent knew what Cliff meant. He meant Carolyn.

When Vincent didn't answer, Cliff prodded gently. "What were you thinking just now?"

Vincent's time with the jacket provoked the memory. He broke himself of sleeping with the yellow coat long ago, but he couldn't prevent himself from becoming lost in Carolyn's death. Not only her death, but the dying. The dying was worse.

Cliff got up and ran water into a glass for Vincent. He mumbled a thanks and swallowed some. He pressed his fingers tightly against the glass until the thumbnail he stared at whitened. Cliff's offering, his sensitivity, deserved something in return.

Vincent and Cliff, a generation apart in years, nurtured an enduring friendship. Later, Carolyn's presence only enhanced the relationship. Carolyn adopted Cliff on Father's Day, with every birthday, and at Christmas. Despite the closeness the men shared, Vincent never told Cliff a certain story, the memory of which he struggled with on this evening in August.

Cliff Walker knew the story's beginnings. Carolyn came to Larkspur to care for her uncle. With a name like Karl Weingarten, there was no question he was of German descent. Carolyn, with a knack for the language, was nearly fluent by the time her uncle died. After she married Vincent, she rarely spoke a word of German. There was no one to understand her.

Absently, Vincent slid the water glass over two inches on the table. "I spent a little time thinking about Carolyn today after Callie's call. She's still on my mind. I try not to dwell on the memories when she was so ill, but…"

A moment later, Cliff finished the sentence. "There is a memory." His voice was barely audible.

Vincent pulled in air until the filling of his lungs set him higher in the chair. "There is one. Carolyn reached the point where she was unable to get out of bed. Two hospice nurses came to change her catheter. It was a miserable process. It hurt. She screamed and moaned. I waited at the foot of the bed. I could do nothing, but bite back screaming myself." He felt his chin tremble. "One of the nurses held her hand. She quieted when the ordeal was over. The nurses went out to the living room to make their notes. Carolyn and I were alone. She gave me the strangest look and asked if there had been a little girl in the room, standing next to me. A girl with long, curly blonde hair."

Cliff's expression of astonishment was the same one Vincent assumed he showed Carolyn when she asked.

"I told her no, of course, but Carolyn went on. She said the girl spoke to her in German. I asked her what she said. Carolyn repeated the German phrase, then told me the English translation. It meant, 'My dear God. My dear God.' I immediately thought the phrasing Carolyn heard—her mind playing tricks— was associated with shock from the child at hearing and seeing such pain."

"You changed your mind?"

"I left Carolyn to see the nurses out, and I told them what she said. The one nurse— It's funny I can't remember her name. She was so nice. Anyway, she said, at Carolyn's stage—which was quite ill and close to the end—patients often reported seeing children in their rooms. They were hallucinations. Carolyn died five days later. Over the course of those days, I came to believe the little girl was praying."

Around him, Vincent's world slowed, matching the pace of his life after Carolyn's death. He lifted the glass to his lips and sipped water. Cliff said nothing, just patted Vincent's shoulder.

The haunt of the little girl, the angel who prepared for Carolyn's arrival in heaven, felt so close. She seemed to call to Vincent on the echoes of Carolyn's remembered agony, knowing comfort was needed.

"We'll need boxes," Cliff said, by way of affirming his decision to pack up a portion of Abigail's clothes.

Vincent wondered if that decision was made out of sympathy, simply to create a distraction for the grieving husband, who said, "I brought some."

So very reticent, Cliff gave the slightest nod. "Of course. Good."

Vincent and Cliff went to the car to retrieve the cartons. All the way there and all the way up the stairs to the second floor and the bedroom Cliff shared at one time with his wife, Vincent felt irrefutable tugs at his heart. Along with the tugs came a drilling whisper: Tell Cliff the truth.

The two men experienced a touching moment in the kitchen with its back door wide open to the neighboring cemetery. The bird on the feeder's perch seemed to look through the glass with distinct captivation and reverence all the while the essence of Carolyn's spirit lingered. Vincent felt a sensation of words on his tongue. The truth crept forward. He pushed it back.

Sitting the brown cardboard boxes on the checkered bedspread, Vincent felt the tug again and heard the whisper. The truth Cliff needed to hear surrounded that one burial in the graveyard when Ned McMitchell spoke solemn words and Vincent strained to keep a deathbed secret. That day was marked in his memory by the bitter taste of bile rising in his throat. He kept his eyes tipped toward the unearthed ground, but his conscience could not block out the man who stood back and watched from a distance. Cliff thought of himself as a grave keeper that day, apart from the burial scene. Vincent knew differently. Cliff was a widower of three days.

Behind him, he heard the rollers of the bi-fold closet door along its track, then the scrape of wire hangers across a rod. He swallowed a sour taste once more. Cliff selected clothes from another age, and Vincent folded them into the boxes, stockpiling hangers. An assortment of nursing tunics found their place inside the box, the fabric both printed and solid. They were made of lightweight cotton with little texture. In contrast, Vincent felt the weight and roughness of the battle gaining and losing purchase inside his head.

Could he—should he—sit Cliff down, right here, right now? The longer he argued with himself, the easier, he knew, he'd find it to delay the telling until Beebe arrived. That was, in fact, the plan he and Beebe agreed on. He invited her home for just that purpose. Even now, her return was imminent. But this was such an opportunity. Although if Cliff's reaction was cataclysmic and Vincent's response was lacking, then he might do more harm than good.

A blouse in a swirling pattern of navy and tan came into his peripheral vision for a half second, then disappeared. Vincent looked over. Cliff stared at the article, considering whether to part with it. Vincent reasoned it might have been a special gift for a birthday or Christmas. For Cliff, indecision reigned. Vincent knew about that. The ambivalence passed, and Cliff handed over the blouse. The memory Cliff just relived would be sewn into the quilt with many others.

Cliff chose a hound's-tooth pleated skirt and lay it on the mattress. Its waistband was pinched to the hanger with special clips. The pleats made it difficult to fold neatly, and finally Vincent gave up trying to keep the alignment from possibly wrinkling during shipment. At the same time, Vincent's willingness to bypass Beebe ebbed.

A pair of silky mint-green pajamas was laid in the carton. The fabric swished in his grasp. That filled the second box, and Vincent reached for the third.

From a bottom dresser drawer, Cliff lifted out several items. They were topped by an organdy apron already folded in a size perfectly fitted for the box. Vincent dropped them in. On top of that, Vincent added a lightweight rain coat. Just touching it clearly transmitted its waterproofing properties. The short coat was dove gray with slant pockets and large buttons. It looked new. Vincent wondered if Abigail ever wore it. The Terri he knew could have wrapped it around herself twice. With Terri invading his thoughts, his justification to delay telling Cliff until Beebe arrived was fully fixed. Terri wanted a permanent embargo. He could concede only a temporary one.

In the same instant, Cliff said, "That's it."

"Yeah," Vincent breathed, feeling battle-worn. "That's it." One by one, Vincent folded down the flaps on the third box, thereby closing the untold chapter of Abigail's life inside.

They got the boxes to the car. Vincent bid Cliff a good night, but didn't leave right away. There was enough light left to find Carolyn's grave.

Staring down at the marble marker, he launched into a conversation at midpoint, as if Carolyn had been present inside the bedroom, aware of his thoughts. "I feel like I had to sacrifice a bit of the father to benefit the daughter. Beebe's entire life for weeks has been built around her reunion with Cliff for just this purpose. To rip it out from under her now seems cruel. Plus, Beebe has training for these situations." He paced, nervously rubbing his hands together. "And what if I told Cliff, and he assumed that meant Beebe was afraid or, worse, indifferent. They're estranged, and this has brought Beebe back. I heard the conviction in her voice when she talked about telling him. How could I take it away from her? And why, in Christ's name, am I beating myself up?"

The volume attached to that last question caused it to echo through the night. He looked up to the house, but saw no movement. In a few days, after

Cliff learned the painful truth, he would hurl a belly-full of angry questions at Vincent. Along with questions would come hateful and indefensible accusations. Those were absolutely the reason Vincent was beating himself up.

Full moonlight went with Vincent a while later when he walked back across the cemetery to his car.

Baptism By Fire

Yates dragged tables and chairs to a central location in the main room at Crossroads. He debated whether the rainy Wednesday, a week into his stay, was the time to involve Vincent in his quest for background on Terri Miller.

Vincent decided to close the center for the day so he and Yates could paint the room. While Vincent rummaged in the stock room for painting supplies, a knock came at the door.

Through the door's glass panel, Yates saw that a woman stood on the stoop. Her face was hidden by the CLOSED sign hanging from a suction cup's hook. He opened the door for the shock of his life.

"I'm Beebe Walker. I'm looking for Vincent. Is he here?" With the rain as a backdrop, he stared at the conflicting aspects of the same stormy eyes and porcelain skin that belonged to the healthy version of Terri Miller.

"He's back in the stock room. I'll…huh…" His feet seemed riveted to the floor.

"Is something wrong?"

"It's just that you, ah, look like someone I used to know."

"Really. Who?"

With his mind already in debate mode, he decided to come out with it. Straightening his shoulders, he said, "Terri Miller."

Behind him, he heard Barleycorn's toenails tapping against the tile floor, but he didn't spin around until he heard Vincent's voice drill his back.

"You knew Terri? You never said that. Is that what this is about, getting me to let you stay? Has this been a hoax of some kind? Why didn't you tell me?"

Each question took Vincent closer to the woman, who slipped two steps inside and closed the door. Each question hardened Vincent's features more. His tone was harsh enough to slice through the trust Yates built with him, until that trust fell away, leaving Yates fully exposed with his less-than-truthful backstory.

Barleycorn's concerned eyes shifted between his master and his new friend, then the dog surrendered to canine curiosity. The new person in the room drew his attention. While he slunk past Vincent's jean-covered kneecaps to give Beebe's gray cotton pant legs a thorough sniffing, Yates stammered through an honest explanation. "I thought you'd claim confidentiality or something if I brought it up, and I'd get the boot."

"Vincent told me the, ah, Terri Miller story," the visitor named Beebe said. "The woman you knew was, actually, my mother. And you are?"

Yates's mind fumbled for a moment. This woman was Terri's daughter. "Oh, sorry," he said. "I'm Yates Strand."

"You left her here." Beebe's words came across as more statement than accusation.

"She made me bring her that night. She wouldn't let me stay. Once Vincent got her inside, she made me promise to leave. I had nursing boards the next day and a long trip back."

"Mother was a nurse." Beebe spoke as if she found herself somewhat adrift in her own mind.

"Yes, I know."

"Yates, I can't believe this—" Vincent revived his chastising tone.

"No, wait," Beebe interrupted. "I want to hear everything he has to say."

For the next two hours, they sat on folding chairs in a close-knit circle and shared stories. The rain outside was a curtain that kept the world at bay.

It seemed Terri talked to Vincent at length during her time in the hospice. She filled her last moments with summer memories, about braces, guitar lessons, and a drum set, about lawn care and ice cream businesses. "As she told those stories," Vincent said, "I knew there was someone she was certainly fond of. That someone was you." Yates's eyes filled. "She died in the early morning," Vincent added, "after the second night."

"I was the one who played guitar," Yates said, "wore braces, cut grass, and shared the ice cream business. She played the drums." He smiled down at the memory. "That was my life. Those were my summers. She was an addict, yes, but she saved my father's life. I knew that sometime before all that, she'd been a nurse, but I don't know the rest of the story. Why she came back to Larkspur. What happened here? At thirteen, I thought it was great that she was on the lam. But now, I need more."

"She didn't tell me the truth about who she was," Vincent said, "until she was very close to the end. The sickness took its toll on her appearance. But even so, I wouldn't have known her. I didn't meet Beebe until our senior year in high school. Her mother was gone by then."

Yates listened, trying not to squirm in his seat. The rest of the story that he wanted knowledge of was not the recent past. Beebe knew what he meant. She told how it happened that her mother left Larkspur.

"Mother was seriously hurt in a car accident."

From that first parallel with his own life, his father's accident, Yates's eyes never strayed from Beebe's.

"She was hospitalized, then Daddy and I nursed her. Eventually, her injuries healed. But she became addicted to painkillers. Percocet. She hid it. Daddy didn't know. I certainly didn't."

Yates tried to picture a younger Terri, struggling to recover, a loving family, and the unrelenting pull of chemical dependency. Beebe told how her mother returned to work at Lakeview General, the very hospital where Yates hoped to gain employment.

Beebe went on. "She pinched the patients' meds to satisfy her habit. Someone caught on. She bolted from town to avoid an investigation and a felony conviction."

He and Beebe shared another parallel, that of abandonment. His mind flashed on the night Terri sat alone on the bench, and he, alone in the Jeep. Terri completed her plan to leave him behind.

As Beebe talked on, another uncanny parallel entered the afternoon gloom. For years, Beebe's father, Cliff Walker, worked at McKinley Hardware, a block over and two blocks down. Yates's father owned a hardware store.

The similarities worked on Yates until they cast Terri in a science fiction movie, existing in a parallel world, trying to do nothing that would change the outcome of peoples' lives, as if she hadn't been there at all. The more he thought about it, the reverse was true. Terri was cast in a parallel world with a second chance to live her life and make a difference. She exceeded with the latter.

"Where did you grow up?" Beebe asked.

"Three hours north of here," Yates said.

"My mother lived there?"

"Only in the summers. The rest of the time, I don't know where she lived."

"She lived with you?"

"No. She wouldn't. Dad asked her. She always said no." Then, when Yates thought he wouldn't, he told them about the year Terri did live in the house and her uncompromising devotion during his mother's illness. "Learning all this must make you angry, or jealous," he said to Beebe after the story was out. "That she walked away from your childhood, and mine with her was, well—something like a revolving door, is how it seems—but I loved her. I really did."

"I've come to terms with a lot of things lately, Yates, especially my mother. I'm glad she made positive influences on your life. I'm glad she found the wherewithal to put your family first while your mother was sick. I'm proud of that. But, today, my father is my first concern. You see, I've decided to move back to Larkspur."

"You don't live here?"

"Not for a long time. But now I'll work here with Vincent and do a little good for my hometown. I hope my decision to return cushions the blow for Daddy when he hears all this. I hope it does. We haven't been close."

Yates pieced a father's and daughter's estrangement with the worry lines around Beebe's eyes. Then Beebe said the oddest thing.

"Of course, there's the question of moving the grave." Yates's confused expression must have prompted Beebe to continue. "We've got to move her to the Walker family plot. She should be buried in her rightful place with Abigail Walker on the headstone. In the end, this will help Daddy heal. Me, too, I think."

Yates bristled. He didn't know this person, Abigail Walker. The name sounded foreign. But it did explain his run of bad luck around town when he searched for clues about Terri's former life. He worked with the woman's alias.

"I came to meet with Vincent and talk this over. You see, my father doesn't know that he's tended his wife's grave now for months. Daddy's the cemetery caretaker," Beebe added the afterthought. Needlessly for Yates's benefit, she pointed toward the edge of town, but Yates already knew the graveyard's location. "I've built my courage. I want to set things straight as soon as possible."

Yates's head spun while Beebe layered on more dizzying details. "I'm going to go see him now," she said to Vincent. "He's at the store. Then, after work, you can meet Daddy and me at the house."

"Fine," Vincent said. "That'll work."

"Wait a minute," Yates exclaimed. "The idea of obliterating Terri Miller's memory and making her into someone else seems criminal."

Vincent started to speak, but Beebe held up a hand. "This is a lot to accept, but you knew there was more when you came here. Give it time to sink in. Each day will get easier. I needed time, too. Vincent came to me a month after she died. She begged him to keep her secret, but he couldn't let the situation ride. Daddy may resist. I don't know. But I will push him toward moving the grave. He'll need time as well, but I think moving the grave negotiates the best outcome. It will set things right. We can pick up our lives with things in the proper place."

Yates couldn't find the words he wanted. Watching him, Beebe's face softened just as Terri's would have. He still had Terri. Beebe was so like her.

"Yates, you can still think of her as Terri. Don't change your memories. Talk about her and use that name. Let your memories live exactly as they are. There's nothing wrong with that."

Yates thought about the recommendation. Outside, the sun fought through passing clouds while memories of Terri floated through many happy summers. He heard her voice whisper in his ear once more: "Be a good boy."

"When do you expect to move the grave?" he asked.

"Realistically, knowing what's ahead of me with Daddy, around Labor Day."

Yates nodded. Another week, and the timeline was fitting. The summer exhausted, Terri Miller would slip away right on cue.

* * *

Beebe dwelled on the ordeal ahead of her involving her father. The shrill ring of Vincent's cell phone cut through those thoughts. He retrieved the device from his shirt pocket and flipped it open.

Instantly, his face changed. "Willa? What's wrong? What happened?" He stared at a point beyond Beebe as he listened. "Yes. Yes, I can." He rose out of the folding chair, and the dog lifted his snout off his front legs in response. "I'm at Crossroads. Give me two minutes." He closed the phone. To Beebe and Yates: "It's Rev. Razzell."

Beebe looked at Yates, recognizing the fact that the young man knew the name.

"He's had some kind of episode," Vincent explained, jamming the phone back into his pocket.

Simultaneously, Beebe and Yates pushed themselves to their feet, their chairs groaning. "What kind of episode? Can I do anything?" Beebe said. Mosie Razzell was an old friend and trusted advisor. He was also a senior. She was an adjutant to seniors, to Vincent, to Crossroads. It seemed imperative that she be involved.

"Yes. That's good," Vincent said. "And Yates. We might need some medical advice."

The three of them and the dog rushed the door, Vincent ahead of the pack. He opened the door and set the lock. Once Beebe, Yates, and Barleycorn filed out, Vincent pulled the door closed behind him.

"Here's my car," he said, directing Beebe toward the passenger door of an older model Chevy. Yates and Barleycorn piled into the back seat.

The curbside parking lane was empty ahead of Vincent so he nudged the car forward and safely around the corner to Standhope without actually maneuvering into traffic. This told Beebe two things: Razzell's situation was truly urgent as Vincent understood it, and Razzell still lived across from the park, two blocks up.

In those two blocks, Vincent told a story that covered the last three weeks. The story included Beebe's father, Cliff Walker, and his involvement with an incident that took place in front of the hardware store. Cliff pulled Razzell back after he wandered into traffic. After that, Willa, the woman who called, and her husband, Ned McMitchell, the current minister shepherding Razzell's former flock, took the reins. They followed up on the older minister, who, rapidly, Willa reported, seemed to "return to his old self."

"There's Willa," Vincent said, pulling to a neck-jarring stop at the curb across the street from the house Beebe remembered as belonging to Razzell. Vincent jumped out.

A young, very pregnant woman stood on the sidewalk. Beebe, Yates, and Barleycorn came around the car. The new arrivals hurried up to the woman.

"Willa, this is Beebe Walker, Cliff Walker's daughter. And this is Yates Strand." Willa nodded. She wore a worried expression. One hand fiddled nervously with the hem of her maternity top. "I thought Beebe should come. She's my new assistant. And Yates is a nurse."

Willa tugged on Vincent's arm. "Perfect. You might need an extra set of hands with Mosie."

Beebe and Yates tarried long enough to exchange ominous looks, then followed in the single-file march up Razzell's front walk, Beebe holding the anchor spot.

"Ned and I decided to come over and check on Mosie. When we got here, the door was ajar. Ned knocked, but Mosie didn't answer. We pushed the door open. The entry hall was a mess. Clothes and papers were strewn all around. We followed the path of destruction. Mosie sat in a chair in his bedroom. The room's condition was worse than the hall's, and Mosie was stark naked."

With that news, Beebe grimaced. Both she and Yates pulled up a half second before proceeding on.

Vincent took Willa's elbow and escorted her up the steps to Razzell's porch and through the door.

"Mosie seemed to be coming around, out of some fog, when Ned asked me to call you," Willa said to Vincent.

They walked over and around the detritus on their way through the house. The men went into the bedroom at the end of the hall while Beebe and Willa waited outside. Beebe held Barleycorn on the leash that Yates carried in the pocket of baggy jeans and clipped to the dog before crossing the street outside Razzell's house.

Willa peeked into the room. "Ned cleaned things up some. There were drawers open and blankets on the floor."

"Like he was looking for something?" Beebe queried.

"Yeah. Sanity," Willa replied, absolutely serious. "You didn't see the look in his eyes." Willa peeked inside again. "Thank God he's dressed."

When Beebe tipped her head to look past the bedroom door, she saw Yates kneeling in front of the drawn face of a man who looked ten years older than he should. Yates took Razzell's pulse. He spoke to a patient who blinked vacant eyes. "I'm Yates, Rev. Razzell. Remember me from bingo?"

"I do. You have the dog."

That's a good sign, Beebe thought, encouraged.

"Right." Yates turned his head and called, "Barleycorn. Come here, boy."

Beebe dropped the leash. The dog waddled over, around the foot of the bed. He sniffed the tall man who stood next to Vincent as he passed. Beebe could assume he was Rev. Ned McMitchell.

When the dog sat on his haunches beside Yates, he said, "Barleycorn, meet a new friend."

The dog raised a paw. After a delay, Razzell took it. The dog seemed to pass a calming influence over Razzell, who then possessed the will to send his gaze out over the width of the room. When he saw Beebe standing beside Willa in the doorway, his facial expression changed to something near horror. He yanked his hand back to his heart. Everyone snapped their eyes around to Beebe.

Vincent's voice was tentative, trying to override Razzell's apparent and unexplainable shock. "You haven't forgotten Beebe Walker? We talked her into returning to Larkspur. Remember, Ned and I came over. We told you she agreed to help me out at the center."

Beebe went into the room. "It's been awhile Rev. Razzell, hasn't it? I'm sorry you're not feeling well today." She had to acknowledge the situation. "If you wouldn't mind, I'll come back another time. We can talk about what I missed by being gone so long."

Razzell stared harder. He leaned forward. "Yes, right. Beebe. Good to see you. You're correct. I'm not at my best. Another time might be better." Razzell sat back. His hand found the dog.

With his words of subtle dismissal, Beebe stepped back out of the room, saddened by the sight. Willa followed her down the hall. Together, they straightened the house. Most of the debris littered the carpet. Willa folded a few articles of clothing.

Five minutes later, Vincent joined them. "That was an odd reaction." He spoke to Beebe.

"I can't imagine what it meant. The last time I spoke with him, I was deciding to study theology."

Just then, Willa shuffled back down the hallway in response to Ned's call.

Even though she was out of earshot, Beebe lowered her voice. "We both know my study of theology was a precursor to disaster."

"Someday soon, you'll need to fill me in on why you think disaster is the right word."

"Well—" Beebe cut off when Ned and Willa McMitchell entered the room. Yates and Barleycorn remained with Razzell.

"I guess we haven't properly met. I'm Ned McMitchell."

Beebe shook his extended hand. "Beebe Walker."

"I'm going to stay with Mosie tonight and make another pitch for intervention."

"Are you sure?" Vincent said.

Beebe followed the conversation with interest and concern for Razzell. But with Vincent's question, she stiffened. Her concern shifted to herself. Was Vincent somehow saying he would make himself available to monitor Razzell tonight? If he did, would that preclude him sitting with her when she spoke with her father about Abigail Walker's body resting in Terri Miller's grave?

"He gave me a great deal of loving care when I came to First Lutheran so he could retire. He probably just needs a good health checkup. Maybe I'll call Dr.

White." To Beebe, he said, "He's Willa's and my family doctor and a church member. I can tell him what happened. Get some advice."

Willa touched her husband's arm. "Maybe you should leave that to Beebe. Those are her duties now." To Beebe, she said, "If you haven't guessed, there have been prior discussions about Mosie Razzell."

"Fine with me if that's Beebe's choice," Ned said, sounding amenable. "I'll just keep him company tonight."

"We'll keep him company," Willa said, her hand rested on her round belly.

"Your plan is fine with me, Ned. Thanks for the help. I just can't fathom his peculiar reaction," Beebe said.

"I don't think he understood why you were here," Willa said, "just out of the blue. He doesn't know you took the new position at Crossroads."

"No. I mentioned it to him two weeks ago." Vincent's expression reflected mounting worry.

"He must have forgot. Given his reaction, it might be best if I team up with one of you the first few times I come back," Beebe said, her eyes sweeping the faces of those in the tight circle around her.

"We'll work that out," Vincent said. "There's enough of us to keep up with Mosie until you have your reunion with Cliff."

"You haven't been home yet?" Willa said.

"Daddy's working. He was out on a delivery, so I checked in with Vincent."

"Wow, then this was a bit of a baptism by fire," Ned said.

Beebe, the minister out of the business, did not grin back at the minister still in.

Pedestal Worthy

Vincent led Beebe, Yates, and Barleycorn across the street to the park. His mention of Beebe's reunion with her father caused missing segments of Abigail's story to press uncomfortably against his heart. The full story should be told to Cliff in one sitting, not in piecemeal fashion. To that end, Beebe must hear it first. And Yates.

The contingent followed Vincent to two park benches sitting in front of a stand of walnut trees. The benches were arranged at right angles and facilitated conversation. Along the way, Yates gave a nursing report.

"He was a bit clammy, but no fever I could detect," said the nurse who lacked instruments for his examination. "His breathing seemed fine until he reacted to Beebe. I still had my finger on his pulse. It shot up to strong and rapid. What was that about?"

"Not a clue," Beebe said. "We had a good relationship when I was a kid. I'm sure we'll get back there. If what happened today is important, I'll let him know I'm open to him raising the issue when he's ready."

Vincent suggested Yates allow Barleycorn a few minutes to romp, and the two went off. Vincent and Beebe seated themselves on separate benches. Vincent gave Beebe a bench-side neighborhood tour of who lived in which house, complete with a thumbnail bio.

When Barleycorn raced to Vincent, he corralled the dog's attention to bring Yates over.

"I kind of like this venue for another talk about Terri. Or Abigail." Vincent looked from Yates to Beebe.

Yates sat down of his own accord. The dog dropped, panting.

Beebe's penetrating gaze read Vincent's face. "Another talk? Haven't you told us everything you know?" Her question carried a hint of accusation.

"No, not everything. But hear me out before you throw daggers at the messenger."

"The messenger? You're an accomplice in disguise."

Vincent decided not to engage Beebe, letting her tone and characterization roll off his back. "She begged me not to tell any of this. You know how she can be." For some reason, Vincent turned the last sentence to Yates, not Beebe. The undercurrent said the young man had greater knowledge of Beebe's mother than Beebe. Vincent steeled himself before he ventured with, "The truth is she licked the addiction. She got the disease breaking up a fight." Simultaneously, Beebe's and Yates's mouths flew open. "Two women were going at it pretty good, scratching, clawing, punching each other. One of them bit her. Broke the skin. The woman was bleeding from a busted lip. She had AIDS."

Yates spoke first, truly injured. "Why didn't she tell me? Why let me think she was less than she was, just an old druggie?"

"I asked the same question because she left me with that impression the night I carried her into Crossroads. She said she didn't want to be looked up to. She was not fit for a pedestal. Those were her words. She meant that nothing she could do could ever pay for abandoning her family, or succumbing to addiction in the first place."

Time ticked slowly by while Abigail's rationale sank in. A yellow butterfly frolicked in the grass. Barleycorn stretched his nose, but laying down and panting, couldn't reach it.

Finally, Beebe spoke. "But if she conquered her addiction, why didn't she come home?"

"The felony warrant, I expect, if one ever existed. That was my take later, anyway." Vincent rested his arm across the bench's seat back.

"We could have gone to her."

Vincent knew this was a scenario Beebe had not thought through. "You and Cliff would be aiding a felon. She didn't tell me everything. Time was short." Vincent saw a wave of anger cross Beebe's face. The daggers weren't far behind.

"You knew all this when you came to my house."

"I wasn't supposed to tell any of it. So I told as little as possible. I don't think you would have appreciated the details as much then. But now, with the two of you together," Vincent said, flicking a finger at Beebe and Yates seated side by side on the bench, "I truly think it rises to the height of pedestal-worthy."

"Why do you say that?" Beebe argued.

"She mastered the addiction. She put it behind her."

"So we're supposed to feel sorry for her because she got AIDS anyway, trying to do the right thing, trying to keep two women from pounding each other senseless. I suppose there's a certain worth to that, a certain irony."

"What if we think about standing her on a short pedestal?" Vincent added a weak smile. It garnered no appreciation from Beebe. "If she tried to stop this fight, she probably inserted herself in other dangerous situations."

"My father's." Yates gave an example. "His car overturned. There was a danger of his car catching fire while she administered what aid she could and while crawling around inside, looking for Dad's phone to call the accident in."

"Why didn't she put her willpower to use while she was here with Daddy and me? She found it on the road? Then she couldn't come home because she faced jail time? In the end, she died of AIDS anyway."

"But she did good along the way. She tried—"

Beebe jerked the sentence away from Yates. "She chose to be homeless! She admitted it. She lived on the streets, and she nearly died on the streets."

"She didn't live on the streets at the end. I took care of her until she needed more than I could give." Yates spoke up for himself. "Then she lived at Gaven House."

"But before that," Beebe snapped, "she was one of the honored homeless."

"What happened to coming to terms with your mother's life?" Yates threw back.

"I came to terms with her death. I didn't know this. Vincent held back."

"Well, you know it now."

Vincent put up his hands, quieting Beebe and Yates, preventing more harsh words. He also had a gut feeling his next revelation would cause Yates to go on the attack. Tipping his gaze toward the young man, he said, "You said you didn't know where she lived during the summers at your house. She told me she lived in a room in the back of a hardware store."

Vincent watched a hurtful astonishment gouge at Yates. It scraped down his face, dulling his eyes, adding slack to his mouth, then it reversed its momentum. Yates pressed his lips together until they were pursed and hard. His pupils full of something short of fury. "I also didn't say my father owns a hardware store." His tone brought Barleycorn's head off his outstretched legs. The dog studied his master.

"She didn't say the store owner and the boy she spent her summers with were connected. I guess I sort of suspected," Vincent said.

"My father—" Yates broke off, closing his eyes and looking away.

"She felt a kinship for you, Yates. Your father must have understood." Vincent sent his next comment to Beebe. "And she was making up for past sins."

Despite Vincent's attempt to move Terri's story into an empathetic arena, Yates ignited. "My father knows more." He dug in his pocket for his phone.

Turning to Beebe, Vincent said, "I know it's hard to hear these things, but you should have the whole story before you talk with Cliff."

"It's not whole yet!" Yates got to his feet. "Not until I've dragged the rest of it out of Dad."

Vincent kept his eyes on Yates's back as he departed. He thought about Terri, how she hid jewels about herself behind, under a veil of misty secrecy that seemed destined to evaporate.

* * *

Yates paced away from the others. Barleycorn followed. Yates listened to ring after ring before he heard his father's hello. He pictured Arthur Strand lifting the receiver, distracted by the business of running a hardware store. Yates's opening line was a shot over the bow.

"You let Terri live in that back room at the store all those summers. Why keep it a secret? She told Vincent all about it before she died. Neither one of you told me. Did Mom know?"

For a moment, Yates thought the connection went dead, then Arthur cleared his throat. "Terri was something of an enigma for your mother, Yates."

"How come? She saved your life. You liked her. She was nothing but good to me. I knew Mom was opposed to her hanging around, but Mom let you win when it came to Terri. I always wondered why. She never let you win."

Arthur's voice was steady, thoughtful. "I had a bit of leverage over her there, son."

"What leverage? What do you mean?" Yates stopped. The dog passed him up, nose sniffing the ground. Yates's free arm crossed his midsection. It held his jumpy stomach in place.

"You had an uncle from your mom's side of the family, Stan Fry, who died before Mom and I were married."

"Wait. Fry? That wasn't Mom's maiden name."

"Stan was her stepbrother. They were close. I knew Stan first. He introduced me to Mom."

Okay, Yates thought. He barely remembered his maternal grandfather having two marriages, but the question was, "Why did Mom let you win?"

"You accepted my perspective about Terri, but it was forced on Mom."

Yates repeated his father's mantra. "Help when you can. Don't judge."

"Mom wanted to judge Terri, but I reminded her about Stan." A second of silence ticked by. "Stan died of an overdose when he was nineteen. Naomi didn't like that Terri hung around. I told her we'd let Terri hang around because Stan couldn't. No one helped Stan. We didn't, and we could have. We got the word he died two weeks after he lay in the morgue as a John Doe."

Yates thought that a measure of shame for the long-ago death of her stepbrother allowed his mother to bend just enough to accept Terri.

"I think your mother fully trusted that Terri would do you no harm."

"She would never. I loved her. From the first." His feelings rushed from him without reserve or embarrassment. Just as hastily, he squinted down at the mysterious side of Terri. There was something about her he could never define as a kid. He couldn't give it words even now. "After Mom died, why didn't you let Terri move in?"

"She didn't want to. That wasn't her life. She adopted us, not the other way around, and on her terms."

Yates thought about that: Life on her terms. Terri had a mantra, too. A worthy one. Not pedestal-worthy. Terri didn't want that. Forgiveness doused his initial fury for both Terri and his father. He was glad she had shelter, glad his father provided it. "Did you know she kicked the habit?"

"Not in so many words, but I never saw her high. She never had the shakes, like she was weaning herself off something in order to spend summers with you. That was an unwritten rule your mother and I insisted on. No drugs if she wanted a relationship with you. But if drugs were behind her—and good for her on that—then the rule and my speech were all for naught." Arthur Strand spoke of a protected time when Yates was a loved and innocent child. The innocence waned, but the love remained.

"Why do you think she told Vincent about living at the hardware store?" He got back to the initial reason he called. This time, the question wasn't delivered as a potshot. He suspected he would not get an answer immediately. His father cleared his throat the way he did when he wanted to interfere in his son's private life—his *grown* son's private life, the son who was twenty-three, a college graduate, and quite capable of taking care of himself and one shaggy dog. "Dad, are we going to do this again?"

"But I haven't said anything yet."

"You're going to." Yates sighed. "Barleycorn and I are fine. We're eating, sleeping, and washing behind our ears."

Arthur didn't let Yates's flippant remark trip him up. "What about money? You wanted to go on this quest and do it on your own. I didn't stop you. But the security deposit your landlady returned isn't much and won't go far."

"I'm fine, Dad."

"You mentioned Vincent twice now. You still at the shelter?"

"Yes. And my interview is still on at the hospital."

A beat passed. "You know I'm proud of you, son."

"Sure, Dad. I know," Yates said, respectful and sincere.

"See that you don't forget." Arthur's dose of gruffness arrived right on schedule. It always signaled the end of touchy-feely moments. "Now let's get back on track with Terri. The reason she told Vincent about living at the hardware store is a simple one in my opinion: She wanted you to know."

"She knew I would come around Larkspur later?"

"No one ever knew Terri's story until she was ready to tell it. We all surmised. We guessed. But our guesses were just animation."

"Where did she go when the summers were over?"

"I don't know."

"You must," Yates hissed. He wanted that puzzle piece of Terri's life.

"I don't, son. That first summer while I was recovering, I told your mother, Terri needs Yates. I won't stand between them. I don't know the story, but I trust."

Yates and his father talked on some. After they said their goodbyes, Yates returned to Vincent and Beebe, waiting on the benches. He told another sliver of the story, not only Terri's, but Stan Fry's, and how that touched his mother. She believed in her husband's good heart, in his trust. Those two elements bridged the summers that followed.

Yates looked off toward the horizon. What would he need to bridge this summer? His first one without Terri. She led him to Larkspur and the first half of her life just as surely as she commanded him. She led him to Vincent. To a hospice. No, a shelter, like Yates's father provided her. Now, Beebe was here.

Yates's thought pattern stumbled over Beebe. Terri may have planned for Yates to meet her daughter, but had she known Beebe left town all those years ago? Even if she had, she couldn't predict Beebe's return. Were these discoveries coming to light by design, or happenstance? Yates felt a measure of anger rumble when he voted for design. Damn the secrets she kept. Were they absolutely necessary? He guessed not, if she told Vincent, a stranger. It pinched Yates that Terri hadn't told him. But if she told any of it, if she told just a little, would he have set out for Larkspur, on a homeless journey himself? That struck him. That made him think. He was doing a lot of that lately.

* * *

On the short drive back to Crossroads, Beebe apologized for her rough temperament in the park. Yates had been quiet all the way, almost brooding, but he perked up and matched his apology to hers.

Beebe took Vincent up on his offer to walk her over to McKinley Hardware, where she'd left her car, so they parted company with Yates and Barleycorn.

Vincent waved away the apology she offered him as they crossed the street. More important to him was the snapshot summary he gave of the stores they passed. The trip was newsy with ownership details. He tied names back to families Beebe might remember from her younger days in Larkspur. Overall, she shook her head more than she nodded. The town had picked up and moved on, just as she had. Either that, or her memory was suspect. In the upcoming weeks, she thought she would enjoy many "aha" moments.

When they arrived, Vincent stepped inside the store with Beebe.

"I can't believe how much things have changed," Beebe said, laughing a bit nervously. She wondered what seeing her father again would bring in the way of emotions now that she was here and soon to be face to face. Anticipation nibbled at her, despite Vincent's entertaining attempts to distract. She felt like a total stranger in her hometown, which was easier to accept than in her relationship with her own father. Perhaps that was better stated a non-relationship.

"It won't take you long to get re-acclimated, especially with Crossroads as a resource point. The seniors will enroll you in an accelerated course of who begat who, and who's doing what now."

"This will surprise you: I know one person from the old days. My stranger status didn't extend to Scott Cotter." She pointed toward the customer service counter, where Scott stood the first time she entered the store two or more hours ago. Their recognition hadn't been instantaneous. There was the split-second of narrowed eyes before they pointed at each other and in a chorus said, "I remember you." After they quickly caught up on each other's lives, she learned her father was out making a delivery.

"So you know Scott."

"We were neighbors during our middle school years," Beebe explained to Vincent. Scott wasn't the skinny kid anymore. His dark hair no longer covered his ears, but was prematurely shot through with gray. "Looks like he's stepped away. I don't see Daddy either." Beebe's gaze careened down those several aisleways within range.

"Scott'll be back soon so this is where I leave you. You and Cliff should have your reunion without me gawking and lurking about." He laid one arm around her shoulders and squeezed. "You still want me there tonight?"

About a hundred times over the last two weeks, Beebe pictured Vincent beside her when they revealed the news about Abigail's death to her father. She let no time pass before she said, "Six-thirty. Will that suit?" Her face was angled up to his and the almost curly chestnut hair that wreathed his face.

"Suits fine."

When he turned toward the doors, Beebe grabbed his arm. "Wait," she said. He gave her an eyebrows-raised expression. "I want to thank you for doing whatever you did to convince Daddy to give up some of Mother's clothes. I hope my friend Callie didn't impose too much on my behalf."

Vincent's face and his tone softened. "It was my pleasure, and no imposition. Callie does deserve credit for the idea and reaching out. I hope the quilt serves its purpose for you."

"Oh, it's more for Daddy," she said, using a flip of her fingers to sweep Vincent's meaning away. "He's the one with the rough road ahead."

"Callie wanted you to have it." Vincent layered a bit of firmness to those words.

"No," Beebe said, ready to say more when he cut her off.

"I spoke with her, Beebe. I know her intentions. No doubt Cliff will appreciate the finished product, and it will touch both of you." He paused to study her. "Don't shortchange yourself. Don't do it." For a long moment, his eyes wouldn't release hers, then he flicked a glance behind her. "Here comes Scott. Chin up."

She complied with his friendly order and added a smile. She was so thankful

Vincent still lived in Larkspur. Vincent waved to Scott, who threw up a hand in return.

"Hi, Scott," Beebe said, when he was close enough. "Is he back?"

"You betcha," Scott said, breezing around her to the customer service desk. He lifted a microphone wired to equipment hidden beneath the desktop. Before she could stop him, he spoke into it, "Cliff. Beebe's here."

Beebe smiled through an inward cringe. A public announcement was not her intended course. His words scratched through speakers all over the store and back in the storeroom. She glanced around. She saw a young female cashier take money from a pre-teen carrying his skateboard under his arm. Intent on their transaction, neither paid any attention to the public address.

The small store felt a bit more cramped than she remembered. There were two cash registers now. The first row of shelving facing the registers held baskets full of dollar items. She reached this decision based on the yellow price tags wired through the wicker.

Distant movement in her peripheral vision brought her head around to reveal her first view of her father in over a decade. His long strides bisected the main aisle and warmed her with the comfort of opening a child's storybook for a one-hundredth reading. How many times as a girl had she stood on the same speckled gray tiles and witnessed her father hurrying to greet her, pulling rawhide gloves off and stuffing them in the back pocket of blue work pants. His first name was stitched in red on a blue striped shirt, just like always. Despite everything, she was so glad to see him.

But when he glanced up to finally take her in, her outlook changed. She saw his even gait stutter, his expression sag. After their years of estrangement, she lost the knack of reading his emotions with any precision. The hand she raised in greeting rerouted itself of its own accord. In the moment it took for one finger to loop strands of chin-length hair behind her ear, she watched Cliff Walker appear to steel himself, before forging a small smile for his daughter.

So far, an auspicious beginning and not how she envisioned it, given his recent sacrifice of Abigail's clothes to be cut and sewed into a quilt. That gift went beyond words. It felt as though he gave up a limb or a vital organ. Now, it took on the connotation of an unwilling act, something wrenched from his grasp.

Beebe matched her father's last steps. "Hi, Daddy," she said, mustering a measure of enthusiasm. She went up on tiptoes, arms stretched toward his shoulders before he bent at the waist to receive her back-patting hug. His embrace did eventually exert pressure. Her heels on the floor again, her chin tipped up, she studied him. She saw that the two swathes of gray around his ears were completely filled in now, but there was no sign of thinning hair. The lines that hours in the sun etched into his skin showed deeper inroads. "You were gone when I got here before."

"You're a day early," was his snappish excuse.

She flinched at his tone. Mouth open, but stymied as to what to say, she was relieved when Scott stepped in with an upbeat reply. "It's called a surprise, Cliff. It's a good one."

After that, Cliff's attitude shifted. Beebe believed he received Scott's padded rebuke as a lesson in manners. Cliff drew a breath. With its exhale, his shoulders relaxed. "Well," he began anew, "you know Scott." He raised a hand to indicate the cashier, but waved away that introduction. Her nails garnered her full attention. She employed an emery board with deft capability. Behind her, the kid sailed past the front window on his skateboard. Scott wandered the cashier's way, leaving the Walkers to their reunion, unchaperoned.

Cliff looked at his watch. "I have three hours yet till closing. What's the plan?"

"When you were out, I went to see Vincent at Crossroads. I'll tell you more about that tonight, or rather Vincent and I will. I asked him over for my first dinner back. You don't mind?" She quickly skirted details, which she knew would leave Cliff to believe they related to her new position at the community center.

"Vincent for dinner is fine," he said, nodding, but offered nothing more.

"I'm cooking. I'll stop for groceries on the way home."

"I won't argue with that. Here, take my keys."

If the inference was to rush her off, she received that message. He worked his pickup's ignition key off the ring. Pocketing that key, he handed over the others. Their eyes met, and she saw gears churning behind his hazel pair. Whatever he was thinking would not and should not be pried out of him here. "Well, see you later, Daddy."

She made her way out, her anxiety at full boil. He certainly seemed more amenable to her return when they spoke on the phone than he displayed face to face. She lost ground already, but maybe it was better to start in an inferior position. She knew so many things he did not. Knowing what lay ahead of her, any ground gained at this stage will most likely be trampled by the time he climbed the stairs for bed.

From Hanna's Market, with groceries in the front seat, she headed north, out of town.

Graveside Reunion

Beebe crossed the bridge over Kettle Creek and automatically reduced her speed. In the distance, she saw the countryside open up off to her right. There was the cemetery and the two-story caretaker's house at its northern edge. Larkspur Cemetery had the capacity to bury the town's dead for 250 years. A good seventy-five years were still ahead. She wondered about the person who would take the last grave. Who would it be? The first person was a child, seven years old. Billy Rightmeyer died of typhoid. It always seemed such an unfavorable start to Beebe. Had the first caretaker, Joseph Jenkins, felt the same way? Had it saddened him to first bury a child?

Beebe turned into the driveway. She shifted into park and sat there a minute with the engine running as if a quick getaway might become necessary. The red brick house itself looked the same with its wide mahogany front door and black iron accents. Cliff's middle name was upkeep. Although he repainted on a fixed schedule, he hadn't varied the color scheme of white window frames and spruce green shutters. She shut down the engine and got out. Her gaze climbed the maple tree in the side yard. Its expansive girth blocked the winter wind and shaded her bedroom windows.

She bypassed the front door and followed a narrow walkway around to the side entrance into the kitchen. Her unhurried pace allowed her a moment to relive the past. There was no order to her memories. She was a minister, schoolgirl, college student, stepping off a yellow bus, nearly running over a lilac bush at the foot of the driveway the day she obtained her learner's permit. She raced around the house, chasing butterflies, and shoveled snow from the kitchen steps. The corner chip off the bottom step was still there. Of course, it was. Some things upkeep couldn't repair.

She searched her father's keys. They jingled when, by trial and error, she tried a few until one turned the lock. She stepped inside, through the mud porch, and up to the kitchen. The house greeted her with the wave of pink gingham curtains at the open window over the sink. Nothing of substance had changed. She could have left an hour ago, gone shopping, and returned. Why, though, didn't it feel like home? She set the three bags of groceries on the countertop just inside the door. The feelings that stirred weren't unfamiliar. She knew them since her teenage days. The empty house didn't feel like home because her mother wasn't there. She looked behind her, through the screen door. Her gaze ran the length of the cemetery.

Beebe shivered with the oddest sensation. She didn't know where her mother was. She hadn't known at sixteen, not during the thirty years when Abigail Walker lived another life, and not now. Her mother was buried in the cemetery, but where? Beebe knew how to find out. She rushed to put the groceries needing refrigeration away, then grabbed her father's keys. She trundled down the porch steps, hung a left, and speed-walked to the block building.

She remembered seeing the drafted plans for the cemetery's layout once. There, the block building was officially labeled the Monument Office. The name never stuck. It was differentiated from the other outbuildings by its composition. Its cement blocks were dressed up with a coat of beige paint and a surround of bushes with red berries. They appeared recently trimmed.

Beebe unlocked the door, passed through, and left it to stand open. She was surprised to see a computer screen occupying the desk on the office side of the building. She could not imagine her father sitting in front of any type of new-fangled contraption. If the cemetery's records had been entered digitally, she was sunk. She doubted she could defeat any password protection, let alone negotiate an unfamiliar software program. Hoping against hope, she went to a card-file unit on top of shoulder-high filing cabinets. The unit's five drawers were sized for index cards. Scanning the clips of paper slipped into metal holders, she found the one where Terri Miller's burial data should be filed. Using her fingernails, she picked through. The last Miller filed contained the first name, Terri. She verified the grave coordinates with the cemetery map on the wall, closed the card drawer, grabbed the keys off the desk, and retraced her steps to the door where a cone of afternoon light blazed through.

She reached for the doorknob and suddenly, Yates Strand appeared. He came around the door with a panting Barleycorn beside him.

"Lord, Yates, you scared me." Beebe's heart raced with his surprise appearance. She gripped the keys so tightly, their rough edges hurt her palm.

"Sorry." His soulful eyes pleaded his case. "I knocked at the house first, then I saw the door open. Figured it was you."

"Why are you here?"

"Same reason as you, I bet. I want to see the grave."

"You haven't been yet?"

"Just couldn't make myself. Like standing next to it would make it more real." He shook his head." I don't know why, or where that comes from."

"No, no, I get that. And yes, I just looked up the location. I didn't know how I could just ignore the fact and begin breading chicken for supper. You know, it didn't seem respectful."

"Can I go with you? You wouldn't mind?"

"I count myself fortunate for the company."

They headed off, down an asphalt lane that curved back toward the house, then south toward town.

"How'd it go with your father?"

"Fine, really. It was a little not like us, if you know what I mean."

"I suppose."

"We were out in public," she explained.

"How long has it been, if I'm not being too nosy?"

"You mean since I came home for a visit?"

"Yes."

"Nearly fifteen years. Vincent met, married, and lost his wife, and I never knew her."

"And the trouble was Terri? Or Abigail." He quickly corrected the name.

"Either is fine, Yates." She touched his arm. "I can't say the problem didn't start with Mother. Of course, it did. But I was a kid, and I needed a little more out of Daddy. He just kept swinging back and forth between being a regular father like nothing happened and being a man mad at the world. You know?"

"I guess."

"He made me feel like it was my fault."

"How could that be?"

"I look remarkably like her."

"You do. It stopped me in my tracks back at the center."

Then Yates should understand, Beebe thought. "In Daddy's heart, the blame for his wrecked life belonged to a woman who had my face. That's all he could see."

Yates said nothing. He just nodded, seemingly deep in thought.

"The grave ought to be in this row."

Yates led them into the row Beebe pointed out. They traipsed single-file, Barleycorn between them.

"Here it is," Yates said.

They stared, their eyes downcast. The marker was a rough stone etched with her mother's alias and the only other information known about the woman: her date of death, March 11. Beebe became lost in the realization that she hadn't cared enough to ask Vincent for the exact date when he brought the news of Abigail's death to Maryland. Her cuttingly neglectful lack of concern clawed at her heart, now suddenly bereft. Beside her, Yates barely held himself together.

Their grief was matched by Barleycorn's. The big dog moaned a heart-wrenching sound, lay down on the grave, and pressed his snout across the grass. She didn't think dogs cried, but Barleycorn seemed on the verge. Her mother's spirit appeared to reach out and touch the dog's. His devotion, so naturally guileless, spoke, Beebe thought, to Abigail's good heart.

Until that moment, Beebe never connected her mother and the dog, but clearly, she nurtured a relationship. Yates's comment confirmed it.

"How could he possibly know?" Yates grasped Beebe's hand.

The three wept. Silently. Briefly.

"We'd better go back," Beebe said, sniffling. "You ready?"

"Yeah." Yates wiped his eyes. He followed Beebe a few steps. "Barleycorn, come," he said. Beebe looked back when Yates added, "Come on, boy."

The dog would not move. Yates went back. He tugged gently at his collar. That prompted Barleycorn to a sitting position. Yates squatted. His arms encircled the dog's shoulders. Beebe watched the scene through fresh tears.

"Maybe you should stay for dinner." The instant she asked, she wished she could pull the invitation back. It was a mistake, given the conversation she and Vincent were determined to have with her father that evening.

"No. I don't think so."

Although she felt relief, she pushed the issue. "Daddy will have to meet you sometime. You're not opposed to that?"

"No. Just not tonight. Tonight when he's hearing the story for the first time, I think he'd somehow perceive me as Terri's illegitimate child."

"But you're not," Beebe exclaimed, stunned he cast himself in such a role.

"I know. But my story is so different from yours. It's not going to be easy. Honestly, I don't want to be here. It's too much."

He gave her such a pained expression, Beebe thought Yates would rather be Barleycorn, happier to lay down on the grave with memories not spoiled by the two Walkers.

Lies at Sunset

Cliff Walker drove with the wrist of his right hand draped over the top of the steering wheel. His thoughts were mixed. His speed was reserved. Someone waited at home at the end of a workday. He shouldn't think of his daughter as someone. Beebe waited. But these days, they hardly knew each other. Perhaps that was the reason he didn't push the speed limit.

In the five weeks since discussion of Beebe's return began, he thought he accepted the idea. He admitted he was grateful, though, when she called with the news of a two-week delay for emergency counseling in West Virginia. Cliff didn't hound or chastise himself for his sigh of relief over the reprieve. It was natural. This was *his* life. He owned it. The two weeks massaged and softened his resistance to change. Those were points in his favor.

Only God knew how many points he should receive for managing his first meeting with his daughter, not only a day early and with his coworkers staring, but unprepared as he was for the shock. His mind ratcheted and his heart squeezed when he laid eyes on Beebe. Had father and daughter not been estranged over the past dozen or so years, he would not be dealing with the remnants of that sudden jolt of comprehension.

There had never been a time in his life when his daughter looked older than his memories of his wife. Beebe was forty-six. Abigail ran away at thirty-six. Until Beebe stopped returning to Larkspur, Cliff couldn't help but make the comparison year by year. Their features were identical. He knew nothing else.

Three hours earlier, he forced himself to walk the main aisle while internally, brakes screeched. Train cars piled into one another. The tracks were gone. His future took no form. It contained no content. He still felt dazed as he turned into the driveway and parked behind Beebe's car.

He went in the front door and called a greeting to Beebe in the kitchen. She called back. He saw the dining room table laid for supper. The aroma of a home-cooked meal followed him upstairs. While he washed up, he heard Vincent's voice in the living room. How odd. A conversation in the house that didn't include him. Voices. Laughter.

So much change, he thought. Too much. Too quickly. It seemed an intrusion. But then, he reasoned, it was one evening meal. Beebe's first night home. A celebration of sorts. Soon they would settle into the sedate life of an old man whose matronly daughter lived with him. Beebe did not lead the wild life. As for Cliff, the solace of his cemetery, its never-wavering gift, would carry him and provide respite and familiarity when needed.

Conversational banter ringed the dining room table while they ate baked chicken and mashed potatoes. Cliff, Beebe, and Vincent talked about Crossroads, Beebe's new job, and Vincent's new spur line: senior programming. Cliff listened and agreed the two of them together would address a need in Larkspur.

Cliff looked from Beebe's face to Vincent's. They chatted easily. They picked up the thread of their friendship without a hitch. Cliff was not a betting man, but he'd lay odds these two would not relight their childhood flame. He just couldn't see it.

To combat the unease of finding less and less to say to support the discussion, and because dessert would cap the evening, he suggested ice cream.

"Not right now, Daddy." Beebe shared a look across the table to their guest. "Come into the living room. Vincent and I have something to tell you."

Just that quickly, the tenor of the evening changed. Dread filled the space when his heart jumped a beat. Cliff felt something akin to premeditation scurry around the threesome as they passed under the archway and into the other room.

Beebe and Vincent perched on the edge of the couch. Cliff grasped the arms of the upholstered chair and sat.

It was late summer. On evenings such as this, a bright sun swept through the window behind the couch, creating long shadows across the room. Cliff's eyes dragged the length of those shadows back to their source. Vincent's hands were folded between his knees. Beebe leaned forward, her forearms resting in her lap. Both their faces were solemn.

She spoke first. "Daddy, you need to prepare yourself. This is going to be a shock."

He felt himself stiffen, ready to take the brunt. Not another shock, he thought.

"Daddy, last March, Mother died."

His head swam instantly. How? Where?

The "how" was a two-part question. How did she die? How did Beebe know?

Where she died staggered him.

"Mother died from complications related to AIDS. I found out about her death nearly a month later. Vincent came to me in Maryland."

"Vincent?" Cliff knew his mouth formed the name, but he did not hear the spoken word.

"She died at Crossroads, Cliff."

"She was here?" Cliff scratched out the question.

Vincent nodded.

"Where is she buried?" He turned his head away slightly, trying to cushion the brunt of the answer coming his way.

"Daddy, she gave Vincent a fictitious name. Terri Miller."

The name struck like a gunshot. It forced him back against the chair. "Oh, my god. She's buried here. Abigail's here. In that grave. Why Terri Miller? I don't understand."

"At first, Vincent didn't know who she was—"

"Why would you do this to me? Abigail's here." Cliff routed his accusation toward the man he counted as a friend. Cliff's forearms rested on the chair arms. He watched his left hand while he loosened the fist, then he loosened the right. His eyes squeezed tight. The tremor was back.

"Cliff, I never met Abigail. The woman showed up one evening just as I was closing. She was weak, barely able to stand," Vincent said, looking Cliff straight in the eye. "I could tell she was quite ill. She told me her name was Terri Miller. I couldn't know otherwise. The next night, she started talking. That's when she told me the truth."

"Why keep this from me?" Cliff watched a pained look cover Vincent's face. Cliff imagined the sparse, gloomy room where his wife died.

"She begged me. She had tears in her eyes. She said she wanted Terri Miller to take her from deathbed to grave to eternity," Vincent said. "Those were her words."

"She didn't want to be my wife?" Cliff said, hurt carving through his heart.

"It's not that. She thought she lost the privilege. I tried to tell her differently.

She just wanted to be nearby and not intrude."

Cliff thought about that. Nearby, without intruding. What were his earlier thoughts on intrusion? Beebe and Vincent in his house. Their laughter was a precursor to this revelation. All the while, Abigail lay buried within a two-minute's walk from the kitchen door. What if years and years passed? What if Vincent successfully kept his promise? For months now, Cliff tended to his wife's grave like all the rest. He didn't know. A sickening, surreal feeling grew inside him, one that darkened around the edges the longer he bore down on it.

"How could you just leave it at that?" Cliff asked.

"After I promised, she slipped into a coma. I kind of thought I'd have time to turn her around. But that's how it was left." Vincent pushed his glasses up with his middle finger. "I got to know her some. I could picture her with you two. A family. I knew how that ended from high school. I knew that side of the story." Vincent and Beebe dated their senior year. Abigail abandoned her family just before Beebe's sixteenth birthday. "After hearing her story, it weighed on me for weeks." Vincent's confession faltered there.

Cliff looked at his daughter. "And you knew? How could it go on this long?"

"Vincent came to me in April. But, Daddy, I was coping with depression, trying to get my life back on stable ground. It was hard. I'd left the church by then."

"Just like Abigail left me."

"What does that mean? Don't make it sound like I did the same thing Mother did."

"Didn't you? You gave up your church family. Abigail gave up her family. Weren't promises made, vows taken for both of you?"

"Daddy, do not, do not treat me this way," she said, her face flushed. "She left us! After that, whenever you looked at me, all you could see was her. I look like her, yes, but I'm not her. It wasn't until recently, with all this churning again, that I realized how, subconsciously, I must have chosen the church to break the connection *you* always made between us. I wore a clerical collar for years, so in your eyes, I would stop resembling her. You'd probably argue the point, that it wasn't much, but it was something, and I think it's true. Her absence has controlled our lives since the day she left."

"So you left, too."

She banged her fingertips against her chest. "It was better for *me* to get away. I couldn't stay."

"But you're back now, just like her." Cliff stated his comparison emphatically, then watched reality whoosh by Beebe.

Her chin lifted. "You're right. I'm back because she's back."

Between mother and daughter, a pattern existed. They came and went from Cliff's life in unison.

He turned his unflagging persistence Vincent's direction. "Why didn't you call me about Abigail?"

"It was all over so quickly. I think she used all she had left just to get here."

"And in that depleted condition, she kept you from calling."

Vincent's Adam's apple bobbed. "She didn't want that. I respected her wishes."

Neither did Abigail call her husband the day she drove off in the new Caprice he scrimped to buy. Abigail's orthopedist and neurologist released her, and she returned to her nursing job at Lakeview General. There, she had access to medication that fed her addiction. Seasons passed. She slipped up one day and didn't cover her tracks. She got wind of a hospital investigation and panicked. She raced home to fill a suitcase. Beebe came home from school that day and found the bedroom Cliff shared with Abigail a wreck. The Caprice wasn't parked in the driveway. Hospital and law enforcement authorities pieced together Abigail's downhill slide out of town to Cliff the evening of her departure. Cliff's grief turned him bitter, then numb. He never recovered. The best he could do was weather.

"The last call I got about Abigail was when she sold the Caprice for drug money. I put the title in her name. They always say, put the vehicle in the wife's name because the husband goes first. It's easier when the time comes. Abigail flipped that scenario to her advantage." He felt his lips turn up with a cruel grin. "You had to call the authorities when she died, Vincent. What did you tell them?"

"I told them just what happened. She showed up at the door. She gave her name as Terri Miller. She said she had AIDS. I didn't have to do anything else. The county coroner confirmed the cause of death and automatically contacted you for a spot in the cemetery." His tone softened. "You took it from there."

Cliff gritted his teeth. His right fist shook violently. The day the call came ripped back through his memory. An indigent burial. The cemetery had such a burial every three or four years. He felt bad for the poor indigent, so he asked Hal Garrett to add a marker. It was small, but something. He didn't like burying all the indigents together. There was always a straggler grave left here or there, and he liked to fill the sections in. It gave the indigent a family of sorts. Abigail's grave closed the gap between the Paulsons and Thorndykes. Funny, he thought, Abigail never liked Patsy Thorndyke.

Suddenly, another thought bombarded Cliff.

The quilt.

Vincent's disloyalty continued with the packing and shipping of Abigail's clothes. "The other night." Cliff sneered at the other man. "You said nothing. You came in here like a thief."

"No, Cliff. I want that quilt to help you both. It was just the timing of the thing. The clothes had to be shipped, but I knew Beebe wanted me to wait before we talked about Abigail."

Cliff waved Vincent's excuses away. "The point is, Beebe gets a quilt from her friends. I get scammed from mine."

"Daddy. No."

Cliff recognized his daughter's best reasoning voice, but he shot his gaze through the dining room to the window and cemetery beyond. "It can't end this way. This isn't an ending I will permit. Not this time." He pushed himself out of the chair.

Beebe and Vincent got to their feet.

"Daddy?"

"Where's he going?" Vincent asked.

"To see Mother."

Their voices drifted away. Cliff entered another time. He stepped out the back door and hurried down the porch steps. He glared at the glider under the sycamore as he passed.

By the time he reached the bend in the asphalt road that wound south through the cemetery, a sheen of perspiration covered his face and neck. A warm August wind skirted the blue spruce that marked the section he sought. The wind met the perspiration and chilled him, making him feel like, on top of everything else, he fought the flu.

Ignoring the shiver and lightheadedness, he marched between two rows and proceeded six plots down. He watched his scuffed shoes cross the grass. Soon his steps slowed. The sod covering the new grave still resembled a checkerboard or, God help him, a quilt. Lifeless blades of grass succumbed to summer's heat and dryness. They outlined the squares in a brown crosshatched pattern.

Cliff came around to face the grave and the small headstone that misidentified its occupant. In the distance, the caretaker's house watched.

At that moment, he wanted so desperately to hold something in his arms, draw something of substance to his heaving chest. His arms and heart ached with the need that something should exist between them. He collapsed to his knees when emptiness would support him no longer. Finally, he hugged himself and wept. Two columns of hot tears streamed his cheeks. He swiped at them and spoke to the stone marker with a seriousness that begot the ages.

"I am so angry with you. I can't get my head, my feelings around this, Abigail. Why come back, just to do this?"

Silence rang in his ears. With it, he realized he didn't know Abigail Walker any better than he knew Terri Miller. He couldn't imagine what Abigail would say in response. Her lack of argument, even in his mind, caused his fury to retreat. He sank to the ground at the foot of his wife's grave. He sat with his back bowed over bent knees, his fingers laced at his ankles, the tremor still visible. A slow, passing cloud dimmed the scene.

Staring back at the grave, he pictured his wife's gray eyes, her china-doll face surrounded by loose sienna curls.

Resentment for her ability to somehow rule his thoughts caused Cliff's red-hot anger to bear down anew. "I have not had one pain-free moment since you left. It's been thirty years. My life stopped! How could you come this far and—" He choked. "Not ask for me? So close. Did you think I hated you? Did you think I ever could?"

So many questions that simply pulsed and died.

He stumbled to his feet. "All right. Fine. I fully shoulder the blame. I saw the signs," he said, crossing back to her addiction, "but wouldn't let them register with enough force to intercede. How could you not come to me?"

His silent partner remained so.

"I thought I lost you after the car accident. I thought God was with us when you weren't paralyzed. But He was just setting us up for another horror."

He growled a shout toward the heavens. His frustration rained down on the headstone carved with a stranger's name.

"After you left, your life was my life, too. The awful need, Abigail. I craved you! How can I describe it? How can I make you understand?" He ran desperate fingers through his hair. "I felt helpless. I worked at the hardware store, and I couldn't fix this. No tool existed." He laughed bitterly. "How's that for irony? Funny, huh?"

Pulling a dingy handkerchief from his back pocket, he ran it across his nose. He balled it back into his pocket while his chin quivered viciously. "You don't know how watching faces has consumed me all this time. How I searched every crowd for you." His throat nearly closed with the swell of heartache. "Thank God I knew Beebe was coming because I would have taken her for you. God forgive me. I would rather she *be* you. God forgive me," he sobbed. The railing truth pulled his shoulders down with its weight.

The sun warmed his back, superimposing his shadow along the narrow path separating two rows of graves. Long-ago memories stretched into view.

He spun to face Abigail and the house. "We sat there in that glider every night, weather permitting." One finger jabbed the air. "We talked about our lives. We talked about everything." His hand flew up. "Wait a minute. Back up. I guess it's really supposed to be one life for a husband and wife. Two people in love, one life." His fingers reiterated the numbers in play. "God, I loved you. Why didn't I help you? Why didn't you reach out? Those moments are indelibly etched on my mind." His sigh skidded across a choppy breath. "I sat in that glider the night you left, my heart bleeding. I watched the sun go down and prayed you'd come home. I flat out refused to believe this day would come. Your loss shattered me. Not knowing. That's what dug in and twisted in the wound. I told myself a year later, it would have been easier if you died. Three, four years later, I believed you must be dead." His hands flapped to his sides.

Cliff needed time and space. He followed the road back to the house. The chill dogged him, as did doubt, anger, and numbness—characters he knew well from three decades past.

Weakness, too. Weakness crept up as the sun crept down. Feeling bruised, he lowered himself gently to the glider. The empty seat beside him seemed to mock the ancient ritual.

He heard the screen door squeak behind him, then quietly close. Seconds later, Beebe eased onto the seat, just like her mother.

Cliff reduced the tally for this awful day to one lingering thought. He spoke it to his daughter. "Every night for too long, she told me lies at sunset."

The Day After

The bedside alarm drilled into Cliff's sleep. Eyes closed, he batted at the clock, silencing it. He dragged his pajama-clad legs out from under the sheet, dropped them to the floor, and waited for the cobwebs to beat themselves down. That was aided by the aroma of coffee. He sniffed, and in that instant, time receded. Yesterday hadn't happened. Abigail was downstairs, getting breakfast. He turned his head toward the door, slightly ajar after she wandered through barefoot. Then the memories subsided. They clouded and darkened. Reality took shape.

His bedroom door shouldn't be open. He latched it last night when he came in to sleep alone.

He heard the barest sound behind him. He twisted around. His heart leaped. "Beebe! Jesus Christ! You stopped coming in here when you were ten."

She sat on one hip in the chair beside the other nightstand. She wore a lightweight cotton gown and matching robe and held a coffee mug in both hands. Her fingernail tapped the ceramic. Her face was drawn, her eyes puffy.

"Funny how old habits creep up. Of course, you slept well. I didn't sleep at all," she said casually, then sipped the brew. "I thought we'd talk a minute."

He whisked his eyes away to the bedside rug, a rectangular weave that corralled his slippers. "I need to get moving. I don't want to be late."

Unruffled, she said, "I knew you'd want to work so I reset the alarm. We have half an hour."

"Reset?" Only one foot shod, he shot a look at the clock. It read six-thirty, not seven.

"As you can imagine, I spent my sleepless night deep in thought," Beebe said, speaking to his back. "I thought and thought. I weighed options, and I decided I want you to know what my life was like after Mother left. Not that I'm minimizing your feelings, either then or now. With Mother's actual death, and me back in this house, it's like she's left us all over again. Here we are, Daddy, you and me, doomed to repeat history. I can't go through that again. So I've come up with the two worse moments that defined my life back then. I want you to hear about them. They involve Grandma. She's gone, too. So there's nothing you can do about them, or her involvement, at this juncture."

The grandma Beebe referenced was Cliff's mother, Emma Walker. She lived her whole life in the farmhouse on the other side of town, where she raised her son.

"First, I want to explore the phrase you used last night: 'Every night for too long,'" Beebe said.

Cliff heard the coffee mug tick against the glass lamp on the bed stand and knew Beebe put it down. For all intents and purposes, Cliff allowed his mulishness to drape his shoulders. He wore it like armor. It instantly became protection against his own words, drudged up by Beebe and reloaded as ammunition against him.

"You connected those words to you and Mother, but it covers you and me, too," his daughter claimed. "After Mother left, I felt cut off from you. All I had was Grandma. She missed Mother, too. I could talk to Grandma. She kept me going. She told me to keep trying with you, that women need to be strong, that it was good I learned that early. But, Daddy, nothing worked for us. Every night for too long, I went to bed in misery."

A trace of that misery grazed Cliff. He heard it in her voice even now, but her next revelation rocked him.

"After a while, I asked if I could live with her. I begged. I pleaded. I gave her excuse after excuse, example after example. She gave me encouragement, but she would not let me give up. Then, like always," she said, with attitude, "the guilt rolled over me, and I said, 'Grandma, please, please, don't tell him.' Mother had secrets, yes, but Daddy, Grandma and I kept secrets, too."

The chill from his slipperless foot ran through him.

"I remember the words I blurted out to Grandma the afternoon she came over with the doctor's diagnosis." Beebe moved the story ahead in time.

About eighteen months after Abigail's departure, Emma's mitral valve deterioration progressed to serious. The doctor gave her six months before her health would fail.

"Grandma didn't sugar-coat anything, and she didn't sugar-coat that. She'd be gone before I left for college. Without a second thought, I said, 'Grandma, I want to go with you!'" Then Beebe strung a matter-of-fact quality to her commentary. "So there it was, splat on the cushion between us, words I couldn't take back. As always, guilt flooded to the surface, and I said, 'Oh Grandma, don't tell him I said that!'"

Her words stung. They were meant to. His retaliation carried a little spitfire. "You can't really mean you wanted to follow your grandmother into death, just to be away from me?"

"I couldn't stand the thought of being on this earth without her, with no confidant in sight, for the rest of my life."

Cliff heard the chair's one squeaky spring release. Beebe rose with the rest of her life dramatically left in the balance. The cup scraped across the nightstand's wood surface. The floor took her weight as she crossed toward the door. From the corner of his eye, Cliff saw that her hand rested on the knob.

On the tail of this eye-opening experience on the first morning of their reunion, Cliff sputtered a question. "Did you hate me?"

"I probably did then. A little. I don't, now." She delivered her words without a shred of emotion. "I understood what Grandma understood: She might have let me live with her, but she knew she was sick. If she died after I moved in, what would that do when I realized I had to move back to you? Until that day on the couch, she kept the secret of her health to herself."

"Do you think your mother told her about her addiction? Did she keep that secret?"

"No. Grandma didn't know about Mother's drug dependency."

"I wonder. Those two were close. It didn't start out that way. Early in our marriage, Abigail seemed standoffish with my mother. Emma Walker could intimidate. Quickly though, the relationship changed. Something smoothed it out. I'll never know what it was," he said with a skim of defeatist's pity in his voice.

Learning certain things now that he knew he would never learn back then seemed unbelievably important. Beebe showed her disinterest to his long unanswered question by closing the door after she stepped out on her bare feet.

Cliff entered the kitchen twenty minutes later. He wore the McKinley Hardware uniform of striped shirt, blue trousers, and work boots. Beebe was dressed in a long cotton shirt, white pants, and pink clogs. She prepared breakfast. Now, *her* back to him.

"There'll be bacon and toast in a minute, Daddy." She sidestepped away from the skillet on the stove to plunge two slices of bread into the toaster.

He passed behind her neutral attitude with the cup he snagged from the small table laid with breakfast dishes. He was finally within reach of coffee. He carried the cup back to the table. The spatula rocked the spoon rest. While Beebe stood at the counter, buttering toast on a paper towel, he picked up the plate sitting at his place and went back for bacon. She dropped the toast on his plate beside the bacon, then headed outside to retrieve the newspaper from the mailbox by the road. With her absence, she didn't witness the tremor, still prevalent when he poured milk over Cheerios.

Beebe lay the folded-over paper at his elbow. Along the way, she must have dug down to go another round with her father.

"You won't argue with me about moving the grave? Mother should be reburied in our plot next to Grandma."

He frowned. "Why would you put it that way? Of course, I won't argue with you. But I want things done right." This time, he grabbed his ground early. "The day the grave is moved, I want Abigail's obituary to run in the newspaper." He tapped the morning edition on the tabletop. "I want the rest of the town to know there is an ending to this story. That's the process. That finishes things. We won't run from this. There's respect in holding our heads up through controversy. The obit closes the book." He focused in on his daughter. "Are you going to argue with me?"

"Well. No. It surprises me. I would have thought the…" she paused for a word search.

"Notoriety?"

"No. The undue attention isn't necessary. This is a private matter. A family matter."

"That's not how things are done in Larkspur. Better get it out in the open. There's value in that." The two Walkers eyed each other. He referred to their discussion upstairs, how past secrets cost them so much. He sensed she understood his meaning.

"You're right, really." She threw her shoulders back. "People will know then that we're grieving and give us some space, make allowances."

"Allowances for what?" His question came out snappishly, and she snapped right back.

"You're going to need time, Daddy. Don't pretend Mother's death will roll off your back, and you'll just swim quietly away."

"We'll see what happens." Roughly, Cliff got his cereal bowl in hand. When he pushed his chair back, the legs scraping viciously across the aged flooring, synonymous with drawing old battle lines in the dirt. He nearly spilled several swallows of milk he'd have drunk from the bowl if Beebe hadn't been there, pushing the issue of his expected grief. He set the dish on the porcelain with more care. The sink faced the window and graveyard. His gaze darted from the sycamore, to the glider, to the blue spruce, and that grave.

He would cling to the safety of routine. He could do nothing for the situation or himself by sitting at home, grieving. Just as his fingers touched his key ring that lay on the counter by the door, Beebe angled in again.

"Let me take care of writing the obituary. You can read it when I'm done."

This was her peace offering. He nodded, pressed the keys into his palm, and went out into the August morning.

* * *

Cliff steered McKinley's delivery van into its parking place behind the store. He opened the door and dropped his feet to the pavement. His knees were old, but they took his weight without complaint.

All the way back from Newton, a hamlet just off County Road 810, he kept his speed below the limit. The entire round trip was spent reliving the hateful part of his life. Deep down, he just wanted the hurt to go away. As for the memories: If he could remember without the tightening clamp crushing his heart in the process, he thought he might just survive the recent blow that did buckle his knees in the cemetery.

He climbed the dock stairs, let himself in the walk-through door to lay the clipboard, paperwork, and van keys on the back workbench, then he retraced his steps. He continued down the alley, his head tipped to the graveled passage, hands deep in his pockets.

Two minutes ago, he waited for a green light at the intersection south of the store and his wandering spirit focused on Rosemary's at the end of the block. In his heart, there was no greater comfort than putting his work boots under Rosemary's counter and his hands around a warm mug of her coffee. That luxury didn't exist today.

Rosemary beamed at him when he dragged through the door. "I kind of thought I'd have seen you for lunch," she said.

"I made a delivery over in Newton and ate there." He slid onto a stool and put his feet on the rail just above the floor. His eyes met her gray ones. Her intuitiveness took over.

"What's wrong? Is Beebe coming in today as planned?" she asked.

"She got here yesterday. Ahead of schedule."

"She did." A beat passed. "Okay." She studied him a moment longer. "Then, let's go back to my first question: What's wrong?"

Cliff fiddled with the salt shaker. "Is Larry here? Can you get away for a half hour?"

She didn't hesitate. "Doable," she said.

Rosemary went back to the kitchen to let her employee know she'd be off the premises. She returned minus her apron, and they headed out the restaurant's swinging front door.

He hooked a thumb down the side street. "Why don't we walk over to the park?"

"Sure, that's fine." He matched his pace to hers. The sidewalk was narrow. She brushed against him. "Tell me what's going on," she said quietly.

He held his story back. A dog barked. Three boys on bikes rode by. The half block behind the restaurant was lined with old doubles. At the curb, gnarly trees shaded the street. They crossed Battlefield. Cliff began to talk a block later, just as they entered Engle Park.

"It seems Beebe's reason for coming back was twofold," he said, leading her around a hedgerow and onto an asphalt walkway.

"She took the job with Vincent at Crossroads. What else?"

"Vincent and Beebe sat me down after dinner last night to tell me that Abigail died."

Beside him, Rosemary's step faltered with his unfettered revelation. She stumbled over her words, too. "Died? When? How did they know?"

"She came back, Rosemary. Abigail came back to Larkspur in March." Retelling the sad tale issued the same kick in the gut he felt last night when he sat across from Beebe and Vincent. He pressed his right arm against his side, but his fist trembled still.

Rosemary grabbed his elbow, stopping him. He would have trudged on and on. He felt her worried eyes hanging on him. She pulled him toward one of the park's benches. "Sit down," she said, "before you collapse."

Rosemary was rarely speechless, but the circumstances of Abigail's return achieved that state. Even her expressive hands lay still in her lap.

"Vincent's conscience got the best of him. He didn't know how to tell me, so he went to Beebe for help. She put him off. Couldn't deal with her mother, or me, the both of us. She was at odds with her own life."

"Till recently," Rosemary managed.

"Yeah. They hooked up again when Vincent got funding for an assistant. Five months passed." He bent the fingers of his right hand around the front edge of the bench's seat. They shook shamelessly. He let them.

"You have every right to be angry and hurt over this. All of it. It's difficult," she said.

"That's the thing. I can push myself into anger. I should rightfully feel damn offended. It was an insult. But part of me could just let this float away and never think of it again."

"Avoidance instead of acceptance. That doesn't sound right, Cliff."

Stepping over that assessment, he said, "The grave will be moved, of course, to the family plot, and a new headstone erected. Beebe wants that."

"You do, too?"

"Yeah. I think that's all I need to get through this. And I want the town to know. Beebe's taking today to write an obituary."

"An obituary? Why? That's not necessary. Why go public?"

"That's the way things are done. There is no reason to hide from this. Someone will get a breath of something. Someone will walk by and see the grave. No, better to get out in front of this. I just wanted you to know." He swallowed. Abigail's death would fit into Rosemary's plan. "Since our last conversation, and your thoughts of—"

"A relationship."

"Well," he started, his mouth drying a bit. "Things are going to be messy for a while."

When he thought she would repeat "avoidance, instead of acceptance," she made a show of looking around for gawkers.

"Speaking of going public," she said.

He had to admit, from the moment she pulled his trembling hand into her lap and held it tight, he felt a binding of the strength Rosemary possessed.

* * *

After he returned from the Walkers, Vincent and sleep remained strangers for most of the night. They were separated by chatter inside his head. Randomly, Terri, Cliff, Beebe, even Carolyn, and occasionally Yates, popped up. Their nattering felt like border attacks, vying for his defenses, but he lay on the hot sheets without any. There was no remedy, no fix for the situation. Weary and overburdened, he imagined wild scenarios requiring super-human Vincent

Bostick feats. Carolyn always said he took on too much when others were involved and gave up a piece of himself every time. When would there be nothing left? After her death, he threw himself into his work at the center. Wasn't he just begging to be eaten alive?

He awoke in fetal position, clinging to the top sheet like it was a shield deflecting rocks and spears. He looked at the bedside clock. Of course, he overslept. He knew his entire day would now become a race to stay ahead of a road roller.

Shaved and dressed, Vincent was coming down the hall when he saw Yates staring out the picture window to Battlefield. Listlessly, Yates shuffled to the front door. Beside him, even the dog moped.

Vincent looked around the community room. He was disappointed to see that while he overslept, Yates had not taken up any of his duties. That was not like him. When Vincent looked back, he saw the tail end of man and dog going out the door. This was odder still. Visits to the park were better served via the facility's alleyway door, making the trip a half a block closer.

As Vincent crossed the room to peek out the window, he saw Yates passing, again in the opposite direction a trip to the park would take. Stepping to the door, Vincent opened it and peered out. Yates's motivation took him as far as the sidewalk bench stationed at the far end of the building. He stared down at the bench for the longest time. When he reached the decision to sit, he eased himself down. Vincent knew why. He did not want to jostle the memory of Terri sitting there. Yates watched the people passing by. The town percolated, not knowing a young man grieved.

Yates mentioned his drive to Larkspur Cemetery yesterday. His comments were sparse, and Vincent hadn't pressed.

He stepped out.

The activity caught Yates's eye. "You're up."

"Yeah. I think we can both say yesterday was a little out of the norm."

"A little," Yates confirmed.

"Who are we fooling? It was a lot out of the norm." Vincent waited until Yates patted the other seat, then he knew Yates cleared his mind of Terri's presence beside him.

Yates's movement attracted Barleycorn's sad eyes. Vincent reached down to scratch the dog's noggin. Perhaps, if they were inside, he would have shown similar comfort to Yates. But outside, he diverted it toward his pet instead, hoping its benefits would soak into the young man by osmosis.

Sitting back, Vincent said, "You miss her, don't you?"

"I think about her every day. Mom, too," Yates said, uninhibited. "Can I tell you something, just between us?"

"Sure."

"Beebe's going to make it harder because she looks so much like her. Her actions. Everything."

"I think you'll get past that in a hurry. You'll come to know Beebe for the kind of person she is, and you'll separate the two just enough to make things easier on you."

"I suppose. But right now." He shook his head. "Geez."

"Listen to me, Yates. Someday down the road and not too far in the distance, you'll find yourself making that same comparison, and it will be a happy one. A beat will pass. Then it will occur to you the comparison didn't bring you down. That beat means progress has been made in conquering your grief." Vincent threw up his hands. "Let's just say it, you're grieving. My wife's been gone seven years. These circumstances have stirred up my memories, too. It happens. But the human spirit is an amazing thing. And the women who we've lost would not want us to dwell on our sorrow."

"I'm not dwelling, but I can't seem to work up any energy. It was the same when Mom died."

Three men crossing the street distracted Vincent. They were the pool-playing group, and they gave him an idea.

"Oh, and Beebe called a little while ago," Yates was saying. "I asked her, but she's not coming in today."

The mention of Beebe's name tagged Vincent's attention. "She got home a day early, so I wasn't expecting her to begin work till tomorrow." But that didn't mean grief wasn't making the rounds out in the caretaker's house, he thought.

"She wants you to call."

He would, but first, he tracked the men coming their way. They were all in a good mood, and he was confident it would rub off on Yates. Already, Barleycorn's tail thumped the sidewalk. Calling them over, he said, "Morning, guys. Have I got a deal for you."

Everyone in the circle around him perked. Vincent suggested that today's game be painting the community room, the job that got pushed to the wayside yesterday by the needs of a senior. Vincent left Rev. Razzell's name out of it. All the men rolled up their sleeves without complaint. Five men could knock the painting out in no time. Before he picked up a brush, he went to his office and put in a call to Beebe. It was just after ten.

When she answered, "Walker residence," he said, "Sorry it took so long to get back to you. How's it going?"

"I'm just walking around inside the house, absorbing the place again, wondering about Daddy, and when to get Yates involved. He said he would speak with Daddy."

"I'll help anyway I can. You know that," he said, being true to his super-human self, despite the wakeful night and other wakeful nights that might lie ahead.

"Vincent, your responsibility ended last night. You told Daddy all you knew."

"I don't think Cliff is ready to absolve me that easily."

"Well, no, not in Daddy's mind. He still blames us. I don't want him to take that attitude with Yates. He's too fragile right now."

Vincent felt certain she referred to Yates, but Cliff was fragile, too. Certainly, she understood that. He listened while Beebe told him about her conversation with Cliff at breakfast, about moving the grave and the obituary she wanted to complete that day. "An obituary. I wasn't ready for that. That will set the town rocking."

"Not with everyone. A lot of people don't know the story."

"But a lot of people do," Vincent said. "They'll tell the others. I'm sorry to say this, but I hope you're ready for flashbacks to high school. Sounds like you're rushing through everything with your mom."

"There's a process Daddy is used to. Structure. He wants to stick to it. Like—"

"Like you all had a normal life, and your mother's ended on a normal note."

"It's all very new to him right now. He's only talking about routines and rituals. More must be going on inside his head. Someday, it's going to slam him hard."

"Would you rather have the grave and the obit out of the way when it does?"

"I would, now that you put it that way."

"Then get past these two things and wait for the fallout."

"I tried to bring up Yates this morning. Before I even got the news out that there's another person involved, he shut me down. He said I should hold everything until tonight."

"So, he's over at the store?"

Beebe's answer told him his assumption was on target. "Wouldn't be distracted from his day."

Vincent's eyes shot to the open office door. He heard a whoop from the men in the main room. Barleycorn barked his typical series of three. "Maybe it's for the best. Despite everything, Yates is having a pretty good time right now."

"I hear something going on, and Barleycorn's in the middle of it."

"We didn't get the painting done yesterday after the rush over to Mosie's, so the pool-playing crowd agreed to pitch in today. They gave us yesterday for the center to be closed, but I knew they wouldn't forgive us for today. They rallied around the project, and Yates is getting the treatment."

"Which means?"

"Good-natured teasing. They're an outstanding bunch."

"You know Yates came out to the cemetery yesterday?"

"After the fact. How'd it go?" He was eager to hear another point of view.

"We had a private moment…"

Beebe's end of the conversation faltered there, although the hesitation combined with the choice words said so much. He could have picked up the ball conversationally and told her about the board meeting the Monday after next, but there was time for that. The thought of a bunch of new faces bearing down might not be what she needed. As she said, she had an obituary to write. Vincent walked that road with Carolyn. It was one fraught with the perils of too many memories, not the right words, and tears staining the paper.

Forgiveness

Beebe talked to Vincent on the kitchen phone. It was the black, wall-mounted model of ancient days. Its rotary dial would stump today's kids. She hadn't hung up right away after Vincent disconnected. The curly cord that kissed the floor when the receiver was cradled on its hook also stretched to the farthest cabinet and countertop.

While Vincent spoke, Beebe leaned against that far counter. She looked back along the cord strung like a taut clothesline through the kitchen. Memories dangled from the wire, alive and bouncing with her every movement.

Her mother talking on this phone was a common sight from Beebe's childhood. Just about the time Beebe turned fourteen, the year of Abigail's car accident, she grew tall enough to walk into the outstretched cord and play-act a choking scene. Her mother teased her in return, rushing to wrap a section of cord around her neck and follow that up with a strong hug. Most times, the caller didn't mind the interruption. Most times, the caller was Grandma Emma Walker, Abigail's mother-in-law. Even as a young teenager, Beebe knew about mother-in-law jokes. Somehow it happened that Emma and Abigail became dear friends. No joke. After Abigail ran away, the phone cord hung lifeless day after day. A week later, her grandmother took matters into her own hands and began calling regularly, after school. The seed of tradition took root and grew. The relationship blossomed. Beebe prayed nothing would change that highlight to her day.

She returned the receiver to its hook, then looked over at the kitchen table. The family Bible and several picture albums lay there. None opened. She felt she needed their contents in order to complete the task of writing the obituary.

She searched out the books earlier when she dared become reacquainted with the house. After climbing the carpeted stairs, she entered her parents' room at the end of the hall. She doubted her father, driven by routine, moved the Bible and albums from the bottom drawer in her mother's dresser. Abigail kept them under her best tablecloth for gatherings around the dining room table and a couple of pairs of summer pajamas.

Beebe knelt and pulled open the drawer. The Bible and albums stared her in the face. The cushion of family dinners and warm fragrant nights with the windows up vanished. Quickly, she slid two more drawers out. Just a hodgepodge of objects remained. Why?

Oh, the lap quilt.

The lap quilt Callie MacCallum promised to sew with the articles of clothing Vincent talked Cliff into parting with. Beebe tried to imagine the two men here in this room with cardboard containers on the bed, boxing up her mother's clothes. How awkward and difficult that must have been. She hoped the awkwardness shared by the men lessened the difficulty. They did that for her so she might have a keepsake. She viewed firsthand Callie's many quilted keepsakes, each sewed together with clothes belonging to the dear departed. They were all treasures.

Numbly, she hoisted the books up in her arms and carried them to the kitchen. The image of the nearly empty drawers stayed with her when she sat down at the table with a tablet of paper and a pen. The scanty belongings left behind in those drawers visibly represented the holes in her life after her mother's departure. The missing clothes, shipped away for a time—for alterations, let's say—would come back, just as her mother had left home, then rather unceremoniously returned. The altered clothes would reenter Beebe's life in the form of a quilt with all her memories pleasingly arranged when, in reality, they were not. Not now, anyway.

Suddenly, she didn't feel a standard obit could be pried out of her. These were not standard times. Despite her father's pretense, these were not days of routine. If her mother's obituary printed in the local paper would shock the townspeople, then Beebe must write a distinctive one. The composition poured out with ease. Like a child who completed a book report, she went to read it to her mother.

She stood at the foot of the grave, her gray eyes latched to the rough stone marker. "Mother, you're going to hear this before Daddy. We both miss you. We have for a long, long time. I put my best words into this."

She held the freshly recopied tablet page in both hands, cleared her throat, and spoke aloud.

Abigail Marie Walker died in the early morning on a day in March that woke to greet a dawn saddened by the knowledge that one less soul existed in its midst.

Abigail's trek through life was no different than most. She chose a loving husband in Clifford Walker, and she blessed her daughter, Beebe Walker, with her open heart, her values, and ever-emerging examples of her influence on the lives of others. Those blessings live on, although Abigail's physical presence is lost. They are her legacy.

Abigail rose from despair and claimed her place on this earth. She lived with fear, but was not overpowered by it. She fought addiction and won. She gave her life in defense of another. The giving of that life, in the world she knew, the sacrifice that came later, touches her family and friends.

Her life inspired many who remain unknown. But those who step forward and speak of their unique friendship with Abigail tell a story of kindness and redemption, of generosity and humility, of selflessness and love.

When her memory passes through our hearts, multiply that number tenfold and know there are those unaware of her passing and yet they live each day stronger for the moment her life crossed theirs.

With the rising sun, Abigail Marie Walker shall be interred in Larkspur Cemetery with private services.

When the tribute was read, tears rolled off Beebe's cheeks. "Mother," she cried. "Mommy. I am so glad you came back."

Letting herself become lost in grief for a moment, she released a pair of heart-wrenching sobs. She slogged back to the house, then couldn't stand to be there. Nothing felt right. Not her silent mother. Not the confusing mix of her mother's absolute closeness, while at the same time, the estrangement swelled to gigantic proportion.

Beebe drove to town for groceries. Upon her return, she sifted her lingering emotions into the ingredients for the applesauce cake she baked.

She heard her father's truck pull into the drive at half past six. After her return from shopping, she made a point of opening the front door and leaving it wide. The welcoming gesture would greet Cliff at the end of his workday, and it would direct his path through the house. If he sought her out upon his arrival, he would pass by the dining room table on his way to the kitchen. Abigail's obituary lay within easy sight on the table.

At the stove, Beebe felt the vibrations of Cliff's passage along the old homestead's floorboards cease. She heard the crackle of paper. Wooden spoon in hand, held aloft over a pot of homemade vegetable soup, she awaited his approval or his grumbling disgust because she had the day and wasted it by not following protocol.

"Have you forgiven her?" His voice startled her. He was suddenly inside the kitchen. He used a level tone for his simple inquiry.

The spoon she held jerked on its way to the spoon rest. That he blindsided her with that particular question caused her head to cloud with something akin to the steam rising from the simmering soup.

She must have space, she thought, not the closed walls of the kitchen where she spent the afternoon, mixing dry ingredients with wet for the cake, chopping vegetables, and keeping company with memories of her mother completing the same tasks. Mechanically, she turned the flame down on the soup, all the while mulling over an offshoot of her father's question. Was it ever about forgiveness?

"By reading this," he said, "it sounds like you have."

She turned to go outside. Her father followed on her heels. She stopped at the edge of the side porch and inhaled deeply. Finally, she faced him. "Let's sit on the glider." She forced a smile to cap this emotional day.

"No," he said firmly.

Her smile dissolved. Again, he tipped the scales.

He walked instead to the picnic table positioned a few yards away, at the corner of the house.

When they were seated, he asked again, "Have you forgiven her?"

She made a quick study of his hazel eyes and concluded he really wanted to express himself, but she didn't mind going first.

"I guess my forgiveness came gradually without even realizing it. I was so focused on myself and my failures that I could barely let the knowledge Vincent brought register. It was there, hanging out in the ether, but I didn't think about it. And Vincent kept asking me to come home, then he switched my focus to the job he lined up. In reaching that decision, I accepted Mother's part, her place in that, meaning her death." Up in the sky, patches of clouds passed behind Cliff's head of salt-and-pepper hair. "My life was such a mess. Mother did very little to add to my depression. There wasn't that much room left. She took only a small part." She produced a weak smile. "When I began to consider returning, the thought of home, and you, Vincent and the job, still took the largest part of my concentration. Mother had her share, but not a crowding share. I'm sorry I took the last five months to come to terms with everything, and now it's come down on you without warning."

Cliff listened intently. He held his right fist to his mouth, the bend of his thumb hooked on his lower lip. He dropped that hand to overlap the other at the table's edge when he spoke. "How could there be warning? No one is prepared for this. I always thought that because she'd been gone so long, with time and distance as cushions, I'd barely feel the blow. You're a cushion, Beebe. All day, knowing you'd be here when I got home, knowing I wouldn't go through this alone, got me through."

Beebe leaned into the table so her outstretched hand could pat her father's to convey how truly touched she was by his words.

"You will stay, won't you? Work with Vincent. Be here." He raised a finger to point back toward town, then to the house.

"I'm staying, Daddy. That part feels right."

"What doesn't feel right?"

"I guess *right* isn't the best word on the negative side. The negative side is that we're not going through this in a vacuum. There's human nature to consider and acceptance. People are going to be people, and those people who remember Mother and our problems are going to talk. These people on a smaller scale must come to terms with her death themselves. When they talk to each other, whether gossipy talk or concerned words for us, that's them also dealing with Mother's passing. Their grief, their knowledge of our grief—" She broke off to arch one eyebrow. As she did, she slipped into counselor mode. "Well, let's just say, people don't deal well with grief. They don't know what to do. Most people give a heartfelt attempt to express kindness and sympathy. Some seem unfeeling. We must send our focus solely inside ourselves, our hearts, our minds, our memories of Mother. Tune everyone else out. Listen with half an ear at best. Then look inside yourself and find a measure of solace. As each day passes, that measure will increase. Maybe a day or two for backsliding, but each day gets us closer to the people we'll be at the other end. We won't be the same. I'm not the same person I was when I passed the new school at the edge of town. I know I'm not. The key is, we need to talk, you and I."

"You changed since yesterday?" he said, baffled.

She had. Yates Strand and his Terri Miller stories precipitated that change, but she would not mention Yates for two reasons. The first, she thought, was a bit selfish. Her father's swinging-door disposition found a decently calm plane for thoughtfulness without anger. She wasn't about to disturb that. Secondly, it would be wrong to prejudice Cliff in any way, give him any precognitions before he met Yates, and they talked.

She waved away Cliff's question about change. "Daddy, you talk. Tell me what thoughts keep swimming around in your head. Things that don't necessarily seem on target with Mother's death or the arrangements. Don't think about it. Just spit something out."

"The empty grave." The words fled off his lips with all the force of a pistol shot. "Moving your mother will leave an empty grave. There once was a casket inside, then it's gone. And I keep thinking about disturbing the graves around hers. It feels insensitive. It feels like I caused it because Abigail was my wife, and she's the reason for the disruption, so by association, it's my fault. After the disinterment, what do I do when I come through that section? How do I fill in that spot?" His eyes begged for answers. "There's no way to bury the memories. I used to say that to surviving family members like it was a good thing. Not this time."

"You want to bury Mother's memories?"

"There are so many reminders. And the thought of an empty grave out there will not go away." He caught his head in his hands.

Beebe knew of his obsession with tidiness when it came to "his" cemetery.

Quickly calm, he raised his chin. "Your ole dad's loony, isn't he?"

She answered his question with a question. "Daddy, why not the glider?" The empty-grave scenario halfway made sense to her, but his near hatred for the glider stumped her.

"Huh?"

"You didn't want to sit on the glider earlier."

He swallowed. "You remember how Mom and I sat there after supper. We talked about everything, or so I thought. But she didn't talk from her heart. She came back and wouldn't see me. Begged Vincent not to call. Shot back into town and brought a passel of lies for him to peddle."

Within Beebe's counselor persona, she reasoned that a hurting Cliff fixated on the glider. Instantly, the glider became Beebe's yardstick by which to measure her father's progress for his return from grief. Someday, passing the glider without a second thought for its prior significance would be the test of accomplishment. Actually sitting in it would blow his recovery off the charts.

"That bothered me, too," she found herself saying.

He looked over.

"But I'm glad she came back. I'm glad to have closure."

"But we wouldn't have had closure if Vincent kept his promise."

"I think she knew Vincent wouldn't keep her secret. Deep down, I think she knew."

"What was the point?"

"She couldn't face you, Daddy. What if you wouldn't come? All these years, she abandoned us. She couldn't hope to think you'd come running."

"Vincent told her I would."

"The fact that Vincent knew enough about you to make that claim probably told her he wouldn't keep the secret. She couldn't bear it, knowing she asked, and you refused her offer."

"You have a lot of empathy for her."

"I have experience with counseling. In that unimpassioned place counselors go, I see the situation from Mother's side. I could imagine if I asked you to come to my deathbed, and because of the distance built between us, you wouldn't come."

"Don't think that. I most certainly would."

"But I know what that would do, the pain I'd feel if you didn't. She couldn't know what you'd do, and she couldn't take the chance."

"Not very brave."

Beebe wanted to argue with that all-too-brief summary. Perhaps it was better though if Cliff altered his own conclusion. She hoped he would after he spent some time with Yates. Beebe firmly believed a person shouldn't be judged by the worst thing she did in her life.

With Yates back in her thoughts, she wondered how she could get around this moment, this conversation, without leaving Cliff on the edge again, knowing someone was out there, someone close who knew his wife, but who wasn't quite ready to meet him.

Neither had she been ready to invite Yates to supper as she thought she would. Writing the obituary, then spending time in the cemetery drained her.

The question of her mother's bravery needed to be addressed soon, but on another day. Yates would answer that question best. Cliff would hear that answer better from the young man her mother influenced for ten years.

Another day, it would have to be.

Duties

Beebe spent another basically sleepless night in the caretaker's house. Only the two hours before dawn came with dream-filled sleep. She dreamed about slithering telephone cords and angry phone calls. The revolving dream reached the place where her mind stepped in and forced her eyes open. She rolled onto her back, dragging the sheet with her, and stared at the ceiling. There in the dark, the dream jarred loose a memory. The memory dated back to a teenage Beebe and included a quick-to-anger, barely coping Cliff.

She climbed out of bed, wandered the house, weighed her options, only to lay back down. She thought about the morning before in her father's room, then snuck down the hall, opened the door with care, and reset Cliff's alarm clock. She measured her time, brewed coffee, pinched several bites of applesauce cake, and then returned upstairs with two mugs and two minutes to spare.

When the time came, her father groggily answered the alarm, threw off the sheet, saw her standing at the window, gave a cockeyed look at the bedside timepiece, and shook his head. An errant clump of hair bobbed.

"Geez, Beebe," he complained.

"I brought coffee," Beebe offered happily. She transferred one cup from the window ledge to the nightstand.

"What is it with you?" He rubbed his beard-stubbled face.

"Actually, what it was, was a bad dream. Those are rare for me."

"Is this where I say, tell me all about it?"

She smiled. There was, in point of fact, a pleasant quality to his tone. "I've been up for a while, Daddy. I've churned out several topics for discussion."

He heaved in a sigh, then raised the coffee cup to his lips. She carried her own coffee to the cedar chest at the foot of the bed and sat.

"But first," Beebe said, "I need to walk something back. I haven't come to terms with my grief. I know last evening I said I had, but scratch that out of your memory."

"Yeah, I pegged that as a bunch of hooey."

When her grin faded, she said, "I spent a long night deliberating, but I thought I might whittle the two hotspots I chose down to one."

"No, no. If you want to let me have it with both barrels, just do it."

This morning, they spoke with a better demeanor between them. Her father relegated himself as the alleged wrong-doer.

"Okay, get your broad shoulders ready. The hotspot that precipitated the dream actually got its legs when Vincent called yesterday morning. I automatically answered the phone 'Walker residence.' I only use that greeting here. The dream tripped a memory of the day you called after I got home from school. I said hello." She looked past her father and drifted back to another season in time. "Your voice was a mix of desperation, hope, disbelief. You spoke one word. Her name. Abigail. I felt your whole world shatter again, standing right there on the kitchen floor when your disappointment registered. It was just me on the phone. Not Mother. She hadn't come back. Hadn't come home. What hurt me was that you accused me of sounding like her on purpose. You thought I should have known it was you calling and should have tried not to sound like her. How could I? That wasn't reasonable, but you scolded me anyway. On that day, 'Walker residence' was born. Mother never used that greeting, so I did. For your sake."

"It was unfair, what I did. I'm sorry."

"You made me feel like a cheap imitation," Beebe said, remembering her sixteen-year old heavy heart.

"Don't say that. You weren't. I'm sorry. I am." His eyes reflected his shame. "Okay. Now give me my punishment. What's the next hotspot on your list?"

Beebe found compassion. In truth, she revived the compassion she found last night. "If you're looking for punishment, this will blow you out of the water."

Cliff managed a wary look.

"Do you remember the summer festival the Larkspur Men's Club held at the high school during my senior year?" She waited for his nod and received a quizzical frown, too. "It was a fundraiser to purchase school supplies for families who struggled financially. Vincent and I went. You knew we were going. You were there, too. You were the handyman. The club hired you to put the games and booths together, but I didn't know that before I arrived because you didn't tell me. You just rolled on with your life like I wasn't part of it."

"You called me on it back then."

"I was embarrassed. Vincent pointed you out, and I had no idea. But what I didn't tell you was how I felt after I heard your explanation. Well, it was sort of an explanation. I caught you right outside this door." She poked a thumb over her shoulder. "Vincent brought me home. I came upstairs. You just finished brushing your teeth. And yes, I called you on it. I asked you why you didn't tell me. You shrugged it off. You said it wasn't a big deal. I told you my feelings were hurt. Your response stuck in my heart. Your response made me think of your feelings when I hadn't before. 'They pitied me,' you said."

In profile, his jaw tightened.

"The hall was dark. Just the light from the stairs. Your voice was low and pained. Then you came straight in here and closed the door. I got it then. I knew who 'they' were. They were the club members who asked you to join. Membership would have given you a certain status in the community. Mother left, and you never joined. Then you ended up their handyman. That was a comedown."

He wiped his nose with the back of his hand.

"I stood there in the hall and stared at the closed door for a long, long time. I realized you didn't tell me ahead of time because it would force you to think about their pity because we needed the money. The Walkers were a family who struggled financially," she said, repeating the words she used earlier. "We didn't have Mother's paycheck. I felt self-centered when first I felt justified. You shared a confidence. That confidence was greater, it meant more than my hurt feelings. But how could I have known? I couldn't know you were calling on the phone, and I couldn't know your feelings until you confided them. That night, I saw a different side of you."

She got up, kissed her father on the top of his bowed head, and quietly left the room.

Cliff left for the store on time that Friday morning. Beebe sat on the living room couch, reading the *Larkspur News*. She had another hour before she was due at Crossroads for her first day.

She heard a vehicle rumble past the house on one of the nearest cemetery roads. Such a happening was only slightly odd. Most visitors used the main entrance farther south. Less than two minutes later, she heard a knock on the kitchen door. She lay the paper aside and went to answer it.

A tall reedy man stood on the other side of the screen door. He tipped his hat when she stepped down to the mudroom floor. "Remember me, Beebe? Hal Garrett."

"Hurdlin' Hal," sailed out of her mouth. "Larkspur High track star!"

"Now, now, you'll turn my head." His full grin exposed the space between his front teeth.

She pushed the door open. "Come in. Have some coffee."

"That's a fine offer." He followed her into the kitchen. "Cliff said you were moving back."

"And here I am." She pointed him to a chair.

When she passed the window on the way to retrieve coffee mugs from the dish drainer, she saw a pickup parked on the road that curved out and around the block building. "You help Daddy out now?"

"I do. Digging the graves and seeing to the markers."

She was glad her sixty-six-year old father took on an assistant at some point. She carried the two mugs of coffee to the table.

"I handle the big equipment. The backhoe loader," he explained.

She slid out the silverware drawer. Crossing the floor with spoons in her hand, she noticed his hat lay on the table now, along with two napkins he helpfully pulled from the dispenser that never left the tabletop. He declined cream. The sugar bowl was passed from one to the other.

"So, last I saw you, you were chasing Lorrie Lamont," Beebe said, her spoon clipping the side of the mug as she stirred her coffee.

"Chased her. Caught her," he said, obviously pleased with himself and his life.

"Praise be to Coach Fenimore," Beebe said of the school's track coach.

"Not so politically correct by today's standards, but he got the job done."

"What did he call the under-performers?" Beebe cocked her head up, thinking.

"Pantywaists," Hal jumped to say. "And if you really disappointed him, flaming pantywaists."

"Back then, I suppose that would make any of the boys get the lead out. But today—"

Grinning, he cut her off. "Today, it'd be a lawsuit in the making."

They laughed.

"It's nice that you and Lorrie still live here."

"Not right after we were married. Lorrie had an airline's job in Lansing she wanted to pursue. That meant travel for her, so we put off having kids. I went to heavy equipment operator's school near there, and here we are. We have a ten-year old, raising us." He grinned.

"Boy for you, or girl for Lorrie?"

"A girl who plays with heavy equipment toy trucks. Go figure."

"Sounds perfect." Between the chatter, their coffee disappeared. "More?" Beebe asked, raising her mug.

"I'm good."

"I'm glad you stopped by. I want to make arrangements for a grave," Beebe said, ever the opportunist.

"Who are you talking about? Cliff usually leaves paperwork, but I haven't been back there yet."

Beebe assumed the paperwork went to the desk in the block building, the desk on which she observed the computer screen and keyboard. "Now, don't think I'm going to be involved in cemetery operations. That's purely you and Daddy. No, this is a special situation. Just this one time. I need a grave dug in our Walker plot."

His surprised expression said, "Who died?"

Beebe passed on that question and kept going. "I'm sure I can count on your discretion about this. The obituary will run Tuesday. There's a grave out there by the blue spruce. Terri Miller."

He nodded slowly, though comprehension had not fully registered.

"That name was an alias my mother used."

"That's your mother!"

"Yes, she was brought here for burial." Beebe decided to skip around the part of the story that involved Vincent, hoping Hal was unaware.

"I'm so sorry, Beebe. Cliff didn't say anything."

"He only just learned. But now that we know, Daddy and I want the grave moved. Daddy's decided on private services for Tuesday. I'm sure you don't work on Sunday and with Labor Day Monday, I thought you should know in order to plan. How do we accomplish this?"

"Well, I'll dig the grave today."

"Not tomorrow?"

"Cliff doesn't like that kind of activity on a Saturday. Folks visit on the weekends, and they don't need to see the housekeeping phase of things, if you know what I mean." She nodded. "Then I'll wait till Tuesday on the disinterment." He paused. His eyes drifted to a point over Beebe's shoulder, then returned. "So your mom, huh? That's gotta be tough. And you're running an obituary?"

"Daddy wants it. I was surprised, but I suppose it gives closure. This is her last chapter, and he wants it done right."

"Maybe, but—" He winced. "You know."

"People will talk."

"Some will. I know high school was hard on you."

"I'm not so worried about me."

"If Cliff's made this decision, then he's decided how to handle it, too. I wouldn't worry."

Beebe tossed him a look.

"But I suppose you are."

"A little bit," Beebe said. She set her coffee cup over to the side. It felt like there should be more, but she just couldn't share details with Hal Garrett. Abigail Walker's life while she was away was no one's affair. After the obituary ran, she could conceivably have dozens of discussions just like this one.

"You know, since Terri Miller was thought to be indigent, I tried my hand at the old ways. I practiced and engraved that headstone with chisel and hammer."

"You're a craftsman," Beebe said, truly impressed. "You did a fine job. I'm sorry it won't stay on the grave."

The two people who knew Cliff Walker spoke back and forth with their eyes.

Then Hal said, "I'll keep everything to myself."

"Thank you," Beebe mouthed.

Beebe looked at her watch once she walked Hal to the back door and let him out, then she went to the phone and called Crossroads.

The phone was answered with the words, "Crossroads. Yates here."

"Hi, Yates," Beebe returned, grinning at his uniqueness. "Vincent around?"

"No, he just hightailed it out of here when he heard about an auction over in Harrelsburg."

"What kind of auction?"

"Gently-used hospital room accessories." It sounded like Yates read from some kind of advertisement. Beebe knew Harrelsburg was three hours away. An auction of any length would tie Vincent up all day.

"Well, I'll tell you then. I'm ready to leave the house, but I need to stop at McKinley's to speak with Daddy a minute." She wanted to fill Cliff in on her conversation with Hal Garrett.

"Fine with me. Vincent wanted me to tell you he finished writing up the program policies you'll be implementing. He wants you to read them over this morning."

Amenable, Beebe said, "I'll take care of it first thing."

When Beebe arrived at McKinley Hardware, Scott Cotter told her Cliff was out making a quick delivery. She reshuffled her day, asking Scott to let her father know she'd stop back in an hour or so. She'd be over at Crossroads if he asked.

The senior center's main room was empty when Beebe entered. As she scanned her surroundings, she saw Barleycorn. Well, his head anyway. He stuck it around a corner from an area behind the kitchen. After eye contact was made, he lifted his nose up and ducked it back from sight in a way that beckoned her. She found Yates cleaning out the storeroom. He anticipated her next question.

"To make space, now that the painting is done. One of the roof-over-my-head chores." His extended job description amused Beebe.

He took a break to show her where Vincent left the reports and led her down a side hall off the main room. Barleycorn trailed dutifully along, his nails tapping the floor tiles. The tight proximity of closed doors in the hall told her the rooms beyond must be small. Her pace slowed with the progression of that thought. Was this the hospice wing?

She was suddenly aware that behind one of these doors, she suspected her mother died. For some reason, she looked down to Barleycorn. His brown eyes darkened with confirmation. They did not let on which room.

The walk became burdensome with the additional weight of insight. She knew first-hand now of the depth of pain and sorrow others experienced. It took full effect. She could empathize with the wife who must lay back into the bed where her husband died the night before.

A few steps ahead, Yates pointed out his room. He opened the door. She glanced quickly around. The room was sparsely furnished and tidy. The next door opened to Vincent's office. Beebe walked in, passing Yates, then a scarred credenza. Once she was settled into one of the four chairs around the table, Yates disappeared.

On the tabletop, under an old gray stapler used as a paperweight, were four program descriptions. At the bottom of the pile, as she thumbed through, was Crossroads' board member listing. She scanned the list first. The president was Donald Thorndyke. Larkspur was such a small town, she thought. Donald's parents were buried next to Terri Miller's grave. Other names on the list sounded familiar, but she could only put definition to Ron Smith, the board's legal counsel. Vincent mentioned his name as the author of her employment agreement.

Getting down to reading, Beebe made notes on the last page of the program Vincent titled, Registration Canvass. The idea was impressive and would prove time-consuming to ensure that no senior was overlooked. Once the canvass was fully completed, the value of the data collected would be priceless. She had just laid the pen down when Yates appeared in the doorway with the dog.

"Barleycorn needs a visit to the park. Can you keep an ear tuned out front? Some of the guys just showed up for pool."

Beebe agreed.

The next program description seemed fairly straightforward and limited to just the few months prior to the annual April 15 tax-filing deadline. Folks schooled in completing tax returns would be lined up to assist seniors by appointment.

Distantly, she heard a commotion from the guys so Beebe wandered out to the main room. She found a woman in a business suit, chatting with the men and checking out the paint job. The wall tint used was a soft blue.

Beebe instantly recognized one of the three pool players. It was Myron Fyffe, her high school algebra teacher. Her mother's abandonment led Beebe to adopt a self-protective personae as a student. She stuck to the books, stayed out of everyone's eye, and, as a result, made the honor roll every semester but one. She carried a solid B in algebra.

"Do my eyes deceive? Is that Beebe Walker?" Fyffe said, placing forefingers and thumbs on the side stems of his glasses.

"Mr. Fyffe. Good to see you."

He came over, still light on his feet, with his hand jutted out. "Not as good as it is to see you."

"Why, thank you," she said. He held the hand she gave him in both of his.

The woman, so out of place in her expensive gabardine jacket and skirt, and fifteen years too young to be of retirement age, showed obvious interest. Beebe turned her attention away from Fyffe. "Hi. Can I help?"

"Beebe? You're the one I came to see. My name is Mona Gabriel. I'm a member of Crossroads board of directors," Mona said.

Beebe remembered the name from the list Vincent provided. She went to the woman. They shook hands.

"I knew you were due in," Mona continued, "so I thought I'd welcome you, see how things are going."

"I'm glad you stopped in." Fortunate timing, Beebe thought. "In fact, I'm familiarizing myself with the programs Vincent designed. I understand the board gave preliminary approval, and it's my job to implement them."

"Implement under Vincent's guidance," she corrected.

"Of course." Beebe applied a grain of diplomacy. "We're a small force around here. We stand together."

"Fine. Excellent. And again, welcome. See you at the next board meeting." Turning, she offered the pool players a stylish salute. "Gentlemen," she said, then clipped on her heels out the door.

Well, Beebe surmised, watching Mona pass the front window, she would be a personality to deal with.

"So, you've got a job here," Fyffe said.

Beebe took a step his way. "Just started."

"Good luck. We'll be the better for your participation."

Smiling, she tipped her head in appreciation of his comment, flicked a wave, and returned to her reading.

She finished just as Yates returned. Barleycorn rushed over to get his ears scratched. "The reports are read," she said to the young man. "I put a few notes in the margins. I'm going to run back over to McKinley's and see if Daddy's back." When she scooted her chair away from the table, Barleycorn made room for her to stand. She raised her eyebrows to Yates. "You know, I still want you to meet Daddy. I'd love to have you and Vincent for dinner. You can share Terri's stories." She used the name he liked best.

"Well..." he trailed off.

"I know this really isn't your problem, but I don't want to wait. Waiting this long hurt him badly enough. I don't want to compound it."

His nod came with no words.

Tilting her head, she looked up to find his downcast eyes. "You came searching for the truth. Can't you imagine how her husband would feel?"

"I can, but Vincent won't be back till late."

"That's right," she said, remembering Vincent's long drive back from the auction.

"What if we put it off one more night?"

She sensed his anxiety. "Okay. Saturday night it is."

"Yeah. Okay."

When she drew alongside the young man inside the office doorway, she lay a hand on his shoulder. "Yates, you have just as much right to Terri's love as anyone. Don't undervalue that, and don't undervalue yourself." She patted his shoulder twice, gave him a firm nod, and moved out into the hall.

A Season Not To Forget

Beebe scuffed down the center aisle at McKinley's Hardware, looking for her father, but having no luck. When she reached the last aisle, Scott Cotter stepped out of the warehouse.

"He's back," Scott said.

"May I?" Beebe asked, pointing at the double doors.

"Sure. He's out by the dock."

"Daddy," Beebe called to catch her father's attention. She saw him disappear behind a stack of boxes. Half a second later, he reappeared. The smile she offered was not returned. "Daddy, I spoke to Hal."

"I know you did."

"You went by?"

"Yes."

"You're angry."

He glanced behind her. Wondering about Scott's proximity, she guessed, then walked her out to the dock.

"Yes," he said, "I'm angry. Why didn't you let me handle it?"

"I wasn't trying to push you out. Hal was right there. I knew the plans. I asked him. He considered your policy about Saturday work." She maintained an informative tone.

"Look, managing the cemetery is my business. Mine alone." He pounded an index finger on his chest. "Do you understand?"

"Yes. I do. Did you and Hal change any of the plans?"

Their conversation was cut by a beat of silence before Cliff said, "No."

"So, everything's just as Hal and I left it." Beebe's words carried the intended jab.

"That's not the point."

She studied him. Despite his stiff posture and clenched fists, she thought him ready to cry. "Are you okay, Daddy?" she asked sympathetically.

Cliff was exhibiting his old trait of swinging wildly, if not symmetrically, from one extreme of the emotional spectrum to the other. He needed to get his arms around the whole story as soon as possible. She reached a decision: Yates must come to dinner tonight. Having more time pass before the full truth was out would only hurt Cliff further. She couldn't let that happen.

And quite frankly, she wanted father and daughter to get along better. They were picking up where they left off with petty squabbles. She was glad Yates seemed to understand that, just as he wanted answers to the Terri Miller mystery, Cliff wanted and deserved answers, too.

"Why would you ask that? Am I okay?" Cliff threw back at her. "We're talking about digging your mother's grave."

She maintained composure, lowered her voice and slowed her words. "Yes, I know we are. And it's hard. But you know what?" She ticked up her enthusiasm. "I'm going to invite a young man working over at Crossroads to dinner tonight. He's new in town. We need some company, and he's got time to fill. It won't be just us tonight."

"You think I need a distraction?"

"I think if I get away from Crossroads early, I can have lasagna ready, plus garlic bread and mint-chocolate-chip ice cream. How's that sound?"

"Fine," he said, sounding more exhausted than exasperated now.

"I will not interfere with your cemetery. I got it." She poked playfully at his no-paunch stomach. "Listen to me: Save yourself for a lasagna dinner."

Rushing back to Crossroads, Beebe swept past the pool players with a wave. Yates gravitated to cleaning out kitchen cupboards.

When Barleycorn's tail thumped the floor, Yates looked around.

"I need a big, big favor," she said.

"What?"

"Come to dinner tonight. I know I agreed to Saturday, but I just talked with Daddy, and I can tell, grief is creeping up on him. This can't wait. Another full day can't go by and he not know what the rest of us do. You can understand that." She added that last sentence to draw him in with a degree of ownership.

The measure was absolutely necessary.

By the look on his face, Yates started to retreat. "Beebe, uh..."

"You can understand, can't you? This is important. Very important. It's got to come from you. You can do this. Please." The determination in her voice dropped the last word to a whisper.

"But Vincent's not here. I'm supposed to close the center." Nervously, he moved some glasses around on the counter.

"It's Friday. There's nothing scheduled for tonight. Lock up at six, and be at our house by six-thirty. I'm checking out early, too. I'll square it with Vincent. You know he'll understand."

"But the guys..."

"I'll handle them. No problem."

She went down the short hall. The same three men stood around the pool table with cues in their hands.

"Hey, Mr. Fyffe, can you guys clear out by six so Yates can have a nice home-cooked dinner at my house?" She passed her glance among the trio. "Come on, give the kid a break."

A tall man stepped up and spoke. "You don't know me. I'm Mick Nettleman. I worked in maintenance at the hospital. Whatever happened to your mother?"

"Mick, don't ask that. What's wrong with you?" Fyffe said, berating the man for his manners. "It's none of our business."

"No, fellas." Beebe patted the air between Fyffe's complaint and Mick's offensive stare. "The truth is, Mother died recently. I'm home now, and Daddy wants to have memorial services." Cliff Walker would just spit it out, she thought, and so would she.

"Oh," Fyffe stammered. "What are the arrangements?" Behind Fyffe, a small-framed quiet man watched and listened.

"That's sweet," Beebe said. "But, you know, it's just going to be us."

"We'll be thinking about you. And we'll be out way before six."

Thanking him, Beebe turned away just as Fyffe smacked Mick on the arm. She waited out of sight at the near end of the hall to gather herself. The conversation had its effect. While she pulled in a deep breath, she heard Mick's voice and turned an ear toward the large room. "But I worked with her mother. That was a disgrace, what she did."

"Leave it, Mick," Fyffe said in a low tone. "Didn't you hear? The woman is dead."

"But she was never punished for stealing narcotics from the pharmacy. It's not right. That Mrs. Gabriel ought to know. Isn't she a doctor's wife?"

"What's your point?" Fyffe asked.

"I talked to her once before when she was in. She cares about this center's reputation. I bet she doesn't know the whole story with those Walkers."

"What makes the difference? It was thirty years ago. And, 'those Walkers?' Don't tell me you're going to bring up the men's club festivals again?"

Every sentence the two pool players spoke felt like a punch to Beebe's gut, up to and including the festival she unburied herself that morning.

"Cliff was shown special consideration, and you know it."

"You still harping on that?"

"I was the one they always hired to get that festival up and running, then Cliff comes around moanin' and sobbin'."

"Stop it, Mick. I'm not going to listen. You should never have taunted him like you did back then. It was petty. So what if he did the job for a few years?"

"Five years."

"Forget it."

"I don't think so. Some crimes don't have a statute of limitations."

"Only crimes against Mick Nettleman don't have a statute of limitations is what you mean."

Beebe experienced a wave of mixed emotions. While her hands formed fists, compassion for her father swelled inside her chest. He hadn't told her the full story. Of course, the Cliff Walker she knew wouldn't. But she understood. When she set out to tell Cliff of her feelings about the festival earlier, she began with her embarrassment. But to be taunted publicly, and with regularity, was something a man rightfully kept from his daughter. Was it true that the Walkers were so financially strapped that he went back year after year and tolerated the abuse?

Out front, Mick wasn't done. "Well, we'll see what Mrs. Gabriel thinks."

"No. Leave it. Too much time has passed," Fyffe said. "Rack 'em up, Quincy, so I can beat the tar out of this bum. Then, I can go home."

Beebe heard pool balls drop onto the felt-lined table. Apparently, the third man's name was Quincy.

Throughout the eavesdropped conversation, her focus remained on the brown-speckled and time-yellowed floor. She decided to take her algebra teacher's advice and leave things in the past. She would not confront the man named Mick Nettleman. One must pick one's battles. Mick, however, seemed determined to place her at odds with her boss. If Mona Gabriel was the kind who attracted those who carried a grudge, then Beebe must tread carefully.

Silently, Beebe thanked Fyffe again for expressing his convictions. The town still remembered. The pool players were probably an accurate cross-section of Larkspur's population: One voice spoke for the Walkers, one voice against, and one appeared neutral.

From the corner of her eye, she saw a pair of dingy athletic shoes step into her line of sight. She glanced up. A sorrowful look hung on Yates's face. She knew he heard the men's conversation.

"About tonight, Beebe. I'll be there."

She forced a smile of appreciation. Inside though, she fought to keep from being transported back to those awful high school days when her mother's absence was an untamable force of nature.

Staying in the present, though, aligned her with the brutal realities that were her father's life. Despite everything, he stubbornly chose the course where rituals required that a death notice be published in the local newspaper for all to see. His stubbornness was exceeded only by his strength to endure.

In tribute to her father, Beebe thought, To thine own self...

* * *

Cliff rode in his truck, heading home. He cruised past the city-limits marker a mile back. When he crested the next hill, his gaze rolled out to the cemetery, tracking the house and the block building. Far off, in the gap between them, grew a tree line. In the foreground, his eyes locked on the newly dug grave, Abigail's grave. Hal Garrett completed his job.

In reality, it was the cut of carpeting Hal laid over the open grave that Cliff saw from a distance. The carpeting disguised the sheet of plywood beneath it and was designed to imitate grass in texture, but it was too bright for August's drought conditions. Twenty-five yards away, equal to the reach of the backhoe's swing arm, lay mounded earth, exhumed, exposed, there for the end of the story.

He pulled into the first cemetery entrance that came up on his right, not the one nearer the house. His speed slowed. The old pickup crept along of its own accord, giving Cliff the time necessary for his heart to accept what happened in his absence.

The thought seemed funny and ludicrous at the same time. Acceptance? His absence? One afternoon. What about his wife's absence? And the last thirty years.

The next blow fell when the cemetery road took him past the blue spruce and the grave that would remain intact until Tuesday's disinterment. What Cliff thought of as "Abigail's other life" had not been disturbed, and the life she should have had existed as a gaping hole. Both graves gouged his heart.

As if that damage wasn't sufficient, in the grassy area where the sycamore stood beyond the curve of pavement, the glider swung a living memory, pushed into motion by a swirling August breeze that would not bring rain. It took all his control not to ram the swing with the battered truck. He might have gunned the engine and done it, but his heart skillfully conjured an image of Abigail and sat her there, one leg folded under her on the seat, the toe of the other foot barely skimming the ground. The glider gently rocked.

In the next heartbeat, she was gone. The leafed-out branches of the old tree fluttered, and a breath of wind took the mirage with it. He made the turn. Two seconds later, that same breeze lifted his hair and raised goosebumps on his flesh. It filled the cab, stayed but a moment before slipping out the passenger window without even the whisper of a goodbye.

He shut down the engine, stepped out to the asphalt, and closed the door with care. The grave so close to the caretaker's house seemed to beckon him. He walked the path this first of many times to stare down at the carpeting. As protocol demanded, Hal placed four decent-sized rocks at the corners. He found them through his excavation work. He drilled a central hole and filled it with a wire flag. Yellow squares spoke of caution. These four sentinels would guard the open grave for the interminable four days between now and the funeral.

How would he get through? Longing for his wife swelled in his throat. Grief bore down, pressing a shuddering feeling through him. It felt like his spirit wanted to drain away, flatten itself out on the ground, and slip beneath the barrier. A measure of fear, that might better be called survival, made him break off his stare and back away. Turning toward the house, he took the first few steps with his eyes closed to the world.

Cliff made an effort to strip off the melancholy when he changed out of his McKinley uniform. He washed up and dressed in clean clothes for supper. Back downstairs, he looked up from his newspaper when an old Jeep rattled into the driveway and stopped behind Beebe's car. Beebe must have been on lookout in the kitchen because she streaked through the living room and out to the front yard. Cliff pushed himself off the couch and walked over to the screen door.

Beebe stood on the far side of the Jeep, her head together with a young man.

They apparently became close in just the three short days since Beebe's return, Cliff thought. He studied the man, but didn't know him.

Beebe and her new friend moved single-file between the bumpers. Even from this distance, Cliff could see the man owned a pleasant smile and apparently, to Cliff's surprise, a long-haired dog. The mongrel trotted out from between the vehicles on the man's heels.

Cliff pushed the screen door open. Beebe took it. Cliff stepped back. The dog tramped through in front of his daughter.

The man found Cliff's eyes and extended his hand. "Hello, Mr. Walker. My name's Yates Strand, and this is Barleycorn. Thanks for having us to dinner."

When Cliff released Yates's hand, Beebe motioned him to a chair. Beebe slid into another one.

Cliff settled himself back on the couch. "Beebe says you're new in town and working over at Crossroads." There, Cliff thought. That was the sum total of his knowledge, and he politely expressed it. Truthfully, Cliff wasn't that interested. If Crossroads was involved, their dinner guest was probably just passing through Larkspur. He suspected Yates's plight, whatever it was, became one of Beebe's care-package projects. Which was how Cliff described all the down-and-out folks Beebe took on in her determination to rescue others from the plight of their own lives.

"Yes, sir—"

"Please, it's Cliff."

Yates nodded. "Vincent's making me earn my keep, just until I get work."

Work, huh, Cliff thought. Maybe he intended on pulling his weight in society. "What do you do?"

"I'm a nurse. A rookie nurse, but a nurse." The grin he used drew Cliff in. He had misjudged the young man. Yates went on. "I have an interview lined up at Lakeview General."

"Nursing is a good profession," Cliff said. He was thinking that maybe Yates wasn't quite the care package he thought when something in Yates's personae showed a miniscule crack. The freshness of his youth darkened. He sat up straighter. Cliff shot a glance at Beebe. It bounced back when Cliff heard the timidness in Yates's tone.

"I chose nursing," he said, "because Terri Miller was a nurse. And this isn't the first time I've been through Larkspur."

Barleycorn got up and came over to Cliff. The dog fitted himself between the coffee table and sofa while words rolled off the shock in Cliff's voice. "Terri. Abigail. My wife."

Yates nodded.

"You knew my wife, and you were aware—" Accusation lived in the incomplete sentence. He dragged his eyes away, his anger percolating.

"Daddy, I met Yates my first day back." Beebe spoke softly. "I learned then of the connection. It just seemed too much to pile on you so I waited. That was my decision. Just listen now. Yates has a lot to tell."

Cliff's ears rang. He was speechless, and the dog just stared at him.

"I don't quite know where to start," Yates said.

"Start at the beginning, jump around, it makes no difference. We just want to hear you talk about her," Beebe said, carrying the conversation.

"Beginnings," Yates repeated. "There are so many beginnings with Terri. I hope you don't mind if I call her that. Beebe said it was okay."

"Sure. I guess. Go ahead," Cliff managed, befuddled, still processing.

"The fact that I'm a nurse and Terri was a nurse isn't the only parallel. She was my inspiration in choosing that field because she came on a one-car accident about ten years ago. The car flipped, and the man was partially ejected. His leg was cut badly. That man was my father. He would have died if Terri hadn't been there."

Cliff realigned the scenario. "You mean if Terri, or Abigail, was here with her own family, your father would have died."

"Well, I guess that's one alternative, but given she was homeless and wandering, she could have been anywhere. But she wasn't. She found my father's car accident."

"I lost my wife for thirty years, Beebe doesn't have a mother, but you get your father." Cliff's voice was harsh.

"Daddy, you've got to accept that Mother left. She was scared. She didn't want to go to jail, be convicted of a felony. I'm glad someone benefited from her life. I had sixteen years with Mother. Yates had ten."

"Ten years?" Cliff raised his voice. "She stayed around? Where?"

"Up north. Otsego County. She came and went from my life, but she showed an interest in me. And quite frankly, I adored her from day one. Dad allowed her to hang around. He trusted her. She told me parts of her story. I knew she was running away from somewhere. I knew drugs were the reason she left, and there was a warrant out for her, no doubt. As a kid, I thought that was cool. I saw her as a female Robin Hood, almost. Bobby and I were her band of merry men. Bobby lived down the street. My best friend. She was all about saving lives and doing good deeds."

Cliff watched Yates's eyes cloud over for a moment before he went on.

"After Beebe invited me over, I spent some time wondering what portions of Terri's life were most important to tell. I decided on the two things I didn't understand until *after* she was gone. First, she was sober by the time I met her. I knew about the addiction, and based on the homeless life she led, I assumed she still used. That was wrong. From the day she saved my father's life, she was sober. I guess as a kid, I would have been disappointed. As an adult, I find it amazing. On the streets. The willpower needed. Awesome."

Yates glanced from Beebe to Cliff, his pride showing for this Terri Miller woman who Cliff did not know. He tried to take in all that Yates related. It came too fast, and Yates pushed on without a breath.

"She only spent summers in town, but just like clockwork, she showed up the first day school was out. I never saw her again once summer was over. She and summer were synonymous, like fraternal twins. I didn't cry around or mope. I just couldn't wait until summer came again. Which was always the case for any boy, but after Terri, it was different. Better."

Cliff's emotions melted. He felt the same about his wife. She was a season he could never forget.

Beebe eased Yates out of the reverie he'd fallen into along with Cliff. "You said there were two things?"

"Yeah, and this one is even news to you, Beebe."

Cliff watched his daughter. A morsel of Christmas anticipation lit her face.

"But let me start back a bit farther. Terri's disease began to get the best of her during my junior year at college."

"Wait a minute," Cliff interrupted, needing to clear his confusion before the young man continued. "First you said you knew about the drugs, then you said she was sober. How did she get AIDS? I assumed she used an infected needle."

Beebe clarified. "She told Vincent she stepped in to keep one woman from being beaten by another. That woman bit her in the scuffle. Her mouth was bleeding. The bite broke Mother's skin, and the disease was transferred."

Cliff's thoughts wound around the facts. It seemed so unfair to be killed by a disease related to the addiction she successfully fought.

"She moved into my apartment off-campus. I wanted to take care of her. She never let on that she was planning a return to Larkspur. She found out about Crossroads on the internet, printed the directions attached to the website and kept them somewhere, hidden among her things, waiting for the time when she felt she was close to the end. Before that happened, she moved to Gaven House. She needed more care than I could give. In March, she said she wanted me to drive her here. The thing is, we didn't go straight to Crossroads. We spent about forty-five minutes parked outside, across the road."

The meaning behind those words hit, and Cliff instantly dissolved into tears. His chin and right fist trembled. "She came here?"

"Yeah. She didn't tell me why. I saw the house and the cemetery. She could be stubborn, and that night, she wasn't answering any questions. We sat there until the light went out in the upstairs window. When the house was dark, we moved on."

"She came back," Cliff cried.

"She came to find you, Daddy. You were on her mind." Beebe got up and came to sit beside Cliff on the couch. He felt the weight of Barleycorn's head on his knee.

"She still loved you guys," Yates said. "I knew that. She never talked about a family, but she never forgot. I knew I benefitted because of something she gave up. It was you two." His eyes welled. "I'm so glad she led me here. Like Vincent said, she wanted us to learn each other's story. She didn't say it. In fact, by working the secret the way she did, I couldn't resist. I had to dig for answers."

Though a flood of tears hindered Cliff's vision, he never took his eyes from Yates. Beebe held his hand, squeezing it hard. A warm droplet slipped from her cheek onto his arm.

"I'm sorry, Cliff. It's hard," Yates said, his voice choked. "The hardest thing I ever did was drive away from Crossroads and leave her behind. I always thought she was leaving me, but really, I was leaving her. I know what that feels like. So I know what she felt leaving you. I never want to feel that again."

Yates's words assaulted Cliff, pelting him, making him somehow feel deficient. In his time, he did not know the pain of leaving someone. It segregated him into a lesser category. Yates knew the pain. Abigail knew. He could imagine the long ache of being torn from another, of knowing the way back, but life's uphill battles not permitting it.

He knew the agony of standing at the open front door, and wondering. The aimless, hopeless wondering. All these years, he kept his life just as she knew it, in the same place she knew, so if she tried, she could find him. He was home, and he felt lost. She escaped her addiction, but died an addict's death. No, not a lesser category, Cliff thought. There was symmetry between his life and hers.

162

The idea of symmetry was borne out when they went into dinner. Yates talked of other parallels between Abigail's life in Larkspur and Abigail's life up in Otsego County. Cliff devoured every word Yates spoke, like his stories were the sustenance he needed, not the lasagna. Yates's fond memories told of a woman who lived in the back room of his father's hardware store, of an ice cream truck, and a grass-cutting business.

It was difficult knowing Abigail lived a life without him. But Cliff had to wonder: Was she somehow trying to share his and Beebe's lives? He looked at his daughter, always fond of hot fudge sundaes. He thought of his endless hours on the cemetery's extra-large riding mower. Were husband and daughter there in the distance, guiding her? He thought they must have been.

He went to bed that night feeling better for having played this small part, but that feeling deteriorated in the darkness when he couldn't find sleep, as thirty years ago, he couldn't find his wife.

Companionship

Saturday morning, Cliff woke at odds with the world. He was overjoyed that his first sight of Beebe didn't take place until he saw her in the kitchen, pouring two glasses of orange juice, rather than hovering over his alarm clock. Cliff was dressed for mowing the eighty-five acre cemetery. It was an all-day job.

"Good morning," Beebe said.

"Have you taken the obituary to the paper yet?" he asked, instead of returning the courtesy.

"I just called. The counter is open until noon. I'll go there first, then I want to see what Crossroads is like on Saturdays."

"I was thinking about the obituary," Cliff said, struggling to maintain level composure.

"Yes?"

"I want you to rewrite part of it."

"What part?" Beebe's eyebrows drew down.

"I want Yates included."

Her face lit. "Oh, Daddy, that's sweet."

Cliff didn't respond in kind. Stepping out the kitchen door, he realized how so much of Beebe's tribute to her mother made sense now. She had time to process Yates's stories before she sat down to write the death notice—actually, volunteered to be the sole author of the death notice. In her years away, Beebe learned the trick of conspiracy. He capped his thoughts in that vein. In spite of his daughter's acquired talent and her ability to use that talent while, metaphorically, leaving him out by the cemetery's back gate, he wanted the sensitive young man mentioned in the obituary.

With a day of cutting the grass ahead of him, Cliff would drive his pickup out to the equipment garage. It was a hike from the house so he always took the truck. The first thing he saw through the windshield when he started the motor was Abigail's grave. On this morning, his beloved cemetery haunted him.

Fifteen minutes later, he sat astride the large mower. He pulled on work gloves and pushed earplugs into place. All routine. But today, the earplugs he wore to protect his hearing seemed to act as stoppers that captured the most oddly vivid scene, and the sounds that accompanied it, inside his head.

The scene was the one he had not witnessed yesterday. His mind chose to dispense an eerie view of the backhoe's scoop as it dug Abigail's grave. Over and over, the scoop's full weight dropped. It met firm resistance from the hard-packed earth. With each attempt, a reverberating mechanic clamor jolted the scoop's attached arm. When the earth cracked and gave way, he swore he felt the ground tremble. He gripped the mower's wheel tighter while the backhoe's large steel hand forced itself past the top layer of grassy soil. It returned to view with a measure of dirt.

Cliff heard the hydraulics of the arm's passage over to an unsuspecting spot where the bounty would be released. The fall and tumble of dirt were audible. First, a long swish, followed by a finishing twang as the last clots of earth bounced off the pointed fingers of the scoop.

He saw the movements and heard the hydraulics so keenly that he kept glancing out to the front section, expecting to see the working backhoe. Nothing met his gaze. Clearly, he fought a losing battle with reality.

Soon, the repetitive sounds became melodic. The cascade of dark earth took its place as a backdrop for the many memories of his wife that he relived. Its effect was bittersweet.

Cliff stopped mowing when lunchtime rolled around and went into the kitchen. He saw that Beebe left a copy of Abigail's obituary on the counter. He scanned the page. It contained the revised sentence:

She chose a loving husband in Clifford Walker, and she blessed her daughter, Beebe Walker, and her young friend, Yates Strand, with her open heart, her values, and ever-emerging examples of her influence on the lives of others.

This was what he wanted. The few words Beebe added were enough. Cliff took a deep breath and let it out. By now, Cliff knew the job of getting the obituary placed in the newspaper was behind them.

The remainder of the mowing task left him feeling boxed in by the mismarked grave, his daughter having returned from town and sitting in that swing, and the waiting grave in the Walker plot.

Still, he attempted to shake off the ravages of his day during his short drive back to the house, before he spoke with his daughter. He came around the bend at the block building, steered the truck just off the road, and parked beside the house.

"Hi, Daddy. Home from the wars?" Beebe said when he was close enough. She was the image of her mother. He blinked back the reverie of his day. It was not Abigail who smiled up at him, but Beebe, perched in the swing, setting it adrift with the toe of her pink clog.

"Home, and glad it's over. I saw the copy of the obituary you left. I'm glad that chore is done. It's one less—" His daughter cut him off.

"Um, Daddy. I'm sorry." Her words stumbled out, tentative. "I didn't get to the paper this morning as planned."

There it was, all the reason he needed to allow the torment of his day to lash out. The pressure built, and Beebe's pitiful explanation continued.

"I stopped at Crossroads and spent some time with Vincent on programming policies. Time got away from me. Before I knew, it was past noon. The newspaper counter was closed. I'll get it there Monday. Despite the holiday, the counter's opened. I checked." Her words dragged a bit. He knew she gauged his rising anger.

"So, your mother's obituary was not placed," he said, hands on hips. "Makes sense, though. Here you sit in the glider where she sat to tell me lies."

"Daddy, what's wrong? What happened?" She wore concern and confusion on her round face.

He spat an answer back. "The cemetery is not a haven for me anymore. You should know that. I spent the day consumed by an open grave and a closed one." Repelled, he shook, like ants crawled beneath his clothes. "An open wound, and skin having grown over an abscess."

"An abscess? Why are you fixating on Terri's grave so?"

"Do you understand? An emptiness is oozing out of me." His hands were in motion from shoulders to waist. "I feel covered in it. I've spent thirty years without my wife."

"I do understand—"

He stepped in front of her words. "Don't use that grief-counselor voice. Tell me how to bury this emptiness in that grave after the disinterment." His finger jabbed first at himself, then in the general direction of the blue spruce. "And tell me how to put it behind me."

Beebe rose. He could see her try to straddle the line between a daughter's anger over her father's wild and overly sensitive ranting and a grief counselor's patience with a client. "Daddy, we will get through this."

She patted his arm. He shook it off. "What's for supper?"

"Leftovers." She sighed. "We have oodles of leftovers."

Stomping off, he said, "Fine."

Cliff allowed his frustration to carry him up the stairs to his bedroom. He did not slam the door, but he threw himself with such force into the chair beside the nightstand that he felt it hop. He scrubbed his face with his palms and left them like blinders over his eyes for a moment. The desire to calm his spirit was strong. It was necessary. He wanted peace. Shortly after Abigail left, he discovered a path to the very serenity he sought.

He opened the nightstand drawer and took out a hinged picture frame made of gold metal. It was tarnished in places, he thought, because he held it so often.

He stared down at two photographs he took on the same day. Abigail's likeness inhabited the black-and-whites. She looked so young at twenty. In the picture on the left, Abigail stood at an angle to the camera, gazing off. The scene was set on the wooden railed porch of the tiny two-bedroom cottage they rented. The lens captured the effect of an unseen wind. It blew her long hair off her shoulders and caused her small-print cotton dress to press against the swell of her womb. She was six-months pregnant.

After he snapped the picture, they walked hand in hand around the cottage. He squeezed hers. She recognized it as his way of starting a conversation.

"Hmm?" she said, lazily.

"You gave me confidence when I had none," he confessed. "But for you, I would still have none."

"How could anything I did give you confidence?" she asked her husband of ten months.

"But you did, Abigail." He stopped, and she, with him. "You married me."

She smiled and tugged him into motion.

Living in that tiny home, carrying his child, she smothered his worries, every one.

Abigail posed for the photo on the right side of the frame a few minutes later. He caught her sniffing the lilac bush in the front yard. The smell of that sweet summer—as if it was there, filling the room—infused him once more.

Memories of that woman, on that day, still beat in his heart.

Proper Goodbye

* * *

Cliff stood on the front walk, fists planted on his hips, eyes trained on his daughter, who was bent down, deadheading a circle of marigolds around the maple tree.

"Beebe!" Cliff drilled, and she jumped.

With her hand on the tree trunk, she pushed herself to her feet. She worked off the gardening gloves and let them drop to the grass. She came over. "You look nice."

Cliff wore his gray suit and burgundy tie. "I looked for you everywhere. Why aren't you ready?" His hands moved in an up-and-down motion. It was just after ten on Sunday, and Beebe was dressed in a long cotton shirt, a pair of denim capris, and those wretched pink clogs.

"Daddy," she said with a laugh, "I haven't gone to church since March."

"Well, I didn't know."

"I take Sundays for myself. I do other things." Despite his cranky tone, Beebe remained pleasant.

"But you were a minister, for heaven's sake." That did it. He saw her eyes narrow. His one-sided argument had an opponent now.

The lilt to her words was gone. "Yes, and God found me guilty of a litany of crimes and unpardonable sins. Then He spoke to the deacons board and got them to fire my ass," she said with shock-value added. His eyes widened, and she read his thoughts. "The new Beebe has learned to swear."

"I don't know where this attitude is coming from, but I guess I'd just as soon you did stay home."

"I'm pretty sure my attitude comes through the Walker line."

He took a step. "We're not going to make living in one house work if we can't find common ground."

She gave him a defiant look. "Leave me alone about Sundays, and we'll be fine."

"I don't know how you're going to get along in this town if you don't go to church."

In a heartbeat, Cliff watched Beebe resolve her anger, something he could rarely do. "Daddy, really? That's a bit of an exaggeration. Not everyone in

Larkspur goes to church. I'll get along fine. Enjoy the sermon," she said. "I'm sorry I snapped."

Then she straightened his necktie. Her mother always did that.

* * *

Cliff whipped his pickup into the church's parking lot and drove straight to the last row, parking with his back to the building. For a long time, he stared across to the ivy-covered sidewall of a brick apartment house. He fumed. He couldn't even slow it to a simmer.

A snapshot from yesterday flashed through his mind: Beebe perched in that glider, setting it into motion with those god-awful pink clogs.

That scene fizzled when conjured imagery appeared. A scoop of loose dirt fell from Hal Garrett's backhoe, dug from his wife's "final resting place." Abigail's death brought new breadth to the meaning behind that phrase. All this represented the future rising up to haunt him in its unending horror.

Around and around, it went. A dizzying carousel ride. The past, the future. Beebe, the glider. The empty grave, a simple sifting of dirt—when there was nothing simple about it.

With a glance in the rearview mirror, he saw Rosemary and Vincent, heads together in conversation. Alternately, they sent worried glances his way. He stayed in the truck too long to deny anything was wrong. Rosemary separated from Vincent. She wound through the cars. He snagged his Bible and climbed down.

She rounded the truck's side panel, her own Bible and purse strap corralled at her bent elbow. "Cliff, is everything all right?"

"Sure. Let's go in." He started to move, but she blocked his path.

"No, I don't think so. By the vibes I'm getting, you might punch out a deacon for saying good morning. It's not a good morning, is it? And where's Beebe?"

He followed her questions up with a nervous array of ear-pulling, collar-stretching, and quick thinking.

Ever intuitive, she posed an option to her own questions before he answered. "Do you want to skip services? Play hooky? We could."

That suggestion evoked a fiery response. "I'm not going to change my life because of Beebe."

"So this," her one free hand indicated his rigid posture, "is Beebe's fault?"

"She says since the church fired her ass, she takes Sundays for herself."

Rosemary emitted a quick chuckle. "She didn't say that." He shot her a look that peeled the amusement right off her face. "Maybe she did."

"She could have told me she didn't plan on attending church. I get ready. Search the house. No Beebe. She's outside, picking weeds out of the flowers." Anger elevated his voice a few decibels.

"Cliff, you need to calm down. Just do it. Just let it go." Rosemary closed her eyes, letting her head loll this way and that. Eyes open again and realizing the futility of her example, she pushed on, "Look, Beebe had her own life away from Larkspur. Things happened to her. They couldn't have been easy to handle. She gave up the ministry. Wow! I think about that, and I can only compare it to no longer knowing how to breathe." She shook his arm playfully. "Come on. Give Beebe a break. Let her take the time she needs."

"Yeah, well, we all need time." He spat the words before he thought. They raised Rosemary's awareness antennae.

"Is there something else? More than your disagreement with Beebe?" She leveled a pair of unwavering gray eyes on him.

Scenes flipped through his mind. Beebe's pink clog tipped to the grassy earth, then a shovel full of dirt fell, taking his heart with it. He couldn't even begin to put his feelings into words so he didn't try. "Are you going to walk in with me?" he said, sidestepping her. He could see her thought processes grind forward, but apparently, she couldn't find words either. He tried a small smile. "Forget it. I'm sorry. I'm past it." He added light-hearted banter. "All the deacons are safe in my company."

She wasn't fooled, but she put one foot out, then the other. Side by side, Cliff and Rosemary cut an angle to the corner of the church. Vincent waited, leaning against the railing for the front steps. His eyebrows went up, a silent appeal for an explanation.

"Good morning, Vincent," Cliff said, several degrees too cheerful.

"Hey, Cliff," Vincent said, not sounding genuine either.

As Cliff passed him, he observed Vincent flick a look to Rosemary and imagined her nearly imperceptible head shake, clueing him in not to elicit details.

Cliff mounted the cement stairs, head high. His burden churned inside him still.

* * *

After services at First Lutheran Church, Vincent followed Rosemary and Cliff down the main aisle and into the line that formed to shake hands with Ned McMitchell. Rosemary, then Cliff complimented First Lutheran's pastor on his fine sermon addressing obedience to God's teachings. They stopped and turned when Ned asked Vincent a question.

"Can you stay a minute?"

"Sure. No problem." Vincent wandered a step or two away with his friends.

"Should we wait?" Rosemary said.

"No. Go ahead. I don't know how long I'll be." Vincent meant their usual after-church trek to a restaurant in a nearby town for dinner.

He pushed them off, shoved his hands into his pockets, and ambled over to an unoccupied spot in the vestibule. Half a minute later, Willa McMitchell separated herself from a small group she conversed with and came over.

"How do you feel?" Vincent asked the preacher's pregnant wife.

"The baby and I think we're in for a hot one."

He smiled. "Babies are so smart these days. Probably all owed to the mother's genes."

"I do what I can."

"And a little more," he judged.

"Ned asked you to wait?"

"Yeah."

"He said he would. Did Rev. Razzell leave already?"

Vincent nodded. Razzell and his white head of hair were several places ahead of him in line. "Is that what this is about?"

Willa's mouth opened, then she saw her husband walking their way. He put a hand on both Vincent's and Willa's shoulders. "We need to talk about Mosie."

The three of them adjourned to the pastor's office. It was large with a nicely apportioned sitting area. A couch and two chairs were stationed around a coffee table. The McMitchells took the chairs, leaving Vincent the couch.

"Between us," Ned said, "we've all been over to Mosie's since his Wednesday meltdown. And we've all pushed him to consider Crossroads' senior watch program."

"I don't think Mosie likes the title," Willa said.

"Beebe fine-tuned it to Senior Life," Vincent said.

Willa nodded approvingly. "Better."

"Mosie came to me just before services. He said the strangest thing. He wants Yates to be his companion, like the program calls for." Ned sent a look toward his wife.

"Companion is better." Willa nodded again.

"And there's more," Ned went on. "He said he'd even let Yates and Barleycorn live in his house."

"He'd give Yates a home?" Vincent said, surprised. "What, some kind of compensation?"

Willa spoke up. "But this is good. For Mosie, of course, if Yates accepts, and it would solve Yates's homeless problem."

"The program doesn't call for live-in companions. That's not how it was designed. It calls for seniors to step in and assist other seniors," Vincent said.

"Well, Mosie wants Yates and the dog." Ned tugged his ear.

"But Yates hasn't even been back to see him. All he did was take his pulse."

"Yates was kind to him," Willa said. "Ned told Mosie Yates is a nurse and looking for work. That must have got him thinking."

"He's got an interview at Lakeview next week," Vincent said, speaking of Larkspur's only hospital. He turned his next question to Ned. "Did Mosie say why Yates?"

"I asked him. He clammed up. Just Yates was all he'd say. Then, almost scornfully, he added, 'and the dog.' But I can see what you're saying, if it's a senior-to-senior program."

"Hmm," Vincent said. "It's Beebe's program to implement. Protocol says I should speak to her first. I'm sure she knew this wasn't going to be a five-day-a-week job, so I'll get with her this afternoon." He got up. "More than the senior-to-senior thing, my concern is, if Yates gets the hospital job and these arrangements with Mosie go forward, they'll be short-term. That might do more harm than good."

"Yes, I thought of that," Ned said. "Yates will have a presence, then withdraw."

"Mosie's needs seem most definitely headed down the long-term road," Willa said, rubbing her belly. "I suppose it's too much to expect Yates to do both. He's young. When would he get to have any fun in his life?"

Vincent left the two McMitchells in the pastor's office. He walked down the hall toward the vestibule while he chewed on Willa's last question. He thought he'd head on out to Beebe's. He knew Cliff and Rosemary were off together for dinner. That was a common occurrence. If not for the impromptu meeting about Mosie, he would have accepted the dinner invitation and joined them.

After the church's front door closed behind him, Vincent decided one thing: He definitely wouldn't mention church. He suspected that topic was the impetus behind Cliff's mood earlier when he barreled into the lot. Beebe bit Vincent's head off before about the subject. Shades of his to-hell-in-a-hand-basket visit in her Maryland living room remained fresh in his mind.

Barleycorn to the Rescue

Beebe jumped back to consciousness. From the glider where she apparently dozed off, she came out of her haze to see Vincent's face staring down.

"Oh, Vincent, where's Daddy?" Beebe twisted in her seat toward the driveway, only her car and Vincent's sat there. "Daddy and I quarreled." She barely got the last word out before she understood from the expression on his face that he was fully aware of the situation. "He told you?"

Vincent laughed. "We're talking about Cliff, here. He's not the most open man on the planet. It didn't require too much of a leap."

"I wanted to make amends so I put in a pot roast as soon as he left, but he didn't come home."

"Well, it's sort of a tradition to eat out after church around here. I would have gone too, but Ned and Willa stopped me."

"He went out? We never did that when I was a kid."

"Well, things are different. I'm sure he wanted to introduce you to Rosemary Olmsted. It's usually the three of us."

"Who's Rosemary?"

"She owns the diner downtown. Nice lady."

"I guess I missed that introduction." Beebe was curious about the woman, but she fed her curiosity into another subject. "So, what did Ned and Willa have to say? Can I offer you some dinner?"

"Sorry, I grabbed a burger." Vincent jerked his head back toward town. "I didn't know there'd be pot roast."

"Don't worry. It will keep."

"Anyway, Ned, Willa, and I had a conversation about Mosie Razzell. Ned and Willa have checked in on Mosie since Wednesday's incident as promised. Ned pushed the new programming you'll oversee. This morning before the service, Mosie told Ned he'd like to have Yates and the dog be his companions."

Beebe sat up straighter. "That's strange. That doesn't sound like Mosie. He's going from one extreme to the other."

"I agree. That's why I'm here. I told Ned and Willa you needed to evaluate—well, because," he shrugged, "it's your job."

"Well, the first thing I see is, the program was written to place seniors in a position to assist other seniors," she said, getting up. "This pairing would derail the program before it got started." Beebe paced some. She thought. Then she stopped and turned to face Vincent, smiling.

"What?" he said.

"As I understand it, the program, as it's written, hasn't been approved by the board yet."

Vincent perked. "Right! So why not sneak this in at the last minute."

"I can't imagine there'll be an epidemic of young men with dogs around to be parceled out to seniors."

"So, this is probably a one-time deviation."

"And what a great idea if it works." She felt her excitement dim. "The real problem is, will Yates have the time when he starts working, if not at the hospital, then somewhere? I'd hate to not use Yates—if he's willing—if it means Rev. Razzell loses ground at the outset. I do think it would behoove us to get on this while the good reverend is in this mindset." She snapped her eyes up to Vincent. "I know! I'll pack up some of my pot roast and give him a visit. He doesn't go with the crowd for Sunday dinner?"

"No, I expect you'll find him at home. With his clothes on."

Beebe laughed. "Oh, please, don't even joke about that." Vincent followed her inside the warm kitchen. "If Yates would rather not live with Mosie, I still think the combo plan is a good one," she said, finding a plastic container sized for a large serving of pot roast.

"Combo plan? What do you mean?"

She expanded on the initial idea she first mentioned in Razzell's living room. "Yates and Barleycorn could visit Mosie. The next time, the two of them and me. If Yates gets the job and is on shift, Barleycorn and I could go. You know, mix it up. See how that works."

"I can see each situation we uncover with a Larkspur senior will require a tailor-made course of companionship. Ned coined the word companion earlier when he spoke of Mosie and Yates."

While Vincent talked, Beebe pulled the roaster pan of meat and vegetables out of the oven and spooned a generous serving into the clear plastic dish. She fitted a lid over the container. "We'll try that word out. Of course, I knew Rev. Razzell years ago, but I need to get some sense of him now and, hopefully, in a lucid moment."

Beebe turned the oven dial off, then made room in the refrigerator for the large pan. She'd store the food better when she got back.

At their cars, Vincent said, "Good luck. Let me know how it goes."

"Are you going to say anything to Yates?"

"Since we're deviating from programs, I thought I might, Beebs."

Beebs, she thought. Hearing him use her nickname warmed her. She began to feel immensely rewarded for the position she undertook with Crossroads.

Vincent's car was out in the road facing town when Beebe looked down her chunky frame to her pink clogs. She ran upstairs and quickly changed into a loose cotton dress and sandals before driving to the reverend's house. She stood on his stoop, checked her watch, and then rang the doorbell.

Razzell answered promptly, fully dressed in church clothes.

"Hi, Rev. Razzell. May I come in?"

She observed his somewhat quizzical expression, but took hold of the door when it was unlatched. The dark room she stepped into was simply untidy, not crazily chaotic. Somehow, she knew the difference. Several sections of the newspaper were spread about, folded on the couch, over the chair arm, his suit coat draped the wing of a wingback chair.

He closed the door, cutting off the light beaming through the doorframe. It was then that she saw recognition in his face. She wondered if, while she stood silhouetted by the sun on the porch, he hadn't realized who she was.

She offered the pot roast. "There's extra because Daddy went out to dinner." She covered their quarrelling by saying, "We got our wires crossed."

His hands remained at his sides. "You didn't attend church, young lady. I saw Cliff. I didn't see you."

"No, I didn't attend. God and I have gotten our wires crossed somehow, too," she said, lightheartedly repeating the theme. "Have you eaten? Are you hungry? I could put this in the microwave. We can talk while you eat."

"No."

She had started to pick a path to the kitchen, then, with the blunt answer, stopped. "We could talk first, then I can warm it for you before I leave."

"No!" He swatted at the plastic dish, jarring it loose.

She worked to catch it. "Rev. Razzell! What's wrong?"

"It's my fault. Stay away."

Her heart lurched. She squinted at his collapsed expression, his chastisement of her replaced with fear.

"What does that mean, Rev. Razzell? What's your fault?" For a second, their eyes met and held. She innately knew he had not employed "fault" to construe a connection to nearly knocking the container from her hands.

"Go away. Get out." He pushed her toward the door, fumbled with the handle, then pushed her out to the porch.

For two seconds, before the door slammed, she stared back at the man, wondering about his state of mind, wondering if he should be left alone.

Those thoughts and others spun around in Beebe's head all the way down Razzell's driveway. She looked back at the house before stepping behind a thick evergreen. The tree would block her actions, just in case the retired minister watched through a slit in closed curtains. She set the container of pot roast down in the grass to search her shoulder bag. With her cell phone in hand, she noted the time when the screen lit.

Vincent answered her call on the second ring. "My visit inside Rev. Razzell's house lasted three minutes. He was dressed, but not himself."

"He wasn't lucid?"

"I honestly can't say. But it was odd. For all intents and purposes, he threw me out."

"My God! What do you recommend we do?"

She bit her lip. This was not a spoiled-child situation where producing the cried-for object only further engrained the unwelcomed behavior. "Come over. Bring Yates and the dog. Does he know what Mosie's asked of him?"

"I told him," Vincent said plainly.

Beebe rushed on, her thoughts jumping ahead in Razzell's therapy. "Maybe after two or three visits, Yates and I can sit with him for a rational discussion. Your protocols mentioned medical evaluations to go with the program. Is a physician on board?"

"We need to retain one. Dr. Gabe's the one I'd like to have. That presents a small problem though."

"Either the problem gets resolved, or we find another doctor. Rev. Razzell isn't a simple case of senior loneliness, where a meal here, some groceries there, or running the vacuum does the trick."

Vincent's sigh was audible through the phone. "To repeat Ned's description, Mosie is baptism by fire."

Beebe didn't like the expression the first time around. She substituted, "A hurdle right out of the gate."

Since her departure from the church, she no longer peppered her speech with biblical overtones.

* * *

Yates noticed Beebe first. Waving back, she waited several houses down from Razzell's house. He elbowed Vincent and tipped his head her direction. The two men and a leashed Barleycorn altered their course.

Beebe met them halfway. "I moved the car so he wouldn't think I was stalking him and call the cops. I didn't realize you'd come this way."

"I had to go to the park to get them," Vincent explained.

Yates, a little overwhelmed by the request immediately before him and more than a little overwhelmed by the live-in companion idea, remained quiet. Barleycorn panted, needing water after his romp in the park.

"Did Vincent fill you in?" Beebe asked.

"I understood what he said, but I don't understand why Rev. Razzell became so attached to Barleycorn and me."

"None of us understand that. But it's not a bad thing. It's kismet. Karma. Something. You'll find you have it with certain patients, don't you think?"

"I suppose you're right."

"Are you willing to try?" she asked him.

Try, Yates repeated to himself. Not a permanent arrangement, not yet. He wanted to ease in slowly. It felt daunting, but he was willing to try. He was also a bit tongue-tied.

Beebe, with her counseling experience, made sure he understood Razzell's wants and needs were not all that mattered here. "No decision has to be made today. You and Barleycorn must benefit as well. Get to know Rev. Razzell better. There's no rush. You've got the invitation. You're testing the waters, spending more time each day. Mention your interview. Tell him a job is important, necessary in your life. Tell him you need time to think. You are not required to do this, Yates. Negotiate if you feel that's necessary. Promise continued contact.

Daily, unless something prevents it. Playtime in the park with Barleycorn."

"That's good." Yates jumped on the idea Beebe threw out. He liked the expansion of possibilities outside Razzell's house. "Do I wait for him to ask me directly?"

"I think you'll know how to play that. He made the offer through Ned. He didn't want me to show up, so he's holding out for you. Get him to talk. Listen. Both of you, listen on all levels." She drove the point home. "What is he saying?"

When Beebe included Vincent in today's equation, Yates said, "You'll go in with me?" His nervousness crept up little by little, although he was not a stranger to responsibility. There was his mother's illness and Terri's. Their bodies gave out. For Rev. Razzell, it appeared that his mind was suffering. That had not been proved medically. But still, he would bet that something physically on this earth caused it. If that something was brought into the light, that something might also illuminate Razzell's discomfort around Beebe. It was not too far afield to think Razzell's situation moved down a psychological path. Beebe might be thinking the same since she asked Vincent and him to listen on all levels.

"Sure, I'll go in," Vincent said. "After that, we'll see where Mosie leads us."

Yes. Yates liked that premise. He reached down to pat Barleycorn's shoulder. Let Razzell lead. They would learn more that way.

"I'm going to head out," Beebe said. "I'll wait for you, where? The center is locked, isn't it?"

"We'll come through the park. If it takes too long and you go on, I'll call. Okay?"

"Fine," she said, backing away.

The men and the dog walked on.

"So, what should I say? I don't know how to start the conversation," Yates said.

"We can't pretend this is a normal visit."

"He's not going to believe that," Yates agreed.

"Then we'll go with absolute honesty."

"Honesty like, hi, we think you're nuts and came to help?" Yates rolled his eyes.

Vincent grinned. "Professional honesty might be a better choice."

When they reached the walkway leading to Razzell's front door, Vincent let Yates and Barleycorn go first. Barleycorn sat next to Yates on the stoop. Yates knocked, then knocked again. Barleycorn barked at the unanswered door. That brought Razzell.

When the door opened wide, Yates, still without an opening line, let the leash fall. Barleycorn raced in, then Yates had his icebreaker. "Barleycorn to the rescue."

Razzell's features softened. "Thank you, son. I so needed rescuing right now."

"Barleycorn could use a little rescuing, too. He needs a drink. A big drink."

Vincent followed Yates inside. Yates moved in the direction of the kitchen, slipping his backpack off his shoulder. It was standard practice that he carry the dog's bowl for playtime in the park. There, he filled the bowl with water from a drinking fountain. That didn't happen today. Vincent arrived after Beebe's call and rushed Barleycorn and him across the street.

Razzell stepped in. "No. Let me. You're my guests."

Barleycorn watched Yates pass his bowl. The dog padded after Razzell onto the kitchen linoleum. When Yates heard water running, he tipped his head toward the other room, indicating that he and Vincent should follow.

"Barleycorn is not a neat drinker," Yates said to Razzell. "Better not get your living room carpet wet."

"Fine," Razzell said. He carefully lowered the dish to the flooring. Barleycorn lapped up the water with zest. "I'll fill it up, boy, as many times as it takes." When the hound drank the dish dry, Razzell repeated the exercise.

The three men took seats around the kitchen table. Barleycorn lay his belly on the cool floor, his eyes half-closed.

On this visit, Yates saw another side of the senior. All Yates did was ask if Razzell ever had a dog. Razzell took it from there. His mind was sharp about a dog from his youth. The stories began with a spotted brute misnamed Sweet Pea and ended when Razzell's father came home from the war. At some point, Vincent got up and ran paper towels through the puddle on the floor around the dog's water dish.

"Despite the fact that Sweet Pea was Father's dog, and they were always like this," Razzell said, holding up his hand, the first two fingers crossed, "she and I got into boyhood scrapes anyway. No matter that we spent a Saturday afternoon together, traipsing through the woods, when we got back home and she saw Father, she ran to his side and stayed there."

Yates felt his eyebrows draw down when he saw the expression on Razzell's face slip. He wondered if the older man was about to experience another episode. When Razzell took up his story again, Yates decided the shift was emotional, not mental.

"Then the world changed when the war brought in the United States. Father became a soldier. I was the man of the house while he was gone, and Sweet Pea got old." His next words were reticent, his gaze far-off. "After Father mustered out, Mother and I got him home from the train station and steered all the talk toward other things. Father drove the car into the garage. It was big and stuffed with junk, but his eyes went straight to it, half hidden on a nail. Sweet Pea's collar. We were going to sit him down on the bench under the oak tree and tell him. All that stuff in the garage," Razzell said, shaking his head, "and his eye went straight to it."

If Yates had any question about the man's lucidity on this day, it was thoroughly trounced when Razzell tied his closing sentence back to Yates's conversation starter. "So to answer your question," he said, "no, I never really had a dog of my own."

A solemn moment passed, then Yates said, "How about tomorrow, Barleycorn and I come back for a visit and another talk?"

"I'd like that. We can talk about the companion idea. I counted on Ned to pass the word, but I know a smart young man like you will take time to consider." The reverend gave Yates and Barleycorn a true smile. He was fully energized again. He looked down at the dog, who raised his head. "Right, Barleycorn? Make sure you weigh in, too."

"Would you like to walk to the park and watch him play tomorrow?" Yates made the offer Beebe suggested. Although he pushed for Vincent's accompaniment with Razzell on this visit, he thought he and Razzell would make better progress alone.

"Most definitely."

Yates returned his smile. He categorized Rev. Razzell a first-rate mystery. And he thought Razzell knew it, meaning the mystery would not be solved until Razzell was ready.

He reclaimed Barleycorn's bowl and his backpack. The dog's leash was clipped on at the front door. The men said their goodbyes. Yates and Vincent walked across to Engle Park where Beebe waited at the squared-up benches.

When Yates got close enough, he dropped the leash. Barleycorn announced his and Vincent's return to Beebe. She watched two boys pass the football, safely out of reach of any "Hail Mary" throws. Her purse and a clear plastic dish with a blue lid occupied the seat beside her. Barleycorn immediately took an interest in the dish.

"What happened? How'd it go?" Beebe said, roughing up the dog's fur.

Yates sprawled onto the seat beside her, and Vincent grabbed the other bench for himself. "In my opinion," he said, "fine."

"He was calm?" Beebe gave Yates a curious look.

"He wouldn't answer the door until Barleycorn barked. I don't know if that was just how it seemed, or if it took him time to get there."

"So what's your evaluation?" Beebe asked.

Yates noticed Barleycorn trying to get the dish between his teeth. "Barleycorn, leave that alone."

"Oh," Beebe said. "He can have this. It's pot roast. Is that okay?"

"Sure. He's never had a Sunday meal like this before."

The dog's tail wagged madly in anticipation of tasting what his nose already told him was a canine's delight. Beebe managed to get the lid off and the dish on the ground before Barleycorn pounced. He ate with fervor. Chasing the bowl around didn't seem to distract him in the least.

Back on the subject of Rev. Mosie Razzell, Beebe frowned. "He nearly knocked the dish out of my hand when I offered it to him. Then he said, 'It's my fault. Go away.'"

"Meaning it's *your* fault or *his* fault?" Vincent asked, lifting his eyeglasses into his wavy hair.

"His fault. What did he mean?"

"I can't imagine."

Vincent glanced at Yates, who shrugged. "I couldn't even guess."

"I've been sitting here, thinking about it. The last time I spent any time with Rev. Razzell, I was seventeen and considering the ministry as a career. I went to talk with him about that. Today, for the short while I was inside, he chastised me for not going to church this morning. I told him something like God and I got our wires crossed. I wasn't specific. I couldn't imagine he understood that to mean I'd broken with the church. But if he did know somehow, maybe he thought sending me in that direction as a career path, when it didn't suit, was his fault."

Vincent made a face. "Unlikely. I can see the connections, but..."

"It doesn't seem to gel, does it?" Beebe seemingly made her decision. "Should we try to get to the bottom of it, or leave it?"

Yates tabbed back into his prior thoughts of the mystery surrounding the senior. "You're sure he has guilt about something?"

"Yes." Beebe was adamant. "He smacked at the dish and told me to get out and stay away." She looked past Yates to Vincent. "I know I told you I wasn't sure about his lucidity, but I've had time to think. He was fine, mentally. He was angry. The guilt was real."

"I like the old guy," Yates said, feeling an inner spirit lift. "It seems mean to grill him over it. We've got to wait him out. Maybe he'll confess whatever was his fault, if confess is the right word."

"The companionship idea took a step. Razzell, Yates, and Barleycorn made a date for the park tomorrow," Vincent said to Beebe.

Beebe laughed. "You've definitely got a leg up on me. I nearly didn't get out before the door slammed."

Vincent pointed at Beebe. "You, my friend, have been Razzelled." His eyebrow arched over the animated expression.

"Is that what you call it?" She laughed again, and Yates with her.

The plastic pot roast dish, now empty, skidded to a stop at Yates's feet, followed by the dog lunging for it. "No, Barleycorn. What have you done?" He wrestled it free of the dog's clenched snout and held it up, the rim fluted by teeth marks.

Beebe didn't seem to mind. She took the dish and tossed it for Barleycorn to chase.

Which he happily did.

Offense and Defense

On Labor Day morning, Beebe and her father met at the top of the stairs. She was surprised to see he was dressed for work. "You're going into McKinley's today?"

"I thought I would."

"But it's a holiday," Beebe said.

"The store's open. People do odd jobs on the holidays. That never changes."

The inference here, Beebe thought, was that she had. No doubt Beebe's swearing off Sunday church services was the very change he intimated.

Cliff led the way downstairs and entered the kitchen ahead of her. "I made a change in Abigail's obituary. Just one word." He took the typed page from his breast pocket and unfolded it. He handed her the sheet. Near the bottom, he struck through the word rising. With his revision, the sentence read:

With the setting sun, Abigail Marie Walker shall be interred in Larkspur Cemetery with private services.

"Setting sun?" Beebe queried.

"Services will be held just before dusk."

"Did you give Pastor McMitchell that detail Sunday?"

"No."

"No? Why not?" She squinted one eye.

"Why would I?"

"Didn't you ask him to preside?"

His hazel eyes were firmly latched to hers. "I didn't think I needed to. I

184

thought you would do it. Ned said a few words when Terri Miller was buried. I thought you'd speak for your mother. I didn't know you'd stopped being a minister."

Beebe bit her tongue. The fact was he did know. Was he embarrassed of the need to line up Ned and admit his minister daughter lost her faith? Now, he could author a new chapter in his lifelong disappointment with her. His cross words were matched with a swift walk toward the mudroom and side porch.

"Will you phone Ned McMitchell?" she called after him, knowing better than to make that contact herself.

The answer she got was the slap of the door.

Beebe swore. Her fingernails bit into her palms when she squeezed her fists tight. She tried not to let her anger with her father's stubborn silence mount to fury. He was grieving, she reminded herself. And the situation was so bizarre. She had months to come to terms with the idea of Abigail Walker reappearing as Terri Miller; Cliff, only five days. The poor man, she thought scornfully, was saddled with a daughter struggling with her life's work and just at the time when a minister in the family was a needed resource.

When her father's disappointment in her welled up, she drowned it with a cup of hot coffee. For good measure, she pushed that disappointment down into her gut with a layer of crisp toast.

Beebe set her dishes in the sink and heard her father's truck just firing up. That was odd. She went out to the side porch in time to see him backing the Ford down the driveway.

Huh, she thought. Then she noticed Hal Garrett's pickup parked beside the block building. When had he arrived?

She went back. Opening the door and stepping over the threshold, she said, "Morning, Hal."

Hal occupied the chair behind the desk. He looked up from some paperwork. "Hey, Beebe. How are you doing?" His inquiry was appropriately sincere for a family in mourning.

"I'm worried."

"Oh?"

"It's Daddy. Was he just back here?"

"He was. We discussed the change in timing for the reburial."

"Yes. Sunset? Is there some ritual about reburials taking place at sunset?"

"Not that I ever heard of. In my life, I attended one burial at sunset. My wife's father. But he was navy. The sun over the yardarm and all that was my take. A color guard attended. Someone played *Taps*."

Imagining that scene caused goosebumps to prickle her skin. Involuntarily, she rubbed her arms. "Can you see well enough at that time?"

Hal sat back. The chair emitted a squeak. "Cliff asked me to get here at eight. We'll lower your mother into the ground at nine. Earlier in the day, I'll do the preliminary work, then wait until evening to get the vault handler in place to exhume the vault. That'll take a little time since we're doing things backwards, but I can keep the schedule and see well enough."

She hung onto the words, "see well enough." First, she spoke them, then Hal. Admittedly, she, too, saw well enough to know her use of "rising sun" in the death notice was a poetic approach. Her father intended his choice of "setting sun" to be a literal, time-specific one. What simple analogy better highlighted the differences between father and daughter? She had no expectation that a small group of mourners would gather around the new grave in the chill of the morning with dew still clinging to the world.

Thanking Hal, she stepped out into the warm morning, feeling the weight of— Of what, where her father was concerned? Obligation? Yes, but the air around Cliff when she was in his company seemed charged, the way static electricity feels, like a kind of force field. Static electricity sometimes pulls the inanimate object toward you. Sometimes, it repels contact. When she braved to stand close enough, how would she find her father's force field charged? Negatively or positively? That test must wait until after the funeral.

She raised her face to the heavens, eyes closed to the surrounding scene. Her father's heart and soul fell the night he learned about his wife's death. So many others who spoke of their grief described a great emptiness. She imagined the crushing emptiness in his chest, the painful emotions, all bathed in the hot red the sun painted behind her eyelids.

When she lowered her chin and opened her eyes, her line of sight found the sycamore and glider. The glider seemed to be a trigger for her father's grief. An idea formed and she pushed herself into motion toward the swing where she sat with him at dusk after his first visit to the grave back by the blue spruce. His words came back to her. That night he spoke of "lies at sunset." In his mind, was the burial at sunset Cliff Walker's way of mending one jagged rent to heart and soul caused by grief?

Beebe corrected that. She thought burial at sunset was Cliff Walker's way of giving honesty its due. And grief had a name. That name was Abigail Walker.

* * *

Beebe swung into town on the main drag. She got caught at the traffic light guarding the mid-block crosswalk. Up at the corner, she saw her father coming out of Rosemary's restaurant. A woman with a long braid walked out with him. She patted his back. This must be Rosemary, Beebe thought. From this distance, it was difficult to peg her age, but not so difficult to say that Cliff and she were good friends. Curiosity first surged when Beebe heard about Rosemary from Vincent yesterday after church. Beebe wanted the story that so far Cliff neglected to shed any light on.

Cliff crossed the street and walked the half block to the alley that ran behind the hardware store. By the time Beebe got the green light, the woman Beebe assumed was Rosemary disappeared back inside the restaurant. Neither observed Beebe's right-place, right-time nosiness.

Before she delivered her mother's obituary to the newspaper building for publishing in tomorrow's edition, she stopped at Crossroads. The flashdrive in her purse contained two versions of the death notice. Yates would determine which one got printed.

She parked on the street and walked over to the community center. She knew it would be closed due to the holiday. If she couldn't raise Yates or Vincent at either the front door or the back, she'd head to the park. When she peeked through the glass in the front door, the men were sharing a bucket of sudsy water. They each dipped and wrung a rag, then worked at the task of wiping down the tables and chairs. Her knock brought Barleycorn in from the side hall, but it was Vincent who admitted her.

"Morning. Come to help?" he said.

"Oh, how I wish I could."

"Liar." He grinned and closed the door.

"Actually, I came to speak with Yates a minute." She scratched Barleycorn's noggin.

"Me? What about?"

"Can we sit a minute, hopefully on a dry chair?" Beebe teased.

"Over here," Yates said. He led her to a cluster of chairs by the wall. Vincent stood nearby.

"I'm in town to place Mother's obituary in the paper so it runs tomorrow. That's what Daddy wants: the obituary in the paper the same day the grave is transferred." Beebe spoke directly to Yates. "Daddy was so taken with you and your love for Mother that he asked me to include you in the obituary. I've written it out. I didn't want to turn the obituary in without gaining your permission." She pulled a printed copy from her purse, opened the folds, and handed it to Yates. Saturday, when she spent time at Crossroads, she got distracted and forgot to approach Yates about her father's revision.

Yates read the obituary through. His face registered a measure of surprise when Beebe thought he reached the phrase containing his name. He looked up. Clearly, he was moved. The first few words of his answer were choked. "Yes. I'd like to be included. Thank you. It means a lot."

Yates passed the sheet to Vincent.

"Will you two come to the funeral?" Beebe sent her gaze from Yates up to Vincent. "I first thought there'd be a conflict with keeping Crossroads open and both of you couldn't be there, but Daddy's planned the services for evening."

"Setting sun?" Vincent's quick read of the death notice reached the end. The quizzical look he sent her said the timing Cliff chose was definitely out of the ordinary.

Beebe downplayed it. Cliff's feelings were personal, and she would not discuss them. It went without saying that Cliff hadn't shared his perspective, so there was really nothing to discuss. "Yes, he wants Mother reburied at sunset, so it works out if you two want to attend. Hal will start the retrieval process around eight. If you could get there after eight, we'll be ready for the reburial, which is set for nine, or thereabouts."

"Sunset? Do you know why?" Vincent pushed again.

"I talked with Hal about it. He knew of no ritual, so..." Shrugging, Beebe trailed off. She withheld her deduction that the timing for the reburial was a symbolic gesture, meaningful only to Cliff.

"Can my dad come? I said I'd ask." Yates's raised eyebrows disappeared under his mop of tousled hair.

Beebe, touched by the request, would have jumped with an affirmative response, but for Cliff. What would his reaction be? His emotions bounced around with great agility lately. With her next breath though, she decided the Walkers would be hospitable. "Yes, we'd love to have him. Apologize for the late hour."

"I don't think he'll mind."

Beebe patted Yates's knee. The motion attracted the dog. A cold, wet nose routed its way under her elbow. Barleycorn would not be ignored. She moved her arm. The dog's snout took its place on her thigh. She scratched the spot between his eyes until they closed with contentment, then she scratched a little longer.

* * *

A young woman tagged Tiffany Clark looked up from her work at the front counter of the *Larkspur News* when Beebe walked in. Tiffany chose a short cut; her hair stood straight up at her crown. Her smile of greeting was so bright, it seemed to light up the ends of her hair.

Beebe handed her the flashdrive with a brief explanation. Tiffany plugged it in and downloaded the second version into the newspaper's specialized software. When she turned her computer screen around so Beebe could proofread, Abigail Walker's obituary had quickly been massaged into a narrow column. Beebe double-checked for Yates's name, then setting sun in the closing sentence, glanced through the rest, and gave Tiffany the okay. She pressed a few keys on her keyboard and an invoice printed from the Epson nearby.

While Beebe selected the correct bills from her wallet, she heard the door open and close behind her. She handed the money to Tiffany. Beebe looked up when Mona Gabriel sidled up beside her at the counter. She recognized her as the Crossroads board member she met last week.

She didn't bother to say hello. "I heard some interesting news the other day. About your mother. Well, not perhaps interesting. More startling. Maybe you can confirm it. Someone told me your mother would have been arrested on a narcotics charge for stealing drugs from the hospital, but she fled the jurisdiction instead? I understand it was quite a hot topic when it happened."

Beebe stammered a bit, shocked by Mona Gabriel's blunt side, in complete contrast with her soft, feminine wardrobe of the day. Then Beebe managed her best smile. She fully suspected that story wended Mona's way through Mick Nettleman, the pool player she met at Crossroads. She overheard Mick speak openly of his intentions to search Mona out. He called her the doctor's wife.

On the other side of the counter, she knew Tiffany took in every word and nuance. She held Beebe's change. Beebe would have preferred discretion. Situations like this were just what she and Cliff would face after the obituary ran the next day. She might as well begin developing a tough skin now, just two seconds after she placed the death notice, before it even hit the doorsteps of every home in Larkspur.

"Yes, that is true. It happened thirty years ago," Beebe said casually, turning to take the coins Tiffany offered. She eyed Tiffany whose face revealed an expression that was a cross between sympathetic and engrossed. For Tiffany's benefit, Beebe played a bit of Mona's forthright game. "You know Mother died several months ago. My father and I wrote this obituary for tomorrow's paper. We Walkers don't run from adversity. We meet and deal with it." Beebe held up the invoice, which contained a printed copy of the obituary.

"May I?" Mona said.

"Please."

When Mona's eyes stopped following the lines of type, she raised them to Beebe's. "A bit glowing for my tastes, considering."

Beebe held her tongue. Tiffany sat down.

"We'll continue this discussion at the upcoming board meeting," Mona said. "The members should know."

"Are you saying I'm not suited for the position? How is my mother's background tied to my work at Crossroads?"

"It's tied to perception, my dear, to the perception of the people who remember what *she* did. Those people are older now. Those people are the ones Crossroads serves. Please excuse me, I have a meeting upstairs."

Mona's closing statement was said to Tiffany. The clerk nodded. "Yes, ma'am."

Beebe wondered what kind of a meeting would take place on a holiday, but then newspapers never took a day off. She folded the invoice in half twice. Holding it up, she said, "Tiffany, thanks for your help."

The young woman's eyes merely widened in response, pulling the corners of her mouth up into a macabre smile, what with her hair standing on end.

Beebe crossed the tiled floor to the double front doors, wrapping a simple rhyme into her memory: Silence from young Tiff, just like silence from old Cliff.

Apparently, Beebe was the only one talking.

In an afterthought, she tallied up two more: the partnership of Mona Gabriel and Mick Nettleman.

* * *

At the foot of the newspaper's front steps, Beebe looked down the street to Rosemary's restaurant. She wondered if Rosemary might offer insight into Cliff's current emotional state. Surely a restaurant owner, like a bartender, was congenial, open, a people person, full of advice. Beebe was determined not to push Cliff to open the lines of communication until after the reburial, but that didn't mean she shouldn't prepare herself in advance. Nor did it mean she shouldn't figure out if Cliff and Rosemary were sweet on each other.

Beebe pushed through the diner's door, catching Rosemary's eye immediately. She appeared to be organizing invoices. Business was slow; Labor Day, the cause. Most people headed toward backyard barbeques with family and friends. The Walkers would not celebrate the day with a holiday feast.

Beebe selected the third booth and sat down with a view out the long expanse of glass. Rosemary cut a jagged path through a warren of tables, carrying a menu.

Up close, Beebe estimated Rosemary's age to be within the late-fifties range. "Hello, I'm Beebe Walker," she said right off. "I understand you're friends with my father."

Laying the menu down, Rosemary thrust out her hand. "Rosemary Olmsted. Nice to meet you."

There was a straightforwardness about the woman Beebe liked. "Sit down if you have time."

"Thank you. Today, there's time." She slid onto the booth. "I've known Cliff for ten years, I expect. I opened the restaurant about that time. Of course, the hardware store is just down the street."

Beebe found the time frame so coincidental, she couldn't help but comment, with a dash of straightforwardness herself. "About ten years ago, we now know my mother was saving a man's life in a car crash."

"Yes, I heard." The woman's folded hands rested motionless on the table.

"Daddy filled you in, then?"

"He confides in me."

Beebe accepted that without craving details. She did not feel any tinge of unfaithfulness on her mother's behalf. In fact, she was glad for Rosemary's closeness to her father for his sake. "I hope he's giving you the full story."

"Since I don't know the full story, I can't confirm or deny. But he is sharing, and he knows I will listen to whatever he has to say."

"Good. But I'm wondering, have you noticed a difference in him these last few days?"

"He's upset. Reasonably so. He talked about you and Abigail and himself, how you've all changed."

"Of course, he's grieving." Beebe watched the other woman.

"You're not?" Her gaze never wavered.

"I accepted my mother's death several months ago when I heard." Beebe considered what might have passed between her father and Rosemary on the subject of timing, since Beebe heard in March, but said nothing until late August. "I'm worried about Daddy, though. I have the benefit of living once before through Mother's escape from her troubles and how Daddy responded. The background I've acquired since gives me knowledge into the way people grieve. I can apply that. Daddy seems headed for a rocky period. I'll need help. It's difficult to counsel your own family. Can I count on you for help? You have the knowledge of the man you've known for ten years. There's value in that. We may need to pool our resources. I want to curb his suffering. Can we work as a team?"

Rosemary waited a moment, then said, "I don't know."

"I don't want you to feel that you're betraying him, but the change I see and the comments he makes have me concerned. Truth is, I may need a confidant, too. He's not explaining himself. No, that's not accurate. When I ask for an explanation, I get anger. Directed at me. I understand. It's because I'm here, not Mother." Beebe watched a look of something very near sympathy or, perhaps, she thought, a specific memory—surrounding Cliff, since he was the subject— pass across Rosemary's face. "What change do you see? What comments do you have? Can you tell me?"

Rosemary's eyes searched Beebe's briefly. She said nothing.

"He's trying to handle some deep-seeded emotion with Mother. There are several specific things. Has he said anything to you about the glider in our backyard?"

Beebe could tell Rosemary thought that a strange statement. Immediately, she shook her head.

"About the empty grave nearly haunting him—my word," she said, "after Mother's casket is moved?"

"Sorry."

"Has he told you he wants her reburial at sunset tomorrow?"

"Yes. I guess I did think that was odd. I asked him, why so late? I assumed some ceremonial rite with reburials. I didn't know."

"What did he say?" Eager for the answer, Beebe leaned forward.

"Just that it will set things right. Does that help?"

"I think it does." Beebe felt she followed the correct path with her "lies at sunset" scenario as an explanation for Cliff's rationale. "I'm still analyzing since these things are such an odd mix, but I believe they're all tied together. I'm stuck on how to help Daddy, or fix it. I can't fix it." She shook her head as if to erase the implication. "Fix is a bad word. I need him to express himself without the anger. Assign words to the anger he's feeling. Maybe it's simple. Simple grief. Maybe I'm over-thinking. I do that. I just need to walk the cemetery and give Daddy's situation the—" She broke off her ramblings midsentence when her mind flashed with understanding.

"What is it?" Rosemary's brows knit.

"I was going to say, give Daddy's situation the time it deserves." New energy emanated from Beebe's voice. "Time. Time is the missing component. I keep going off on tangents with the glider and the reburial at sunset."

"Those aren't important?"

"They are. Very. But the time perspective needs singular attention."

"You've lost me."

Before Beebe explained, she made a quick decision to loop Rosemary into the solution. "We," Beebe began, wagging a finger between the two of them, "we need to remember and consider how thirty years of not knowing what happened to his wife affected Daddy. Of wondering. Of hoping. Of beating himself up for thinking she must be dead, only to revive her spirit in his heart to hope and wonder all over again."

While Beebe spoke, she watched as Rosemary's eyes darkened. Her father's friend seemed to empathize with the intense emotions that must swirl around Cliff. Over the last thirty years, those emotions moved at a slower pace than today, Beebe thought, but never, for a moment, were they quiet. Always at a simmer. Ready to heat. Prepared to ambush with the slightest provocation. Then the blow came. It had not fallen by degrees, but with one swift motion that sent his emotions into a whirlpool to circle him like prey.

Now that she imagined it, she felt the pull of the whirlpool. It took real effort to wrench herself back, and that effort forced out her next words. "All he needs is a handhold, Rosemary. The strength of one *or two* people. To let the dregs of those long, awful years pass." Beebe envisioned the rough waters receding and sensed acceptance rolling in on the foam of the morning current. She sent a knowing gaze across the table to the woman who rubbed her father's back earlier, outside the restaurant. "You love my father. I know you do. Will you be a handhold?"

Rosemary's reaction spoke in advance of her words. She sat taller. She smiled. Her eyes softened. "Yes. I do love your father. And I will be a handhold.

I'll be one for you, too, if you want one."

Beebe waved away any interest in herself. "Just knowing you'll help Daddy helps me." Then surprisingly intuitive Rosemary struck on the very thought going through Beebe's mind.

"And don't think that just because I love your father, I want to somehow replace your mother. I'd like to be friends, yes, but it's been the same thirty years for you. Let me know if I can help."

Rosemary's sentiment dazed Beebe for a moment. In response to her sincere words, she said, "Thank you, Rosemary. I'm sure we can be friends and team our efforts on Daddy's behalf. He's going to need strong support. Certain people in this community will talk and say hurtful things." Mona Gabriel and Mick Nettleman easily slipped to the forefront.

"Every community has them."

"But this is Larkspur, where Daddy and I make our home. We're a united front, he and I, but he's hurting. I don't know how much more he can endure from the neighbors he thought were his friends." Beebe shifted her sights out the window to quiet Town Street. She remembered Cliff's comment when she confronted him about the fundraiser for school supplies. That night, he spoke of friends who pitied him. Rosemary was not that kind of friend. Her commitment to Cliff and Beebe confirmed that.

Still Beebe shivered with her next worried thought. It was a conclusion, really, one that a sixteen-year old missed all those years ago, but the woman with a few trips around the block could perceive. "I think Daddy is afraid of his grief. It terrifies him. That's why he behaves as he does."

Another Emotion Visited

At McKinley Hardware, Scott Cotter directed Beebe to the electrical aisle. There, she found Cliff mechanically placing packaged light bulbs on a shelf, straight out of a shipping carton.

"Daddy, can we talk a minute?"

He gave her a weary smile. "Hi, Beebe."

"Daddy? Can we go back to the dock?"

"What's wrong?" he asked, low-key.

"I want to tell you something."

"Okay." He sighed.

They passed through the dimly lit warehouse. She didn't want Mona or another board member walking up to her father, blithely mentioning the "perception" problem involving Beebe, Abigail, and Crossroads—and by extension, Vincent—and Cliff be unaware.

"Something happened while I was at the newspaper, placing the obituary."

He frowned.

"Mona Gabriel came in. You know she's a member of Crossroads' board?"

"Sure."

"Well, the other day when I was at the center, Mona dropped by for a minute, and Mr. Fyffe was there. My old algebra teacher. We spoke. He was nice. After Mona left, another man, Mick Nettleman, told me he worked with Mother at the hospital. He did not say nice things." Cliff frowned. Beebe understood. "You know him."

"I do."

"He threatened to tell Mona about Mother's past. Clearly, he did because she caught me down at the newspaper and said she needed to inform the board of the situation with Mother at the next meeting."

"She's trying to cause trouble," Cliff said, his statement lacking vigor. "Mona sits on several boards. Vincent calls her a board bouncer. You know, a professional board member around town. That's how she gets the gossip." He seemed completely uninterested in the fact that the gossip concerned him and his family.

"Well, if that's the case," she said, conceding to his opinion, "Vincent will know how much to worry. He knows the makeup of the board. I just wanted you to be aware that Mona may be spreading the story, and you may hear it from someone who comes in the store."

"But you got the obituary placed okay?"

For a moment, Beebe was speechless, confused by his lackluster concern for a serious problem and his focus on a relatively minor issue in the scope of things. "Yes, Daddy, the death notice will run tomorrow, just like you wanted."

"Good," Cliff said. He showed no anger, but seemed almost lethargic.

Another emotion visited, Beebe thought. Since she wondered if her words truly sunk in, she decided she'd leave her acceptance of Yates's father's attendance at the reburial for later. She suggested reheating the vegetable soup.

He gave the requisite, "Sounds great."

* * *

Hours later, when steam rose off the soup, Beebe had to climb the stairs to pry Cliff out from behind his bedroom door. She knocked, and true to his words, he joined her at the table "right away." Dinner conversation was minimal and led by Beebe. She did broach the subject of Yates's father, Arthur Strand, attending the services. Cliff nodded, thoughtful, his mind elsewhere. He declined a second serving of soup, carried his dishes to the kitchen sink, and then went back upstairs.

She was running a wet cloth over the table when he returned, carrying a sheaf of papers.

"I found the life insurance policy on your mother," he said.

So, he's been sorting through documents, Beebe thought.

He followed her to the sink, where she ditched the rag and dried her hands on a terrycloth towel hanging nearby.

"I want to file a claim, but I don't have an accurate death certificate," he said. "The one delivered with the body for burial says Terri Miller."

Beebe hadn't thought about the paperwork surrounding her mother's death being filed and recorded incorrectly. "Surely, we can have it changed. I'll take care of it, Daddy."

"It's not much."

She knew he meant the policy amount. "What will you do with the money?"

"What everyone else does," he said grumpily. "Pay for the funeral."

"You mean it will go to the cemetery?"

"Some. And some will go back to town hall. Town coffers pay for indigent burials. Then there's Hal's time for the marker. There's more than needed. So, the remainder will be used for the next indigent burial."

"Will you use the same grave for the next indigent burial?" She prodded a bit further toward another comment he made the same night he learned about Abigail.

"Don't ask me now what I'm going to do! Your mother hasn't finished ripping open old wounds yet." His snappish words told her he still hurt over the many layers of this muddled situation: the empty grave, his tidy nature, the tarnished blot on his cemetery that equaled a scratch on painted metal, one incapable of being rubbed out with a special compound. "There's always a burial you can't forget," he concluded dully.

Although it appeared Cliff spoke purely for his own benefit, Beebe added a quiet plea. "Try, Daddy."

His eyes widened, alive with an intensity that made her recoil. "You know nothing about how hard I've tried!"

He stomped off and left his resentment for her naiveté behind.

* * *

The day of the funeral, Beebe crossed the grass. Her father stood on the cemetery road that passed the house, speaking with Hal Garrett, who had just driven in. Before she reached them, Hal drove on, out to the equipment building. The morning paper was folded under Cliff's arm. The open grave in the Walker plot was ahead of him on the left. The symbolic glider was behind him on the right.

He heard her approach and turned.

"Is the obituary in the paper?" she asked, coming up to stand beside him.

"Yes. It's very nice. I'm still glad we did it."

She thought, Hmm, still glad? Had he wavered at some point? Rather than broach that subject, she chose another and braced herself for his blustery reaction. "May I say a few words at the service?"

He tipped his chin down to her. "That's a change in tune. Are you sure you want to?"

"Yes, Daddy. Not as a minister. Just as a daughter."

He sent his eyes to scan the acreage of stones. "So, that means you won't pray for your mother at the conclusion?"

"I think a moment of silence would be more appropriate. Please try to understand, I don't think my prayers have gotten through. Not for some time."

He nodded. "It'll work out, I'm sure."

She heard his dismissive tone, but surprised herself when, on tiptoes, she kissed his cheek. "I'm going to Crossroads, then to check on the correction of the death certificate. I'll be back in plenty of time. There's gobs of food in the refrigerator if you get hungry. Invite Hal, so you don't have to eat alone."

* * *

Cliff worked in the block building for an hour or so, dealing with paperwork. Outside, he heard the rumble of an engine float through the open windows. He pushed his chair on casters back to see out the paned glass. Hal and his backhoe marched slowly to Terri Miller's grave. Cliff scooted the chair back to the desk. Shortly, he would hear the engine idle. That meant Hal was out to spread tarps on the ground nearby. Dirt scooped from the unearthed grave would be mounded there.

Cliff's eventual arrival at the site was timed to speak with Hal when he was again out of the backhoe. Hal lowered a long sturdy broom into the open grave. He used it to brush away dirt clinging to the handles of the burial vault. Inside the vault was the casket. Inside the casket lay the remains of Abigail Marie Walker.

It was the other grave, the one in the Walker plot, and Hal's duties there that were on Cliff's mind. He wanted to intercede before Hal wasted his time placing the short scaffolding-like framework around the open grave up near the house. The scaffolding aided in the lowering of the vault.

"I want to use the leather straps for Abigail, not the scaffolding. Can you work it out?" Even to himself, his words sounded abrupt.

Many times over the years, Cliff picked up the first ledger for Larkspur Cemetery. Joseph Jenkins, the cemetery's original caretaker, approached his tallying of accounts more like a diary than a financial recordkeeping. On this day, Cliff was glad for Jenkins' wordy summaries. Cliff wanted to be a personal part of his wife's burial. The idea gnawed at him for days now. The ancient leather straps would substitute for the pallbearer ritual that time never forgot.

"Really?" The tenor of Hal's voice shot the one-word question up and, when meshed with his facial expression, produced a result that was thoughtfully agreeable.

Cliff nodded.

"Well, an old-fashioned service. A nice touch, Cliff. But we'll need at least four strong men."

"We've got them. Me. Vincent Bostick. A young man Abigail knew, Yates Strand. And his father, who Yates says wants to come."

A flash in Hal's eyes told Cliff he wanted to know the story of Abigail Walker and the Strands. Too polite to ask, Hal said instead, "If the father doesn't make it, I can step in. Beebe can ease off the vault handler's lever until the straps take the weight. It's a lot of weight. The lever must be moved correctly. So let's hope the fourth man shows."

"It'll work out, I'm sure." Those were the same words he said to Beebe earlier. If he maintained positive thoughts, maybe they'd take hold and prop him up, and he'd get through this awful day.

"By the way," Hal said, "the obituary was nicely written. Beebe's hand?"

Cliff swallowed. His daughter's sentiment for her mother touched him deeply each time he thought of or read the obituary. "She did a good job." Despite the complimentary nature of the response he managed, Cliff turned and walked off so Hal wouldn't see his face crumple. Sunset was hours away, and already, everything was coming down on him.

He pointed himself in the direction of a walking path. He met up with the path at a century's-old cypress and stepped behind it. Screened from Hal, he fished a red bandana handkerchief from his back pocket and dried his eyes. Roiling emotions governed his life since he learned about Abigail's death, but in this moment, those emotions were merely packaging.

A hot tear streamed his cheek. He spoke aloud all that really mattered. "Thank God, I know where you are, Abigail. I know where you are, and I can keep you with me, always."

Thirty years was a long wait. But the wait was over. He would care for Abigail's grave until the last breath left his body.

* * *

Vincent looked up when Beebe stuck her head around the doorframe of his office. He offered her a seat, then listened quietly while she retold her story of running into Mona Gabriel at the newspaper building. When she finished, Vincent added tangential information that shed a new and different light on the overall situation.

"Mona's husband's a doctor," he said. "Remember Sunday when you asked about a physician on retainer for situations like Razzell's, and I said that presented a small problem? Well, the physician the board has in mind is Dr. Hershel Gabriel. His practice is geriatrics."

Beebe's eyes widened. "Sunday, you called him Dr. Gabe, short for Gabriel. I didn't put it together with Mona."

Vincent pushed away the papers stationed in front of him on the table. "Yeah, well, we say retainer, but no money changes hands. It's an agreement to become involved with some degree of priority given to our seniors. If Mosie's condition hadn't cleared itself, we had no one to call. We can't force a senior to seek medical help, go to the hospital in an ambulance. Your mother, for instance. She told me right out, don't call for medical aid; she wouldn't participate. And in her case, the treatment wouldn't have changed the outcome, just probably made her more comfortable. I can't even be sure of that. People decide how they want their lives to end when the time comes. I'm not interested in forcing my opinions on them. I hope you don't either."

"I will do my best to encourage attention if it can make a difference, if clearly there's hope."

"I agree. There has to be hope."

"That hope comes from medical advice," Beebe said, sitting back in the chair. "Currently, we're not set up—with just you and me, and a rookie nurse, if we count Yates—to deal with true life-threatening situations. So many things can influence seniors. They could be the newly infirm, or those heading that direction through lack of intervention, or those having lost companionship—there's that word again—or those with no family, or family members who don't care. All these things can bring a senior into the center's circle of light. On the flip side, as people grow older, family and friends die. Being the last one alive in your group is a lonely prospect. It wears on people quickly."

"That speech should spur Crossroads' active members into action to work to complete the inventory of seniors in this community. The program's already been approved, and what a benefit to have a general idea of the breadth of population that might tap our services."

"We're getting a little far afield from the *perception* situation." Beebe emphasized Mona's word choice, using it to clarify.

"Right, and I'd prefer to call it the Moaning Mona situation. The problem is not you or perception; it's her. I'd like to get an opinion from the board's attorney. You haven't met Ron Smith yet. Mona shouldn't go around speaking publicly as if she's speaking for the board."

"She didn't. She was clear. She wants to raise the matter at the next board meeting."

"Well, we'll head it off. Ron should be made aware. Gabby—"

"Gabby?"

"Yeah. Another Mona nickname used by many, just not to her face."

"Gabby and Dr. Gabe," Beebe said with a giggle.

"Gabby doesn't want it to look to the board members that her committee's choice was a poor one. She doesn't want the spray-back to get on her."

"Then why bring it up?"

"Honestly, she can't help herself. She thinks this is juicy, and she wants to be in the middle of things. Always. She'll play both sides of the street, mark my words. A few wanted to wait to interview you. Ron and Mona followed my recommendation. Events from thirty years ago, when you were a child, are not germane. We can turn this around."

"Mother's obituary will fuel the flames under this, don't you think?"

"You knew it would. Cliff knew it." He shrugged. "Nothing new. You were upfront. That plays in our favor."

"Well, I was upfront accidentally. Daddy wanted it out in the open. He wanted the community to know the end of that ancient story. He wanted to follow standard procedure. This is what people do when there's a death."

"Timing. Coincidence. It's just as much my fault as anyone's."

"Why is it your fault?"

"I asked you to come back because your mother died. Then I offered you the job to keep you here. I struck the match."

Beebe patted Vincent's hand. "Mother struck the match. None of this can be laid at your feet. It's just like Daddy said: For a while, the obituary in the paper will stir those in the community who remember. A week, maybe, then people forget. Daddy and I are not going to hide. So let's you and I bring it up with the board. I'm willing to let them vote again on my suitability for the work. My contract can begin after Monday's meeting. Everyone can have their say, ask me questions, whatever."

"I'd like Ron's opinion first. He may agree, but he's level-headed. I think he can paint a clear picture of the situation Mona is tainting for the members, and almost in words of praise for her."

"That, I'd like to see."

"Oh, you will. If anyone can turn a phrase, it's Ron Smith."

"Hmm. I feel better."

"This little hiccup will pass. Be ready with your thoughts on the programming. I want you to dazzle the board with your insight and creativity."

"A *Razzell* dazzle." She winked.

"Something like that."

"That reminds me. What about confidentiality matters and privacy issues? Rev. Razzell, for instance. I don't think he'd want the board to know the level of care or his medical history without his consent."

"I agree. I assumed that, but didn't stress it to the board. Another matter for Ron. And you get credit for the thought. We need a policy in writing. More will evolve as time goes on and we get experience under our belts."

"Oh, please, I don't wear a belt these days." She patted her belly.

Vincent was happy to have her back. She was the best choice, and he would do whatever was necessary to smooth out the road before her, one that currently included a hairpin turn for her mother's funeral. Yeah, he worried, a hairpin turn at dusk. Those can be dangerous. He would stick close, very close for the next few days.

Sunset

Beebe stepped out onto Battlefield without saying a word to Vincent about her next task. At some point, he might become involved with the death certificate issue. She didn't know.

She felt the oddest sensation on her walk to the Holmes Building, where the health department was housed. She felt, well, discombobulated was how she'd describe it. A crazy word for the crazy feeling. She shook her shoulders. She walked faster. She couldn't outrun it. The feeling persisted. She was dogged by her mother's death revisiting her, tension with her father, reasons for denial, numbness, fear, and anger, perhaps not quite depression. Those emotions were the full menu of grief's first two stages before recovery kicked in.

At the door to the Holmes Building, she rolled her neck without relief, then pulled the door open. She read the lobby registry, then shuffled into an elevator to the second floor.

She wondered if it was considered poor manners to discuss the life insurance before the funeral. Maybe some kind of social blunder. She guessed not. Those gears needed to turn, in most cases, to pay the funeral home, medical bills, and the deceased's debts. In reality, the life insurance policy was a side matter. She wouldn't mention it. A death certificate simply should be correct. The closest the certificate might get to correct is one that documented both names: Abigail Marie Tanner Walker, and Terri Miller, scribed as an "also known as." That may be the only way to satisfy the powers that be.

Earlier in the morning, she saw the insurance policy lying on Cliff's dresser when she went in with clean shirts. His idea for use of the money was laudable. When it came time in the future to put the funds to good use, he would look back, she hoped, and see a positive track running from Mother's life. A benefit paid forward.

The door to the health department in the old building stood wide. She entered and was immediately noticed by one of the clerks behind the counter. When the clerk rose, Beebe recognized her from high school. She was Heidi Wells back then. Beebe couldn't say she and Heidi were close friends. Beebe had no real close friends until Vincent in high school. It was alphabetical order that placed Heidi and Beebe in close proximity. Always Walker, then Wells for those teachers who followed the ABCs for their seating chart.

"Heidi!" Beebe said.

"Beebe!" the other woman cheered, rushing over. Her face slackened when she reached out to Beebe's forearms resting on the old scarred wooden countertop. "I'm so sorry about your mother. I just saw it in the paper. How sad."

"Thank you. Of course, you remember what happened back in high school."

"The whole situation was a shame. Just terrible. Well, now it's over," she said, always a silver-lining kind of person. "You're dealing with it. And your father. How's he doing?"

"As you said, we're dealing with it." Beebe pointed to the nametag pinned to Heidi's striped cotton shirt. "Looks like you married Bud Cranston. I can see you two together."

"Better be able to see it." With a smile, she leaned forward. "We've got five kids."

"Five!"

"And two dogs. The kids would hate it that I didn't include Bossy and Spike as members of the family."

"Sounds perfect."

"It is. So, are you back in Larkspur because of your mother?"

"Yes, and no. I'm back because I took a job over at Crossroads."

"Working with Vincent. That'll be nice."

"So far, so good. I'm still getting started. But, back to Mother."

Heidi's eyes widened inquisitively.

"I have a bit of a story to tell and, hopefully, you can give me advice."

"I'll try."

Just then, a man appeared at Beebe's elbow.

Heidi turned. "Alice, can you help this gentlemen? Come around, Beebe. We'll use this office over here." She gestured Beebe toward the pass-through at the end of the counter.

Inside the cramped office with the door closed, Heidi went behind the desk. Beebe slid onto the padded metal chair that faced her.

"Daddy and I had no further connection with Mother after she left," Beebe said, "but when she got sick, and it was apparent she would not recover, she came back to Larkspur. She learned that Crossroads was a hospice, and she showed up on Vincent's doorstep one evening. Vincent never met my mother, and I'm sure her appearance had changed. She was homeless, as I understand, and now ill." Beebe watched and appreciated Heidi's empathetic expression. "She told Vincent her name was Terri Miller."

"Terri Miller!" Heidi jerked her shoulders straight.

"You know that name?"

"There was a young man in here, maybe ten days ago, asking for records for that name."

Beebe nodded. "Yates Strand. I met him. He can corroborate that Mother used the name Terri Miller for at least ten years. Perhaps the entire time she was gone, I don't know. Her last request to Vincent was that Terri Miller be the name that carried through to her grave. Before she died, she did tell him who she was, and she begged him to keep her secret. She didn't want Daddy or me to know. It's been hard. Vincent said he didn't think she wanted to intrude, but she obviously wanted to be back home and be buried here. Vincent tried to keep her secret, but he couldn't."

"What an awful position for Vincent! With you, your father, and Crossroads." Heidi's hands were in motion. "And your father's position. Oh my stars. To find his wife buried in the cemetery. Of course, this has been hard."

"Now, you see, Daddy knows, and he wants things made right. He wants a death certificate with her true name on it. How do I get the certificate corrected?" Beebe reached down to her purse sitting on the floor and pulled out the folded certificate by an exposed corner.

"The coroner signed the death certificate," Heidi said, scanning it. "He must be notified, and he must issue the replacement if one is to be issued. He's going to ask questions. He's a stickler for accuracy, protocol, rules."

That sounded ominous, Beebe thought, but stoked her resolve. "Well, okay. I'll take him on. What do I do? Should I meet with him? Is there a form of some kind?"

"You should write out the background. You can do it now if you want," she said, her palms touching the desktop, "or bring it back in. I'll attach it to a copy of the certificate and take it to him."

"Should I take it? Can you make an appointment for me? I just don't want this to sit around on his desk."

"I doubt it will. He's going to ask questions."

Beebe smiled at the repeated phrasing. That was Heidi. She remembered Heidi's mumbled comments made from the school desk behind Beebe's. "What about some kind of affidavit from Vincent and Yates to go with my statement?" Beebe thought Ron Smith could be encouraged to help.

"Let's keep it simple at first. Let Dr. Jeffers take the lead."

"Dr. Jeffers? I don't know that name."

"Comes from over in Butler. He resides here now. But Larkspur and Butler are still Stryker County."

Beebe nodded her understanding of public office requirements. "Well, I'd like my statement to be neat, so I'll print something up and come back."

The women rose, and Heidi came around the desk. "You have my sympathies." She patted Beebe's arm and offered a wan smile.

The gestures were two points against Mona Gabriel's assertion that the Walkers would present a perception problem in an unforgiving community.

* * *

Cliff was filling a glass with water at the kitchen sink when he heard the front door open and close. Beebe called out.

The two Walkers sat at the kitchen table while Beebe explained everything she learned at the health department. She asked him for patience. Her intention was either an appeasing one or a convincing one when she said, "Dr. Jeffers is fond of rules. In his job, he has to be."

Cliff got it. He was also fond of rules. In the cemetery business, he had to be. And, really, how far was the coroner's business from the cemetery business?

Beebe went straight upstairs to her laptop to write the statement for Dr. Jeffers. The next time father and daughter saw each other, they were dressed for Abigail Walker's second funeral.

A two-car convoy pulled onto the cemetery road alongside the house a few minutes after eight. Vincent got out of the lead car. Yates Strand and a man Cliff guessed to be forty-five or forty-six opened doors to a black sedan.

Cliff and Beebe met Arthur Strand, standing in the grass of their front yard. The man limped, not badly, but noticeably. Beebe invited everyone inside. Cliff watched Vincent slip away, back to his car, where he retrieved a bouquet of flowers. He would spend a few minutes with his beloved Carolyn.

While Beebe served everyone either coffee or lemonade and laid the dining room table with a selection of sweets from the bakery, Cliff and Arthur stood in the living room, talking.

"I'm glad you came," Cliff said to the elder Strand. Arthur's nodding head stopped, surprised when Cliff corrected himself. "No. I'm glad you *wanted* to come."

"Yates says he's told you about Terri's—" Arthur cut off with an instant look of regret over the perceived fumble with the name.

"In this house, either name is accepted without reservation," Cliff said with genuine sincerity.

"Well, anyway, you know how we Strands appreciated and loved Terri Miller. She was integral to our lives for so many years. When my Naomi got so sick, we couldn't have survived as well as we did without Terri." He cocked his head up to Cliff, wearing a near frown. "I know this must seem very strange to you."

"At first, yes. But I'd rather know the story than spend the rest of my life wondering. That's what the last thirty years were. Wondering."

Arthur's bobbing head dropped, his chin to his chest. "Yes," he said. He understood.

"If only she'd reached out to me when the addiction took hold. If I'd forced the issue. In the back of my mind, I knew. If only she'd gone to someone for help here in Larkspur if she couldn't come to me. I just wish that had happened. Knowing that would somehow soothe my heart more than I could say." Cliff found he could easily share his deepest emotions with this man who knew his wife. "But, then look at her influence on your life, her nursing skills put to work for your wife's care."

Arthur sipped his lemonade. "It's one of those things. We didn't deserve to have her if it meant you and Beebe lived without. But it wouldn't be truthful if I said Yates and I could have endured my wife's illness on our own. Terri was a blessing during those horrible, horrible days."

Cliff did not know what it was like to care for a loved one from illness to death. Yates did. Arthur did. Just then, Vincent appeared in the dining room. Cliff thought of Carolyn. Cliff did all he could for Vincent and Carolyn through her decline, but he didn't bear the true weight there. It was painful enough for him, but it was not a husband's unbearable suffering for the helplessness and hopelessness felt deep in his soul.

After a moment, Cliff said, "Abigail conquered her addiction. She got help somewhere. I just wish the help started here."

"Completely understood."

Vincent took on the duties of lookout. He informed Cliff when the vault handler crept toward the house, a burial vault suspended from a crane-like arm preceding the handler.

The fivesome quietly and reverently filed outside, their pace a match for the vault handler's trudge. They formed a straight line to receive Abigail Marie Tanner Walker. No one spoke. They watched, then participated in the grimly odd procession. When Hal Garrett drove the handler past them, Cliff and Beebe broke ranks. Yates and Arthur formed the next row. Vincent anchored the rear.

Before Vincent and the Strands arrived by car, Hal positioned a solid, one-piece wooden framework around the grave cut in the Walker plot. While the soon-to-be graveside party was gathered in the living room, Cliff explained the ritual of the long leather straps. He compared the duty of the four men to pallbearers. Cliff, working across from Vincent, and Yates across from his father, would very slowly and cautiously lower the vault of the woman with two names into the grave. No need to worry. The straps would move smoothly over the wooden framework's edge.

Once Cliff completed the explanation and saw everyone understood and approved, Beebe spoke. She stood beside him. "It's our job to keep the old ways in good repair," she said.

Her repetition of his words from a day long past stunned him into speechlessness, a condition that lasted until after the service concluded.

From the controls inside the handler, Hal positioned the vault over the grave to a place several inches below the ground line. The men held the two leather straps taut while Hal lowered the vault by increments until the straps and the men took the weight. He jumped down and expertly released the chains attached to the vault handles. "Slowly, gentlemen," Hal said before he climbed into the idling vehicle and backed away what would be an intrusion on the ceremony.

Cliff caught the eye of the other three men. With darkness waiting in the wings, the ground received Abigail Walker.

The weight was more than Cliff could ever have anticipated. His heels dug into the grass, his knees bent. His shoulders ached down into his back. The width of one hand after another, red and cramping, the ungodly job continued.

He stared into the grave. He could do nothing but stare into the grave. Soon strain absorbed every joint. He gritted his teeth. His neck muscles tensed until he thought he could not breathe. Then all that had been the pain of burying his wife reached bottom. The leather strap went slack.

When they worked the straps free and Hal retrieved them, Beebe moved to the head of the grave. Cliff watched, quite aware she carried no Bible, but the story she told got its beginnings from the Great Book.

"I thought and thought what I would say at this moment with Mother's family standing here." She raised her hands to include the men on both sides of the grave, then interlaced her fingers in front of her. "No matter what words I began to organize, a memory of a small boy, a six-year old towhead named Jonah Young, pushed every grouping of words aside and looked up at me.

"When I left my last church, Trydestone, I accepted the position of grief counselor for Swanson Funeral Home. I was inside the carriage house behind Swanson's on a Monday morning, oh," she thought, "about three weeks later, getting the room ready for the morning's session. From behind me, I heard Jonah's voice call my name. I asked my parishioners to call me Pastor Beebe, so that's what rung out in triplicate, as Jonah liked to do. I turned around to find him racing across the room. His mother, Lynn, followed in close pursuit. Jonah didn't disappoint. He did what he did every time he stood in my company. He grabbed my hand and swung it. Every time, that connection captivated my attention."

Cliff watched his daughter's right hand drop and swing at her side. She remained lost inside herself for a second before continuing.

"After my last sermon at Trydestone, Lynn explained that Jonah begged her to bring him to see me with every Sunday that followed. She told him he had to wait till his spring break from school. So that Monday, he was dressed and ready, and Lynn brought him over." Her gaze scanned the circle of faces. "Jonah was a part of my life at Trydestone from my initial Sunday. I remember retreating to my office to pray and ready myself to meet my congregation for the first time from the pulpit. When I opened my office door, there stood Jonah. His white shirt was tucked into navy pants, his shoes were shined, and his face glowed. It was so clean."

She smiled down at the memory, and Cliff imagined the multitudes of people, young and old, that his ordained daughter encountered and touched.

"I hadn't yet matched up children with parents," she went on, "so he took my hand, and together we walked the side corridor to the pastor's door that led straight in to the front of the auditorium. Jonah spotted his parents in one of the front pews and off he skipped. The next Sunday, and every Sunday after, the same thing happened. Jonah stood outside my door. He raised his hand. He wanted to walk me into services again. Why not? In that moment, I thought: Let the children lead them. I told him that morning while we strolled along the corridor that there was a story in the Bible about another Jonah. Of course, he wanted to hear the story right then, but I asked him to wait. The next Sunday, the sermon was about one of the Bible's most recognizable stories: Jonah and the whale. The story begins with God's command that Jonah preach repentance to the wicked Ninevites. God's Jonah found this unbearable, so instead, he ran away from the Lord."

In the dim of the evening with a sprinkling of fireflies joining the gathering, Cliff watched Beebe's eyes glaze.

"Partway through Jonah's tale, an odd thing happened. I sensed I would follow suit. After that sermon, every time Jonah dropped my hand and skipped away, I felt the need to escape from Trydestone. In the Bible story, God sent a whale to save Jonah. I wonder if God didn't send Jonah Young to save me, or at least to prepare me for this day. I savored Jonah's dimpled grin that first day of spring break and his choking hug 'round my neck. It upset me for weeks to realize I hadn't given Jonah a proper goodbye, a moment just between the two of us. Something seemed unfinished in his life; so much so that he begged his mother to come find me. We meet people. We touch their lives. Some connections become special, meant to grow and blossom. Why does it happen? How do we find them? Who brings us together? The answer to those questions are not as important as realizing that those special people are to be cherished."

Beebe reached out a hand to Cliff, then to Vincent. They took hers before grasping hands with Yates and Arthur Strand, who stretched arms across the recently dug grave to complete the circle.

"Today, I stand here at Mother's grave with those people who cherished her, and she cherished them. *This* is a proper goodbye."

As if Arthur Strand had some innate sense that Cliff Walker wanted a graveside service that included a prayer, he converted all that Beebe said to that prayer with one word.

Head bowed, eyes closed, he said, "Amen."

The word was repeated in unison by Yates and Vincent, and finally Cliff. He squeezed his daughter's hand as he said it.

From nowhere, Hal stepped up with two long-stemmed roses. He handed one to Cliff and one to Beebe. He must have kept them all this time beside him on the vault trailer's seat.

When Beebe kissed the scarlet bloom and handed it to Cliff, he passed the one he held to Yates. Taking Beebe's, Cliff kissed it and let it fall into his wife's grave. Yates and Arthur Strand followed suit. The second rose fell on top of the first.

Cliff raised his head to witness the stunning vista across the road. The sun ducked down behind a border of trees. The full foliage glowed a burnt orange, outlined with the slightest trimming of crimson.

"It's beautiful, Daddy," Beebe said, observing the same scene.

"Your words were beautiful, too. Perfect. Thoughtful." Beebe stepped forward for a hug. With his mouth close to her ear, he said, "I do wish I heard you preach, just once."

"Daddy, you just did," Beebe said, tightening her embrace.

Wigged Out

The morning after the funeral, Yates left Barleycorn to bark at Rev. Razzell's front door. Yates couldn't raise him by knocking, so he tried looking through the windows. He found no success until he discovered the back door unlocked. He let himself in, then Barleycorn. The rooms he walked through looked much the same as the previous day, but Razzell occupied none of them.

The two men, fifty years apart in age, decided on a schedule of morning visits. For two days, all went well.

Yates raced directly to Razzell's bedroom at the end of the hall. From several steps away, he saw layers of clothing and papers littering the floor.

"Not again," he prayed, but the undeniable signs were there. He bit his lip and slowed his pace. When he reached the doorway, he stopped and looked inside. Razzell, wearing nothing but a brown sock on his left foot, sat as limp as a ragdoll in the chair across the room. His white hair looked tousled from sleep, but the bed was still made and covered with clothes. Most of the dresser drawers hung open and were empty. It appeared to Yates that Razzell flung armfuls of clothing up in the air. In Razzell's state at the time, he must have enjoyed watching the clothes rain down. Somehow, Yates could tell by the room's condition that Razzell had not been in a state of fury, rather, he, in effect, wigged out.

In as normal a tone as Yates could muster, he spoke to Razzell. "Hey, Mosie," he said, carefully making his way to the man. He grabbed Razzell's robe off the bed, shaking off a half-unfolded dress shirt. "What're you doing? Barleycorn's here."

Razzell blinked his empty stare away. His eyes raised to Yates.

"Here, let's get this around you." Yates used the robe more like a blanket.

He covered Razzell's genitals and legs, then tucked the robe into the cushioned chair to insure it stayed in place.

A full three seconds passed. Yates watched realization dawn on Razzell's face. The minister nearly cried. "I did it again, didn't I?" He scanned the trashed room, took in his state of undress, and lifted sad eyes to Yates. "I never remember taking my clothes off." Razzell understood he participated in a repeat performance.

Yates squatted down. That was an invitation for the big dog to come over. "Barleycorn's going to stay with you while I go out and get you some breakfast. Just stay in the chair. Don't get up until I get back." He tipped his head to find Razzell's eyes. He thought shame caused the older man to withdraw his gaze. "Okay?" Yates said, smiling.

Razzell nodded briskly, then glanced away. Barleycorn scooted in to take Yates's place when he rose and stepped back. The dog lay his nose on Razzell's robe-covered knee. For that, he was rewarded. Razzell scratched his head.

Out in the kitchen, Yates made toast and tea and called Vincent at Crossroads. Their conversation was short. True to his word, Vincent's call to Dr. Hershel Gabriel produced the tall, distinguished physician standing on Razzell's doorstep within forty-five minutes.

Gabriel placed his medical bag on the nightstand. He examined Razzell, who wore pajamas now and sat propped against pillows and the headboard. The room was tidier. Doctor and patient talked. Yates looked up from folding clothes at the foot of the bed when Gabriel asked about Razzell's medications. He studied the older man for a handful of seconds. Gabriel completed the standard examination. He returned his stethoscope to his bag, then broke the tongue depressor used for Razzell's throat exam. He removed his Latex gloves and quite nimbly captured the depressor's two halves within the inside-out ball of Latex, all while he reassured his patient.

"We're going to get you better, Mosie. Just leave it to me. And to your buddy Yates, here. And Barleycorn." Gabriel reached out to pet the dog, who kept a close watch on the proceedings. "We're your medical team."

"I'll show you out, Dr. Gabriel," Yates said. But when the men were out in the hall, Yates motioned the doctor into Razzell's bathroom. "Mosie wasn't exactly truthful about his medications. I saw all this when I brought him in to brush his teeth." Yates spoke quietly and opened the medicine cabinet door. A dozen orange pharmacy jars lined the shelves. "Look, different doctors, different pharmacies, conflicting side effects." He picked up bottles and set them down.

"Sleeping pills. Antidepressants. Some good stuff, yes, vitamins and supplements. But if he's taking all this…" Yates's question trailed off.

The nurse-to-be saw the alarm in the doctor's face as he read the labels Yates faced forward.

"For some reason, he rips off his clothes and trashes the place," Yates added in frustrated summary.

"I can't explain that, specifically. In medical terms, though, his mind tries to cope with all the mixed meds. It can function for a while, then it—well, short-circuits—is the best description. We need to get him off this medication, slowly. He'll go through withdrawal."

"At his age, what will that do? Will it be difficult?"

"It's difficult at any age. He'll probably think he's got the flu. Let him." Gabriel's manner of speech assigned Yates the job of carrying out his orders. "Push rest, fluids, small meals, soup."

"I can move in here and monitor him constantly." Yates felt his heartbeat quicken as he absorbed the implied urgency and the importance of his role.

"Who have you got if you need help?"

"Well, the McMitchells, Vincent, and Vincent's new assistant, Beebe Walker." Yates was hesitant to suggest Beebe. Razzell didn't always show a good reaction to her, but if Yates needed errands run on Razzell's behalf, other background duties undertaken, or advice issued, Beebe would certainly step up if asked.

"That sounds fine. I wouldn't suggest strangers be inside the house. On top of everything, we don't want him agitated." He paused. "Beebe Walker, huh? My wife Mona is a member of Crossroads' board, you know. She mentioned Beebe."

Yates bit his lip. Given the agitation comment, then specifically calling Beebe out made Yates wonder what passed between husband and wife. Mona witnessing Razzell's reactions to Beebe couldn't possibly be the issue because she'd never been present. Yates decided to glaze over the doctor's aside. "Don't worry. I'll sleep in the chair in his room. Barleycorn will alert me if Mosie makes a move in the night."

"Given the situation, I want to get a physician on the phone from mental health to give me a course of action."

"Mental health? He's not crazy. It's the meds."

Gabriel sent him a look that said, "Think about it, Yates."

"Of course, that makes sense. The meds have made his mind sick."

"The reduction of the meds must be strictly choreographed. I'll get you the dosages recommended. Don't let him get a hold of these bottles." Gabriel wagged a finger at the cabinet. "Hmm. I wonder about caffeine and sugar. There's no way to know his daily consumption. Best to let the mental health physician decide on that as well. When he's drug-free, I'll take the pills for proper disposal. We don't flush them anymore."

"I know." As a nursing student, he read article after article about how flushed medication tainted local water supplies. Proper disposal, these days, meant burning the medications at extremely high temperatures in a controlled environment and by law enforcement agencies.

Yates watched Gabriel make notes of the medication names and their strengths. One by one, Yates set pill bottles back in the medicine cabinet. Ninety minutes later, a uniform-clad worker from Gabriel's office showed up at the door with a timeline and a pill cutter. The timeline covered five days for a slow, steady reduction.

Yates called Vincent in order to get some food in the house. "Bring Barleycorn's kibble and bowls. Bring my clothes. What the hell, bring everything. I have so little. I might as well move out of Crossroads."

* * *

Vincent was bent over the bed in Yates's room. He shoved the young man's shaving kit into the bottom of his backpack. A folded-over pair of jeans went in next. He threw underwear in, then squeezed two T-shirts on top. He looked around for anything he missed.

Beebe appeared in the doorway. "Hey, what are you doing in here?" In the next instant, she and her worried frown stepped into the room. "What's going on?"

"Mosie had a real bad spell. Yates found him and called. I got Dr. Gabriel over there. Evidently, Mosie's been self-medicating," Vincent said of Rev. Razzell.

"What?"

"Yates found pills in his bathroom. With his nursing knowledge, he was concerned. Dr. Gabe says Yates was right with his diagnosis. Mosie takes too much of the bad combination and makes himself dopy."

"So?" She pointed to the backpack Vincent zipped closed.

He hung the pack on his shoulder. Beebe followed him through the center to the kitchen for Barleycorn's possessions. Along the way, he explained, "Yates is going to move in. Dr. Gabe has a plan to get Mosie off the medication. The withdrawal won't be fun. Yates is willing to take that on and follow doctor's orders to the letter."

"I want to help. This is my program to implement."

To Beebe's firm statement, Vincent smiled and handed her Barleycorn's water dish.

"I want to do more than this." Beebe grinned. She dumped the remainder of the dog's morning drink into the sink and shook off water droplets. Being a good sport, she carried the stacked dog bowls in one hand and a half-full sack of kibble in the other.

"You'll oversee and document. Dr. Gabe approved Yates as primary because Mosie seems close to him. The McMitchells and I are backup if Yates needs assistance to get him through. The estimate is five days."

"I'm proud of Yates for wanting to take on a project of this proportion."

Vincent knew Beebe would not be proud of him if he didn't share Yates's decision to keep Beebe at arm's length of Razzell and that the reasoning for that was derived from Dr. Gabe's agitation comment. "You'll oversee and document," Vincent said, slowing his words to match his pace through the community room, "because Yates said Dr. Gabe mentioned to him that he and Mona had a conversation about you at some point."

Beebe's mouth flew open.

"Dr. Gabe was cryptic, but I thought Yates should know the position Mona's taking, which, although the good doctor didn't elaborate, is what Gabby must have *gabbed*."

"So, Dr. Gabe is an enemy, too."

"I don't know about that."

"Do you think he used Yates as a backdoor effort to get to you?"

"I don't know that either."

"This may interfere with getting Dr. Gabe to act as the center's medical advisor?"

"Slow down, Beebe. I'm not going to speculate any further than to relate Yates's decision about you and Mosie, which was made for Mosie's benefit. You know that. Yates would never hurt your feelings purposefully. But I will go out on a limb and confirm that Mona's the interferer here. And then, yes, I'll scoot out a little bit further and say I know Dr. Gabe can think for himself." Vincent grabbed Beebe's elbow and steered her toward the front door. "Now, come on. Let's go. Yates is waiting."

He flipped the reversible message sign to the CLOSED side, let a solemn Beebe out, and then, from the stoop, tested the lock.

Beebe led him to her car parked at the curb. Quickly, Vincent loaded the backpack on the floorboard behind the front seat. When he reached for the dog bowl, Beebe wouldn't release it. His eyes met hers.

"Prepare yourself, Vincent. In addition to Dr. Gabe's cryptic assessment, I came over here to tell you something."

"What?" he said warily.

"Daddy came to me before the funeral. He wants the name on the death certificate corrected. I made that request of the county coroner. I provided background information. Which means I had to mention you and Crossroads and Mother's statements to you."

"I see." He thought the situation a messy one to clean up. He handled the bowl now, and placed it on the back seat. The kibble went in next.

"I was clear that Mother used the name, Terri Miller, for at least ten years. She was insistent it go on the death certificate."

Vincent stepped back, and Beebe closed the door. "Don't worry. It'll be fine. That's exactly what happened."

"We've got your story, and Yates can corroborate. Arthur, if we need him." She walked around the rear bumper to the driver's door.

"It's a simple case of putting both names on the certificate." He sent his words over the top of the red car.

"That's what I think."

"Abigail Walker, A.K.A. Terri Miller."

At Rev. Mosie Razzell's house, Beebe parked. Items from the back seat were unloaded. The front door stood wide open so they walked straight into the house. Yates must have heard their footsteps because he was out of the chair in Razzell's room and coming around the foot of the bed, heading their way, when Vincent stepped into the bedroom. The seventy-eight-year old man lay under a sheet, his eyes half-closed.

Before speaking to Vincent and Beebe, Yates stopped to assist Razzell in raising his head. A glass of water sat within easy reach on the nightstand. With Yates's urging, the patient took three sips from the straw. Vincent thought Razzell seemed only semiconscious if he could interpret the faraway look in his eyes and the lethargy of his reactions.

The appearance of Barleycorn, who wandered around the footboard, sparked Razzell's attention. The dog came to Beebe and whined. His tail wagged. She held his dog food bag.

Over on the bed, Razzell pushed the water glass away, spilling some. His eyes were wild with fear. White stubble covered his jowls and chin. He fought the bedclothes. His voice trembled. He spoke directly to Beebe. "It can't be. Why are you here? Why are you doing this to me? Abi—" He bit off the rest.

After a split-second delay, Beebe took a step. "Rev. Razzell, it's me. Beebe Walker."

Razzell reared back, still frightened, clutching the sheet. "No. No. Barleycorn. Where's Barleycorn?"

Yates, a little flustered, moved to usher Beebe from the room in order to calm his patient. Belatedly, Vincent realized he and Beebe should have remembered that she needed to keep her distance. This was just the kind of agitation it was better for Razzell to avoid.

"She's taking his food," Razzell exclaimed.

Vincent read the silent exchange between Yates and Beebe. Yates gave her a "We need to play his game" look and took the bag out of her hand. Then Yates whispered, "I'll be out in a minute. We can talk."

Vincent waited with Beebe in the living room. He turned around when Yates came in.

"Did he start to call me Abigail?" Beebe asked the young man.

"He wigged out. That makes him confused. The meds have caused his mind to short-circuit. I just gave him the first dose from Dr. Anthony's instructions. He's the physician Dr. Gabe contacted at mental health. Mosie will sleep some now. Barleycorn's with him."

"If the medication is the problem, why give him more? That can't be right," Vincent argued.

Yates repeated what he heard from Gabriel on the subject. Vincent translated that to mean Razzell couldn't quit cold turkey. "Stay in touch. Call if you need anything. I may just stop by periodically. Can I let myself in?"

"Sure. Five days from now, I hope Mosie's himself." Yates shrugged. "Of course, I don't know what that looks like."

"I wonder if something happened that pushed him to escalate his medication." Vincent scratched his jawline. "We need to get to the bottom of that. He didn't just start popping pills for no reason. Just looking at his eyes, I can tell he's worse than the last time." Then he grinned at Yates. "Wigged out. Is that a medical term you learned in college?"

Tormented Days

From Cliff's position at the rear of McKinley's main aisle, he stood with his back to the double doors, ready to push through into the warehouse and drag two large, but empty cartons with him. He had a view of Scott Cotter, waving his arms wildly. He wanted Cliff's attention. Cliff lifted his chin, and Scott held up the telephone receiver at the customer service desk. Cliff pushed the two cartons to one side and went up front to take the call.

The receiver he picked up lay on the waist-high desktop. Scott stepped away. Cliff answered with his full name and, "How can I help you?"

"This is Allen Barker."

Allen Barker was one of McKinley's customers over in Newton. His tone told Cliff something was wrong. Automatically, Cliff picked up an ink pen laying on the counter next to a box of 500-count trimming nails.

"I just got around to looking at the order you delivered this morning, and I checked the paperwork. It was four bags of cement and two bags of gray grout, Cliff. You brought four bags of grout and no cement. I need that cement. I can't grout the tiles until I lay the tiles. That's how it works."

Cliff's eyes closed against Allen's grating voice and condescending attitude. "Yes, Allen, I understand. I'm sorry for the mix-up." The order Cliff delivered also included three tins of a product to keep water from penetrating the handmade Saltillo Mexican tiles the customer wanted laid on a large outside patio. Two dozen boxes of twelve-inch square tiles were delivered, too.

"I paid the delivery fee. I'm not going to pay it again."

"Of course, you won't. Should I run the cement out today?"

"There'll be too much downtime if I hold my guys and wait for you to get here. You've got the cement, don't you?" Allen asked as if Cliff was dim-witted.

"Sure. It was my mistake." Cliff fought to keep his reply respectful. He wanted to throw back the argument that it was an *honest* mistake, like Allen never screwed anything up. "Will you be back at the site first thing tomorrow?"

"I'll be here until the job is done."

"Then look for me before nine tomorrow," Cliff said, wanting to move the conversation to a conclusion. "I'll load the cement in the van tonight so I can get moving right away."

Two insults back, Cliff stretched out his arm toward the day's delivery slips where they lay in a file tray. The limitation of the telephone cord and the grinding machine for keys immediately to his right worked together to shorten his reach.

"Get it right this time, Cliff."

His arm at an awkward angle, Cliff caught the edge of the tray and scooted it just enough so he could pinch Allen's order between two fingertips. "Yes, Allen. I will. Sorry this happened. I'll make it right."

"You bet you will." With that final jab, Allen hung up.

A dial tone buzzed in Cliff's ear as he drew his arm back, his eye on the snagged delivery slip. Cliff's anger reheated when he noticed Allen's signature in the corner confirming delivery. If Allen compared the written order with the products delivered, he would have caught the error immediately. Cliff could have returned to McKinley's for the cement and made a second trip. But oh no, this foul-up was totally Cliff's fault. Cliff made a mental note of the route his argument would take tomorrow with the belligerent Allen just as his elbow chucked the box of nails off the counter.

Something near rage bored into the top of Cliff's head as he watched an exploding scatter of five hundred nails skitter across the waxed floor and up to a pair of brown loafers.

"Are those my nails?"

He looked up to see another man employing a disgruntled tone. Quickly, he returned the receiver to its cradle and slapped the delivery slip down on the desktop. "I'm sorry, sir. My elbow caught the box."

"I went back for some wood glue. I told Scott I'd be right back," the man said as if this accident was foisted on him personally and with pleasure, like Cliff relished the idea of sweeping up all these nails. "Yeah well, Scott's not here," was all Cliff could think to say and not take a bite out of the customer. And by the way, where was Scott? If he'd stayed up front, he could have handed Cliff the delivery slip and none of this would have happened.

Cliff glanced over to the cash register girl for some form of assistance, but she tapped out a message with flying thumbs into her phone, oblivious and most probably useless.

He returned his attention to the customer. In as courteous a tone as he could manage, he said, "Let me get you another box." He used the side of his booted foot to scoot the largest portion of the nails up toward the counter, clearing a pathway. Spilled nails could be slippery underfoot. The man did not attempt to duplicate Cliff's method. He just stepped out of the way when Cliff's boot-scraping progress reached him.

They stood near the front door. A "wet floor" warning sign hung on a wall hook. Cliff rushed to retrieve it. The sign received a lot of wintertime use on snowy days, but set open now, it would at least alert incoming customers.

"Just let me get this in place, then—" He broke off. He couldn't get the hinged sign to cooperate. Twice, he tried to catch the sign's rubber feet on the floor and stretch the sign open. The man sighed his impatience at the delay for safety's sake. Finally, Cliff opened it manually and lowered it to the floor.

That done, he raced off for the replacement box of nails and cut down the lawn and gardening aisle, his frustration mounting to full peak. A plastic watering can sat on the floor where a customer left it. He wanted to kick it. It begged to be kicked. He was nearly ready to pull his foot back when a woman walked within view. Dousing the urge, he walked past her. The simple act of nodding to the woman felt like some inner shell cracked.

He couldn't process. Things wouldn't stay pigeonholed. They flopped about. In his mind, he tacked up the jobs in an orderly fashion before him: the replacement box of nails, then a broom to sweep up the contents from the broken box, then the cement loaded in the van.

It seemed to Cliff he slogged around in a wet-concrete concoction made from the four bags he hadn't delivered to Allen Barker. The concoction covered his shoes, working against him, threatening to stop him permanently, hold him fast to these last tormented days.

He arrived at his destination. The next box of trimming nails on the shelf was pushed back from the front. He started to reach in through the tunnel between other stocked boxes, but stopped. He let his wrist hang on the shelf's edge. He felt so tired. He closed his eyes to his trembling hand and heaved one wrenching sob. Thank God, no one heard his suffering.

* * *

Beebe stood at the cemetery's back gate. She drew her gaze away from the apple orchard across the road, ready to walk back to the house. Her pink clogs were silent company on the narrow asphalt lane. She let her eyes rake the landscape and came up with Hal Garrett's truck, partially backed through the raised overhead door at the equipment garage. She picked up her pace. She wanted to thank him. Earlier in the day, he put in another appearance and installed her mother's headstone.

She eased through the opening between the truck and garage wall. Hal was bent over an old army footlocker. The lid was up. He dug through and pulled out a small cloth tarp. From the color splotches smeared across both sides, it served itself well as a drop cloth.

When Beebe spoke Hal's name, he jumped. "Sorry," she said, grinning.

"Oh, geez." He lay a fist at his heart as if to steady its beating. "I thought you were Cliff."

Her grin faded, and she walked over. "Why? Are you hiding something in there?"

He looked her dead in the eye. "No. I'm hiding something over here. Well, not hiding, really, just keeping it out of sight for a little while. I thought it was best."

He led her and her piqued curiosity toward a dark corner. A wheelbarrow leaned upright against the wall. The wheelbarrow shared its spot with a sledge hammer, rake, shovel, and an ancient hand-held piece of equipment. Attached to its wooden handle was a long, narrow rod made of forged steel and used to pierce the ground. It was pushed through to determine if a casket rested beneath the earth. The need for such a device came, most probably, during a time when the records weren't so meticulously maintained, somewhere after Joseph Jenkins and before Clifford Walker.

Beebe felt her face form a questioning look. She saw nothing worth warranting Hal's nervous spirit until he lowered the wheelbarrow and rolled it several feet away. In the shadowy gloom, Beebe recognized the Terri Miller grave marker.

"Your father hasn't mentioned it. You know," he said, shrugging, "we've never had a gravestone leftover before. And with it being this one..."

Beebe laid a hand on Hal's arm. "You did the right thing. This is cemetery business, and Daddy decides such things. Especially this one. But let's keep it covered for another few weeks. Maybe he'll ask sooner."

Hal went to retrieve the tarp, half-draped over the footlocker's edge. Beebe stared at the hand-chiseled marker. There was no need to force her father into a decision. Decisions were difficult enough while he grieved. This decision would touch that place where bereavement still dug at his heart. It would be better if that wound healed some.

Hal folded the tarp down to size and tucked it around the marker. Beebe did her part so they were equal cohorts. She wheeled the barrow over, but then repositioned it, laying it on its side for better coverage. They both dusted their hands, then climbed into Hal's truck for the ride back.

The truck was parked beside the block building, and they stood at the door. Hal sorted through his keys for the proper one when they heard the office phone ringing inside.

"I need to catch this call," he said, jamming a key into the lock. He rushed through the door and snatched up the phone, saying hello. "Yeah, Bill, what's the word?...Okay...That's the address...Not until Monday, huh?...Okay, if that's the soonest...Sure...No, we've got nothing pending. Thanks, Bill." Hal replaced the receiver and said, "You saw the backhoe sitting out there?"

Although inside the building, Beebe turned her head toward the place where she remembered the backhoe sat on an internal cemetery road. "Uh-huh. Why? Is there something wrong?"

"Alternator belt broke. It started okay this morning. I got your mother's site filled in," he said, seating himself in the swivel desk chair. "Another maintenance item caught my eye on the way over to the old grave. I turned the backhoe off while I took care of that. The thing wouldn't start again. It was running off the battery by then. I walked back and found the broken belt."

Beebe leaned an elbow on the olive drab file cabinet. "So? You can't get a replacement before Monday?"

"I gave Cliff a call at the store when I suspected the delay. He wasn't happy."

"It can't be helped."

"Oh, I understand. This is a beautiful cemetery. A piece of heavy equipment sitting for days detracts from that."

"Still, it can't be helped." Neither could Cliff help his dark disposition, but she could help. In fact, she should have already found a grief counseling group so he could attend the minute she got him to admit the benefit.

"He's not himself. I understand. He'll come around. He just needs some time. The new belt will be here by late afternoon Monday. I'll get back over here, get it put on, then charge the battery. I should be able to finish the job at the other grave before dark."

As she nodded in agreement, she heard a raised voice outside. Hal heard it, too. He pushed the door open and stepped out ahead of Beebe. They both stopped in their tracks.

Angry words spewed from Cliff Walker. He yanked at a long hose connected to the back of the house. A kink in the hose caught on the glider's leg. He whipped the hose, but the gyration that created died before it reached the kink. Swearing, he threw the nozzle down and stormed off toward the swing.

"It's the sod on Abigail's grave," Hal said. "He's right to water it. We need to keep it going if there's no rain."

Beebe's gaze traveled over to the Walker plot. The area disturbed for the burial was level and covered with sod.

Beside her, Hal made no further comment about Cliff's poor showing. His remark reminded her that the job wasn't done just because the burial ritual was complete. Tending to Abigail's grave was a task that would continue indefinitely.

"He's got a hatred for that glider that's tied to Mother and this whole thing," Beebe said.

"He'll get better. Things will calm down for him in a week. You'll see."

Hal's simple conclusion brought Beebe's eyes up to the man's solemn face. In Beebe's estimation, there were complexities involved that would take root like the sod, would grow and flourish, and would become a covering over a bereft Cliff for a long time to come.

Cliff twisted the kink out of the hose. Beebe thought he must know she and Hal watched. She called over. "Hi, Daddy. We didn't know you were home."

Hal bravely stayed on-point long enough to absorb Cliff's glare, then Hurdlin' Hal retreated inside the block building.

Beebe's bravery didn't materialize either. She knew better than to console or counsel Cliff when he adopted a hateful frame of mind. She bypassed him, stepped over the hose with one Mother-May-I giant step, and went inside. She anticipated another evening spoiled by a sulking Cliff. He would let his fight with the hose be the tangible reason. If he didn't, he might be forced to acknowledge that behind the fight, a grieving man cried out for help.

Change a Memory

The next morning, Beebe left a group of seniors at Crossroads filling out surveys. She thought she'd walk over to the health department and, hopefully, receive some good news about her mother's death certificate. She desperately wanted something to raise Cliff's spirit.

She spent part of her morning searching for grief counseling services in Larkspur. She contacted the funeral home, completed an internet search, and finally called Ned McMitchell. The pastor actually recommended his wife once the baby came.

That was something to consider. Beebe thought back on the conversation and sighed as she mounted the steps outside the Holmes Building. Her father could not wait for Willa to recover from childbirth. In the interim, it would not be appropriate to counsel Cliff herself. With the door handle in her grasp, she paused. A stray thought prodded. There just might be a benefit to attending whatever out-of-town classes she located with her father. Surely, he would perceive this as a supportive measure on her part. Then, from the place where his wounds began to heal, they could move forward together. Giving herself tacit approval, she vowed to give the idea continued consideration. With that, she yanked the door open and stepped through.

Beebe's passage into the second floor office caught Heidi Cranston's eye. She broke off her discussion with a small man who had sandy hair and wore wire-rimmed glasses. She waved Beebe over. "Here's luck for you. Dr. Jeffers, this is Beebe Walker. You remember, she—"

"Why, yes. Of course. Pleased to meet you." Dr. Samuel Jeffers smiled. He and Beebe shook hands over the counter. A ringing phone took Heidi away from their conversation.

Beebe started to speak, but an anticipatory Jeffers eased in front of her question.

"I'm afraid I've only given your request a cursory review. Time has been short recently," he said apologetically. For proof, he showed her a handful of paperwork. "Give me a day or two to study things in depth."

"Should I stop back?"

"Heidi will call. Or I will."

To Beebe, his words meant the doctor might be explaining why the certificate would not change. Her mind instantly jumped to the affidavits she would gather from Vincent and Yates in order to appeal his decision. If necessary, Ron Smith would become involved. Her voiced comment, though, tracked a positive vein. "I'd rather pick up the new copy over having it mailed."

"Understood. Of course."

Nothing in his words or manner were a clue as to which direction he leaned. She forced a smile and thanked him for his time before she made her way toward the old wooden door beneath a transom.

"Miss Walker," Jeffers said.

She turned. He rounded the end of the counter and closed the gap between them.

"Part of the delay is—and I hope you'll forgive me—but your request raises some issues, some broader issues." He spoke in a confidential tone. "I can't explain them now, but I want to devote the time needed to study policy. I'm talking about policy in my office. I know you're not interested in the inner workings of the coroner's office, but the subject matter is important. Just a few more days, please."

She read his pale blue eyes and thought he wanted to say more, but he swallowed whatever words were there and excused himself. She watched his back until he disappeared through the doorway into the small conference room. Her gaze drifted to Heidi, obviously interested, but too far away to hear the muted conversation. Heidi shrugged. Beebe's nod conveyed a positive result, although she was left confused by the turn of events

Back out on the street and heading toward the community center, Beebe either received or imagined she received a lot of attentive looks from her fellow Larkspurians. The obituary, of course, was the culprit. It seemed to lift the veil of anonymity that accompanied her throughout her first week back in her hometown. Looking around, she was surprised to recognize Donald Thorndyke, Crossroads' board president, in the crosswalk. Donald was ten years older than

Beebe. They attended the same church as children. He appeared to look right at her, then avert his eyes. She decided it wasn't an obvious snub. He was deep in conversation with a woman whose hair was a mass of dark curls that shielded her features.

Beebe closed Crossroads' door behind her and went straight to the comment box where she instructed the seniors to deposit their completed questionnaires. Inside were an even dozen. She read and walked toward the kitchen for a drink of water. She liked the idea described in the first survey she unfolded. It suggested a warm weather/cold weather exercise class. The participants would exercise outside when possible, even form a bicycle club, then come inside to avoid the chill with fun-packed muscle-stretching aerobics. The last questionnaire held a phenomenal idea: an introduction to social media. This suggestion went so far as to propose that a high school kid teach the class. What fun, Beebe thought. Who knew social media better? It would be a joy to work with a teenager—the right teenager—to prepare a class syllabus. Not a social media wizard, she would take the class herself.

Her thoughts were interrupted by a noise overhead. She raised her nose to the ceiling. From somewhere, a draft ruffled her papers. Turning, she found a set of double doors in the short hall to the kitchen stood open. She hadn't noticed them before. Stepping forward, she looked in at a decently wide staircase that angled back on itself.

She climbed the stairs and began looking around as soon as her line of vision cleared the top step. At the back end of the floor, she saw Vincent sliding storage boxes around. The boxes left skid marks in the patina of dust on the floor. She walked his way. "Wow, look at this," she said, startling him.

The air was musty and humid. Her eyes arched over the high ceilings and wide-open area of the former department store's second floor.

"Roomy, isn't it? The grant money includes dollars for rent or refurbishing."

"You want to refurbish this area?"

"Yeah, you'll need an office, perhaps a waiting area, maybe even a small library. I'm just thinking ahead. I thought we'd turn this into a game room. Move the pool table up here, then put up some walls for your office downstairs. We'll close off what isn't needed up here."

"Why move the pool table to the back of the floor when the stairs leave you off up front?"

"There's an old freight elevator back here." He pointed into a dark corner, and she looked. "It'll need some work. Not all seniors can handle the stairs.

What have you got there?" He nodded to the survey sheets she carried.

"There were a dozen questionnaires in the suggestion box."

"Any good ones?"

"Yeah, two. I guess there's a bike and walking trail nearby."

"Out on Old Mill Road by the lake."

"A suggestion was made to form a bicycle club for the warm months and bring the exercise inside for the cold ones."

"Sounds fine."

"The other suggestion got me thinking. The seniors want to understand social media. Facebook and Twitter were mentioned. What do you think about finding a high school student to teach?"

"A teenager and seniors. Wild! And if I know you, you're thinking that same integration might be woven into other programs."

Vincent's use of the word *wild* dislodged Beebe from the discussion and transported her back through time.

"Earth to Beebe." Vincent waved his hands.

Ticking back, she returned his smile.

"Where'd you go?"

"Actually," she said, taking a breath, "to a place you'll remember."

The way he tipped his head said, "Tell me."

"Do you remember the song, *Your Wildest Dreams?*" This memory hailed from the college days they shared at Michigan State. The song had been out for a while, but that day, she heard the words in a new context.

He snapped his fingers. "The Moody Blues."

"You remember."

"Of course."

"Your VW."

"A bucket of junk, but the radio was great."

"Spring day. Windows down."

"The two of us."

"And our wildest dreams."

"I thought we were on our way to something. But you had other plans."

His words caused something to clog in her heart. She walked over to the windows and looked down to the street. The song's lyrics strummed through her mind. How did it go? Once upon a time, once when you were mine, in your wildest dreams.

She heard his footsteps and imagined the petite swirl of disturbed dust.

"That evening," he said, "you told me you were going on to seminary, you weren't coming back to Larkspur."

"I almost changed my mind that afternoon after hearing that song. We had such a good time."

Vincent looked at her like he saw directly into her soul. The day of her seminary announcement, she hid behind the words, once upon a time. The announcement surprised and crushed him.

That day, she worried he would try to change her mind. He could be very convincing. Witness the fact she was back in Larkspur at his beckoning. But while they tooled around in the Volkswagen, he didn't try, and she anointed him on that occasion with a certain quality of wisdom.

Thinking about his powers to convince, though, led her to raise a question and store another one for some other time. She might have asked him about seeing and being ignored by Donald Thorndyke, but she decided to list Donald's actions as unintentional, and her reaction as overly sensitive. His concentration was simply given over the woman with him, and so completely so that nothing else came into focus.

And besides, Beebe, Vincent, and the ghosts of this old building were firmly lodged in the past, not the present. Wisely, she let Donald Thorndyke fade. Was it possible wisdom rubs off with close contact?

"Vincent," Beebe began her question timidly, "how did you get Daddy to let go of Mother's clothes for the quilt?"

Vincent's reaction wasn't what Beebe expected. For a long moment, he drew in on himself. When he spoke, his words carried an inner peace.

"I talked about myself," he said, "about being a widower. I told him a story about a little German girl."

She was intrigued, but the counselor knew better than to interrupt for clarifications. She just let him go at his own pace.

"But maybe it wasn't that. Maybe Cliff just knew the time was right. He was ready. You were coming home, and someone thought enough of you to ask for this small concession for a larger gain. Cliff did it for you." He stood close enough to nudge up against her arm with his. "Not for him. Not for Abigail."

Beebe pursued one word from Vincent's explanation that seemed caught by the cobwebs hanging all around. "This is the first time I've heard you refer to yourself as a widower," Beebe said tenderly.

"Yeah." He raised his glasses to nearly be lost in his thick curls.

She waited.

"I was a raving mad lunatic." When she smiled, he said, "What?"

"Those are three words that all mean the same thing."

"Oh, you're a great counselor," he teased, "criticizing my choice of words the first time I decide to talk about Carolyn."

"You've never talked about her since her death?"

"I closed up that part of my life, like this second floor." He lifted his hands palms up. His eyes raked the ceiling. "I shut myself down into a small room and coped. That's the best I could do for a long time. Cope. I closed the house we lived in and called an auctioneer over in Butler. He took care of everything. I had the few things I wanted."

"They must be precious keepsakes. All totaled, it couldn't be much."

"Memories. I have memories, and they keep me going. I make myself remember. Every night before I go to sleep, I run down a half dozen memories. The best ones. I make myself relive those moments. Others crop up when I least expect them."

"Have you written down any of them? That's good therapy."

"No. I want to hold it all inside. That's where my memories of Carolyn belong. Inside. Not out in the open. Not on a cold flat page with regular lines. She was none of those things."

Beebe thought about that. Holding things inside can cause certain people to explode or implode. She didn't know which was more accurate. For Vincent, it brought comfort. Grief wasn't fighting to get out.

"Vincent, why do you live here?"

"Because I couldn't live where Carolyn and I lived together. I never understood Cliff keeping Abigail's things all those years. I would have curled up and died if I stayed at home."

"Do you think you would have benefited from counseling?"

"Probably. It's easier now to look back, but I probably wouldn't have agreed if counseling were available. I did better not talking about Carolyn." Barely audible, he said, "And her death."

Beebe thought it was true. People handle grief differently. Vincent and her father occupied opposite ends of the grief spectrum. Vincent navigated through his recovery following his own course. Softly, she said, "I think you did better, too."

* * *

Yates's days of detox with Rev. Mosie Razzell were broken up by the occasional visits from Ned and Willa McMitchell and Vincent Bostick. Beebe Walker stayed connected. She stopped by, but only after calling first, to determine if Razzell was not then in the front part of the house. Everyone agreed Beebe's interaction with the reverend might cause a setback so she made notes from a distance, which Yates assumed were related to the senior life programming Crossroads would soon undertake in full force.

Only once did Yates call for help. His panic set in just after midnight, making it Thursday morning. Razzell was shaky and incoherent. Following Dr. Gabriel's earlier lead, Yates told Razzell he had a bad case of the flu. He tried to push herbal tea, toast, and saltines off on the minister, but a mumbling Razzell declined them all. Yates was afraid to leave him even for the length of time it would take to let Barleycorn make a quick pit stop out back.

Vincent answered Yates's call and rushed over at one in the morning. When Vincent arrived, Razzell was wrapped in a blanket on the couch, his knees pulled up to his chin. For all intents and purposes, he adopted a sitting fetal position. A worried look crossed Vincent's beard-stubbled face. Yates couldn't imagine Vincent was as anxious about Razzell's socked feet peeking out from beneath the coverlet as he was about the glazed look in the old man's eyes.

Razzell shook. By way of greeting to Vincent, he said he ached. It was a pitifully feeble comment, full of pain and something unknown.

Barleycorn, sensing his new friend's misery, spared no time for doggie pleasures. He ran to the closest bush, lifted a leg, and when the job was done, raced back inside. From the back door, he trotted directly to Razzell. So very gently, he climbed onto the couch to warm and comfort the suffering senior. Over the next six hours, whenever Razzell moaned, Barleycorn snuggled closer. The message was clear: Barleycorn would never forsake Razzell.

At sunrise, just like a fever breaking, Razzell rallied. He had not reached full recovery, but the residual effects of the narcotics broke their hold on his system. More clashes were expected, but victory was closer.

The worst, Yates prayed, was behind them.

Dr. Gabriel arrived Friday afternoon on Razzell's third day of detox. Razzell was bathed and dressed in fresh pajamas.

The doctor's daily visits surprised Yates. He found him personable and dedicated, but he misconstrued Yates's connection with Crossroads. Yates set him straight. The doctor thought the hospice hired him, not that the young man was homeless and in need of shelter until, hopefully, he gained employment with the local hospital—employment that included a much-needed paycheck.

"My interview is next Tuesday," Yates said. "Ned and Willa will stay here with Mosie while I'm gone." They talked on the front stoop, out of earshot of Razzell.

"Mosie may not need an aide by then. He's doing great. This is better progress than I expected. You're a fine nurse, Yates. I enjoy working with you."

Yates was pleased beyond words with the compliment from the doctor who, days earlier, he began to truly admire.

* * *

"Hi, Daddy."

Cliff turned from slicing open a carton with his box cutter. His shift at McKinley's was nearly over. Beebe, to his surprise, wore a business suit. He couldn't imagine why. "What's up?"

"I just wanted to let you know I stopped by the Health Department again to ask about Mother's death certificate. I got a few minutes of Dr. Jeffers' time. He said another day, maybe two." Beebe's tone was matter-of-fact.

"Christ, it's been since last Thursday." This was Monday. How much time would the coroner take? He slammed the metal case of the box cutter against one of the metal shelves in the aisle where he worked.

While the reverberating echo died down, Beebe's nervous eyes darted from the shelf back to Cliff. "I know, but we're almost there, Daddy. Tomorrow or the next day. Heidi will give us a call. She has our number. I told you it's Heidi Wells from school. She married Bud Cranston."

Beebe ended her tale on a light note, like it was some kind of mood stabilizer guaranteed to have an instant effect. Cliff could care less who was married to whom. He felt his frustration heating. Couldn't Beebe do more? She seemed content to merely let the situation ride.

"Daddy, are you okay?"

He forced a smile. "Yeah, I'm fine. Just wish the news was better."

"Maybe just another day. Heidi will call. Well, I've got to get off to the board meeting. After I meet the members, Vincent and I will talk about the programming he's set up. Wish me luck."

So that was the reason for the suit. He forgot about the board meeting. That worked in his favor because Cliff just wanted to be alone. He kissed her cheek as a way to push her off. "You'll do well," he added when, after a few steps, she turned to wave.

He finished stocking the incoming shipment of furnace filters, grumbling when he fought to fit the larger ones on the shelf. He broke down the now empty shipping cartons with a vengeance. Gathering them up in his arms, he banged through the hinged doors into the warehouse, tossed the cardboard into the recycling dumpster at the bottom of the dock stairs, and kept going down the alley until he came out on Cramer Street. He turned left and looked up the block. Rosemary's restaurant sat across the intersection.

He stopped. Autopilot took him this far. His longtime friend and confidant was his intended destination, but did he really want to talk about the death certificate fiasco? He got this far. He thought he did want to talk. What to do? He rubbed his eyes and massaged his temples. Three minutes later, he swung through the diner's door.

The look Cliff gave Rosemary dimmed her high-wattage smile. Staying behind the counter, she matched his steps to the far end. He propped a hip on the last counter stool. One foot remained on the floor. Rosemary leaned forearms onto the counter, ready to listen.

He rehashed every nuance attached to the death certificate in infinitesimal detail. His arms waved. The foot on the floor tapped. He opened with his desire to correct the name on the document. A simple request. How it started with his search for the life insurance papers. The quest was now on hold for nearly a week despite Beebe's three or four visits to the health department. He lost track. He closed with his deduction that the coroner couldn't be bothered to make a decision, or he was too inept to grasp the concept.

"Maybe Beebe didn't articulate the request clearly enough," Cliff argued, running his hand through his hair.

Rosemary finally broke into his rant. "I'm sure she did. It's not her fault. The doctor is probably just busy."

"God, I hope when I get home, Hal's got that damn backhoe repaired and that grave filled in." Cliff thought to latch onto another aggravating topic.

"That grave is still bothering you?"

"You know how it is. Something out of place. It's a trigger for my memories. I can't prevent all these thoughts from winding up when I go out to that section. First, it was just the grave. Now I've seen that backhoe for five days. How long will it be before I can walk that row and not think of these last two horrible weeks?"

Rosemary studied him closely. "Are you done for the day at McKinley's?"

"Yeah. I'm done," he groused.

"Hang out here then for a while. Let me fix you a plate. What do you want?"

Cliff heard the door, then people chattering. Rosemary's attention veered away. What he said next brought it back.

"I *want* to do something," he said with grit stuck to his words.

"Huh?"

Cliff looked from Rosemary's questioning expression to his hand. He clenched his fist to cover the tremor. A rant of fury spiked with such energy that he thought his brain would explode. This duplicated his agony over the undelivered cement and spilled nails.

"Cliff, are you okay?"

He looked her straight in the eye. "No. Not yet, but I will be." He spun off the counter stool.

"Where are you going?"

"Home. To change a memory."

Small Town Fears

After Beebe arrived, Vincent hung a slightly worn sign from the hook suction-cupped to the glass in Crossroads' front door. The sign read: Center Closed For Board Meeting.

The large recreation area was fashioned into a makeshift board room. Four tables were placed end to end with plenty of folding chairs spaced along both sides. To gain enough room, the board table at the room's center point ran parallel to the front window, the pool table, and the half-wall dividing off the kitchen. A straggle of tables and chairs lined the room's outside walls.

Vincent stood by Beebe, making introductions. Board members arrived in groups of two and three. The tally of Crossroads' board membership numbered eleven. Several days ago, Mona Gabriel introduced herself. Beebe's path crossed Donald Thorndyke's last Thursday although he was locked into a conversation with a woman at the time and unaware. Ron Smith came in. She knew his name as both a voting member and Crossroads' legal counsel. Beebe was glad to finally attach a face to the name. Other board members stepped forward to be introduced.

When the crowd around her cleared and Beebe took a breath, she was caught by surprise. Donald Thorndyke stood, talking ultra-privately with Dr. Samuel Jeffers in the kitchen. Her skin prickled. Why was the county coroner here? Both men entered Crossroads unobserved by her and, she presumed, by Vincent as well. Vincent said nothing earlier about an agenda item involving the coroner. She lay a hand on Vincent's arm to ask him just that as the door opened and board member Mona Gabriel walked in with pool player Mick Nettleman.

Concern quickly ground itself into a lump in her stomach.

In the second it took for Vincent to lower his ear in response to Beebe's touch, she jumped topics to the second unexpected guest.

"Why is he here?" Beebe nodded discretely the pool player's way. Nearly a week ago in a private moment with Vincent, she described the "perceptions" conversation she had with Mona in the lobby of the newspaper building. The beginnings of that conversation were attached to the man with his head turned to Mona's, listening to her whispers. Days before that encounter, she remembered his oh-so-righteous complaints about her mother.

"Mick Nettleman," Vincent said grumpily. "Well, I guess we know what this is about."

Beebe felt numb. She juggled so many balls since her return to Larkspur that she really wasn't surprised that one of those airborne balls dropped instantly to the floor when Mona and Mick sent her duplicate sneers. That done, Mona directed the pool player to a chair along the wall.

Before Beebe and Vincent could comment further, Donald Thorndyke approached with Jeffers. Another juggled ball representing a trial plaguing her life fell through her peripheral vision, hit the tile, and rolled away.

"Beebe," Donald said, "there you are. It's been awhile." Up close, Donald's left eyelid drooped noticeably, putting Beebe in mind of a big cat that perpetually dozed. He wore a finely tailored suit. The hand he placed in hers was chilly.

"Good to see you, Donald. And Dr. Jeffers. Nice seeing you again." The doctor's warmer hand was also smaller, suitable for his delicate autopsies. His eyes smiled pleasantly through round spectacles.

Since Donald made no attempt to introduce Beebe to the good doctor, and was now offering no curiosity about their prior acquaintance, she assumed he owned some awareness of recent events. That cleared Beebe's bafflement over the doctor's presence. The kitchen conversation apparently covered details involving her mother's death certificate. In Beebe's head, there existed more than enough space for conspiracy thoughts to loom.

"My pleasure seeing you." Jeffers released her hand for Vincent's. The men exchanged a few words.

"Back in town, what, a week now?" Donald said to Beebe.

Still wary, she calculated. "Closer to ten days."

"I wish I'd gotten over earlier to welcome you."

"Mrs. Gabriel did."

"Ah," Donald said noncommittally. "Any of the others?"

"Not while I was here."

"Still, I should have come," he said in conclusion. His tone was almost too sincere. No, she thought, it was more apologetic than sincere. She got the sense it was directed toward an immediately upcoming event, not toward his past lapse in etiquette.

"Well, let's get started," Donald said.

He moved to find his seat at the head of the table and others quickly found theirs. Beebe and Vincent sat at the far corner, opposite Donald, who counted heads. Beebe watched Mona. From her seat at the table's center point, she sent a reassuring glance to Mick Nettleman. The man responded with a firm nod. Dr. Jeffers moved a chair within range of the table, but at a level removed from the voting members.

Donald called the meeting to order. "Well, perfect attendance," he said. "This rarely happens. I thank you all for arranging your schedules so we could meet Beebe together. Of course, that was the original plan a month ago when Beebe signed and returned our employment contract. In the meantime, one of our members," he indicated Mona, "uncovered a detrimental situation. That was how I believe she put it. I asked Mona to make a presentation of those facts."

A flash of stomach-twisting déjà vu resonated within Beebe. For an instant, she occupied the board room with the deacons of Trydestone Lutheran Church. She cast a glance into a dark corner beyond the pool table, expecting to see Olney Jones waiting beside his custodial cart, dust mop in hand, a couple of packing boxes at his feet.

As an aside, Donald said, "I hope the members don't mind an interruption of our standing agenda for some—well, new business, I guess. Before I turn the meeting over to Mona, let's talk about our guests. Mona requested that Mick Nettleman be present for this new business, and I agreed. You'll hear about that."

In unison, the board's contingent turned toward the pool player, but Beebe raised her eyes to Vincent. He wore a look of consternation, blindsided as well by the direction Donald sent the board meeting.

"On a related note, Dr. Samuel Jeffers, our county coroner, is also present. His topic of conversation was brought into the light, as Mona well knows, because Beebe made a request of him to correct the name on a death certificate. That was the death that you recall occurred here in one of our hospice rooms." He put his hands together. "Now, please give your full attention to Mona."

Beebe's mouth dried to dust as she watched Mona.

Wearing a brocaded summer suit and gold jewelry, she rose to her full height. She placed her fingertips on the table. "I think first I want to review the order of events. Last March, Vincent promptly made us aware of the passing of a hospice patient. The summary he put together named this woman as Terri Miller, who lost her battle with AIDS. The same summary was given to our county coroner when the body was transferred. Dr. Jeffers completed an autopsy and issued a death certificate for Terri Miller, an indigent. He also contacted town hall and requested funds—public money, mind you—for this homeless woman's burial." She made eye contact with every face around the table. "When Mr. Nettleman came to me with his knowledge that Beebe Walker's mother stole narcotics from Lakeview Hospital, I didn't know that Terri Miller operated under an alias."

A murmur passed among the members at the word narcotics. Several members shifted in their seats, also uncomfortable with the word alias.

"It was Terri Miller's name that Ms. Walker wanted removed from her mother's death certificate, so Abigail Walker's name, a wanted felon, could be added. You must all admit, this is shocking. I can only imagine that Dr. Jeffers is present to express his outrage. As a result, we have a darkening blot on Crossroads."

Behind Beebe's hot face, thoughts of conspiracy mutated to confusion. She assumed Jeffers must have abandoned confidentiality and took her request to correct the death certificate to Donald or Mona, with one of them speaking to the other. If so, if Donald and Mona operated as a team, why wouldn't Mona be aware of Jeffer's invitation to the meeting? Beebe bit her lip and let the court of public opinion rattle forward.

"As Mr. Nettleman remembers Abigail Walker," Mona went on, "so will the seniors we look to serve. Thirty years have passed since Abigail Walker's theft of drugs and her escape from capture. In that thirty years, the people who remember are now seniors. We can all see that picture come into focus. The community will perceive collusion between Vincent Bostick and Beebe Walker," she said, looking down her nose at the pair of them, "and the fleecing, if you will, of our town funds for a free burial. Free burial, falsification of a death certificate, and free reign to put who knows how many seniors at risk for abuse, neglect, or some other type of scam directed at the very population these two swear they are here to protect. It's villainous and disgraceful."

As if rehearsed, Donald said, "And your recommendation to the board for its next step?"

"Someone has to resign." She seemed pleased with her haughty and non-specific answer. Nose properly elevated, she sat.

Low rumblings rounded the table. Only four or five of the members dared to look at the accused. Beebe met their unspoken accusations with a straight back and shoulders.

"Do any members want to add something?" Donald asked.

Of course, they didn't, Beebe thought. They were a flock of sheep, rallying around their shepherdess.

"Fine." Donald sat forward, so poised. "Vincent and Beebe, I'm sorry for the ambush. If either of you want to comment, we will listen."

Vincent started to push his chair back. Beebe clamped her hand onto his arm. She could not wait a moment longer to address her accusers. She rose in defense of three people.

"My mother, Abigail Walker, did not ask to be badly hurt in a car accident. She did not choose to be born with a weakness, what we term today, a disease. The disease of addiction. She needed help, but she didn't ask for any. She was scared, and she ran. I ask each of you to imagine the degree of fear it would take to cause you to run from your families." Her gaze jumped from member to member. "To run from prison, yes, but she ran from her family. That must have been more traumatizing than the accident. Realizing after she left what she'd done must have damaged every filament in her soul. You would know, if all the details were disclosed, that she sought forgiveness." Beebe meant her mother sought forgiveness through her relationship with Yates, but she would not let this disgrace for a board meeting come down on him and release his identity. "My mother made a supreme effort to do good with her life, and she succeeded. Evidence exists. She found sobriety." Beebe took a breath to be sure that message sunk in. "And yet fear lived within her still, as fear of so many things lives in a small town." Quieter, for emphasis, she wondered, "Will we run from our fears, too?"

She sent that question to Donald. He sat with his elbows on the table, hands together, both index fingers propped against his mouth. She was surprised to find an attentive look on his face when she expected one of contempt.

"Vincent Bostick never met my mother when she lived in Larkspur," Beebe said, laying a hand on his shoulder. "But when a stranger, a dying woman, showed up and literally collapsed in his arms on this very doorstep, his heart expanded to include another. She told him her name was Terri Miller. Do you know, if this hospice is allowed to continue, how many strangers may ask for his

239

help? A stranger tells you his name, he has no identification, he's sick, and this man will help him."

Vincent must have felt a dozen sets of eyes on him. His were focused on his one knee crossed over the other.

"My mother used the name Terri Miller for over ten years. Was it legally changed? We don't know. Terri Miller wanted to die with dignity. She wanted control of her life at the end of her life. Those decisions are difficult for the dying. Those decisions are difficult for the caretakers. You all better get a grasp of that right now. Difficult decisions are made by those who show up. As Mr. Thorndyke said, perfect attendance today, and for a sideshow. But who will be here when difficult decisions face you, like the decision that faced Vincent?"

Silence dimmed the room.

"My father," Beebe said. "He did not want to hide from any of this. He insisted an obituary run in the paper. And he insisted that the name be changed on the death certificate so the proceeds from Mother's life insurance policy could be used to reimburse the town for the so-called free burial. Whatever funding is left will be set aside to make final arrangements for as many future indigent burials as it can. He will not profit."

Board attorney Ron Smith, in his crumpled suit, sat, informal and unpretentious, on one hip, his dangling elbow hooked over the chair back. At this point, he waved Beebe unceremoniously into her seat. Dragging himself forward to lean on the table, he said, "My dear Mona, Dr. Jeffers is not here as a witness for the prosecution. We do not have a perception problem. We have a family member who, from her teenage years, has lived in the trenches, and despite that, *despite that*, went into the service of others as her mother had. Both have returned to us. What does that say about these women who faced adversity and the pull of this town? This is a good town with ties that stay tied, that stretch and accommodate. You are new here, Mona. I hope you come to learn— and if not learn, then appreciate—and feel the connection the rest of us have to each other and to Larkspur. At least the vast majority of us." His eyes darted to Mick Nettleman, who stared at the door and escape with longing, Beebe thought.

Mona opened her mouth to respond, but didn't when Ron stretched his neck to a point beyond her. Mona's husband, Dr. Hershel Gabriel, and a woman with long, dark curly hair walked past Crossroads' window. Ron shot a glance down the table to Donald. Board members' heads swiveled in all directions, finally to focus on the two who entered. Dr. Gabriel closed the door behind them.

Several people talked at once. Husband barely glanced at wife. Ron was up quickly. He moved two more chairs to the corner of the table across from Beebe and Vincent for the new arrivals.

Even before Donald Thorndyke introduced the woman, Beebe knew who she was. She looked more like her mother, Patsy Thorndyke, than Donald did, and she had now reached the age her mother attained when Beebe last saw Patsy.

"You all know Dr. Gabriel and my sister, Melinda," Donald said. He leaned his head out for a view of Dr. Gabriel. "Thank you, Gabe, for driving her here." He gave himself a moment. "When Mona called with her plans to *prosecute* Beebe and Vincent, I well remembered the days when Abigail Walker fled our community. Good people are often placed in complex positions with complicated decisions to make. As was Abigail Walker. As was Vincent Bostick. As was my sister. Melinda asked to come here today to add her words personally to this discussion."

Stunned, Beebe's heart nearly stopped. She felt a shift in the proceedings. Donald, at least, changed sides in this sham, which, Beebe decided, was a word of which he would approve.

Melinda stood. Closer, Beebe saw the dark hair was streaked with gray. Melinda was years past fifty. Her face was rounder, her eyes sadder than Beebe remembered. Those eyes were tipped to Beebe.

"I'm a nurse. I worked at Lakeview Hospital with your mother." Abigail Walker's nursing career had a ten-year tenure over Melinda's. "I remember her return to work after the car accident. I liked her very much, and I was the one who reported the theft of drugs." She swallowed. "I thought I saw her substitute meds once. After that, I watched closer. I saw her repeat the process several times. I debated, but I reported it." She turned her head toward the others at the table. "If any of you have come through your lives without facing a decision like that, then count yourselves lucky. It took me days to decide, to find the courage, and I blame myself for the results. I had two choices: I could go to the administration, or I could go to Abigail. Clearly, I didn't have the courage to go to Abigail and disregard hospital policy. I went up the ladder. Rumors spread, and Abigail was off the floor by the time the hospital's CEO came looking for her. Police officers showed up a moment later. I was so ashamed of myself at that moment, I wanted to run, too. I understood exactly what happened. Abigail's accident, the pain, the reliance on medicine to relieve that pain, but she was to be treated like a criminal, not like a human being who needed our help. The hospital protected my identity. My family knew, but the hospital would not protect Abigail. That was disillusioning, and I never forgot."

Melinda held the members' rapt attention. Based on Dr. Gabriel's concentration, this was the first time he heard Melinda's story.

Donald startled Beebe when he spoke. "With my family's involvement, Mona, should I resign from this board?" The question was expressed evenly, without malice.

Every head turned to Mona, who threw her shoulders back. Beebe saw Mona's mind slip into gear. One glance at her husband told Beebe no help would come Mona's way from him.

"Well, no," Mona stammered. "There's no real connection."

"But the perception, Mona? With this community's long memory, and as you would have us believe, a long and spiteful one, what about the perception?" He allowed two beats to pass while Mona stiffened to stubborn silence. "Well, let's put my resignation on the back burner for a while, shall we? I invited Dr. Jeffers to attend and speak to us."

Jeffers rose. Beebe turned. His position placed him over her left shoulder. He spoke directly to her.

"Let me express, again, my condolences on the loss of your mother." Then Jeffers' composure slipped with a grin to the others. "What goes on in the world outside my autopsy suite is quite—in a word—alive. I must get out more, and I plan to." Hands in his pockets, he began in earnest. "Beebe's request to correct the name on Terri Miller's death certificate to her mother's name and the explanation behind it prompted me to contact Donald. He asked if I'd bring my decision to the meeting today. The decision I bring is not about the death certificate. That will be handled privately with Beebe. The decision I came with concerns the need this county has to inform hospices of the legal aspects affecting their function and the policies of the coroner's office so the two don't conflict. That has been lacking. I see the need to educate. I'm hoping Crossroads will host directors from similar agencies so I can be involved, answer questions, skim the ethics, and create ongoing communication. As I said, I feel the lapse resides on my side, and I want to rectify that."

Donald cleared his throat. "With the details to be worked out later, does this board agree to host as many meetings as Dr. Jeffers finds necessary to open a line of communication between hospices and the like with the coroner's office? All in favor?" Hands shot up. "Opposed?" None. "Unanimously carried, Dr. Jeffers. You have our thanks. I'm sure from Dr. Jeffers' talks, we'll learn that we need to set policy for Crossroads so our employees have guidance and our agency does not again find itself in conflict with the coroner's office. One other thing. Will you speak to patients' rights?"

"We've talked." Ron Smith took the question. His chair creaked as he motioned to Jeffers with the hand that boasted an onyx pinky ring. "We'll handle these meetings with a tag-team approach. I'll add the patients' side of things for a nicely balanced presentation."

"Fine. Excellent. We're in good hands," Donald said, as Jeffers resumed his seat. "Dr. Gabe? Something to say?"

Gabriel got to his feet. "Dr. Jeffers, I am very pleased to hear your plans for in-service meetings. Well done." Head down, lower lip out, obviously in thought, he took a step away from his chair. His comments started with an intake of breath. "Daily life is a real challenge for our seniors. The last chapter of that challenge is often told on the autopsy table. I complement each of you for your desire to provide Larkspur seniors with so many possibilities here to improve their quality of *long* life. There is a beloved senior in this community with whom I had the opportunity in the last few days to spend time. I couldn't give my full attention, by any means, so representatives of this agency stepped in and provided amazing care with a full recovery. I am so impressed with Crossroads' superior personnel and the results they gleaned that I spent a great deal of time considering a true opportunity opened to me by Vincent on Chairman Thorndyke's behalf. Well," he smiled, "it was months ago now. If the offer still stands, I would like to sign on as Crossroads' medical liaison, to support senior programming as it relates to geriatric needs."

Donald clapped his hands. "This vote will be an easy one, I'm sure. We need this association with Dr. Gabriel, just as we need a working relationship with Dr. Jeffers. Although I'd like to see more of Gabe than Sam, in the professional arena, of course. You're more than welcome, Dr. Jeffers, to join the crowd on bingo night. All in favor of accepting Dr. Hershel Gabriel as our physician-on-call?" Hands raised. "Opposed?"

The entire group watched Mona. Her focus pierced the tabletop in front of her.

"Abstentions?" Donald queried. The question seemed to hang in the air.

Beebe thought she could almost see Mona's anger burning behind her eyes. The tips of her hair would smolder next. As Beebe rankled earlier with conspiracy, Mona must suffer the same. Her husband participated in battle against her. This was public humiliation, and her husband spoke not one word in her defense. But then, humiliation was a two-way street, Beebe thought. She felt a pang of sorrow for Gabriel as well. His wife was an object of disrespect among Crossroads' board members.

"Our dear Mona has obviously concluded that her husband's involvement as service provider will create an irresolvable conflict of interest for her as a principal board member." Sitting sideways to the table, Ron Smith put his elbow on the faux Formica top and led his eyes around to Mona's. "That resignation you saw coming," he paused, "I believe it's yours."

Conspiracy was exactly the name of the game for the entire ordeal. The game's goal: bait a trap for Mona Gabriel. Beebe's first encounter with Ron Smith revealed his cruel streak. He matched it with a crooked smile. What a force the man would be in a courtroom.

From the faces around the table, Beebe saw not one morsel of disgust over the attorney's malicious intent, but a moment of emotional release, of internal glee. These people suffered a long and trying history with Mona Gabriel.

The savoring of Mona's demise was cut short when Rosemary Olmsted burst through Crossroads' door. Her frazzled look was emphasized by deep lines cutting into her face. She came from the diner. Rosemary's apron was still tied around her waist.

"Oh, excuse me." Rosemary wrung her hands. "I'm so sorry. Beebe? Can you step out?"

Vincent came with Beebe. They huddled on the sidewalk while Rosemary hurried into an explanation. "Cliff was just at the diner. He's upset. He headed home. It's Abigail. It's everything. The glider. The grave. How he wished Abigail had asked for help from someone. Anyone. The death certificate delay. Everything's collapsing around him."

Beebe's gaze shot to Vincent. His brown eyes reflected his concern.

"Go," he said. "Call me later. Call me if you need help."

Inching toward the door, Beebe said, "I don't have my car keys." Her purse was inside.

Vincent stopped her. He dug in his pocket. "Here, take mine."

The translation meant every second was important. But Beebe took time to put a hand on both Vincent's and Rosemary's arms. "Thank you. Thank you."

At a trot, she crossed the street to Vincent's car.

Secondhand Grave

Yates entered Razzell's bedroom. "How do you feel?" he asked Razzell, who was dressed and sat in the room's upholstered chair, reading *National Geographic.* "We could walk to the park. Let Barleycorn play."

The dog's ears perked when he heard his name. He lay on the carpeting beside the chair. Yates's first weekend in the house was behind him. Since then, the reverend's overall health and stamina seemed greatly improved. He spent most of the day resting, but not in bed.

"Let's sit on the front porch," Razzell said. "Barleycorn can amuse himself in the yard."

"Deal." Yates hoped for a little more, but the compromise was welcome. He handed Razzell a comb and grinned. "Here, make yourself presentable in case some women walk by. It's shady out front. I'll get your sweater."

Out in the living room, Yates pulled the lightweight tan sweater from the couch where it occupied the far cushion since Yates arrived six days ago. A folded section of newspaper, unseen all this time, slipped off the couch onto the floor. Yates picked it up and stared at Abigail Walker's obituary.

He looked back down the hall, wondering about the man who knew her. Yates thought there were probably papers all over town folded in the same manner when the death notice ran. He decided to leave the matter. He called the dog. Barleycorn appeared with Razzell close behind. Yates thought his patient's gait was good. Stronger. His eyes were clear. He needed a little weight.

"Here, let me help you get this on."

Together, they worked the sweater over his arms and back. A few seconds later, Razzell was settled out on the porch, sitting in a webbed lawn chair. Barleycorn had his nose stuffed in the bushes.

"I'm going to pour us some juice," Yates said. "I'll be right back."

"No, wait. I think I can do without juice for a minute."

Yates, surprised by the determination riding his tone, leaned back on the porch railing and watched the man. The man watched the dog.

"Barleycorn is an unusual name. Do you know its meaning?"

Yates did. Terri told him the meaning when she first came home with the mutt. "It's an old unit of linear measure equal to one-third inch."

The expression on Razzell's face seemed to flatten out. Yates first thought the reverend was just disappointed that he knew the answer, but then he repeated Yates's next sentence with him, word for word. "Nine barleycorns equals three inches."

Yates stared at the man who struggled so hard to return clarity to his life over the past days. "How did you know I was going to say that?"

The answer to Yates's question came in the form of a tear rolling off Razzell's cheek. "Yates," he said, "I need a lift somewhere. Will you drive me?"

"I guess," Yates said, confused. "Can Barleycorn come with us?"

"Yes, please, bring the dog. It's time to speak with Beebe."

* * *

Beebe skidded Vincent's car to a stop on the service road alongside the caretaker's house. Out of the driver's seat, she winged the door closed and ran to her father. Cliff lifted a sledge hammer over his head. It fell on the glider. Both swing and framework lay on the ground. By the looks of the poor mangled metal object, Cliff made contact a half dozen times.

"Daddy, what are you doing?"

When he reared the hammer again, she jumped back. "Why can't something go right for me?" he complained. "I've done nothing."

"Daddy, you're going to hurt yourself."

Out on the cemetery road, Beebe saw Hal Garrett, his head under the hood of the backhoe. Couldn't he hear the hammer hitting the metal? Then she heard the backhoe's motor rev and knew it shunted Cliff's racket from Hal's ears.

"Your mother left. You left. I've been here. Now I'm just trying to pick up the pieces." He groaned with the effort to slam the sledge hammer again at one of the glider's legs. "Do something nice for the cemetery, for future indigents, now that I know the story of one, of what happens." Breathing hard, he let the hammer head rest on the ground while he voiced his conclusion a second time. "I've done nothing."

She became panic-stricken when he got his grip around the hammer again. "Daddy, please stop!"

"No."

She looked down to Hal, still oblivious. Cliff slammed the heavy mallet against a cross-member. It screeched in pain. "Daddy, will you stop."

"No."

"All right. Go ahead. You know," she said pointedly, frustrated, "because you're right. You did nothing when Mother was getting hooked on drugs." Boy, she was going to have to apologize for this later, but she had to jolt him free of his destructive path. The glider was a lost cause, but his actions were feeding his mood, his psyche, and his soul.

Cliff glared at his daughter and reiterated his feeble excuse. "She told me lies, in this glider, night after night. It will never end."

"It will end. You need to talk about this. Give it time."

"No. I like this better." He got the sledge hammer over his shoulder.

"Smashing the hell out of the glider?" She dodged a piece of flying metal. "We'll find a grief support group." In that odd, bizarre instant, Beebe thought everything seemed to happen for a reason. She triangulated between the broken backhoe, the open grave, and the smashed-up glider. The solution was so obvious. She and her father must bury the memories and the lies in that grave.

A good two-hundred yards away, Hal closed the backhoe's hood. He climbed onto the seat and gunned the engine.

"Wait, Daddy. Stop. We've got to catch Hal."

"No. One more."

The hammer head rested on the ground. Beebe slapped at her father's hand. "Stop. Help me," she pleaded.

She reached for one end of the swing and lifted it and her eyes to the befuddlement on Cliff's face. "Do you want to bury the memories and the lies?" He stood dumbfounded, arms at his sides. "Grab the other end. We need to get this to Hal."

"Hal? What are you talking about?" The hammer's handle fell back onto the grass with a soft thud.

"We're going to take care of things ourselves and right now. We're going to bury this swing in that grave." Her head swung fore and aft. "It's fitting, don't you think? The memories of the lies told on this glider buried in the once-used grave you don't know what to do with. Don't you see? We can solve everything. Grab it. We've got to hurry."

Beebe saw realization and a new purpose flood hungrily into Cliff's body. Leaving the crushed framework behind, they lugged the dented and paint-chipped swing. Father and daughter traipsed off in an awkward sidestepping march that the cemetery, in all its years, never before witnessed.

The words, one has to be flexible, ran through Beebe's mind. She once thought the glider would be an instrument to measure her father's return from grief. One day, he would sit on it of his own accord, and she'd know progress was made. She guessed if her father sledge-hammered the hell out of it, that was another form of measurement. She flexed her thinking and reasoned this latter, more aggressive form made all the sense in the world.

A section of chain dragged the asphalt, but Beebe kept her eyes glued to Hal and his progress to position the heavy piece of equipment near the loose mound of dirt he would scoop back into the empty grave. Luckily, Hal stopped to use his forearm to wipe sweat off his face. Beebe could almost see his eyes cover the distance to the unusual sight she and her father presented.

Hal shut down the engine and jumped to the ground. He hurried out, wanting to take Beebe's end.

"No. I've got to do this with Daddy."

"Do what?" He was still at a loss, but he plugged forward, alongside her.

"This piece of bad history is going in that secondhand grave."

"Okay," a puzzled Hal said, drawing out the word. His eyebrows rose so high on his forehead, it looked painful.

Beebe and Cliff sidled up to the open ground. Their eyes met, sending a calculating gaze between them. They positioned the glider over the six-foot deep hole. Cliff nodded, and they dropped the pitifully twisted swing.

Its creak, when it landed, was muffled by the loam. After a second of indecision, the trailing chain scraped over the swing's metal backrest. A victorious silence rose up from the grave.

Beebe went to her father. They embraced. When they broke from the rocking and back-rubbing hug, the two Walkers began to heal.

Beebe saw movement in her peripheral vision. It was Yates's jeep. It stopped. Razzell looked out the passenger window. Yates leaned forward, staring. Barleycorn's head hung out a lowered rear window. Three mouths gaped open. A panting tongue protruded from the dog's.

Yates climbed out and came over. He looked in the grave and pursed his lips. So much energy flowed through Beebe in the last few minutes that she hadn't stopped to think that their actions might be perceived by Yates as a desecration of Terri Miller's memory.

Yates's eyes shifted from Beebe to Cliff. "There's a great story here. One, I bet, Terri would appreciate. But right now, I think I'm going to need your help. Mosie wants to see Abigail's grave."

"Why?"

"I don't know, but I bet it's another great story. I can squeeze you guys in the back with Barleycorn."

"You sure I won't set Mosie off?" she asked.

"Not a problem. Detox has finally gotten his wig on straight." While the young man's grin was infectious, he followed it up with, "And besides, he specifically mentioned meeting with you."

Beebe felt her lips part in surprise. Rev. Mosie Razzell definitely turned a corner with his recovery.

Before they piled into the Jeep, Beebe rolled her hand at Hal, giving him the go-ahead to scoop dirt into the open grave.

Just past the Walker plot and its one newly sodded grave, Yates put the Jeep in park. Everyone, including the dog, kept their eyes on Rev. Razzell as they trooped over. He led the entourage.

Beebe reached for Razzell when his face crumpled. He turned wet eyes to Yates. The older man's words surprised Beebe. Now her mouth gaped. "Barleycorn is Abigail's dog, not yours." It was not a question, but a statement of fact.

"No. Not Mother's dog," she countered.

"Yeah, he was. She brought him home during my junior year in college," Yates said. "She was living with me by then. She already named him. When I asked her about the name, she told me the definition for Barleycorn. She found the word—"

Razzell cut him off. "She found the word magical."

"Yes. The most magical word she ever heard."

Razzell nodded. Beebe watched his face. For a moment, he left their presence and went off to another place. He came back to them when Barleycorn moaned. The dog lay down on the grave just like he did before. The name on the grave made not the slightest difference.

Razzell turned away, and Yates helped him over to the picnic table. He got him seated, then came around to speak in Beebe's ear. "Kind of wish we had a swing to sit him in."

She smiled. "Where were you forty-five minutes ago?"

The others found their place on the two benches.

"Barleycorn is an old word, an old measurement," Razzell said, speaking to Beebe and Cliff. "Abigail came up on my front porch one afternoon after her shift. I was working a crossword. She was walking just as good as ever, given her broken hip from the car accident. I complimented her. She was slow to get started about why she was there, so I supplemented with the clue for the word I just filled in. I gave her the definition and followed that up with an example: nine barleycorns equal three inches."

Beebe warmed to the expression on Cliff's face when Razzell said to him, "She turned to me with childlike delight in her eyes. She said, 'That's the most magical word I ever heard.' I had an impact on her that day. Or I thought I did. Eventually, she told me of her difficulties. The drugs, the stealing, her desire for help."

Beebe rubbed her father's back. His wife *had* asked for help. This was what Cliff so desperately wished had happened.

"I wanted her to stay while I made some calls." Razzell went on. "I could counsel her soul, but her mind and body needed an expert better than I. She wouldn't stay. She wanted to get home to Beebe and you. Dinnertime and all that." He studied the grave. "I thought I made an impact. By the end of the next day, there was a manhunt for Abigail Walker. I failed. I couldn't even come forward with what I knew. I had no real information on her whereabouts, so I kept quiet."

"The day after she talked with you," Beebe said to Razzell, his eyes downcast, "hospital administrators got word of her thefts. That pushed her to run, Rev. Razzell. Not you. Why would she rekindle the Barleycorn memory if she was disappointed in you? She wouldn't. That was a tribute, I think, to you. You didn't judge. You instantly wanted to help. That's how I see Mother responding. You should, too." She patted his hand. "You are not a failure. Period."

His eyes came up. "But then you came to me one day after school. You walked up on my porch, looking so like your mother. You wanted my advice about the life of a minister. We talked."

"We did."

"But you're not a minister any longer. You've taken a step, or two, back from the church."

"I have."

"Another failure for me."

Beebe watched the old man. She heard his words, but she focused on his slumped shoulders and sunken cheeks, the tiny twitch in his right eye. She looked past the physical, the evidence of recent illness, to his fight for sanity. That fight sapped his strength and deflated his soul. Mosie Razzell would recover because Mosie Razzell had won. Later, she knew Yates would tell him the Terri Miller story that bridged her mother's life in Larkspur with her death. Her death set so much in motion.

"You're absolutely not a failure," Beebe said. "Your guidance was nothing short of exceptional. My decision to study theology was between me and God. And it was God and I who untied that knot, despite the fact that a man named Olney Jones fought against us." She felt her fondness for Olney grow in her heart. "He was a brave man to stand up to God, but Olney had to understand that God wanted me back in Larkspur. Don't you see? There's a place for me here. We're a tight little group, the four of us." She smiled over at Yates. "We need each other. We each carry a piece of Mother. But the four of us together bring those pieces back in line and create a whole. We will heal. Scars will form around those four pieces, but we'll be stronger for this binding of family. A unique family, but family just the same."

Barleycorn wandered over, his tail wagging mightily, and lay his head on Razzell's knee. Razzell scooped the dog's head up into his hands and spoke to him with pride. "Did you hear that, boy? Good news. I'm not a failure."

With that, Beebe recalculated her math. Five pieces of her mother were gathered. Barleycorn was her dog.

Where Do Old Tombstones Go?

The board meeting adjourned after Vincent's summary of the new Senior Life programming. Dr. Hershel Gabriel remained throughout, nodding and tacking on brief, but poignant comments. Vincent wondered how the physician focused after his wife's dramatic exit. The walls still rattled from Mona's door-slamming retreat. She nearly caught Mick Nettleman's shirttail in the jamb as he raced through behind her. Vincent was just a little anxious about Beebe and Cliff as well.

He stood back with Donald Thorndyke and Ron Smith. They waited for Crossroads' board members to welcome Dr. Gabriel and shake his hand before filing out. The doctor was not a voting member, but he was a true and necessary asset for Vincent's programming.

When the four men were all who remained, Vincent stepped over to Gabriel. He issued his own hearty welcome, pumped his hand, and added his appreciation for Gabriel's close attention to Mosie Razzell.

"Young Yates pulled the load there," Gabriel said.

"You know, he's got his interview at Lakeview tomorrow."

"Yes, he mentioned that."

"I'm glad you're on board. We need you," Vincent said solemnly.

"I hope it's a long and beneficial relationship. Speaking of relationships..." Gabriel rocked back on his heels and made a tsk sound.

Vincent knew Mona was the subject, but he could think of nothing pertinent to say. Thankfully, Gabriel reclaimed the lead.

"Mona and I will survive. Mona always survives. She shouldn't be surprised by this turn of events. For weeks, I told her to dial down the rhetoric around town. I specifically cautioned her about this Abigail Walker situation. I overheard her phone calls at home to the board members and pictured disaster hovering. When Donald approached me, it seemed we already etched out very similar scenarios."

"Gabe indicated he was leaning toward helping us out here. Knowing that consideration, the other board members' feelings about Mona, and knowing Gabe thought Mona needed a sharp and heavy dose of reality," Donald Thorndyke said, his droopy left eyelid fully awake, "we sort of plotted against her. In retrospect, I have to say, it feels like a bit of a disservice. But Mona was picking up momentum, like a fully loaded logging truck on a downhill grade."

"There seemed to be no stopping her. She was going to slam into something." Ron Smith's declarative statement was supplemented with his fist striking his open palm.

"No one knows better than I. I better get home," Gabriel said, although his feet remained firmly planted. "I sort of suspect she's backed off to coasting right about now."

"Sorry we left you in this position," Donald said.

"I knew it was coming. Hopefully, she'll take heed. The newspaper board has just about had it with her, too." With that, Gabriel pushed off toward the door. It closed silently behind him.

"So he knew you were plotting against his wife." Vincent could hold his surprise no longer. His spectacled eyes danced from board chair to legal counsel.

"He did," Donald confirmed. "I'm sorry we kept it from you and Beebe, but it had to be. It came down quickly. We were dissatisfied with Mona. Other members complained regularly. Our cohesiveness as a group was suffering. I came to the conclusion we needed and wanted her out. I decided to give her enough rope." He paused. "And she obliged."

"We're not totally heartless sons of bitches." Ron grinned and leaned against what served as the board room table. "I wrote a press release to run in Wednesday's paper. In the release, Donald reluctantly accepts her resignation. He calls it a great sacrifice. Mona realizes she must step down for a greater benefit to the senior community. Her husband is a fine and dedicated geriatrician, who has graciously aligned himself with Crossroads to provide much-needed medical advice. With the conflict of interest, her integrity simply would not permit her to remain a voting director."

When Ron's over-the-top recitation concluded, Vincent said, "It's more than she deserves." Memory of her biting comments ranked high.

"But this is how things are done to minimize blowback," Ron said.

The room breathed quietly for a moment before Donald broke in. "Well. Now the hunt is on for a replacement."

"It should be a woman," Vincent said.

"Yeah, and closer to an age that mirrors Crossroads' membership."

With that, Donald and Ron said their goodbyes to Vincent. Vincent hung the closed sign. Back in his office, the telephone rang. He raced to answer it. Relief followed shortly thereafter. The caller was Beebe.

* * *

In his bedroom, Cliff Walker pulled a V-neck sweater on over a buttoned-up checkered shirt. He was alone in the house. It was Tuesday night. Beebe helped with bingo.

Cliff straightened the shirt's collar and the sweater's sleeves. He gave himself an appraising look in the dresser's mirror. Cautiously, his eyes traveled to the valet box on the dresser's surface and the tri-folded paper anchored beneath the box's front corner. Two weeks passed since he placed it there. Tonight, he thought, it should be put away.

He slipped it out, held it between thumb and fingertips, debating. Slowly, his other hand moved to open the page. He read the contents once more, nodded resolutely, and went to open the closet door. He lifted the lid of the security box he kept there and lay Abigail Walker's death certificate inside. In consideration of the many years she answered to Terri Miller, Dr. Samuel Jeffers filled that name in the block created for noting alternate identities.

He lowered the lid and pushed gently until he heard and felt the latch catch. Cliff closed the closet door and went downstairs.

When he stepped off the last stair, Rosemary appeared outside the storm door. Both he and the porch light awaited her arrival. Her restaurant was locked up for the night. They planned to see a late movie in the next town over.

Rosemary looked pretty with her thick cord of woven hair pulled forward over her left shoulder. She wore a gray sweater, a string of pearls, black slacks, and flat shoes.

Through the glass, he observed her broad smile and rushed to let her in.

"How did it go?" he said, pulling her to the couch. Rosemary scheduled a meeting for dessert and coffee with Ron Smith and Donald Thorndyke thirty minutes before the restaurant closed.

"They wouldn't accept any of my rationales. They talked around me the way they do—quite comically, I might add—and called every one of my legitimate rationales crappy excuses. I told them I worried that, as a small business owner, I'd continually run into problems and time issues that would cause me to miss board meetings."

"And they said?"

"They said the pie and coffee complimented each other perfectly and insisted that I reconsider their invitation to sit on Crossroads' board. I was not permitted to decline. The whole thing left my head spinning."

"They are a formidable duo," Cliff said, watching her catch her face in her hands for all of two seconds before it rebounded.

"When I said I didn't feel qualified, they turned my words back on me. They said I was a successful small business owner and that, in itself, qualified me to make intelligent decisions." Her words came hastily. "When I asked, they said my connection to you and your connection to Beebe was not a conflict, but asking, revealed my integrity. Of course, they were really holding this conversation with each other, not me, even though I was right there in the booth. They considered me far removed from any Larkspur generational link since I moved here from Kerr. Then Donald wiped his mouth on a napkin, pushed his plate back, and asked me if I had any hidden agendas."

"You said no," Cliff answered. He had no doubt she was an exceptional choice.

"They said they'd see me at the next meeting, in two weeks, and slid out of the booth."

"This is great," Cliff said. "Technically, your Beebe's and Vincent's boss."

A laugh burst out of her. "You're in a good mood." She tilted her head, taking him in. "And quite handsome. You get everything accomplished today you wanted?"

"It's done," he said with a weighty exhale of breath. None of the tasks warranted a celebration. "I reimbursed Hal for his time and materials. Well, not for the stone. He found that at an excavation site and set it aside to be a practice piece. It turned out the practice was needed for the real thing." He knew Rosemary understood he spoke of the Terri Miller marker. "I took a check into town hall with the old invoice and reimbursed the town coffers. That went without a lot of explanation. I told the woman who helped me just what happened. An insurance payment was made, and so, in reality, there was no indigent burial. The town should be paid back. It took no longer than the time needed to print a receipt. The rest of the insurance money was deposited into a new account on the cemetery's books for future indigent burials. The balance will cover two, three at the most. I feel good about everything, really."

Quick as a cat, Rosemary pecked him on the cheek.

Cliff shyly looked down. To his surprise, he found he held Rosemary's hand.

* * *

It was Wednesday afternoon when Yates slowed the Jeep and steered it into Larkspur Cemetery. Up ahead, Beebe watered the sod over Abigail Walker's grave. He waved through the windshield and waited while she walked the hose back across the road. He reached across the passenger seat and opened the door for her.

She pulled herself inside and closed the door. "Hal called," she said. "He's running fifteen minutes behind."

"No problem," Yates returned, pressing the accelerator. He followed the long winding cemetery road, then coasted to a stop when the Jeep's back bumper was positioned in front of the equipment garage's overhead door.

They got out of the Jeep. Yates swung the rear door open. Noticing loose grass and dirt on the carpeted bed liner, he quickly hand-brushed the particles over to the edge and out. With a wild flourish, he offered Beebe a seat. It was a joy to see her smile.

"Yates, you are so like the little brother I never had." She made room for him beside her. "So this is your day off. How's the job going?"

"Great. I'm off to a fantastic start, thanks to Dr. Gabe." Dr. Hershel Gabriel fixed it so Yates accompanied him on his rounds through the geriatric floor. Once the patients were discharged, Yates also completed at-home follow-up reports. The young nurse was being groomed to play an active role in Gabriel's partnership with Crossroads. Slow and steady stayed the course. Those words applied to Yates's career, and he repeated them for both his benefit and for recovering patients who were once again up on their feet and looking to him for a path back to a full life.

"How are you and Mosie getting along?"

Yates picked up that story at the point he accepted Rev. Mosie Razzell's offer and moved Barleycorn and himself in the retired minister's two-bedroom bungalow. Over the course of two tear-filled days for both men after the cemetery visit, Yates told Razzell about Terri Miller. He started with first seeing her in the ER, guarding his father's treatment cubicle, gave detailed accounts of summers with her, and concluded with the woman's stubborn determination to be returned to Larkspur to meet death and be buried.

Cut into Yates's tale were Razzell's realizations—now that his head was clear—about how he got started with the excess medication. Feeling his age and feeling useless, Razzell experienced a creeping depression. He was already cooking with more pills than prescribed when Yates and Barleycorn took up residence at Crossroads. Barleycorn's name was the trigger. Yates remembered the long stares and awkwardness Razzell exhibited that first evening at bingo. To his depression, Razzell added a revived guilt over Abigail Walker's disappearance. Beebe's reappearance, looking so much like her mother, did nothing to dissuade Razzell's spiraling condition.

"Dr. Gabe would approve of the term spiraling condition," Yates told Beebe. "He instructed me not to use wigged out." Beebe laughed when Yates couldn't maintain a serious expression.

"Mosie and I are both worried Barleycorn may wander out of the back yard since there's no fence. If that happens while I'm at the hospital, Mosie could never chase him down."

"I'm glad I called with Daddy's offer, although neither of us suspected it would be used in this manner."

Yates felt his enthusiasm dim.

Beebe saw it. "You okay with this?"

"Just where do old tombstones go?" Yates answered Beebe's question with a question. "The idea that it was a useless stone reminded me of Mosie's feelings, triggered by Barleycorn. The next leap was easy. If something has to weigh Barleycorn down, I figure it might as well be Terri, you know." His voice choked just a bit.

Yates purchased two lengths of chain at McKinley Hardware. The shorter one would be wrapped in both directions around the headstone. Once in place, it would resemble a ribbon tied around a gift box. Hooks would connect the longer chain from the headstone to the dog. Yates grinned to himself. His heart swelled. He pictured Barleycorn safely tethered to this last treasure of Terri Miller.

Yates looked up. Hal Garrett's truck coasted toward them. After the greetings were out of the way, the three of them filed into the equipment garage.

Hal passed Yates a pair of work gloves and donned a pair himself. The cemetery man moved a wheelbarrow to the side. Beebe stepped in to retrieve and fold the tarp covering the headstone. Hal moved long-handled tools out of the corner and pushed a red metal toolbox far enough away so he could stand in its place.

"Ready," he said to Yates.

Yates walked over. The two men worked their fingers under the block of stone and, grunting, lifted it. Beebe followed them out and over to the Jeep's rear compartment. Yates barely breathed. Hal's face reddened from the exertion. When the loading was done, they all gave Terri Miller's grave marker a long and thoughtful stare, and all for different reasons.

Yates thought Hal stared because it was a final appraisal of his first attempt at accomplishing the old ways with one's own hands guiding chisel and hammer.

Beebe's eyes also lingered on the stone. Yates easily assumed the stone represented the mysterious side of Terri Miller that Beebe would never solve. Yes, Beebe had knowledge, through him, of the last ten summers of her mother's life, but twice that amount hung in the dark, gray, gloomy mist of the unknown. There, he suspected, it would always remain, although stranger things have happened.

Yates remembered the last time Terri Miller rode in his jeep, how he kept his anger burning to fight the tears, how he tried to tell her he loved her, but how not telling her honored her more. Terri Miller brought the full range of emotions out of Yates: anger, love, honor, and yes, there would be tears. There should be tears. How paradoxical that his life should loom with such expectation, that his horizons should brighten and gather strength on the raveled edge of hers. What an enduring impression, as enduring as a name chiseled into stone.

Hal's voice snapped Yates back. "Should I follow you and help you get it back out? I can."

"No, thanks. I've got Ned McMitchell lined up. That is, unless Willa's decided to give birth in the last hour."

The McMitchells' baby was two days past due.

* * *

258

The day the quilt arrived, Beebe and Cliff sat side by side on the couch, sharing it across both of their laps. Beebe stared hard at the squares, machine- and hand-stitched, all fine-quality workmanship. Tears threatened. Her chin quavered. The pain in her throat bespoke the rush of emotions coming at her so quickly, she simply could not form words. When Beebe hoped Cliff might take up the conversation reins, he failed to speak. He projected stoicism. His rigid posture told her of his fight against expressing emotion. The subject matter was, of course, surviving grief. To his credit, he seemed as mesmerized by the quilt as she.

Perhaps it was enough that their random movements in smoothing the quilt carried their hands across cottony nursing garb, silky mint-green pajamas, a woven skirt, a crisp linen blouse, and other quiet memories. She flipped a corner back. The quilt's backing was cut from the fine tapestry tablecloth Emma Walker gave the couple as a wedding present. Funny how Grandma Emma was stitched into the quilt.

When she suggested that the quilt be folded and kept over her mother's chair in her parents' bedroom, she received nothing more than simple agreement.

A tumble of questions lived inside Beebe's head. Had there been progress concerning Cliff's grief? Was the quilt's arrival a setback? She wanted answers while he remained tightlipped. She wanted him to break through and break the silence. What would it take?

Since that day on the couch, regular reports came from Yates on the emergence of Mosie Razzell's clear mind and full health. With them, a solution presented itself with very little fanfare.

She visited the retired minister and asked if he would counsel Cliff through his grief. "Of course, Daddy has to agree. I haven't approached him yet." She sat in a rocker in Razzell's living room. He occupied the near end of the davenport. Behind his eyes, she saw him putting the proposal through its paces.

"I've returned to life, and that life needs a solid purpose. The thing is, I think I would benefit as much as Cliff. That might appear self-serving, but I'm so hungry for something worthwhile that I can assure you Cliff will profit."

"If the counseling is good for the both of you, all the better. Let me speak with Daddy. Of course, we're talking about evening sessions, two or three times a week. I imagine he'll come straight over from work."

Razzell's brows drew down. "Aren't you joining us?"

"Oh gosh, no. Not me. Just Daddy." Still he plied her with a questioning look, eliciting more. "I admit, I thought I would when the only recourse was a counseling group out of town, but here, at home, with you, I think Daddy will agree and make the effort without me pulling him through the door by his ear." She laughed. Razzell cracked a slim smile, not erasing the studious expression on his face. Rising, she said, "Thank you, Rev. Razzell. And you just look great."

Confidence in her decision to put her father's grief in this man's now steady hands was further backed up by his rosy cheeks and an overall vibrancy that emerged since his detox sessions. The reward he earned was a new life with Yates and Barleycorn as companions.

On his feet, he placed a hand on her back and guided her to the open door. Throughout her brief visit, pleasant sunshine and warm air filtered through the screen.

"So, you'll call?" he said when they stood outside on the porch.

"Yes, I will—or Daddy will—to set up the first session."

"Fine," he said, patting her shoulder.

She descended the few porch steps. Along the front walkway to her car, it dawned on her that Mosie's invitation to attend her father's grief sessions was not merely a polite gesture or a measure aimed at minimizing Cliff's unease. Mosie suggested that her grief still prickled behind the scenes. She settled herself in the driver's seat, her purse on the passenger's side. Leaning over, she searched the leathery object for car keys. Finding them, she sat up straight only to find that Razzell had magically appeared at her driver's door, its window down.

"Are you sure you won't join us?"

Beebe decided to use plain words to set Mosie straight on his miscue regarding her grief. "I handled Mother's loss months ago. I miss her. I always have. I always will. It's kind of you to be concerned. But I'm good. Really, I am."

An odd beat passed while he held her eyes in his gaze. He double-tapped the base of the window frame and said, "Off with you then," and stepped back.

In the rearview mirror, she caught sight of him standing in the street. His stalwart figure topped with a head of white hair. Hands in his pockets, he watched after her as she drove away.

She broached the idea for Cliff's consideration that same evening. She pushed the fact that something meaningful in Razzell's life would cement his convalescence so the sessions would be mutually beneficial for both men. Still, Cliff's quiet nature prevailed. Beebe went on to say that if he decided against

Razzell's counseling, she would make the effort to locate sessions in a nearby town. For good measure, she added that she'd be happy to keep him company on the ride over.

The "good measure" argument produced the anticipated result. Cliff went to the phone and set up his first appointment with Razzell for the next week.

With that decision made by her father, she thought he would feel a weight lift, but he remained reticent. No memories shared. He would not talk about Abigail Walker. Had he nothing to say?

Theme of Family

Since it was late September, Beebe set out to clear some of the flowerbeds around the house. She dragged a canvas catchall with a wide mouth from bed to bed. It caught the now petrified begonias, petunias, and impatiens she yanked up and tossed in. With the bed on the north side of the house devoid of annuals, she angled around the corner into the front yard, towing the catchall up in her arms. Off near the blue spruce, Beebe observed a woman who appeared to be Melinda Thorndyke. Beebe set the catchall down, pulled off her garden gloves, and let them fall to the ground.

When Melinda didn't notice her cutting across the row of graves, Beebe spoke quietly from several graves away. "Am I intruding?" This was their first encounter since the board meeting at Crossroads.

Nearly a month passed since the grave beside Patsy Thorndyke's was disturbed. The dirt there was tapped down. The sod had taken hold. All looked good.

"Hi, Beebe." Melinda looked genuinely pleased to see her. Errant strands of her dark curls blew with the breeze. "No, you are not an intrusion. Today was my parents' anniversary. It was such a pretty afternoon, it just drew me outside. And here I am. I don't come often."

The admission mirrored the impression Beebe felt that a closeness had not existed between Melinda and her parents. Patsy and Kenneth Thorndyke's graves were memorialized with a double bronze marker. Melinda brought yellow mums for the embedded bronze vase that lifted up and out from beneath the marker's surface. The bottom of the vase locked upright into grooves designed for just that purpose. Melinda held a nearly empty water bottle. Beebe suspected the missing contents were poured into the vase to keep the flowers going for a while.

Melinda fiddled with the bottle. The former grief counselor felt she should let Melinda direct the conversation. After a long moment, she did.

"My mother was not always a model to emulate. In fact, I didn't like Patsy Thorndyke very much." She gave Beebe a sad smile. "That's awful to say, I know. And what bothers me about my involvement in your mother's situation at the hospital is whether my actions were driven just a little bit by what my mother would say if I went to Abigail and tried to help rather than turning my back on her and racing for cover under the guise of hospital protocols."

"I hold no grudge against you, Melinda. I haven't even run the scenario of what would have happened differently if hospital administration and law enforcement weren't brought in. Honesty, thirty years have passed, the story is fully engrained just as it played out back then. There are no options, no alternate endings. But Mother transformed her life. I learned about that transformation. Look at things this way, you brought that about. You followed the rules, and, somewhere down the line, Mother found sobriety and came back to us. More often than not, life is not well lit. It's full of dark passages."

Melinda nodded. Her eyes darted from place to place. She brought her concentration back. "Standing here, it feels like I should tell you an unflattering story about my mother. It involves your mother and your Grandma Walker."

"Really? Even Grandma Walker," Beebe said. "Sounds intriguing."

"Well, let's just say it lights my mother's passage through life fairly well for all to see." Off in the distance behind Melinda, a migratory flock of ducks flew silently southward. "Did you know that your parents rented a little house over on Arbor Street when they were first married?"

Beebe shook her head. She knew nothing but life in the caretaker's house.

"My parents owned several rentals around town, and Mother was in charge of rent collection. When I began working the same shift with Abigail, Mother decided to revive a situation involving the collection of rent from Arbor Street. Apparently, your father had his job at the hardware store. Your mother was finishing nurses training, which takes money—I know," Melinda said, fingertips touched her breastbone. "She was pregnant with you, so money was tight in the Walker residence. Mother felt no compunction to show compassion. I guess for two months the rent went unpaid. My mother and your mother had words. In the revived version, my mother told me how she proudly tagged your parents the Two-Warning Walkers. If another transgression occurred, a for-rent placard would go in the little house's window." Beebe thought Melinda replicated her mother's sneer perfectly. "She could degrade people with just two or three well-chosen words. Of course, I found Abigail owned all the compassion my mother did not."

Beebe listened closely. This tale covered completely new ground.

"When the bedpan hit the floor over your mother's problem," Melinda smiled with her insertion of hospital humor, "I explained my part in things to my parents. I was young and scared. The police were called. Abigail disappeared. It was frightening. I was panicky. The hospital was abuzz." Suddenly, her face darkened. Her lips tightened and shrunk. "But my mother looked at me without a hint of understanding. Just as snidely as she was capable, she chirped, as if well-deserved, 'Third warning.'"

The words grated across Beebe's heart even though they were heard three decades later and secondhand. She studied Melinda Thorndyke, who stepped inside herself, leaving Beebe alone to wonder what she thought. "But you're here today. You've forgiven her for her ways?" There was something about mother and daughters who traveled a rocky road and the forgiveness sought at the end. It was an enduring scenario, fit for the ages. Beebe hadn't realized she forgave her mother until her father recognized that forgiveness strung through the words of Abigail's obituary.

"I began to accept my mother and her shortcomings when, over the years, I saw worse examples. My brother and I contribute to society. Whether it's to spite her, who knows?"

Beebe considered Melinda's attitude an odd mix of blasé and providence. She thought the woman next to her seemed entitled to a shared secret, and an uplifting one. "See this grave?" Beebe pointed to the one that bordered Patsy Thorndyke's.

"Yes, I was going to ask you about that marker."

"I'll tell you about that in a minute, but first, you should know that when Mother died under the name Terri Miller, and Daddy had to find a spot for the quote-unquote indigent burial, he buried her there. My mother and your mother were neighbors for six months."

"Beside Mother!" Melinda's mirth was hearty. "Serves her absolutely right."

The stone marker next to Patsy Thorndyke's grave read: HERE LIES ONE MANGLED SWING.

Hal Garrett chiseled the words on another excavated flat stone suitable for a grave marker. He caught on to a technique with the serifs, Beebe thought.

The women walked back down the row and around the blue spruce to Melinda's car. Beebe explained the story behind the words along the way. In

Beebe's opinion, Cliff's outlook improved marginally after the symbolic burial of past lies. When Beebe concluded, Melinda nodded her appreciation of the psychological needs of those who grieve.

Melinda reached for the door handle, and Beebe said, "Wait. What happened with the rent?"

Corralling several long blowing curls with her hand in a combing motion, Melinda said, "Oh, it got paid. I think to the true disappointment of my mother."

"Daddy must have found a second job," Beebe reasoned.

"No. No. I don't think so. Well, he could have, but that's not the story I got from Father."

When Melinda finished the forty-six-year old tale, Beebe upgraded Kenneth from her unjust ranking of him as the "silent one" in the Thorndyke household. Apparently, Kenneth was a husband willing to spill awkward details despite how they tainted his wife. Those details supplied Beebe with an early piece of her parents' marital history that, oh so neatly, bridged the gap that stymied her father all these years.

The women said their goodbyes. Beebe strolled leisurely back toward the house. The air gliding across the cemetery brought a crisp quality despite the bright sun.

When Beebe passed close enough to the side door to hear the phone ringing inside, she rushed up the steps and through the mudroom to lift the receiver.

"Yates here," the caller said. The young nurse sounded giddy. He drew the afternoon shift that day. "Guess what? Willa just came in."

Nearly all of Yates's eight-hour shift ticked by before his second phone call woke the house. Beebe dozed on the couch; Cliff snored in the recliner. Yates proudly announced, "Mother and baby Rebecca doing fine."

On that note and, with their spurt of renewed energy dissolving quickly, the Walkers climbed the stairs for bed.

* * *

Beebe endured a wakeful night. She made rounds through the house. Back upstairs, she eased open the door to her father's room and went in for an armchair visit with her mother. Still hours before dawn, the room was clothed in darkness. She made her way to the chair, though, without one false step, and stretched out her hand to the object she knew was draped there. Her fingertips caressed the squares sewn into her mother's quilt.

Beebe's thoughts wandered to the days she counseled the bereft and what she encouraged family members and close friends to do. There would be no new memories of the lost loved one, so it was welcomed and beneficial to share old ones. This gave Beebe an idea.

Very quietly, she crossed to her father's bedside clock and reset the alarm. Beebe added chance to hope that her idea would nudge her father into opening up.

Stepping down from the last stair step to the entry hall, she wondered if her father sensed Abigail's presence in the house again. That was the quilt's doing. Beebe felt a warmth embrace her every time she came home. To carry the warm feeling forward until her father's alarm woke him, she decided on baking something. A pair of too-ripe bananas caught her eye in the kitchen, and when she sniffed, her nose agreed.

Good, she thought. Banana muffins. They were always a childhood favorite.

She found the cookbook she wanted behind the door of a nearby cupboard. After laying it on the countertop and lifting the cover, she flipped pages to the recipe. She mashed the bananas into wheat flour, added other ingredients, stirred up a batter, and spooned it into tins. The tins went into the heated oven.

With the timer set, the cookbook could be returned to the shelf. She hadn't gotten a firm enough hold on the large book, and it slipped out of her grasp, hitting the counter at an angle. The impact jarred a loose paper stored between the leaves partially into view.

Just the corner of the page was enough to wrench memories free from a long-ago day when she was twelve or thirteen and her mother's vitality filled the kitchen. She placed a steadying hand on the Formica to balance the dizzying effect of her peripheral vision graying out around the sliver of yellow construction paper.

Slowly, she cut the pages to the cookbook-turned-memory book. Within its binding, like a rose pressed between the layers, was a portal back in time to a mother-daughter baking contest at church. The Walkers entered banana muffins. Their entry had not won, but they did go home with a Polaroid photograph taken by one of the judges. In it, Beebe displayed the tray of muffins while Abigail's arm draped her daughter's shoulders. Later in the day, good-natured Beebe set about correcting that error in culinary judgment. She fashioned a blue ribbon out of colored paper, glued it to one side of the yellow backing sheet, leaving room for the photo on the other.

Beebe remembered presenting her homemade award to her mother. Laughing at her funny daughter, Abigail displayed it next to the plate of remaining muffins stored under a clear dome. At some point, Abigail slipped the award-turned-mother's-keepsake inside the cookbook.

Beebe could not draw her eyes from the photograph that transported her to another age. A sad smile crossed her lips. So very slowly, Beebe's trembling hand reached out to touch her mother's face, captured and preserved exactly as she remembered it. Beebe never watched Abigail Walker grow older, never saw her become frail. In the picture, Beebe was grinning and gangly; her mother proud and shapely. But, their faces— Their faces were a twin of the other.

Beebe set about washing up the few dishes while the cookbook and its discovered treasure remained on the counter. While she constantly snatched looks at the photograph, the day mother and daughter baked muffins for the contest replayed in her mind. Her memories ballooned vivid and full until her chest swelled to a painful proportion. When she could endure it no longer, a hiccupping sob burst through.

For the first time since she took up residence in the caretaker's house, she submitted to the ache of misery embedded just beneath the surface, kept buried by all the busying tasks she undertook: the obituary, the corrected death certificate, the reburial, her first board meeting. Now, with Cliff's agreement to attend counseling cemented by an appointment, she finally succumbed to grief.

The cloak of strength she projected for weeks fell away. Her knees buckled, and she slid down the counter with a deep, guttural moan that told of the tremendous sense of loss and loneliness she felt since her mother's death. In a leaden heap on the floor, she hugged herself with sudsy hands and wept.

Her wallow in sorrow measured but a brief moment. Blinking back tears, she struggled to her feet in response to another call to duty. The oven timer chimed.

With the tins of golden brown muffins cooling on the stovetop, Beebe gazed down at the photograph and spoke to her mother. "Thank you for saving my artwork. Thank you for coming home." With that, she closed the homemade ribbon and its accompanying photo inside the book. She returned it to the shelf and smiled. The aroma of banana muffins curled around her like a warm hug. She welcomed it as one last act of love from her mother.

But a mother's love has the power to transcend all barriers. With Beebe's next breath, she sensed Abigail Walker's encouragement to accept Rev. Razzell's invitation for counseling. Her "miscue" terminology veered way off the mark. It seemed to her that he knew the scorching pain she just experienced waited to ambush. He knew she would stumble around lost in a world of emptiness if she didn't attempt to resolve her grief.

Razzell knew.

He came through his own haze aided by the careful attention of others, and he knew. She decided a call to the minister for her own appointment was in order. She would not upset Cliff's and Razzell's private sessions.

Her mind drifted ahead to the end of this day. She just might sleep through the night.

A glance at the kitchen clock reminded her of her initial mission for this morning, the reason she reset her father's alarm.

In the dark bedroom upstairs, she sat down in the armchair and arranged the quilt over her legs.

Eyes open, but her sight useless, her random movements along the quilt brought forth a unique and startling realization. Her fingers touched varying textures. She thought how that element of change, from one second to the next, aptly and accurately represented a person's life, one's characteristics, moods, even smiles. A person owned several smiles. Each could be interpreted. Often, a smile could be enough by itself. No words spoken. The quilt was like that.

The alarm clock's buzzer snapped her out of her reverie. She watched her father smack at the off button.

He used a half-second to read the numbers, then said, "Ah, geez, Beebe, where are you?"

From the chair behind him, she lay the quilt aside. His head whipped toward the sound of the chair's creaky groan when she got to her feet. She went to open the bedroom door. That ushered in a fuzzy cone of low-wattage illumination from the hallway's overhead light. She wanted enough light to appreciate her father's expression. She cracked a mystery that puzzled him as far back as the days before she was born.

There by Melinda Thorndyke's car, Beebe learned that when Patsy Thorndyke issued her second warning to Abigail Walker all those years ago, Emma Walker appeared out of nowhere on the porch steps behind Patsy. She overheard the threat, understood the monetary shortage involved, and without hesitation, wrote the pinched-faced creditor a check in full for two months' back rent. Beebe pictured her grandmother's arm firmly encircling her mother. An eternal bond sealed around mother- and daughter-in-law as they watched Patsy stomp down old wooden steps in heated retreat.

That day, Grandma Walker foiled all of Patsy Thorndyke's fun.

And that day, Emma and Abigail reached a bargain. Poor Daddy, Beebe thought, always on the outside of one secret or another.

Cliff's chin came up when Beebe artfully drew on the oratory experience of a former minister and brought the story to its conclusion. He looked off into a dark bedroom corner, then swiveled his head to his daughter. "My mother wrote a check? You're right. I can see it now."

Then it happened.

His face relaxed. The texture of his smile warmed Beebe's heart. Full understanding of the relationship binding his wife and his mother was enough to usher her father into breaking the bounds on his silence.

"We got into trouble with a car repair, baby doctor bills, and things for the nursery. I came home from the store and wanted to call Patsy Thorndyke. I actually wanted to speak with her husband because I thought, man to man, he'd be more sympathetic. I worked out overtime with Old Man McKinley, but Abigail stopped me from making the call to Kenneth."

"Because Grandma paid the rent."

"No. Well, yes, I guess. But your mother said she arranged it with Patsy. She sold some of her nursing textbooks. She planned to type term papers for students at the college. She was a fair typist. For weeks, her typewriter sat out on the desk. Papers lay there. I saw her typing. And Patsy Thorndyke stopped coming around. It didn't seem like typing would pay the rent, but your mother knew college life better than I."

"She wanted a special memory, Daddy, just her and Grandma. Maybe she did do those things. The books and the typing. For the extra money. A cushion. You guys were young. Just starting out." When Cliff's expression turned from thoughtful to bleak, her anxiety rose. "You're not thinking that Grandma influenced her lies at sunset?" She used his phrasing. She worried that her morning-talk routine may backfire. They could not go through the whole swing business again.

"Of all the memories I have of Abigail," Cliff said, slow to speak, "the memories of her when she was pregnant are my favorite. Always."

His words moved her because he used the present tense, not the past. Even more moving, his tone carried greater love than Beebe ever heard him express.

Without a word, he pushed himself off the mattress and went around to the other side of the bed. He bent to the bedside table next to the chair, opened the top drawer, and returned with a hinged picture frame. He handed it to Beebe.

She opened the frame and tipped a set of photographs, this pair black and white, away from the hallway's light and toward what seemed the enchanted glow of sunrise meant to reach them around the drawn curtains. Again, Beebe's fingers reached out. Tears loomed. She touched the glass and melted at the sight of her mother, twenty years old and framed in gold.

The photographs set the scene as her father's stories, all firmly rooted to the small cottage, tumbled out. Abigail, well into her pregnancy, posed for the camera on the porch steps of their Arbor Street home. In the second photo, she sniffed a lilac bloom in the yard. Beebe absorbed all the tiny details the lens captured as she knew her father had over and over for the last thirty years.

What Beebe began to appreciate, during her father's retelling, was that he included her. She was not overlooked. His Arbor Street stories drew on the theme of family. For all the while, their daughter was present, like the tense. She grew in Abigail's womb.

Also by Connie Chappell

Wild Raspberries

When Callie MacCallum sews her first quilt after the death of her lover Jack Sebring, she doesn't realize she'll be drawn into a Sebring family battle between wife and daughter-in-law. She simply wants to fulfill her promise to Jack to visit their cabin in the West Virginia mountains, where their long love affair was safely hidden.

Instead, her emotionally reminiscent trip becomes crowded with the two Sebring women, a grief counselor, and the massive role Callie assumes. She must speak for Jack in order to protect his four-year old grandson Chad from his stubbornly manipulative and blame-passing grandmother and his recently widowed and power-usurping mother. Callie understands both women grieve the loss of Chad's father. He died when a raging storm split the tree that crushed him.

Grief isn't the only common thread running between the four women. One by one, their secrets are revealed on the West Virginia mountaintop.

Deadly Homecoming *at Rosemont*

Historian Wrenn Grayson arrives at the Rosemont mansion expecting to receive payment for her services from the mansion's new owner, Clay Addison. That expectation dies when she and Clay find Trey Rosemont murdered on the foyer floor. Across town, police officers race to Eastwood University. Priceless Egyptian artifacts were stolen from the history department safe. Wrenn's longtime love, Eastwood professor Gideon Douglas, heads the department. Only recovery of the artifacts will save his career.

Life in Havens, Ohio, doesn't stop for this crime spree. Wrenn works for Mayor K.C. Tallmadge. He wishes Wrenn would stop searching down clues ahead of the police and pacify temperamental playwright Barton Reed. Barton's play is just days away from opening in the town's historic Baxter Theater.

Amid murder, theft, or curtain calls, Wrenn's instincts prove sharp. But it's her stubborn one-woman approach that places her directly in the killer's path.

View other Black Rose Writing titles at www.blackrosewriting.com/books and use promo code PRINT to receive a 20% discount when purchasing.

BLACK ROSE
writing™

Made in the USA
Middletown, DE
15 March 2017